UNDERKILL

UNDERKILL

LEONARD CHANG

THOMAS DUNNE BOOKS / ST. MARTIN'S MINOTAUR ♔ NEW YORK

THOMAS DUNNE BOOKS.
An imprint of St. Martin's Press.

UNDERKILL. Copyright © 2003 by Leonard Chang. All rights reserved. Printed in the
United States of America. No part of this book may be used or reproduced in any man-
ner whatsoever without permission except in the case of brief quotations embodied in
critical articles or reviews. For information, address St. Martin's Press, 175 Fifth Avenue,
New York, N.Y. 10010.

www.minotaurbooks.com

ISBN 0-312-30843-4

First Edition: May 2003

10 9 8 7 6 5 4 3 2 1

FOR FRANCES SACKETT

PART I

GESTURES OF ANTICIPATION

One

I **f you thought** you knew her, you didn't. If you thought because you had seen her on TV and read her features in the *Sentinel*, and maybe even met her once or twice at a panel discussion or at a news conference, that this gave you some idea of who she was, you would be wrong. Sometimes even Linda didn't know. She would look at herself in the mirror, and I witnessed this many mornings, her restlessness kicking her out of bed and in search of a newspaper, the coffeemaker gurgling, the radio murmuring NPR and the smell of buttered toast filling the kitchen—I would see her stop and stare at her reflection in the large mirror in the hall outside her bedroom. It was as if she suddenly glimpsed inside of herself, and this held true especially in the mornings when her guard was down and the softness of sleep still lingered around her. She stopped. She stared. She wasn't examining her face for blemishes or wrinkles. She wasn't looking at pores or pimples or pouty lips. She was looking into her own dark, drowsy eyes, searching. I kept still, watching from the bed, angled from her view. I feigned sleep. Linda pulled her hair back. She leaned forward, her gaze deepening into itself. I didn't know what she saw, and never asked. Hers was a private act.

Linda and I had been dating for two years, marking not only the longest relationship I'd been in, but the most puzzling as well. The initial rush of infatuation and lust was over. The grinding details of daily life had set in. And something was happening to us. We were—as some seasoned partners might say quietly to a friend over drinks, the lights low and the mood somber—we were having a little trouble.

Trouble? Sorry to hear that. What kind of trouble?

With this, a pained look would cross my face, a look of shame and melancholy as I would weigh the consequences of revealing personal truths that would expose Linda's and my faults, and yet the prospect of having a sympathetic listener would be too great a temptation. I would feel the gentle tug to which weary confessors surrender. I would yearn for compassion.

You see, I would say tentatively, lowering my voice. You see, she might be leaving me.

No lightning bolts. No sudden flashes of insight with this revelation. No, just the dull clang of painful truth.

This is a story about Linda as much as it is about me, about the disturbing events we would witness together and separately, about what happened after she visited her mother and stepfather in Los Angeles. She had flown down for a few reasons, though the most compelling seemed to be that she wanted some distance from me. A few hundred miles of distance. Three hundred and forty-four miles, to be precise.

She needed, as she explained, some time alone. But there were more reasons. Her younger brother Hector had disappeared again, though this time her mother was really worried. Linda had a few weeks of vacation time from her newspaper job, and she hadn't seen her parents in almost three years, despite being only an hour away by plane. So, Linda flew out of San Francisco, and away from me. She flew out of our discord, out of her job as a features writer with which she was growing more unhappy, out of her daily life. She flew away to think, to evaluate.

I could understand that. I am a believer in taking stock.

So, this story begins with her uncertainty about us, and with me vaguely disappointed and confused. This story begins with my pained realization that maybe I had done something wrong but didn't know what, and that the pleasures of discovering someone whom you liked, whom you connected with, whom you've found *engagement* with, once worn away, was quickly replaced by the shocking understanding that these things—these *relationships*—were very, very difficult. This story begins with a phone call from Linda after I returned home from a long run around the neighborhood. I had been trying to wash away a stressful and moderately hazardous day at work, and my thoughts had kept circling back to Linda, to my job, to a strange sense of solitude that I was actually enjoying but then feeling guilty about.

This story begins, as many do, with a sense of regret.

I view my life as a struggle for *engagement*. No, not the engagement to marry, or the engagement of a battle, though the two might possibly be related; rather, a more general sense of engaging with others and myself. We try to connect through work, through play, through love, and yet the forces around us constantly keep us off balance and isolated. We wrestle endlessly in a vacuum, in a suffocating void, reaching out.

But first, this: I was finishing up a surveillance job for Larry, since his workload was heavy. Last year he had taken me on as a conditional partner at Baxter Investigations in order to expand into executive protection and security, something for which he wasn't licensed. Larry, a private investigator, could legally handle client protection only if it was directly relevant to a PI case, but because I was licensed as a private patrol operator, I was certified by the Bureau of Security and Investigative Services to protect people and property. I was a *bodyguard,* a term most security professionals abhorred, but I didn't mind so much. No need for pretensions in this business.

Larry knew where the money was. The hourly rate for executive protection started at twice that of a PI.

The long-range goal sounded good. I would steal clients from my old firm, ProServ, and drum up new clients. Larry would get licensed as a private patrol operator, and we would move into full-scale executive protection. Baxter Investigations would become Baxter & Choice Security. Larry had even mocked-up a business card, "B&C Security," that had a smart sword-and-shield logo in the background.

Although this *sounded* good, the reality was different. I was having trouble bringing over old clients because ProServ and its main competition, Black Diamond, were undercutting each other's rates. The Silicon Valley economy was crashing, and companies were going bankrupt. Everyone was reining in expenses, especially in areas considered nonessential, like executive protection. Also, even with the small amount of publicity I had received two years ago, new clients were wary of small boutiques. Large companies, the best clients, wanted to deal with other large companies. The only steady work I'd brought in was a jewelry appraiser and dealer requiring an escort every three weeks as he transported uncut gems to and from jewelers around the Bay Area. This guy had chosen me, it seemed, because he was Korean and liked the fact that I am Korean American. That was okay. I took what work I could find.

Yet for some reason Larry's end of the business was revving up. He had been getting more insurance companies and law firms asking for research, employee screenings, workers' comp investigations, and general background checks. Executive protection might have been extraneous, but cheating employees were always a problem. Larry had even upped his rates to cool off demand, but the insurance companies weren't blinking. So now he needed help. The only problem was that I wasn't licensed as a private investigator and couldn't conduct interviews or deal with cases in any direct way.

I could tail people, though. I could use a video camera. And that was what I did this afternoon.

The subject, B. B. Smith, was a possible workers' comp fraud case. The insurance company was paying while this guy rehabilitated from a construction-related back injury. They suspected fraud and hired Larry to check him out. Larry had already done all the background searches, the criminal and civil digging, the financial dirt, but had found little to help the case. He had been hoping to point to large debts, maybe a bankruptcy in the past, hints of financial trouble, but the guy was clean, and the next step was to wait and watch. The papers filed by Smith's lawyer detailed Smith's extreme pain and discomfort, the "incapacitating" injury forcing him to leave work.

My job was to catch Smith doing something that pointed to fraud. It was simple and straightforward, and I didn't mind this kind of legwork. I kept the tiny digital video camcorder attached to my hand, poised for recording, and stared out across the street. Smith, a huge bald man with tattoos along his arms and rolls of fat hanging over his belt, climbed slowly out of his truck and lumbered into his house. He had driven around Daly City—running errands at the post office and supermarket, eating lunch at a diner, browsing for hours at a Home Depot—and finally returned home for the day. I hadn't recorded anything interesting, and turned on the camera's night-vision option. The view screen flared brightly, then darkened to a low glitter, the camera searching and amplifying the barest embers of light. I stared through the viewfinder. Night vision was sexy. An aura of green and sparkling white settled around everything. Life shimmered with night vision.

I had told Larry that I'd watch the subject until the evening, but I was getting bored. I tapped my fingers and looked around my car. A box of chocolate truffles I had impulsively bought lay on the passenger seat, a present for Linda when she returned. She liked the walnut-centered kind.

When I had driven her to the airport, she had asked me to collect her mail and water her plants, though she didn't think she'd be longer than a week. I volunteered to fly down there for a weekend; I had never met her parents. She was quiet. The residue of our last argument—about spending more time by ourselves—laced our words. I amended my suggestion quickly by saying that I might have more work to do for Larry this weekend.

"So you're going to move into the PI end?" she asked.

"It might be the best way. Larry and I still have to talk about it. Maybe we'll be licensed in both security and PI work to be more flexible."

She didn't seem to be listening. She stared at the airport signs with no expression, her long curly dark hair pulled back and exposing her neck. Her profile, angular and sculpted, saddened me. Her nose, with the small bump on the bridge, twitched. She then asked to be let off at the terminal—no need to find parking. I gave her a quick kiss good-bye, and said, "I guess this trip is good."

"What?"

"For us."

She turned to me. Her eyes, normally wide and bright, seemed muted. She smiled sadly. "We just need time to think. That's all."

I nodded, and she left the car and walked swiftly into the terminal without looking back.

We needed time to think? *She* needed time to think. Perhaps a bit of both. Our last argument had been a familiar one: I had bought her a new VCR because hers was eating tapes again. But I had surprised her with this, and I had assumed she would be pleased. She was not. Her annoyed expression—a fur-rowing of her eyebrows—and her quick questions as to why I had done this, put me on the defensive. I pointed to the ruined rentals, and the chewed news shows she tried to record. She said she preferred to buy her own things. As the argument grew more heated, it became clear to me that she objected not to the VCR but to my encroaching on her apartment. These were her things, and I had no right replacing them. Yes, she had a point, but I spent time there. I watched her TV with her. I thought she would appreciate the gift.

The realization had hit me slowly. Wait a minute, I thought. It's not the VCR. *It's me.* I fumed. Why was I being made to feel foolish? It was a stupid machine. Linda said, When I want a new one, I'll buy one. This is my place. This is my VCR. Let me handle it.

I said, It won't happen again. I yanked the new VCR off the shelf, and left.

That night I secretly browsed the relationship section of a bookstore. I needed guidelines. I needed checklists. Instead I found meaningless platitudes. I found advice about loving myself first. I thought, Give me something I can use.

I had left the VCR in my apartment, not wanting to deal with it. Now I had missed the fourteen-day return window. So it was mine to keep. What the hell was I going to do with a VCR? I didn't even have a TV.

As it grew darker on Smith's street, I checked the low light option on the camera and considered ending the surveillance. I'd probably have to continue this tomorrow morning. I had plenty of other things to do as well. I had to start cold-calling old ProServ clients again, selling myself more aggressively. I was also looking into the PI licensing exam. Maybe I'd read up on it tonight.

The sound of a screen door banging shut stopped my thoughts. Smith trudged down his front steps wearing a sweat suit and circled his house, head-ing past his truck and toward his garage. I quickly raised the camera and rolled down my window, but I didn't have a good line of sight.

Slipping out of the car while adjusting the settings on the camera, I moved quietly toward the garage. The air filled with static and jumping voices of jum-bled radio stations, and then heavy-metal rock surfaced, wailing guitars distort-ing the speakers. The volume lowered. I moved along the side of the driveway, the shrubbery scratching my back, and paused at the sound of clanging.

Larry hadn't prepped the location, so I had no idea what was going on. I started recording. I heard Smith grunting as he pushed something heavy. Per-fect. More clanging. I watched the viewfinder flare as I inched toward the garage, where there was more light. I stopped and stared into the glowing screen.

Life should always be viewed with night vision, I thought. It filtered out the unimportant details. Backgrounds faded. Shadows blurred. People—their eyes, their expressions—became grotesquely real.

A commercial came onto the radio. Smith let out a long, deep breath.

Inching closer I saw Smith lying on a workout bench, his thick arms lifting up the bar with large iron plates on each side. Large weights lay on the floor around him. He slammed the bar back into position and sighed. I continued recording, zooming in, needing a shot of Smith's face for identification. I smelled talcum powder and motor oil.

Smith sat up slowly, wiping his forehead with his sweat suit sleeve, and I got a clear shot of his blotchy, shiny face.

I wanted to leave but wasn't sure how much the bench presses affected Smith's back. He leaned forward and with each hand picked up a dumbbell. He began curls, flexing his biceps. He exhaled though his teeth, sweat beading on his bald head. I thought, Bingo. There was no way that someone with a bad back could do those thirty-pound curls.

"Yo, what the fuck you doing?" a voice behind me said.

I whirled around and saw a muscular man in shorts and T-shirt approaching, his thighs bulging with each step forward. He noticed my camera and said, "What the hell?"

Smith stood up off the bench and lowered the radio volume.

I thought, Hmm.

The man approached, folded his mammoth arms, and said, "B. B., this Chinese guy is taping your work out. What is this, some sick faggot pervert thing?"

Smith said, "Huh? He's taping me?"

"What's up," the man said to Smith with a laugh. "You into some things I should know about?"

I glanced at both of them as they closed in with a mix of curiosity and hostility, and I was about to try some fast-talking when Smith said, "Oh, wait a fucking minute! It's the insurance company!"

With that, I dove through the bushes and rolled into the neighbor's yard. Smith yelled, "Get that fucking camera! I'm fucking screwed if they see that!"

Smith's friend crashed through the shrubs as I scrambled up and ran toward my car. I looked back in amazement as he zipped across the yard with surprising speed, his pasty white legs blurring in the night. A surge of adrenaline pushed me on, and I stumbled over a lawn sprinkler that spit out a string of water in protest. I almost dropped the camera. A dog barked hesitantly. Smith hefted himself down his driveway, trying to cut me off. I raised the camera, which was still recording, and taped Smith running. He cursed. His face contorted into an enraged grimace.

I reached my car, but Smith's quick friend grabbed my arm and tried to pull me back. I turned and shoved him away, then opened my door. As I jumped in, I saw Smith picking up a brick from the curb and holding it high. He looked like a white hairless bear thundering toward the car. His friend yanked open my door before I could lock it, and he grabbed my neck. His fingers dug into my throat.

"Where you think you going, asshole?"

I gasped and dropped the camera near my feet, and the man choked me while trying to pull me from the car. I started the engine. The man's hands were slippery and smelled of wintergreen. Smith thundered to the passenger side and slammed the brick into the window, and the glass exploded into tiny pieces and sprinkled over the seats. He reached in and lunged for the camera, but I shifted into drive and jerked the car forward. Smith yelped and held on for a second before falling away, and his friend cursed as his grip slipped from my neck and scraped my skin. My door flung wide open and I stepped on the accelerator, losing control as I drove up the curb with a crunch. I yanked on the steering wheel, turning the car back onto the street. I bounced in my seat, the world blurring around me. The bottom of my car scraped loudly against the pavement. I pulled into the middle of the road, still pressing the accelerator, and reached forward to close my door. Regaining control of the steering, I sped away. In the rearview mirror I saw Smith punching his fist into the air, spitting out curses. The night air blew into the car, rattling the plastic around Linda's candy. The box had been flattened by the brick, and little shards of glass sparkled around the cellophane wrapper. My eyes watered from the minty fumes on my neck, or maybe it was from being choked. The red recording light on the camcorder flashed against the dirty floor mat.

I caught my breath and touched my sore neck, the relief making me giddy. I let out a short, nervous laugh, then stopped at the thought of what might have happened if they had caught me, then laughed again.

Two

Linda and I met when I was still working at ProServ. She had looked into the details of the shooting of my late partner, helping me track the chain of events back some twenty years. She ended up writing an extended feature about the entire mess. I call it that—the Mess—because I still haven't quite sorted everything out, including my feelings toward my aunt Insook, whom I learned had been responsible for my father's death when I was ten years old. She had probably fled to Guam or Korea, though no one really knew, and I still think about her a lot.

I was grateful for Linda's help, and we had grown close during that time. We started dating cautiously, and I attributed this wariness to my inexperience and to her early marriage that had ended bitterly. We circled and feinted. We were awkwardly casual by pretending not to think about any long-term plans. At least *I* had pretended this.

Throughout those first few months I had a strong image of Linda, formed from an early meeting, of her leaning back on a sidewalk railing, her cropped leather jacket hanging open, one leg hooked behind her on a low rung; her black thick-soled boots sharply contrasting her faded jeans. She had worn that outfit when we had searched downtown Palo Alto for a contact, and it was the first time I had really *seen* her. I had realized at that moment that she was more than a reporter looking into my partner's death; she was a friend trying to help me. And she had looked so damn good. Her stance said, Don't mess with me. I probably started falling for her around then.

About nine or ten months into this, though, something changed. We were both having job trouble—I had moved to Black Diamond but immediately resisted the highly formal corporate culture, and Linda's promotion to features writer was fraught with colleague envy and infighting. No doubt this bled into our personal lives. I soon left Black Diamond and agreed to start talking to Larry about a partnership. Linda felt more trapped in her job, though. Her mood darkened. Small annoyances mushroomed between us: I splashed too much water around the sink when I washed my face; she'd leave the front door unlocked, which, considering my profession, felt like a willful dig. I wanted to speak ungrammatically just to annoy her.

Then there was Harlan, an editor at the newspaper with whom she began spending more time. What the hell kind of name was Harlan? I imagined a tall, broad-shouldered blond Iowan. I imagined a man who constantly swept back his hair and smiled with bright white teeth. Harlan, Harlan, Harlan. Truthfully, I imagined much more than that.

After my run-in with Smith, I drove to my apartment in Monte Vista, the wind swirling around me and fluttering the seat belt next to the broken window. The sound was oddly lulling, making me think of sailboats. My throat was raw, my coughs painful. I hoped I could get Larry to expense the window repairs. I watched the video in the parking lot, smiling as the camera shook wildly, red-faced Smith coming after me. Larry was going to love this. I could see him raising his thumb and saying, "You nailed him, buddy."

Larry was pushing me to get my PI license, since this would allow me to conduct interviews and help ease his client load. I was stalling, both because I didn't like the subtle rebuke that my end was lagging, and because everyone I knew in the executive protection business looked down on PIs. This wasn't because of the stereotype, of the sleazy antics in which I had just participated, but because PIs had been encroaching on the bodyguarding turf, often without the training and experience. Lately, PIs had been justifying their executive protection by claiming it was part of their investigatory case, but because they often didn't know what they were doing—bodyguarding was more than looking tough and talking into your wrist—they were lowering standards. At ProServ, all the agents logged at least fifty hours of course work and training in executive protection, firearms, self-defense, electronic surveillance, defensive driving, and dozens of other aspects of security.

It was partly ego. I could imagine what some of my former colleagues might say if they heard I was working as a private detective. Peeping through windows. Digging through trash. But I had to be realistic. I had to think about the future. If I earned my PI license, I would be a double threat. I couldn't dismiss this.

I taped up my car window with plastic and brushed out the floor mats. Glass pebbles danced onto the blacktop. The box of chocolates was crushed. I popped a truffle into my mouth and walked up to my studio apartment, rubbing my throat. I said the alphabet aloud, testing my voice. It cracked at "h."

I spent the rest of the evening reading through the PI-licensing application and eating Linda's present. It turned out that my former job wasn't enough to qualify me for the minimum three years' work experience as an investigator. However, I knew my ex-boss, Polansky, was licensed as a private investigator in addition to private patrol operator. I could petition the Bureau of Security and Investigative Services (BSIS) and have Polansky certify my years at Pro-Serv. Technically I hadn't done any investigative work, but the BSIS wouldn't know that. With Polansky's help, I could take the exam immediately.

Mulling this over while cooking instant ramen, I felt my stomach souring from all the chocolate. I thought about Linda. The two things I didn't want to worry about right now—my job and Linda—kept shouldering their way toward me. I changed into a sweat suit and shoved the unfinished ramen into my bare refrigerator. I went for a run.

Night in Monte Vista had a crispness that stung my face. I had been lengthening my route to five miles, twice a week. I no longer felt stitches in my legs or cramps in my gut, and I moved lightly over the sidewalks on the balls of my feet. I hovered, then flew. I had tried to get Linda to join me, but she didn't like it. She didn't see the point. "You just run in circles," she said.

Yes, in circles, but in ever-increasing ones. And with a familiar route I freed myself from the logistics of navigation. I glided outside of myself, my thoughts separating from my surroundings, and found a unique calm that I couldn't duplicate anywhere else. Streetlamps blurred, as did headlights from cars. The world dropped away and left me alone. I thought of nothing and everything.

I returned home, sweaty, panting, and relaxed. I was heading into the shower when the phone rang. My tension returned. I let the machine answer it, but as soon as I heard Linda's voice I picked up.

"Hey! What's up," I said, forcing the cheerfulness. "How's it going down there?"

"My brother's dead, Allen. They found him, or what's left of him, in a car wreck."

I could begin with the first time I had heard about Linda's brother Hector, and the subsequent conversations about him that occasionally arose, especially when we had dinner with Linda's stepsister. I could continue with Harlan, and how I had overheard Linda on the phone with him, telling him about her brother's initial disappearance. She explained it to him at greater length, and I couldn't help but wonder why I got the quick summary whereas Harlan got the details.

Admit it.

Yes, I was jealous. Her voice on the phone had been quiet, almost seductive with a guy I had never met, though his name, *Harlan*, seemed to float around her conversations. This, combined with the recent spate of arguments, had made me instantly suspicious.

I was paid to be alert, to notice innocuous signals that belied a deeper truth. I was trained to see hidden hands and furtive glances. I saw movements before they became movements, gestures of anticipation. I thought I knew what I was seeing here.

Or perhaps I should begin with Larry giving me a heavy-lidded look as I told him about needing a few days off from work. I planned to fly down to Los Angeles to see Linda.

No, I should begin with Hector. His body, or what was left of it—burned, melted—was found in a charred car at the bottom of Luego Canyon in Malibu. Hector had plummeted two hundred feet and into a bed of small boulders and shrubs. His car had caught fire and blazed down to black metal. It was smoldering when a motorcyclist, racing through the quiet canyon roads, noticed the trail of smoke ascending in the breeze. Recent rains kept the fire from spreading. The motorcyclist called the fire department, and they brought in a hazardous material unit as soon as fire officials suspected the presence of chemical products and a strong formaldehyde smell. Haz-Mat found evidence of an acetone-based chemical and anhydrous ammonia in containers in the trunk, ingredients for the production of methamphetamines.

The accident investigation team also found blackened bottles of liquor in the front seat. Using the license plate and the vehicle identification number, the police traced the car to Mr. Luke Sherwin, who had recently filed a missing person's report for his stepson, Hector Gama. The Los Angeles Coroner and the Sheriff's office contacted Hector's parents, then Linda called me, and everything was set in motion.

Three

My flight was delayed, and by the time I reached L.A. and walked from the plane to the terminal, I was ninety minutes behind schedule. Linda was standing against a column, her arms folded, her eyes checking the arriving passengers, but I saw her first. I felt a small rush of pleasure as I recognized her familiar, anxious expression as she searched for me. Her head tilted up, and she bit her lower lip as she scanned back and forth. Some of her hair fell over her face and she tucked it aside with her pinky finger. She had on a familiar blue blouse, the sleeves rolled up, and faded jeans. I waved. She turned to me, and smiled. In that instant both of us had forgotten why I was here. She rolled her eyes and pointed to her watch.

We hugged and she kissed my cheek. All I had was a duffel bag, so I told her we could go. "Sorry for being late."

"It always happens," she said. "It's good to see you."

I checked her expression. She smiled and nodded. A spark of hope warmed my chest. She pointed to the escalators, and we walked toward them. She filled me in about Hector: "The police think he was drunk and probably high, and drove straight off the cliff. No brake marks. The fire was fast, because of the chemicals, and probably burned out quickly. No witnesses."

"Why the chemicals?" I asked, as we left the terminal and walked to a parking lot. "Did he make drugs?"

"I don't know," she said. "My mom and Luke were surprised. Maybe he was delivering it? I just don't know." We climbed into a large black sedan—her stepfather's, she explained—and she drove us out of the airport. Her face seemed tired, drawn down, and her usual tightly wound body, ready to spring, was languid, sinking back into the driver's seat. Her arms flexed for a moment as she held onto the steering wheel. I slid closer to her and put my hand on her neck.

"How are you?" I asked.

"Still in shock, I guess. My mom is worse."

"How?"

"In a haze. She's not fully accepting this. It's very weird."

"Is Julie coming down?"

"Not yet. Her daughter has a bad case of the flu. She might fly down later."

"She didn't get along with him," I said, remembering some of Linda's conversations with her stepsister. Julie and her father, Luke, joined Linda's family when Linda was twelve.

"Not really," she replied. "I told you about when they were kids."

I turned to her. "Hector didn't like them becoming part of the family."

"He was a good kid before that, but after they started living with us, he was impossible."

"He was young."

"Around nine or ten." She sighed. "Maybe I could've helped him down here."

"You didn't know what was happening—"

"Julie and I heard things were getting worse. My mom mentioned it."

"Worse how?"

"He was staying away most of the time, barely ever coming home. He was fighting more with my parents." She stared ahead, her jaw tightening. "I'm sure I could've talked to him." After a moment she said, "My mom's looking forward to meeting you."

"They don't mind me being there?"

"No," she said. "They have the odd idea that you're down here to help me find out more."

"More?"

"About Hector, what he was doing. No one really knows."

"Why would they think that?"

She said quietly, "They think we're a team."

The way she said this startled me, since it wasn't clear if Linda agreed. That glimmer of hope faded. I felt my stomach tightening, and leaned back in my seat. We didn't speak for the rest of the ride.

Marina Alta was only fifteen minutes away from the airport and as we drove along the main boulevard, the sun bright, reflections blinking simultaneously off trafficked cars, I noticed construction sites every few blocks. Skeleton frames rose up into the blue sky, cranes and bulldozers lined up on the powdery dirt. A thin film of dust seemed to cover this town, but once we turned toward the marinas, the rope-entwined masts of tall sailboats webbing the horizon, a cooler breeze filled the car. Linda pointed to a tall building down the street. The top floor had a huge banner with "Condos for Sale" strung over two balconies, the red letters undulating.

"Is that a new building?" I asked.

"A couple years old. They moved into it about a year ago." She parked us deep in an underground garage. Yellow lights shone down on us. I grabbed my duffel bag and followed Linda up the stairs and into the front lobby, the tiled floors unmarred and gleaming. The far wall was mirrored, and at the elevators we looked at ourselves. Linda smiled at me in the reflection.

"Are you okay?"

"I guess a little nervous."

"About meeting my parents?" she asked. The elevator bell rang softly, and the doors opened. She walked in. "It'll be fine."

Her parents were waiting for us and stood up from the sofa as soon as we entered the apartment. Linda's stepfather, gray-haired and thin, almost skeletal, greeted me with a somber hello and offered me his hand, his grip brittle, his movements stiff and jerky. Then he said, *"Ah nung ha seh yo."*

I hesitated. "Excuse me?"

"*Ah nung ha seh yo.* Doesn't that mean 'hello' in Korean?"

"Dad," Linda said. "I told you not to do that."

He said to me, "One of my partners at the firm is Korean. He taught me that."

Linda gave me an apologetic look.

I said, "Actually, Mr. Sherwin, I don't speak Korean."

He said it was too bad and asked that I call him Luke. He then introduced me to his wife. Instead of shaking my hand, Linda's mother hugged me. She was much shorter and heavier than her photos, and when she let me go, she grabbed my forearm and squeezed hard. I looked down. Her fingers were thick and strong, rings and bracelets sparkling. "You'll help Linda, won't you?" she asked. Her face was made over with thick powder.

"Help her? I'll try, Mrs.—"

"Marianne. You call me Marianne."

"I'm sorry about Hector," I said.

She tugged my arm. "Thank you. I'll show you the guest room." She guided me down a long hallway with white plush carpeting and framed generic prints on the walls, her strong perfume trailing her. I heard Linda talking quietly with Luke.

"That's Hector's room," Marianne said, as we passed a small bedroom with the shades drawn. The bed was neatly made, and except for a few small psychedelic posters of DJs and bands, everything seemed impersonal, sanitized, and bare. I smelled pine air freshener, reminding me of a hotel room. Before I could study the bureau and desk, Marianne pulled me along to the next room, which she said was an office, but Linda would be sleeping there now.

"She doesn't have a room?"

"No. She was in the guest room, but we want you to have that."

"I don't mind the office—"

"Please. We already cleaned it for you." She opened the door to the guest room, and motioned me in. "The sofa folds out. Fresh sheets and pillows in the closet."

I wondered whose idea it was to separate our sleeping arrangements. Small potted plants lined the windowsill, framing a view of the marina and the ocean. A portable TV sat next to a desk. "It's better than my apartment," I told her. She was watching me closely. "Is something wrong?" I asked.

"I just need more answers," she said.

"What?"

"I just don't understand how and why . . ." Her face tightened, and she stepped toward me. "I need to understand what was going on."

I was startled by how open she was to a stranger and didn't know how to respond. I had grown up with my aunt, and a cold reserve had always shrouded us. I asked, "He was acting differently?"

"Mom," Linda said from the hallway, and appeared at the door. "Give him a chance to catch his breath. He just got off a plane."

"Did you tell him what Hector said to me?" Marianne asked.

"Not yet."

"Tell him."

"Now?"

"Isn't he here to help you?"

Linda held up her hand and said tiredly, "Mom—"

"Don't do that," Marianne snapped. "Don't dismiss me like that. You haven't been here in a long time and Hector was going through something."

Luke appeared behind Linda and said, "Ladies, shall we convene in the living room and give Allen a chance to unpack?"

"I'm taking Allen out," Linda said.

"Right now?" Marianne turned to me. "Have you even had lunch?"

"Uh, not yet—"

"Mom, I'll take him out," Linda said. "I already called Hector's ex-girlfriend. We're going to talk to her this afternoon."

"Who?" Marianne said. "Why didn't she come to the funeral?"

"She was working yesterday."

"The funeral was yesterday?" I asked. "Not tomorrow?"

"We moved it up," Linda answered.

I said, "I could've flown down yesterday."

"Why didn't you tell Allen?" her mother said.

"Okay, stop," Linda said. "Everyone stop, please." She rubbed her temples. "We need a little quiet. I need to talk to Allen. Can all this wait?"

Marianne was about to protest, but Linda raised her hand. "Please, Mom?" she said. "I promise we'll be back for dinner."

Everyone waited for Marianne's response, and I found myself stepping back, trying to fade away. I heard a clock ticking in the hallway. Marianne glanced at me, then at Linda, then threw up her hands. "Fine. Dinner."

Linda hurried me out of the apartment and pressed the elevator button a few times. I watched her tap her foot as the numbers above slowly blinked to our floor. If the funeral had been yesterday, then she could've invited me during our conversation two days ago. She had purposely kept me away until today. The elevator door opened, and I said quietly, "Didn't you want me here for the funeral?"

She walked in. I followed. The door closed with a hiss. In the following silence, which was all the answer I needed, I felt my balance shifting as the elevator descended, and that strong sense of being unwanted, something I felt acutely as a child, resurfaced. A quiet, insistent voice popped into my head and whispered, *What the hell are you doing here?*

I said, "What the hell am I doing here?"

Hector, two months before he disappeared, had told his mother that he might be leaving soon. He was twenty-seven and barely living at home, anyway, staying out for days and coming home only to do his laundry. When Marianne had pressed him for details, all he would say was that he was tired and knew he had to move on. Linda told me this story with some skepticism, adding that it sounded like her mother had filtered his words. "She seems to think that he was really depressed, how he could've committed suicide, drinking and driving. She kept telling me how he seemed so down."

I stared ahead. The realization that Linda might not have wanted me here had rattled me. I watched her drive, the sleeves of her blue blouse rolled up, and she said, "He could've been drunk and high, and then maybe he drove off the cliff. I could see that." She paused, then said, "You're not listening."

"Why am I here?" I asked.

She glanced at me, then signaled and switched lanes. After a long silence she replied, "You're here because it seems to comfort my mom."

"Why?"

"She knows how we found out about your father and aunt."

"The Mess?"

"She followed my stories."

"Do *you* want me here?"

"I asked you, didn't I?"

I looked out my window. I said, "Whenever you don't want to answer a

question, you ask another question that's supposed to answer it, but doesn't."
I turned back to her. "Do you want me here?"

She let out a slow breath, and said, "I didn't want you here for the funeral because it was just a family thing, and I didn't want to have to think about . . ." She waved her hand in the air.

"About me."

"About us," she said.

"But I'm here now."

"You're here now and I really appreciate it. I can use your help."

"To do what?"

"To see what Hector was up to. My mom wants to know."

"You said you wanted to come down here to think about us."

She nodded. "It's true."

"Have you?"

"Have I what?"

"Have you been thinking about us?"

"Yes."

I waited, then after a minute asked, "And?"

She pressed her fingers to her forehead, rubbing, then sighed. "I don't know if I can do this now. Allen, my brother is . . . I just can't do this now."

"Sorry," I said, chastened. "You're right." I looked up at the sky. Exhaustion brushed my heart. I couldn't see a single cloud, the color a striking deep blue, and this alarmed me. In the Bay Area, I always saw clouds somewhere, sometimes a hint of fog, a marine layer. There was something false about a perfect blue sky. I needed an imperfect view. Maybe none of this was real.

"Allen?" Linda prompted.

"Tell me about this woman we're meeting."

She hesitated, then told me that Serena was Hector's ex-girlfriend, and the only one to send flowers. Linda had called to thank her, then started asking some questions. "I've never seen any of Hector's friends before, so I wanted to meet her."

"What about current girlfriends or friends?" I asked. "No one called or anything?"

"No. That's strange, isn't it? I mean, his death was in the paper and everything."

"Maybe he didn't have friends," I said.

"He must have. He was always going out."

"Did he do drugs?" I asked.

"I don't know. He had some trouble with the law over marijuana, a couple misdemeanor possessions, but I don't know about harder drugs." We pulled off the 405 freeway and began winding through Costa Mesa, a small town with Spanish-styled houses and bungalows. Large palm trees and leafy bushes overwhelmed many of the yards. Linda seemed to know the area, and so I asked her about this.

"We lived down here for a couple of years. Right after my father left we moved into a tiny apartment in Santa Ana."

"How old were you when he left?"

"Nine."

"Why move here?"

"A job. My mom worked in a fabric company." Linda checked the street signs. She began counting off house numbers and told me to look for 320. We found it and parked in front of a small brown house with ivy thickly knotting a trellis. I climbed out and was blasted with sun; I had to stop to catch my breath, and my skin instantly broke out in a sweat. Linda walked ahead. I watched her shimmer though the wavy heat as she bunched up her hair and twisted it off her neck with a flick. She rang the doorbell, and we heard a dog barking. After a minute Linda rang again, and this sent the dog into a door-scratching frenzy. We stepped back and looked at each other.

"Is she expecting us?" I asked.

Linda glanced at her watch. "Oh. We're early. I expected more traffic." We sat on the front steps. Linda fanned her blouse.

The silence weighed us down. I remembered how last year we couldn't stop kidding each other. She used to tease me about my old nickname, the Block. "The Block approaches," she used to say, imitating the narrator of the nature shows I would sometimes watch at her place. "The Block, in its natural environment, sits in front of its dinner and consumes it heartily." She would smile, her eyes dancing. Once, I couldn't resist and looked up slowly, then said, "The Block, sensing its mate in heat, rears its head in anticipation."

"Oh, very funny. Hilarious," she said, grinning.

"The Block approaches cautiously, fearing the dangerous mating ritual."

"Ha-ha."

This memory now brought a small smile to my lips, but I hid it from

Linda. We listened to the dog whining on the other side of the door. We sat a few inches apart, not touching, waiting, and it might as well have been a few miles apart.

A young Asian woman in tight black spandex running shorts and a yellow sports bra jogged up the street. Her lean face and arms shone with perspiration, rivulets of sweat trickling down her neck and bare midriff. When she saw Linda and me, she slowed down, walking up the front path, breathing hard. She wiped her forehead with her arm, slickness dripping. Her short black hair had once been bleached, now only the tips white, small jagged spikes covering her head. She nodded to us. We stood. She then turned back to the edge of the sidewalk, still huffing. She coughed, bent over with her hands on her knees, and spit into the street. Slim muscles curved around her shoulders and down her arms.

I hadn't gone running in a few days, and felt my legs yearning.

Linda said, "It's pretty hot for a run."

The woman nodded, trying to catch her breath. She said, "Too . . . hot . . ." She stretched her arms up, then twisted, giving us a nice view of her ridged abdomen.

"Are you Serena?" Linda asked.

"Yeah. You're Hector's sister. Sorry about him. I couldn't make the funeral."

I knew then that she had been invited, that the funeral hadn't just been for the family. Linda had lied to me.

Linda said quickly, "Sorry we're early. We thought there'd be more traffic. Thanks for the flowers."

"No prob. Who's this?" She turned to me, and I wasn't sure why I was surprised that Hector's ex-girlfriend was Asian American.

Linda said, "This is Allen, a friend. If you want, we can come back later."

"No, it's fine. Hello, Allen."

I nodded hello, disturbed by Linda's lie. Serena waited for me to respond, and when I didn't she said to Linda, "Strong, silent type, huh." She moved between us to open her door. Small knots of muscle flexed on her shoulders as she leaned forward to scratch her dog's ears. Her dog barked, and when she pushed open the door she crouched down and said, "Shh, Gracie. We have guests."

Gracie, a German shepherd mix with black-and-brown fur, nuzzled Serena's hand, then pushed past her to sniff us. Linda held her palm out, which Gracie licked. I had once been bitten seriously as a kid and have never been comfortable with dogs since then. A moment of uncertainty flashed through me, which Gracie sensed. She growled.

"Hey," Serena said. "Be nice."

I bent forward and extended my palm. After a moment, Gracie sniffed it, and moved on. Serena led us into the living room and said to me, "She's protective of me with men. She can sense wolves. Are you a wolf?" She smiled, and I felt Linda tense next to me. Serena asked us to have a seat, excusing herself. I tried not to stare at her while she walked away, her gait smooth and even. Gracie, clicking on the pale hardwood floors, moved next to us, and I petted her carefully.

"You guys want something to drink?" Serena called from the kitchen, a faucet running. We told her we were fine and looked around. Wood and leather furniture surrounded us. African masks hung on the walls. Although dark from the trees blocking the front windows, the interior felt comfortable, lived-in. I had trouble placing Hector here.

When Serena returned with a towel around her neck, her hair wet and combed back, she sipped from a water bottle and asked, "You wanted to talk about Hector?"

"We're just trying to figure out what he was up to recently," Linda said. "There are some things that don't make sense."

"Like what?"

Linda mentioned how Hector had died and what had been in the car. Serena looked surprised, and turned to me for acknowledgment. Linda ended with, "So maybe you can tell us something that might help? Do you know if he used or sold drugs?"

Serena began to answer, but stopped. She asked me, "Did you know him?"

I shook my head.

"So how are you involved here?" She wiped her forehead with the tip of her towel.

"Just a friend," I said. "Their mother also asked me down here."

"He speaks!" Serena said with a grin. "Are you a narc?"

"No."

"You have that clean-cut look of a narc."

"Do I?" I asked. "No. I *do* work in security."

"What kind?"

"Executive protection. A bodyguard."

"Really. I've never met a bodyguard."

"So, did Hector use drugs?" Linda asked. "Did you guys go out for long?"

Serena sat on an ottoman and crossed her legs. Her expression became more serious. "Well, we went out for maybe six or seven months, but this was almost two years ago. He went out with other people since then."

"And drugs?" Linda asked.

"That's odd, all that stuff in the car. He never did meth, not around me. I mean, he did E and a lot of pot, but never speed." She shrugged. "But who knows? When we broke up he was going through a lot of stuff."

"What do you mean?" Linda asked.

"Just real down and kind of confused. Then I started going to night school and he wanted to do something like that, but he couldn't really hack it."

"Night school? What did he want to study?"

"That's the thing. He didn't know. He was trying to find something."

"What are you studying?" I asked.

"Web authoring. Programming. Time to get practical." She winked at me.

"Why'd you break up?" Linda asked.

"Oh, who knows? We were changing. I was getting serious about things, and he was still acting like . . . like a kid." She said to me, "I need to go out with an adult, you know? I have to think about my future. Do you bodyguard actors and stars?"

"No. Mostly executives. A lot of high-tech people."

"Around here?"

"I'm from the Bay Area," I said. "We both are. Silicon Valley."

"Really? I'm thinking of getting a job up there."

Linda said, "Was Hector dealing?"

"I don't think so," Serena answered, turning to her. "Well, he started doing more raves, and I think he sold E on the side."

"Ecstasy?" I asked.

"Yeah," Serena answered. "We both went to a lot of raves, but I got tired of it." Serena wiped her neck with her towel. She caught me looking, and the corner of her mouth raised into a smile. "Tim Jacobs. Have you talked to him?"

"Not yet," Linda said.

"They were friends. Tim and his girlfriend."

"Do you have a number? An address?"

"Venice, near the boardwalk. He's probably in the phone book."

"Do you know why Hector was in Malibu? Did he know someone there?"

"No idea. He liked the beach."

"Hector?" Linda asked.

"Yeah. He even tried surfing for a while."

Linda seemed surprised by this, and I asked Serena, "So, what was he like? How would you describe him?"

She tilted her head at me, thinking. She finally said, "He was . . . lost."

"Lost how?" Linda asked.

"He couldn't really grab onto anything."

"You mean jobs?"

"Jobs. People. Everything. Sometimes he talked about wishing he could go back and redo everything. He once mentioned looking for his father, just to start over at the beginning. To set things right."

"What?" Linda said.

"Didn't your father take off a long time ago?"

Linda blinked. "My father?"

"The one that took off when you were kids?"

Linda nodded, but seemed too startled to speak.

"Hector couldn't figure out why he felt so . . . I don't know . . . empty . . . angry. He was always trying to figure out what went wrong."

Linda just kept staring. Everyone seemed to run out of things to say, so I stood up and asked Linda if we were done. She turned to me and nodded. Serena showed us to the door. Gracie followed us. Linda thanked Serena, then walked ahead to the car. Serena said, "Nice to meet you, Mr. Bodyguard. How long are you in town?"

"Not sure. Not long."

"Give me a call if you feel like doing something. I can show you around. You can tell me about places to live up north."

I hesitated, wondering if Linda could hear this, I said, "Thanks. That might be fun."

She raised her bare shoulder in a half shrug.

I walked away, feeling her watch me, and climbed into the car. Linda started the engine and drove off. We were quiet. I asked, "You okay?"

She seemed to snap back to attention and said, "I'm okay."

"Well, what do you think?" I asked.

She narrowed her eyes. "Could she have hit on you any harder?"

"What?" I asked, with as blank a face as I could manage. "What do you mean?"

She rolled her eyes at me. "Oh, please."

I looked out the window and said softly, "Too bad she couldn't make the funeral."

Four

The reason why I was called "The Block" in high school was because of my build, which some kids thought looked like a square building block, and I played fullback on our soccer team, successfully defending and blocking our end. I quickly regretted telling Linda about it, since it became an endearment. "Hello, Block," she'd say as she settled onto the sofa next to me. After a while I became used to it, but whenever she saw a headline in her newspaper with the word "block" in it, she couldn't resist clipping it for me. So now I had random snippets in my desk drawer such as "Governor's Building Blocks" and "The Blockhead Budget." When things between us seemed to be going well, the term would mutate into "Blocky," or she'd use it to define something that related to me, as in, "But is this truly blockable?" meaning, was it something I liked.

Linda's playfulness had been unexpected, since I'd grown to know her under bleaker circumstances, and I came to enjoy this kind of teasing from her. And when it stopped, when that lighter feeling of play began ebbing, replaced with a seriousness often centering on work problems or reflecting the subtle tension between us, I felt the loss. I almost winced at her use of "Allen" instead of "Block."

After leaving Serena's, Linda and I had a quick lunch at a small pizza parlor. We were attracted to the noisy air conditioner over the front entrance, the promise of cool. Two teenage boys sat in the corner—the only other customers—and the small plastic table rocked every time I reached for my plate. I said, "You're not mad about her flirting, are you?"

"No. It was cute. I always knew you had a thing for hard bodies."

I wasn't sure if she was joking. This difficulty reading her had been happening more often, and I was suddenly unsure if I should be defensive. I felt the urge to confess. "Did you hear what she said as I was leaving?"

"No."

I laughed, trying to lighten it, and said, "She asked me to call her, to hang out."

"Come on," she said. "You're kidding."

"I'm not. When you went to the car."

She raised her eyebrow, but didn't say anything.

"It was nothing," I said, waving it off.

I tried not to dwell on her not wanting me at the funeral. Fine. Perhaps I would've been a distraction, and I didn't know Hector or the family. Frankly, I would've felt awkward there, anyway. I decided to let this fall away. I watched her poke at her small salad. I asked, "Did what Serena say about your brother surprise you?"

"She made him sound more . . . thoughtful than the Hector I knew."

"Selling drugs?"

"That didn't surprise me."

"What about the raves? What do you know about them?"

"We did a few stories in the *Sentinel*. Didn't you read them?"

"Not really. I just look for your articles."

She smiled. "That's nice of you, but you're missing out on a lot of other things. Raves are illegal dance clubs that people put up for a night." She pushed her salad aside. "I guess I barely knew him."

"Even as kids?"

"I used to look out for him. He was so skinny and weak, and I was always dealing with bullies going after him." She turned to the door as the teenagers left. A wave of warm air passed over us, and the air conditioner shuddered.

"Our father, Raul, used to push Hector around because he was so sickly. Raul hated his son to be so puny."

"Push around? Physically?"

"Yell at him for being weak, but yeah, pushed him around. Especially after he'd have a few beers."

I hadn't heard this before, and said, "But not you?"

"No. He left me alone. He actually used to bring home gifts for me. I hated when he did that, played favorites. There was something about Hector that really bugged him. I don't know." She was quiet for a while, then said, "I think I'm feeling it."

"What?"

"Dis-ease."

She used to make fun of my system of removement, the framework I was trying to construct based on the search for engagement. Dis-ease was the opposite of feeling at ease with yourself and others. It pointed to a sense— sometimes unconscious or vaguely hinted—of disconnection, of looking around and suddenly seeing with clarity how strange everyone and everything really was. Dis-ease was when you looked at the person next to you and were simply unsure if she were some kind of alien walking around in human skin. "Describe it," I asked Linda.

She stared down at her hands on the table. "Like that hand isn't mine." She looked at me. "Like I'm not fully here. Like I'm slipping."

I put my hand on hers. "You have to shake out of it."

She said, "Right. Through . . . what was it? Enclosement? No, wait, encouragement?" She smiled.

"Engagement. Very funny. You're mocking me."

"No. I remember what you said. We find it through others, through work, by meeting something head-on."

"You listened."

"I did." She stared out the window. "Once we get through all this I'll feel better."

"Come on," I said. "Let's follow up Tim Jacobs. Should we look at Hector's room?"

"We should."

"You haven't yet?"

"Not yet."

We left the pizza parlor, and hit the heat outside. I said, "Will you be okay?"

She said, "Maybe I should go running and get all sweaty and blink cutely at you."

This stopped me. Then I saw her smile.

"Will you wear skin-tight shorts?" I asked. "Will you show me your cleavage?"

"In your dreams."

"If you insist. I'll start dreaming tonight."

She sighed. "Man, was she obvious."

"She's young."

"Don't remind me."

I glanced at her. "Will you be okay?" I repeated.

She took a deep breath, shielding her eyes from the sun, and said, "Let's find out what we can, satisfy my mom, and then I'll be fine."

Yes, I thought, But will *we* be fine?

I began formulating my notions about the dis-ease during the Mess two years ago. In serious jeopardy of going to jail, my money running out, and unable to trust anyone except Linda, I clutched at the straws of rationality. I tried to break down and analyze everything, including my fragmented thoughts and nebulous feelings, and I realized later that I had been displaying some of the signs of depression. But it had calmed me to postulate theories as to why everything felt so wrong. With some time and perspective, however, I was beginning to see that my attempts to order the chaos had been a good idea. By quantifying my indecision and puzzlement, I had been able to focus.

I had named it, for the time being, a philosophy of removement. We are all displaced from the center, from others. I had no answers, but I continued my search.

When we had left Serena's house and had driven in silence, I wondered if I was attracted to her. Yes, I was.

Why didn't you do anything? Why didn't you respond? I asked myself.

Because I didn't want to hurt Linda's feelings.

Why not?

Because I like Linda a lot.

Love might be a way toward engagement.

I never said "love," and even if it were true, the thought was too scary to admit.

Nevertheless, this might be a way toward engagement, because you fight off the dis-ease by connecting with another.

If Linda didn't reciprocate, though? Then what?

Love is also a way to get kicked in the stomach.

We returned to Marina Alta, intending to search Hector's room. When we entered the condo, we found the dining room table elaborately set with wine-glasses and gleaming china, the smell of roasting chicken assaulting us. Luke was watching TV with a large beer in his hand and said hello to us. "I hope you two are hungry," he said. "She's cooking a feast."

"Already?" Linda asked.

"You know we eat dinner earlier on weekends," Luke said.

I felt the pizza sitting heavily in my stomach. I sat down with Luke while Linda went to talk to her mother. On TV was a business news show with the anchors discussing the stock market. I remembered Linda telling me that Luke worked in real estate and had once tried to bring Hector into his firm. Hector had lasted for two weeks. Luke cleared his throat and said to me, "Sorry about that Korean remark. I was just looking for a chance to use what I learned."

I said it was fine.

"May I ask why you don't speak Korean?"

"My father never taught it to me. He always spoke English to me." I shrugged. "What kind of name is Sherwin?"

He smiled. "Polish. My grandfather was from Czerwin, Poland. His name was Czerwinski, but he changed it to Sherwin."

"Do you speak Polish?"

He shook his head.

"Your father?"

"No. Well, maybe a few words, but no."

I smiled, deciding not to point out the inconsistency. He had expected me to speak Korean, whereas neither he nor his father spoke Polish. Instead I said, "All these different last names in this family."

Luke held up his hand and counted. "Linda Gama Sherwin Maldonado."

"But she only kept her ex's last name," I said.

"Thank goodness for that."

Linda and her mother's voices rose in the kitchen. A very sharp, "Give me a break" came from Linda, and Marianne replied, "I'm just worried about you."

Luke excused himself, rising slowly from the sofa. He walked to the kitchen, the sound of something sizzling, growing, and fading as Luke entered and shut the swinging door behind him. I stared at the stock charts flashing on TV. Luke's calm, modulated voice steadied the kitchen. I looked around the apartment, the wineglasses sparkling under the small dining room crystal chandelier, the furniture around me worn and comfortable, and I thought, So this is what a family is like.

Linda appeared from the kitchen and motioned for me to follow her down the hall. We went into Hector's room and she closed the door behind us. "What was that about?" I asked.

"It was nothing. She tends to meddle in my life too much."

I waited for more, but she didn't elaborate. Looking around, I said, "Not a lot of junk."

"No. I thought she cleaned it, but she didn't. I think he was staying here less and less." She pointed to the desk and bureau. "I'll start there."

"I'll take these," I said, moving to the night table and bed. The clinking of dishes carried down the hall.

I searched through Hector's night table drawers and found condoms, a few small pipes, and scraps of paper with names and phone numbers. I took the papers out, looking deeper into the drawer. Pens, pencils, two pocket-knives, a canister of pepper spray. The book cubby below held comic books, surfing magazines, and old invitations to raves. A few photos lay wedged in between two magazines, and I pulled these out. Night shots. People dressed in odd, garish costumes. I thought I recognized Hector in one shot. A skinny man with a narrow, bony face, Hector had a dark goatee and mustache. He wore baggy army pants and an oversized T-shirt, which made him look skinnier. The photo of Hector in the living room—part of a family shot—showed Hector with a clean-shaven face.

"This is him?" I asked.

Linda looked over my shoulder. "Yes. What is he wearing?" She noticed the slips of paper in my other hand and examined them. "These are good," she said. I looked underneath the bed and pulled out a bag filled with baby pacifiers. I held them up.

"What the . . . ?"

She said, "I think it has something to do with raves."

"How?"

She shrugged. I found another bag, this one with NiteBrite sticks, flexible tubes that lit up in neon colors, still in its packaging. "Maybe he sold these," I said, holding them up. "You find something?"

Linda was studying some papers at the desk. She said, "For someone with no real job, Hector had a lot of money." She showed me old bank statements, with deposits and withdrawals as high as five thousand at a time. His balance had reached thirty thousand before he had emptied the account six months ago.

"Is this the most recent one?" I asked.

"Looks like he closed it a while ago. This doesn't look good."

"Drug dealing?"

"Deposits never more than five grand to keep under the radar. But where's this money now?"

We continued looking for more paperwork, but turned up only half-completed job applications and clipped articles about the Internet porn industry. Linda made a face as she showed them to me.

"Could the money have come from there?" I asked.

"Hector didn't even have a computer. But the phone numbers are a good start." She stared at the desk drawer, and said, "This is a little creepy."

A soft knock at the door. Marianne opened it and said, "Dinner's ready." She looked at the disarray, the papers and bags on the floor, and frowned at Linda.

"Don't worry, we'll clean it up," Linda said.

Her mother nodded and closed the door. I whispered, "I'm not even hungry. That pizza—"

"Shh. You'll have to eat, anyway."

"But why?"

She smiled sadly. "You'd hurt her feelings. You have a lot to learn about us."

Meals for me as a child had been quick and functional, usually take-out or fast food when my father was alive, and when I began living with my aunt I ate better-quality restaurant food that she often brought home for free. She had worked as a bookkeeper for a small Korean restaurant chain, and now I couldn't look at Styrofoam containers and not think of the cold leftovers of my youth.

When Linda and I sat down for dinner, I felt queasy from the sight of all the food before me, huge steaming enchiladas stacked on a platter, a large bowl of rice with chicken and vegetables mixed in, and a meatball dish in chile sauce. Linda's eyes widened and she said, "Mom, there are only four of us here."

"You're too thin. You used to love *albóndigas en chipotle*. And Allen looks like he hasn't had a good meal in ages."

Is that true? I wondered.

"Your mother spent all afternoon preparing this," Luke said. "She hasn't had a chance to cook like this in months."

"Not for Hector?" Linda asked.

Marianne said, "He hardly ate here."

"Or hardly slept here," Luke added. "Or at least spending all night out and sleeping all day."

"Breakfast at seven at night!" Marianne said. "Then he'd disappear for days."

Linda asked, "Do you know where?"

Her parents turned to each other, and Marianne said, "To parties. Who knows?"

"He never told you?"

"No."

Everyone grew quiet, and I ate slowly. The silence continuing for too long, I cleared my throat and they all turned to me. I said, "Well, Linda and I met his ex-girlfriend, the one who sent the flowers. She was nice."

"You did?" Marianne said, her voice rising. "What did she say? What was she like?"

Linda froze, then shook her head. My stomach fluttered as the energy of the table suddenly shifted toward me. Marianne said to Linda, "Why didn't you tell me this when you came in?"

Then I realized why Linda hadn't mentioned it. The news wasn't very good. I said, "Well, they hadn't gone out in a while—"

"Mom," Linda said. "Let's talk about something else."

"What did she say about Hector?" Marianne asked Linda.

"We still need to sort things out."

"Why? Did she say something bad? Is there something I should know—"

"It's too early to tell, Mom, but once we find out more—"

"You must be able to tell me something," Marianne said. "What did this ex-girlfriend say?

"Let us talk to more people."

"Oh, you just love this, don't you?" Marianne said, her voice tightening. "You love being able to control the information and leave me thinking the worst."

"What? That's not true."

"Honey," Luke said quietly.

"No, no," Marianne said, throwing up her hands. "Why should I be told anything? He was only my son. I ask her to help and this is what she does—"

"All right," Linda said, sighing. "You want to know what we found out so far? Are you sure you want to hear—"

"Please, you two," Luke said.

"We haven't confirmed it, but Hector might have been dealing drugs on the side," Linda said, glancing from her mother to Luke.

"What else?" Marianne asked.

"That's about it."

Marianne eyed her daughter and said quietly, "What else?"

Linda nodded. "She mentioned him being lost and aimless. She mentioned that he was thinking about his father."

Marianne turned to Luke.

"No," Linda said. "I mean the other one, Raul."

"What?"

"The ex-girlfriend said Hector sometimes talked about finding him."

Marianne's face paled, and she opened her mouth to speak, then closed it. She shook her head and said, "What are you talking about? Why would he do that?"

"I don't know. Maybe it was nothing. If you give me a chance, I might find out."

Marianne's forehead wrinkled as she looked down at her hands, which she lay on the table, palms down. She kept very still for a few seconds, then asked me, "Were you there? Did you hear this?"

"Yes," I said. "But there's a lot we still don't know."

She took a slow breath and said to Linda, "See? That's all I wanted. The truth."

Linda watched her closely.

Luke asked his wife if she was all right.

"Of course," Marianne answered. "We suspected the drugs, right? Didn't we? Those strange phone calls in the middle of the night. His going out like that all the time."

"And looking for . . . Raul?" Linda asked. "Did he ever mention that?"

"No." Her body deflated.

When she didn't continue, Linda said, "Why would he want to find Raul?"

Marianne said, "I don't know." She said to Luke, "He was always so sensitive. He remembered everything and stored it away." To Linda she said, "Do you remember when I yelled at him for breaking our window, and he wouldn't speak to me for weeks?"

"I remember," Linda said. "He was like that, brooding all the time."

"I had to yell at him. But he acted so . . . so . . ."

"Devastated," Linda said. "Yes."

"Devastated. What did he think, that I wouldn't get angry?"

"He always felt wronged."

Marianne said to Luke, "I was working so hard and sometimes I didn't have the strength to be so patient and calm."

"Yes, of course," Luke said. "I remember when I first met you."

Marianne sighed. "Oh yes, I was on my last legs. I was trying to be a good mother."

"You were a good mother," Linda said.

Luke reached out and touched Marianne's shoulder. She smiled sadly to Linda and said, "Thank you. Maybe you can find out more. I just need to know more." She stood up.

"You haven't even eaten," Luke said.

"That's okay. I'm feeling tired. It's been a hectic day." She turned to me and pointed to the platters. "Please help yourself. We have plenty more."

We watched her walk down the hall. When the bedroom door closed, Luke said, "I'll check on her." He left the table.

"Oh, damn," Linda said.

"Will she be okay?"

"I hope so."

"Sorry for bringing it up."

"No, it's okay. She knew something was up. I can't hide much from her." She stared at her plate of food. "Jeez. I can't eat this."

"Neither can I."

"Let's clean up and make some calls." She looked at the clock, which showed that it wasn't even six. "We have all night."

Five

lived down here in my early twenties while trying to figure out what I should do. I had walked out of an organic chemistry class, out of college, out of the Bay Area, and ended up in a studio apartment in Santa Monica with cracked, water-stained ceilings and a cockroach battle that I had lost. The skittering sounds of insects on the vinyl floor no longer sent me leaping up and swatting. I tried bug sprays, roach traps, and roach poisons, but nothing lasted. One trick I used many times was laying a sheet of newspaper on the floor in the dark. When I turned on the light the roaches would zip for cover, and often fled under the newspaper. Then I'd stomp them with satisfying crunches. But they kept coming. I placed my bed away from the walls and kept traps near the bed-posts. I learned to expect their startled surprise if I turned on the lights in the middle of the night. I learned to live with my socks always on. There was nothing more alarming than a roach tickling your bare toes.

When Linda and I approached Tim Jacobs's house in Venice, I flashed back to my roach days. The house was a few blocks from the beach, wedged between a crumbling brick apartment building and two smaller houses in the process of

being renovated, scaffolding and temporary fencing surrounding the proper-
ties. The windows, shrouded in the shadow of the apartment building, had
white flowing bedsheets in place of curtains. Scabs of peeling paint hung from
the door and window frames. The yard, filled with overgrown weeds and rusting lawn chairs, had as a centerpiece a broken picnic table, one leg lame.

I noticed movement in the alley behind the apartment building. There
wasn't enough street lighting. When I had lived here gangs hung around this
area. We walked up to the front door and Linda knocked. I watched the
alley.

Linda had spoken to Tim briefly on the phone, finding his number among
the scraps of paper, and though he had sounded reluctant, he agreed to meet
tonight.

The smell of marijuana eased around us. We heard slow footsteps.
"Yeah?" said a voice on the other side of the door.

"It's Linda, Hector's sister."

The door opened and Tim, a wiry tanned man with stringy bleached-
blond hair, paused at the sight of me. He asked Linda, "Who's this?"

"My friend."

"You didn't say anything about bringing someone."

Linda replied, "He's keeping me company. Thanks for meeting me."

"Could've just talked on the phone."

"No, I wanted to see you, to meet you in person," Linda said, which I
understood. She needed to see and gauge reactions as she dug for information.

The skin around Tim's nose was blotchy from sun damage, and when he
peered behind us, moving near the light, I saw pale orange freckles covering
his neck and arms. "So, what do you want?" Tim asked.

"Can we come in?" Linda smiled.

"What for?"

Linda tilted her head, her eyes curious.

I said, "Because there are some guys in the alley next door waiting to
jump us."

Tim looked behind us again. "Yeah? Probably just a bunch of local kids."
He stepped aside to let us in. "But it does sometimes get hairy out there."

We entered a large living room with three ratty sofas surrounding a low
black coffee table. On one torn sofa, a young skinny woman slept on her side,

her back to us. Her shoulder blades poked against her oversized T-shirt. The smell of marijuana was stronger, a haze clouding the bare lightbulbs above.

Linda whispered, "Is there somewhere we can talk?" She motioned to the sleeping woman.

"We can talk here. She won't mind. How'd you find me?"

"Hector had your number."

"That sucks about the accident. Was there a funeral?"

"Yesterday. How did you hear about Hector?"

"From a friend."

"Who?" Linda asked.

Tim, startled by the rapid question, fumbled with, "No one—I mean just someone who read about it. So, why are you asking about Hector?"

"I need to know more."

Tim sat on one of the sofas and leaned back, spreading out his sinewy arms on the back rest. "How'd you know I was a friend?"

"Serena told us about you."

He smiled. "You talked to Serena?"

The woman on the sofa shifted her position to listen.

Linda said, "She mentioned you two hung out a lot. I figured you'd be the place to start. When was the last time you saw him?"

"I don't know, maybe three weeks, no, four weeks ago? How is Serena?"

"She seems fine. What was Hector doing?"

"Last time I saw him? We went to a rave in Orange County. It was okay. The DJs weren't that good."

"Was he dealing?"

Tim blinked, but didn't reply. He looked at me, then said to Linda, "Why do you want to know that?"

"I'm trying to find out everything I can."

Tim waved this off and said, "He might have had some extra E and sold some, but that night we were there for the music."

"Why did he go to them, these raves?" she asked.

"You've never been to one," he said. It wasn't a question.

"No."

"I'm not going to try to explain it to you. He went because he liked it there. He was kind of fucked-up and went to feel better."

"Taking drugs?" Linda asked.

Tim frowned. "No. Maybe a little, but it's not about the drugs."

Linda began to question this, but Tim cut her off with, "Forget it. You won't get it. But anyway, that's the last time I saw him."

"Was he upset? What do you mean he needed to feel better?"

Tim leaned his head back for a moment, then said, "Man, he was always upset. His jobs were shit, his parent—your parents—were getting on his case. He was just depressed all the time, man. Really down."

"Did he ever mention his father?"

"Yeah, sure. He always talked about the bug up his father's ass. Pissed Hector off."

"What about his birth father?"

Tim paused. "The one who took off?"

"He mentioned it?"

Tim nodded. "I think so. A couple times he got stoned and talked about him."

"What did he say?"

"Just that he wanted to find him, figure out things."

Linda glanced at me, then asked Tim, "He looked for him?"

"Yeah, I think so. He talked about you, too."

Linda waited, then asked, "What did he say?"

The woman on the sofa rolled over, her tangled hair covering her face, and said, "That you ran as far and as fast as you could."

"What?" Linda asked.

"This is Kate," Tim said. "Don't mind her."

Kate pulled herself up, trying to flip back her hair, but it fell over her face again. She pulled down her T-shirt over her thighs. She cleared her throat a few times, and said, "You're the reporter?"

"She's a reporter?" Tim asked.

Linda nodded.

Kate's arms were bone thin, her shirt hanging off her sharp shoulders. She said, "He told me you married young just to get out of the house, then went to Ohio."

"That's not true," Linda replied. "At least not completely true."

I caught Linda's eye and said, "The chemicals in the car."

"Right." Her eyes lingered on Kate, then she asked Tim if he knew why Hector had been driving with methamphetamine chemicals in his trunk. "They were in his car that burned in Malibu."

"No idea," Tim said. "He never touched any of that stuff. Not that I knew of."

"Then why did he have it?"

"Maybe he was just doing a favor. Maybe he didn't know what it was."

"Maybe he did," Kate said, "and crashed on purpose."

They turned to her, and Tim said, "You're full of it. You don't know."

Linda asked Kate, "What do you mean?"

Kate said, "He was really down. I mean, like, the kind of down where he didn't want to think about anything. I don't know, but he was going through some shit. I think his girlfriend tried to help, but maybe he just got tired of it all."

"Serena tried to help? This was a while ago, then."

"Nuh-uh. Gloria. The recent one."

Linda met my eyes, then asked Kate, "Do you have a last name?"

"Nope," Kate said, then waited for Tim to answer.

He frowned at Kate, then said. "That chick wasn't his girlfriend. Just someone he met."

"Whatever," Kate said.

"Do you know her last name?" Linda asked him.

"No. He met her at a rave. I think she just wanted the free E."

"She's always at them," Kate said. "You might even run into her at one."

"Just a vowel hound. I don't think they dated. What's with all this?"

"Do you really think he might have committed suicide?" Linda asked.

Kate said, "I don't know. What did he have to live for?"

"You tell me," Linda said. "You two hung out with him."

Tim said quietly, "The only times I saw Hector happy was when we were stoned or at a rave." He scratched his stomach.

"Did he use Ecstasy a lot?"

Tim raised his voice, "What's with all these questions, anyway? I'm getting itchy."

"Tim-my's getting a rash," Kate sang.

"Like I need to think about this shit?" Tim said. "I'm trying to relax tonight. I gotta be at the café first thing tomorrow morning for the goddamn yuppie Sunday brunch crowd. Look, don't take this the wrong way, but you should move on. Get on with your life. Hector's gone, man."

Linda stared at him without replying, her eyes sad.

We drove out of Venice and stopped at a small bar a few blocks from her parents' condo. We sorted through Hector's pieces of paper, separating the legible names of the men and women, searching for Gloria. There were about two dozen slips, some with just initials, some with no names at all, and Linda planned to start calling some of these people tomorrow. There was no "Gloria" in the piles, but Linda hoped someone among these numbers might know more. She had been quiet during the ride back here, and I asked her if she believed Kate, that suicide might be a possibility.

"That's what my mom mentioned, but I don't know."

"Maybe if we find Gloria, we'll have a better idea. And Tim seemed nervous."

"Yeah. I think all the questions about drugs did it. You look like a narc." I smiled.

"How old did you think they were?" Linda asked.

"Early to mid-twenties."

She shook her head. "Why do they seem so young?"

"They talk young."

"It's more than that. They make me feel so much older," she said, sipping her beer. "Is it me or did they seem young?"

"They seemed young."

"You started working when you were what, twenty?"

"I had to," I said. "My aunt cut me off."

"But you started your career, didn't you? In security?"

"Not quite." I reminded her of my string of lousy jobs. I had worked at a warehouse as a delivery boy and as a furniture mover before getting a mall-walking security job, then moving up from there. I realized that Linda never had an aimless period and said, "Marriage at eighteen must have sped you up."

"Nineteen. It sure did," she said. "I'm glad I didn't have any kids. That would've really complicated things."

"Why didn't you?"

"Oh, Manny wanted them, but I was still in college and wanted to go to grad school. I wasn't about to let some loser tell me to have babies."

She rarely spoke about her ex-husband. I never knew how to ask about him. I had met Manny twice, and both times—during the Mess—he had tried to make Linda's life more difficult, sniffing around for money. He hadn't surfaced since then, but I knew Linda would never let her guard down. She said, "Maybe Hector was right, though. I did leave as fast as I could."

"Why?"

"I needed to get away from my mom. She was overbearing. I wanted to start fresh."

"By getting married?"

"I was stupid." She shrugged, then laughed.

I said, "Two different people mentioned Hector and your real father."

She quickly lost her smile. "I don't understand why."

"Do you think about him?"

"No. Maybe when I was younger I did, but now . . . nothing."

"Why did he leave?"

"He took off. He was never around, anyway, and when he was all he did was fight with my mom and bully Hector. I'm sure he screwed Hector up, putting him down all the time."

"How?" I asked.

"He hated that Hector was so weak and picked on." She frowned at the memory. "He used to try to teach Hector how to box, but Hector just went crying to my mother. Raul was such an asshole to him."

"To your mom, too?"

"Oh, here we go," she said, grinning at me.

"What's wrong?"

"I know that look."

"What look?"

"That look you have on right now. It's a digging look."

I touched my face. "I don't have a look."

"It's when you start digging for stuff about my family."

"I start digging?"

"Remember the last time we saw Julie? You kept asking about us as kids? You kept digging."

Two months ago we had dinner with Julie and her husband, and I had been fascinated by Julie's view of Linda as a teenager. She told us about Linda's weight problem and how she had lost almost a hundred pounds through unhealthy starvation diets. I had trouble seeing Linda like that, not just overweight but so radically self-punishing.

"I was curious," I said. "And you never talk about it."

"You were more than curious. You were insatiable."

"It was obvious?"

She said, "Julie thought it was weird."

"She never really liked me."

"True," she replied.

Linda noticed my surprised expression and added, "I explained it to her later."

"Explained what?"

"How you grew up with no mother, no brothers or sisters. And your father dying when you were young. You're fascinated by this, by my family."

I said, "I am, but I'm interested because of you."

"Not much here, though. My father was rarely around. The only things I remember about him are the fights with my mom, and then his taking off."

"What were the fights about?"

"Money. His drinking. Everything."

"Why was he so hard on Hector?"

"Probably some macho thing." She smiled. "Stop that."

"Stop what?"

"I can see those wheels turning in your head. You're looking for connections."

"You can read my mind now?"

"I know you. Look, my family isn't like yours," she said. "We're all pretty straightforward."

"No family is straightforward."

"Yours was kind of twisted, I admit. But mine is simple. My brother was taking drugs, selling drugs, probably getting in over his head. He drove off a cliff and died. End of story."

"Then why are we doing this?"

"For my mom. But I should listen to Tim's advice."

"His advice?"

"Hector's gone," she said. "We should move on."

I wasn't sure if I believed her.

She finished her beer and said, "Did I ever tell you about the time when my brother got sick of it and tried hitting Raul? It was bizarre."

"No," I said, leaning forward. "Tell me."

"We went on a picnic. What a joke," she said. She explained that Raul had returned from a job and uncharacteristically he had wanted the family to go out on a picnic. Marianne packed a lunch, and they went to a local park, the facade of a family on an outing making everyone uncomfortable. When Hector and Linda went to the small playground at the other end of the park, using the swing set, a few neighborhood kids began picking on them. "Typical bored kids amusing themselves," she said to me. "Telling us we weren't allowed to use the swings, that kind of thing."

"What did you do?" I asked, glancing up at a couple who had entered the bar arm in arm.

"I told them to get lost, but they kept at us. It didn't help that Hector was shaking and on the verge of crying," she said. She told Hector to get their mother, and he ran. But when he returned it was with Raul. "And he wasn't very happy."

Raul sent the kids away but was angry that Hector had left Linda alone with them. She tried to explain that she had told Hector to get help, but her father wasn't interested. "And he decided to see how weak Hector really was. This was strange. He hoisted Hector onto the top of the swing set, the high bar, and told him to hang there, yelling at him to be tougher. Here was this weakling with pencil arms trying to keep his grip ten feet in the air." Hector was crying, a few other kids were watching, and soon her mother showed up.

"Why would he do that?" I asked. A waitress passed by our table, the smell of strong perfume floating behind her.

"It bothered Raul that his son was so weak," she said. "But instead of trying to help him, he just punished and punished him."

"Then what happened?"

"By the time it was over, Hector fell on the ground howling, Raul was red faced and screaming at him, and my mother was yelling at Raul. Then Hector was so humiliated and angry he got up and tried hitting Raul, throwing punches like a windmill, and after laughing it off, Raul got angrier. He swatted him away and left."

"What did your mother do?"

"Tried to comfort Hector, but he couldn't stop crying. I felt terrible," she said. "I was the one who sent him for help."

"How old were you?"

"Seven or eight? He was maybe five. I never understood how hanging from a swing set was supposed to show strength. And in front of those other kids. That's just nasty. I don't blame Hector for hating him." She stared down at the table, then stifled a yawn, covering her mouth. I glanced at the clock. It was nine-thirty.

"You're tired," I said.

"Maybe we should go."

"I'll hang out here for a little bit," I said. The condo was too small to think in. "You go on ahead. Take the car."

"You'll walk?"

"It's close," I said. "Leave me the key so I don't have to buzz everyone."

She lay the key on the table. I knew she was studying me, but I didn't look up. She finally said, "I want to thank you for coming down here."

I nodded.

"No, really," she said.

"I'm glad to help."

"But why?"

"Why?" I said, surprised by this. There were too many reasons. When I had needed help during the Mess, she had jeopardized everything for me. I was helping her because I wanted her to be happy and safe. I didn't know where to begin and just said, "Because you asked me to."

She reached for a glass of water that she hadn't touched; condensation had dripped onto the table, leaving a ring. She ran her finger along the rim's edge, and said, "Are you mad at me?"

I looked at her through the dim light and heard laughter from one of the tables near the bar. I struggled with conflicting feelings, wanting some kind of resolution between us but knowing that this was the wrong time. She wanted me here to help, but at the same time she didn't want me here. A small burst of irritation clouded my thoughts. Why couldn't everything be simple?

"Allen?" she asked. "Are you?"

"Mad at you? I don't know," I said, as honestly as I could.

"If you want to go home, I understand."

"No, I'll help you. In fact, I'll call Larry tomorrow and tell him I might be a few more days."

"Won't that get you in trouble?"

"Yes."

"I don't want you to get into—"

"It's okay. I want to help."

She nodded. "Thanks." She pulled herself up, then hesitantly leaned forward and kissed me on the cheek. She said good night and left the bar. The chaste kiss disturbed me. The cool, damp imprint of her lips still lingered on my skin. It disturbed me because it was the kiss of friendship, a kiss of distance. It was the kind of kiss you gave to say farewell.

Six

Conversations replayed in my head as I finished my beer. I paid the tab and walked out into the cool evening. The buzz of the other customers faded. Beer sloshed in my empty stomach, and I regretted missing Marianne's dinner. The night air made me want to go for a run, but when I realized I hadn't brought any gear, I was suddenly depressed.

Linda's tentative question had reminded me of my confused role here, and I found myself yearning for answers. I needed decisions, ultimate conclusions, rather than this ambiguous state of bafflement. Were we breaking up, or have we already implicitly broken up? Had something transpired that I missed?

I tried to accept what seemed ominously close. I told myself that when I was alone I was usually at some kind of peace. When I was alone I didn't have to worry about conflicts and consequences.

But then there were other dangers. *Inertial deception*, which I saw as the fear of change, and the ease with which we could convince ourselves that what was static and present was best. We feared the momentum of change, since it disrupted our settled or regulated lives. We knew where the canned soups were stored, and we didn't like opening the cupboard and finding them inexplicably missing.

Maybe I had drunk too many beers.

This is hard, but maybe you need a change like this.

"Like what?" I said aloud. "How is being dumped good? To find my soup cans missing? Someone took my soup cans."

A man walking ahead of me glanced back, and sped up. I blinked, embarrassed. I trudged toward the condo, thinking about Linda as a kid, an overweight kid, and couldn't truly picture it. Linda had destroyed or hidden most of the photos of herself as a child, and whenever I asked for stories about herself or her family, she usually dismissed it as "ancient history" and changed the subject. Tonight's story about her brother and father had been a surprise.

Linda, even in sadness, couldn't shake my gaze. Her eyes, large and dark, hadn't quite met mine as she told me the story about her brother, so I was able to stare at her unselfconsciously, absorbing her features. Her face had been shadowed by the poor lighting, but I knew her so well and stared at her soft skin, her cheeks smooth. She tugged at her earlobe when she said I could leave, looking down at her glass and waiting for my response. Her hair curled down her neck.

I touched my own cheek now.

I remembered the feeling of her fingers on my neck the first time we kissed, now so long ago. She had, in her own subtle way, declared her interest in me, and I hadn't believed it. I had thought, Am I hearing this right? But when she approached me, closing our distance and moving within inches, I knew she felt the same way as I did, and more than anything I had been relieved. I couldn't remember a time when I had been happier.

The movement from professional to personal, from partners helping each other to a real couple, was a strange one. In my other brief relationships, the leap had always been quick and determined, from dating to lovers, and always the first meeting, the first date, the first kiss—all these were fraught with the underlying, shared purpose of somehow getting to bed. With Linda, it was different from the start, and because of the scars of her previous marriage, we moved slowly.

As I let myself into the lobby now, taking the elevator up to the condo, I thought about the first time we slept together. We had been dating officially for only a week or so, and an odd cloud of shyness had descended upon us whenever we began kissing. I felt guilty for touching her. I remember reaching awkwardly for her breasts, and then stopping, thinking, Hell, I can't touch her there.

But then she grabbed my hand and guided me. I ended up laughing at my hesitation, and she smiled. She whispered, "It's like we're in high school again."

I said, "I never got any in high school."

"Poor Allen," she said. "Well here's your chance."

I grinned to myself as I walked into the dark condo, listening for sounds of anyone awake. The refrigerator hummed; a night light in the main hallway glowed. I paced in the dark living room, not ready to sleep. Staring out the window, I watched the boat lights in the marina and thought I saw people moving around in some of the larger sailboats.

I heard a door down the hall opening, and hoped it was Linda. Someone walked into the bathroom and shut the door. Running water. A toilet flushing. Then, in the moonlit shadows, the person walked into the kitchen and opened the refrigerator. The door light shone on Marianne's face. She pulled out the bowl of rice. Not wanting to frighten her, I cleared my throat.

She snapped her head up. "Who's there?"

"Allen," I said. "I just got in."

Marianne walked out of the kitchen and saw me by the window. "Are you hungry? Would you like a snack?"

"Actually, yes."

She said, "Good," and hurried back to the kitchen, grabbing utensils and an extra plate, quickly running the microwave, then setting a place at the dining table for me. She said, "Sit."

"I don't want you to go to any trouble—"

"Have some of the meatball dish that Linda likes."

"That sounds great," I said, as she set the platters in front of me. I asked, "You couldn't sleep?"

"I've been having trouble lately."

"Sorry."

She sat down next to me. "What were you doing, just standing out here?"

"Yes."

"Why?"

"I was thinking."

"I knew you were a thinker," she said through a smile. "I told Luke that Linda was dating someone different this time, someone with a brain." She had a fork and ate some rice off the platter. I was pleased that she felt comfortable enough with me to be so casual. Then I registered what she had just said.

"Oh, uh, we might not be dating anymore."

"What? Since when? She never said anything." She stopped eating.

Shit. I cleared my throat and said, "Well, I don't know. We're not sure."

She said slowly, "I see."

"This is delicious," I said, stuffing my mouth with a meatball. The chile sauce warmed my tongue.

She nodded in the semidarkness, and fell quiet. I thought, Stupid of me to say anything. I should never talk. My fork clinked on the plate and I ate too fast. After a while I asked, "Did you know her ex-husband?"

She stiffened, her blurry silhouette contracting. "Why?"

"I'm curious. I'm trying to understand her . . . history of relationships."

"I don't know anything about that, but he wasn't a nice man."

I nodded.

"He tried to break her down. He tried to humiliate her."

I grew uneasy at the tightness in her voice.

"Please don't mention him in this house again," she said.

"Sorry," I said. "I won't."

"Is she going to be all right?" Marianne asked.

I said, "I guess so."

"They were close when they were young."

At first I thought she was talking about Manny, but then realized she had switched to Hector. I said, "She told me."

"Did she tell you that they had their own secret language? They used to talk to each other with me right there, and I had no idea what they were saying."

"A code?"

"Exactly. A code."

"I didn't know that," I said. "Did he feel abandoned after Linda got married, then left for school?"

"Who said that?"

"Hector might have mentioned it to one of his friends."

"Was it so hard for him with us? We gave him a roof, food, even money. Most parents would've pushed him out."

"I agree," I said, thinking of my aunt.

I finished the chicken and ate more vegetables. I was aware of Marianne watching me. "Sorry, I'm being a pig."

"Are you kidding? No one eats anymore. I'm glad you're hungry."

I finished off the green beans. After a minute Marianne said, "The problem with Hector was that he could blame everyone but himself."

I waited.

"If something went wrong, if he lost a job or ran out of money, it was because of someone else. A bad boss, someone cheating him." She looked at me. "How do you make someone like that see? I'm sure he blamed Linda for something. He blamed everyone."

"What about his father, his birth father?"

She put down her fork. "What about him?"

"Did Hector blame him for something?"

"I don't like talking about him."

"Sorry," I said. "I don't know if Linda told you. My father died when I was ten. I imagine her father leaving might be similar."

"It was very different. Your father died. Hector and Linda's father hurt us and then left us with nothing."

I said, "Linda mentioned how he wasn't around much."

"He went on construction jobs far away from us. On purpose," she said. After a moment she said, "You tend to . . . get to the point, don't you."

Startled, I said, "I'm sorry. Was I being too personal?"

"It's fine. We can probably use that around here."

"What do you mean?"

"Nothing. Just that Linda never tells me much."

I almost smiled. I thought, Join the club. Instead I said, "She hasn't mentioned . . . us?"

Marianne said, "No. But she's glad you're down here. I can see that."

I didn't reply, not sure if I believed her.

She stood up slowly. "Do you want some more?"

"I'm stuffed. It was delicious." I jumped up to help with the dishes.

"Stop right there. You're a guest. I'll clean up."

I ignored this and brought my dish to the kitchen sink. She followed with the platters and said, "Really. I'll clean tomorrow morning."

"Tell me something about Linda as a kid."

"Linda?" she said, and smiled. "She tried so hard as a child. Did she ever tell you about kickball?"

"No."

"They played kickball in school. The boys and girls. You know she was a little overweight and not very athletic."

I nodded.

"She was determined to be a good kickball player and made me buy a kickball—those red rubber balls—so she could practice. She made Hector roll it to her, and she'd practice kicking." Marianne sighed. "Her face would get all red and sweaty, and she would be out of breath. Poor child."

"What happened?"

"She never told me. I don't think it went well. She cut up the kickball and never talked about it."

I felt a sudden longing for Linda. I said, "She didn't tell you what happened?"

"Why should she? As I said, she never tells me anything." Marianne sighed, and patted my arm. "Good night, Allen."

I said good night, thanking her again for the snack. She waved it off and moved out of the kitchen. She stopped, and lowered her voice. "Give her a chance. She tries to be tough and hard. She has to be." Marianne's face was hidden in the shadows. "If she wasn't so tough, she might not have made it through her marriage." She turned and walked back to her bedroom.

I heard her door close. I thought, Give Linda a chance? She didn't seem to be giving me much of one.

I washed my plate and utensils, and wandered into the living room, looking at photos and checking book titles on the shelves. Real estate and investment. Paperback romances and spy thrillers. It struck me that the layout of the living room—bookshelves near the TV, the position of the sofa and reclining chair—was very familiar, and then I realized that Linda's apartment was arranged similarly. I wondered if my own apartment was patterned after my father's or my aunt's.

Linda's presence was all around me. I remembered the time we drove up to Marin and spent the day at Muir Beach, lying out in the sun and reading.

We found the nude section in a cove hidden beyond some high rocks, and Linda went topless while I tanned my butt. Naked men and women sprawled on blankets, and an old wrinkled couple held hands and walked along the water's edge, their naked bodies evenly browned. They moved so naturally that they didn't seem naked at all. Linda and I watched them, and she said, "They're so comfortable together."

I nodded. I couldn't imagine my life that far in the future. I asked Linda where she saw herself thirty years from now. She said, "Jeez. I'm still trying to figure out the past twenty-nine years. Maybe when I get up-to-date I'll start thinking about the next twenty-nine."

Now, as I circled the living room, I suddenly had an image of Hector, dancing wildly, wearing a strange costume, and trying to free himself from his depression. I saw him smoking pot with his friends. I saw him lying in bed, staring up at the ceiling. I saw him disconsolate over the fragments of his life. We brood over the past, we fear the future. We are joined in our uncertainty.

Could I have something in common with Hector?

Seven

The next morning I awoke with Linda staring at me from the foot of the fold-out bed. I sat up, confused by the plants on the window. I didn't have any plants in my apartment. My back ached from the bar underneath the mattress, a spasm of pain running up my spine. I groaned. Linda said, "Sorry. I wasn't sure if I should wake you. I found a Malibu connection. We should go over there right now."

Malibu? I needed a few seconds to orient myself. The wall opposite the window was so bright I had to squint. Linda was dressed in khakis and a navy blue T-shirt, her hair tied back. She looked refreshed, with flushed cheeks and an excited smile.

"How long have you been standing there?" I asked.

"Not long."

"You were watching me?"

"Kind of. I like how calm you look when you're asleep. You always look so tense during the day."

"Maybe that's because I wake up with people watching me." I smiled. "What's up?"

"I made some calls," she said. "I couldn't find Gloria, but I found this older guy who was friendly with Hector. I'm not sure about the connection, but he was glad I called. He heard about the accident but didn't know who to talk to." She spoke quickly, and I had trouble taking this in.

"What time is it?" I asked.

"Ten."

I shook myself awake and went to wash up. By the time I was out of the bathroom and changed, Linda had a slice of buttered toast waiting for me, which I ate in the elevator. She told me she had been up early and started calling the phone numbers on the slips of paper, unable to reach many and waking up a few annoyed friends of Hector's. Most either didn't know Gloria or had no idea where to find her. "There were a few cagey people, not wanting to give out any info, but then I reached this guy William."

"Who is he?" I asked, following her into the underground parking garage. When we climbed into her parents' car, I realized I hadn't seen them. "Where are your parents?"

"Church."

Last night's conversation with Marianne felt unreal now. I sat quietly as we sped out of the garage. Linda told me that William Delgado had had a few lunches with Hector about a month ago.

"Did he say why?" I asked.

My sudden voice startled her, and she glanced at me. "No. You awake yet?"

"Yeah. Does he live in that canyon where Hector crashed?"

"No. He lives on PCH, right on the beach. But he knows where it happened. I asked if Hector knew anyone up there, but William wasn't sure."

Last night, I had continued wandering around the apartment, studying family photos, leafing through books and magazines, then watching the small TV in the guest room. I had been up until 3:00 A.M., unable to sleep in this unfamiliar place. There was a small bookshelf next to my sofa bed, and I tried reading a primer on real estate investment trusts. My big discovery, however, was a photo that fell out of a book of crossword puzzles, only a third of the puzzles completed. The photo was a family shot at some kind of amusement park. Luke and Marianne stood at opposite ends, while Julie, Linda, and Hector crowded the middle. What had surprised me was Linda, who was in her early teens and was very overweight. She had thick limbs, with a large apple-shaped body, a full, round face. I almost didn't recognize her. The fragile, sickly boy next to her, Hector, looked brittle, and Julie appeared very much the same as she was now. Very blond, very alert.

After a moment, I had placed it back into the book. Then a few minutes later I took it out again and stared at Linda. I recognized her nose and cheekbones, but her face was so padded that it had changed the proportions. I had an odd affection for this teen, knowing what she had been through, kids teasing her; she was often lonely.

When I looked at Linda now, I was amazed at the change. She caught me staring and said, "What're you looking at?"

"You."

"Why?"

"I found a picture of you and Hector as kids."

"What? Where?"

"In the guest room. In a book."

"Damn. My mom does that, uses anything as a bookmark. Which book? I thought I found all of them."

"Why? It's a record of how you once were."

"I can't look at those. I was so messed up."

"Just because you were a little overweight?"

"No, I was fat. I was very fat. I was having problems."

"Like what?" I asked.

"Just with food. It was a strange relationship with food. Compulsive, almost. I'd rather not talk about it."

"Why not? You never want to talk about that."

"I know," she said, shaking her head. "It's painful."

"Oh."

"And my mom didn't help matters by feeding us burritos and enchiladas all the time. I'm sure my arteries are permanently clogged."

"You should go running with me more often."

"Ha," she said, glancing up at the rearview mirror. "I get enough exercise *watching* you run." She changed lanes and sped up.

"What's the matter?" I asked, checking the traffic.

"Remember you told me about counting cars?"

I nodded, and pulled down the visor with a vanity mirror. I positioned it and began watching the cars behind us. Counting was a way to track cars quickly, simply counting off the cars behind you every few miles. This mechanically registered the cars in your mind and often you'd spot a "mark" that kept appearing. I had learned this at ProServ. "What is it?" I asked.

"A dark green SUV two cars down. I keep seeing it."

I angled my visor and spotted the humpbacked SUV keeping its distance. "Since when?"

"Not sure. I saw it five minutes ago, and it's keeping pace."

"It might just be heading in the same direction. Maybe you should hit the slow lane and see what happens."

She did this, and we watched. When the green SUV moved from the fast lane to the middle lane, and also slowed, still keeping two cars away, I said, "Hmm."

"Who did we talk to? Tim and Kate."

"Serena," I said.

"And a bunch of calls I made."

"Can you see the driver?"

"No. It's staying back, and the sun is too bright."

I looked for the license plate, but the front end was hidden behind the cars ahead of it. "Slow down," I said.

She began coasting, and we watched the SUV drift three, then four cars back. Linda said, "I think the driver has on sunglasses and a baseball cap. I'm not sure, though."

"Start signaling for a turn, get close, then change your mind and speed up. See what happens."

I folded the visor and turned in my seat. Linda signaled, and our tail moved into the slow lane. As we approached a cross street, Linda waited until the last second, then accelerated. She merged one, then two lanes over, and gained more speed, passing cars. Our tail didn't turn but continued in the slow lane. As our distance increased, the SUV moved into the middle lane and crept forward.

"Shit," I said. "He's definitely on us."

"We shouldn't go to Malibu."

"You're right. Head back."

"To Marina Alta?"

"Let's see what he does," I said.

"If Hector really was dealing, then this isn't good."

I turned to her. "You're pretty calm."

"I know. In a way, I'm glad. We have someone curious. Maybe there's more going on here than we know." She turned off the highway and began winding along side streets, working our way back to Marina Alta.

"You want to try to ID this guy?"

"How?"

"Find a smaller street. We can U-turn and move closer, getting a better look. I'll get his plate number."

"All right," she said, checking the traffic and turning a corner. "I'll take the next light."

Our tail was slowing down, probably suspicious of the erratic driving, but as Linda signaled to turn at the next corner, the SUV moved into our lane. "He's a block back, but still following," I said.

"Get something to write down the license plate."

I found a pencil and a car wash coupon in the glove compartment. Linda turned another corner and said, "We're getting close to our neighborhood."

"He's still following," I said.

Linda made a right at another intersection, then turned left into what looked like a commercial neighborhood, small stores and office buildings lining the blocks. But the street was quiet, a Sunday morning calm that allowed Linda to race forward. Then, she made a screeching U-turn in the middle of the street, forcing me into my door, and she said, "Here we go."

The SUV was a block and a half away, heading toward us. It stopped. A car behind the SUV honked, then passed it. Linda slowed. I saw the front end, a large black bumper, but didn't see a license plate. "There's no plate—"

"He's speeding up," Linda said, her voice uncertain. The sun was behind us, reflecting off the SUV's windshield. "I can't see him."

The SUV quickly veered into our lane and was speeding even faster toward us.

"Uh," I said, sitting up. "What the . . ."

"He's heading directly at us!" Linda said. "Is he nuts?"

"Chicken?" I said. I gripped the door. "He's coming faster."

Linda jammed on the accelerator and tried to swerve away from the oncoming SUV.

The SUV swerved as well, matching our lane.

"Damn," she said, yanking the steering wheel in the other direction.

I tried to see through the windshield, but the jarring movements made it hard for me to focus. I caught a glimpse of the baseball cap and sunglasses.

She sped up even faster, and I checked my seat belt, then checked hers. When I looked up, the SUV was only a hundred feet away, and I saw the front driver's side window rolling down. "Wait! He's opening his window. . . ."

And when I thought I saw the barrel of a gun, I yelled, "Gun! Get away!"

Linda cursed and yanked the steering wheel, screeching forward too fast and heading for a parked car. She slammed on the brakes, fishtailing out of control, and we headed straight for a bus stop bench, jolting over the curb and crunching into metal. Both of us were thrown forward, then choked by the seat belts, and my head flung back into the seat, my vision blurring. Linda went forward and back again. Something in the engine raced then died. Then it was quiet. My head and neck hurt.

"Oh, man," Linda said.

"Are you okay?" I tried to steady myself, but my heartbeat was now thumping out all sounds, and I couldn't see straight. I looked around for the other car, but it had sped away. My eyes had watered, and I wiped them. "You okay?" I focused on her and saw blood over her eye. I leaped to her, but my seat belt held me in. Unbuckling, I moved to her and said, "What happened? Are you hurt?"

"I think I hit the steering wheel. Jeez, what kind of candy-ass seat belts are these?"

I checked her forehead and saw the cut. Then I checked her arms and chest and said, "He didn't shoot, did he? Are you hurt anywhere else?"

She turned to me, her eyelids fluttering. "My head hurts."

"Did you hit the wheel hard? Are you all right?"

"That . . . really . . . hurt," she said, her voice slowing. She swooned, and tried to steady herself by grabbing the steering wheel. Her hands missed and she almost fell over. "I don't feel so good."

"Linda?"

"You better get me to a hospital," she said, and her eyelids fluttered.

PART II

FOLLOW THE VOWELS

Eight

When my partner Paul Baumgartner was shot in the eye during the Mess, he died quickly, but afterward I couldn't stop obsessing about his final moments. I had administered CPR and had looked down at Paul's good eye, seeing the attention, the bewilderment, the life flickering. I was giving chest compressions and then moved to give him breaths, and our eyes met for a moment, right before I thought I saw him lose consciousness. I still pictured that moment, and every so often—especially when Paul seemed furthest from my thoughts—I would have nightmares about it. We'd switch roles in my dreams, and I would look up at Paul through a dark red-hazed tunnel and feel trapped in death.

For a panicked moment as Linda almost passed out, I thought about Paul, and I quickly searched her torso again for any kind of bullet wound. I looked for blood. I suppressed my fear and focused on first aid. When I didn't find any wounds, I looked at her forehead, a swell forming. A concussion. She needed a hospital. She needed a doctor. I saw a bystander watching us, a man in a Laker's jersey, and I yelled for help. He hurried over to me, and I asked him where the nearest hospital was.

"There's one just four or five blocks that way," he said, pointing down the street.

I asked the man to help me move her to the passenger seat. I ran around the car to pull her over the center armrest, the man struggling with me, and she said, "Oh, man, my head."

"Hang on. I'm taking you to the hospital." I buckled her in and closed the passenger door. I ran back around the car and thanked the man. He said, "The hospital's just five blocks on your left. You'll see the big white sign." I climbed in and slammed my door shut. I backed off the curb, bouncing us, the bottom scraping against the pavement, and Linda groaned. She steadied herself by reaching out and holding the side of the door with one hand, and her head with the other. "You okay? Does it hurt?"

"Yeah," she said, slurring. "I feel sick."

I kept checking the traffic, looking for the hospital. I had heard of freak accidents where a head injury resulted in hemorrhaging and even death, and said loudly, "Hey, stay awake." I touched her leg. She was rolling her head slowly, her eyes closed. "Stay awake!" I yelled.

Linda grabbed the dashboard, leaned forward, and threw up. Sounds of splashing. She heaved and gagged a few times, spit, and said in a low voice, "Oh, yuck."

I honked the horn, put on the hazard lights, and sped around slower cars. I blew a red light, swerved too close to a couple more cars, and saw the hospital ahead, the sign—Marina Alta Emergency Care Center—in blue, red, and white. I continued honking as I pulled into the lot, and I almost hit a van trying to back out of a parking space. I sped toward the ambulance entrance. Linda moaned.

Stopping the car, then jumping out to open her door, I saw a policeman and a nurse talking on the walkway. I called to them, "We had an accident. She needs some help!"

Both the nurse and cop stared at me in confusion, until I opened the door and Linda almost rolled out, her seat belt holding her in. The nurse rushed into the hospital yelling something, and the cop ran over to help.

Regrets. I punished myself while Linda was being examined. None of this should've happened. Even worse, the gunman could've raised his pistol an inch or two and fired at us pretty cleanly through the windshield. I hadn't been expecting anything like that. I knew I was getting soft. This should never have gotten this far. I should never have suggested that Linda drive so aggressively, because of course our tail would retaliate. He was worried about being identified or even stopped.

I told the Marina Alta policeman what had happened, and he returned to the scene to find witnesses. I also called Linda's parents, but they weren't home. I left a vague message on the answering machine. Now, I was just waiting. Linda had been laid on a gurney and wheeled into an examination room earlier and had then been taken to a different wing for tests. The doctor said it wouldn't be that long, but I kept checking the clock. I asked the nurse where Linda was, and the nurse said, "Getting a CT."

"When can I see her?"

"The doctor will let you know."

I nodded and returned to the waiting area, where six others sat on plastic chairs, two of them in apparent pain. One man had his arm in a sling made out of a sweater. Another man rocked back and forth while he held his stomach. When I sat down, I found that I couldn't keep my hands still. I kept squeezing them into fists and then flattening them. I took deep breaths and closed my eyes. I heard rhythmic banging from a construction site nearby. I shoved my hands into my pockets and inhaled. I should've been more alert, more aware of the possibilities. If I had been on the job, actively searching for threats, I would never have let Linda play tag. We would've headed straight for a police station with the guy on our tail. That's one of the first rules in being followed. Get help.

I had messed up.

I saw the Marina Alta police officer enter the lobby and look around. I hurried to him. "Witnesses?" I asked.

The officer shook his head. "We've got another officer doing more checking, but if there was a gun involved, we're bringing in the L.A. County Sheriff's Department. They handle these kinds of investigations. How is she?"

"I don't know yet."

"Didn't look too bad."

"I didn't get a license plate or a good look at the driver."

"Detective Jay Harrison will be the investigating officer. He's heading here right now. I just wanted to get your information for my report."

I gave him the address and phone number of Linda's parents. When I told him my home address, the officer took this down and asked, "How long will you be in Marina Alta?"

"I don't know."

"But I can reach you at this number?"

"At least for a few days," I said.

After the policeman left, a doctor appeared from the hallway and called my name. I asked how Linda was.

"She's fine. It looks like a minor concussion—"

"But she threw up."

"Yes, but that's not unusual, and it might been partly the drive in the car. I wanted to keep her here for observation, but she's resisting that."

"What could happen?"

"Well, we just want to watch the symptoms, the nausea, any memory loss or disorientation. Sometimes the intracranial pressure poses a danger, but this doesn't look that serious. The tests didn't turn up anything. She can leave, but just keep an eye on her, and make sure she rests."

"Can I see her?"

"Room twelve. She's filling out forms."

I thanked him and flew down the hall. Gurneys and slick linoleum floors were in my peripheral vision, but I focused on the windowed door with venetian blinds. Room twelve was at the end, and I kept thinking, She could've been really hurt. She could've been shot. I opened the door. The blinds swung against the window. All eight beds in this large room were occupied, and everyone turned to me. I saw Linda sitting on her bed, her legs hanging off the side, a clipboard in her hand. She looked up and smiled weakly at me.

"Are you okay?" I asked. Her forehead was bandaged, her hair tied back. Her skin was shiny. "Is everything all right?"

"I'm okay. Sorry about throwing up."

"Jeez, I don't care about that. How do you feel?"

She frowned. "My head hurts, but you know what? I'm just feeling a little pissed off right now. That guy almost killed us."

I let out a small sigh. The relief of hearing the sharpness in Linda's voice almost made me laugh, but I was too wound up and just let out a strangled "Hmmf." I touched her arm lightly.

Detective Jay Harrison of the LASD found us after Linda finished her paper-work and prepared to leave with me. She insisted she felt fine and didn't need to stay here any longer, though she moved unsteadily and admitted she had never had such a severe headache. I cleaned out the car with paper towels, while Linda apologized a dozen times, then collected the dirty paper towels in a plastic garbage bag. Harrison, a short black man in a brown suit, walked by us with a bow-legged gait, then stopped, and circled back, looking at Linda's forehead. He introduced himself and asked if she was Linda Maldonado.

"How'd you know?" she asked.

"Lucky guess," he said, then introduced himself. He had a crushing hand-shake and I noticed his knuckles were callused, a sign of martial arts training. He said, "I just spoke with Officer Carlisle, and we don't have much. You two didn't get much of a look at the SUV?"

We told him what we could, but I admitted I didn't get a chance to see the license plate. "Everything happened so fast."

"Why don't you tell me," he said to Linda. "You first."

Linda explained about heading out to Malibu and spotting the tail. Harrison stopped her and asked why we were going to Malibu. Linda glanced at me and told Harrison about Delgado. Harrison continued taking notes as she went on to detail the run-in, but he stopped her and said, "Wait. You didn't see the gun?"

"No. Allen did. I think I saw the window going down, but he was heading straight for us very fast. I turned the car when Allen saw the gun."

Harrison circled the car while talking. "Did he fire at you?" he asked.

"I don't know," I said.

Harrison bent down to inspect the driver's side door. I knew he was searching for bullet holes, and I said, "I didn't hear any shots."

He asked Linda, "You were heading toward him?"

"He was heading toward us."

"Head-on?"

She said, "Yes."

"Why did you U-turn to face him?"

Linda said, "I wanted us to get closer to see the license plate."

Harrison nodded slowly. "Do you know if at some point you cut this driver off on the highway? Maybe merging or something?" he asked.

"I don't think so," Linda said. "Why?"

"Couple of months ago we had a situation like this. Driver cut someone off, then the suspect started following him. The driver tried to lose him, making the suspect angrier, and finally the suspect took a shot at the driver."

"Road rage?" Linda said. "You think this was road rage?"

"No conclusions, just checking the context."

"The context," Linda said, "is something you might not know about. My brother died recently, and we've been asking a lot of questions about him."

Harrison looked up from his notes. His forehead shone in the sun. "Your brother?"

"Hector Gama. His car went down in Luego Canyon."

The detective cocked his head. "Just a week ago. Your brother?"

"Yes. Allen and I have been trying to reconstruct his movements."

"Why?"

"My mom wants to know. She doesn't understand what happened."

"Didn't I read that he was transporting chemicals for meth, possibly driving drunk?"

"I mean she wants to know *why* he was doing that."

Harrison studied her, then said, "You think the SUV had something to do with that?"

"We've been making calls, seeing some of his old friends, and maybe we got someone interested."

Harrison asked without expression, "Have you received any threats, warnings?"

"No."

To me he asked, "When you saw the gun, did you get a sense that this was a warning?"

"I don't know. I think he was worried we were going to get a good look."

"Are you certain it was a gun?"

"It looked like the short, squared barrel of a nine-millimeter."

Harrison paused. "How would you know that?"

I told him what I did for a living, and Harrison wrote this down. He said, "And you're sure this person was following you?"

"It wasn't road rage," I said.

"Why not?"

"He stayed far behind. If he was mad at us, he would've followed right behind us, tailgating aggressively. Instead he stayed way back."

Harrison thought about this, then wrote more down in his pad. He said, "Let me look into this." He pointed to the car. "You mind leading me back to the scene and giving me the exact locations of you and this SUV? Maybe I can find some bullets."

Linda and I glanced at each other, then shrugged. I said, "Let me finish cleaning this out first."

Harrison nodded while I bent back down. The acrid smell made me nauseous. Linda tried to help, but stopped and steadied herself. She touched her forehead lightly, squinting. The white bandage crinkled. I motioned her away and continued wiping the floor mats.

Nine

had once seen Linda sick with the flu, her fever spiking at 103 degrees. She was sniffling, aching, her eyes watering, and her voice a throaty croak. She had stayed home from work but wanted to finish a story, and so she crawled across the living room floor to reach her computer. Her fingers left sweaty prints on the keyboard, and she shivered as she blew her nose with one hand and tried to type with the other. She gritted her teeth and leaned toward the monitor, unable to focus, strings of greasy hair stuck to her face. I had to leave for the office, and tried to get her back into bed. She waved me off. I warned her that she would get worse if she didn't rest, and she mimicked me good-naturedly and said, "Thanks, Mom," though with her clogged sinuses this sounded more like "Danks, Bob." She added, "But I've got a five o'clock deadline."

I remembered this when we returned to her parents' condo. Linda changed her clothes and wanted to go right back out to see Delgado. She erased my message on the answering machine, not wanting to worry her parents.

"But you have a concussion," I said. "The doctor wanted to keep you overnight for observation. I don't think you should go out now."

"You're coming with me, right? I'll be fine," she said.

The white gauze bandage on her forehead had become a little dirty from our searching the street for bullets. Neither I, nor Linda, nor Harrison had found anything, and I knew Harrison was skeptical about my seeing a gun. We left him at the scene as he began visiting all the stores and apartment buildings along the street, canvassing for witnesses. Linda and I had to meet with him again to sign a statement.

"Maybe you should replace that bandage," I said.

She sighed. "Allen, don't worry. Let me call Delgado again, and we'll talk with him."

She went to the phone while I watched her squeeze her eyes shut for a moment. She then searched her pockets for Delgado's number. She picked up the handset and began dialing, and I suddenly thought of our exposure. I walked over to her and pressed down the hook.

"Why'd you do that?" she asked.

I said, "Do you remember during the Mess two years ago how all our movements were tracked?"

She stopped and looked at the phone. "You don't think . . ."

"That tail changes everything. We have to be more careful."

She lowered the handset and said, "You think we could be bugged? Already?"

"There's a pay phone downstairs, right?"

She nodded.

"Use that, and let me sweep the car before we go. I'll check the condo tonight."

"I'll meet you at the car," she said.

In the underground garage, I inspected the sedan, searching the transaxle and then the fuel tank and fenders, the most likely places for trackers because of their stationary anchors. I checked the brake hose for tampering, the gas lines for leaks. I went through the interior of the car, hunting for bugs. Without radio frequency sensors I could only do a visual and tactile search, but I tried to be thorough. I remembered the shock of discovering two years ago that my car and apartment were bugged. At ProServ I had been trained to screen for these kinds of things, but it had never really occurred to me that my personal life could be a target. I was so used to working with executives and the corporate world that *my* world, my quiet, solitary world, had seemed immune. I quickly learned otherwise.

When Linda came down to the car, she moved slowly, and I noticed that she had put on a fresh bandage. I asked her how she felt, and she said, "A little sluggish."

"I can do this myself," I said. "Just give me his address."

"No. Absolutely not. I want to meet him in person."

I saw the look on her face, her jaw rigidly set, and said, "At least let me drive."

She agreed.

We followed our original route before the SUV had derailed us, and I took us along the Pacific Coast Highway toward Malibu. I said, "Do you remember that time you were sick and refused to rest? You crawled to your computer to write."

"With the flu. Yeah, that was bad."

"You should take better care of yourself," I said.

She smiled. "Yes, but I finished the story. It was pretty damn good, too."

I counted cars, looking for marks, uneasy that we were back on the same road. Except for a dented fender and parts of the underside scraped from the curb, the car seemed fine. I'd have to tell Luke to check the alignment. Had I really seen a gun? I wasn't so sure now. What if we had hit the SUV? A head-on collision with it might have been an even match, this boat of a car is probably as heavy as that SUV, but Linda would've been even more seriously hurt.

The traffic thickened as we entered Malibu. Cars were parked along PCH, beachgoers weaving across the highway to get to the ocean on our left. A cliff of rocks and brush rose up to our right. We passed a family carrying beach chairs and a bright yellow umbrella. Linda leaned back and pressed her fingers against her temples.

"You okay?" I asked.

"I'm fine."

"Truthfully?"

"Yes. I'm okay."

I said, "You scared me."

She remained quiet. When I stopped at a red light, I turned to her. She said, "Thanks, Block."

I smiled. The light changed and I continued along the highway. Linda directed me to a smaller residential road off PCH, tightly packed bungalows only a few steps away from the beach. She said, "Hey, when we're done here, I want to see where it happened."

It took me a few seconds to realize she meant Hector's crash site. This had probably been why she had insisted on coming up here in the first place, and I regretted not thinking of that sooner. The loss of her brother wasn't yet real to me. I had to shift my focus of Linda as a reporter to a sister mourning her brother.

I said, "We'll figure all this out."

"Something's wrong with that seat belt, so be careful."

"No airbags?"

"Old model."

I repeated, "We'll figure this out."

"I know."

I rolled down my window and turned off the air conditioner. The strong salt air filled the car. Linda read off the address from a slip of paper and said, "It's coming up." She pointed to a small brown-shingled ranch-style house with two skinny palm trees in front. I parked in front of the picket fence and waited.

Linda took a deep breath. She said, "It's strange. He was here not too long ago."

"How long ago?"

"Last meeting a month before he died."

We walked toward the front steps, a jagged watermark lining the base of a wooden fence. A thin layer of rippled dark sand had hardened on the pavement. Classical music drifted from an open window. Everything smelled salty. Linda rang the doorbell, and I noticed her somber expression. I touched her shoulder. She said she was fine.

The door opened, and an older, square-jawed Latino man with wavy dark hair and thick eyebrows smiled at us. His teeth were unusually white against his deeply tanned face. Both Linda and I were startled by the force of his good looks. I almost stepped back. "You must be Hector's sister," he said.

Linda replied, "Mr. Delgado, again, I'm sorry we're so late. We ran into some problems."

"Call me William," he said, his voice deep and precise. "I was just reading the Sunday paper. What kind of problems? Is your forehead okay?"

Linda touched her bandage and said, "Long story. This is Allen."

"Allen." William shook my hand tightly. "Husband? Boyfriend?"

I turned to her.

Linda said, "Just a friend. Thanks so much for seeing us."

"Come in please. I'm glad you called."

He led us inside, and I stared at the back of her head, wondering what she had meant by the "just a friend" remark. She didn't look at me. I went to the window and surveyed the street. Quiet. I followed them into a small living room with a view of the ocean, and Linda complimented him on the house. Everything—the carpet, the tables, the sofa—was white. I squinted at the glare.

"Thanks," William said. "Your brother liked it, too."

"Hector was here?" Linda asked.

"A few times. You two want a drink? Juice or something?"

We declined, and I kept thinking about Linda's comment. I tried to concentrate on the room and studied the photos of William on the wall, glamour shots. "Are you an actor?" I asked.

"Was. Not much anymore. I'm producing now. You recognized me?"

"I think so," I lied. "You seem familiar."

He grinned. "I did a bunch of roles on TV." He shrugged it off.

"How did you know Hector?" Linda asked.

I thought, Two years together and I'm just a friend.

William waved his hand in the air. "He called me out of the blue. He was looking for his father and found out somehow that I once knew him."

"My father?" Linda said.

"Raul. Did Hector tell you? Raul and I used to do carpentry work way back."

"No," she said slowly. "He didn't. Was this in L.A.?"

"In L.A., Hollywood, Orange County. All over. We built recording studios and small house projects."

"When was this?"

"About fifteen years ago."

Linda stared at him. "That was after he left our family."

William said, "I didn't know he had one. Hector told me about it."

"I thought he went to Mexico."

"He might have, but I met him through a contractor, and we started doing more jobs together. He was pretty handy with design plans and blueprints. I was better with the tools."

Linda fell silent. I asked, "How did Hector find you?"

"Through my friends still in construction and carpentry. I think he found my name on some old work schedules or tax forms. I'm not sure."

I saw Linda still processing this, so I asked him, "So why was Hector looking for his father?"

He spread his hands out, his snug T-shirt pinching his arms. He gave us an easy smile. "Sounded like unfinished business, I suppose. He didn't want to talk too much about himself."

"And what did you tell him?" Linda asked. "About my father?"

"That Raul and I worked together for a few years, but then I started getting the acting bug and was doing bit parts. I left the business and he continued for a while. The last time I saw him he wanted me to invest in some company of his."

"When was this?"

"About five years ago—"

"*Five* years ago?" Linda said, shocked. "You saw my father five years ago?"

William nodded. "Your brother had the same reaction. I think Raul might still be in the area. Last I saw him was in Burbank."

"Doing what?"

"Not sure. He saw my name in some industry news—my production company got a deal with VH-1—and he looked me up. We had lunch and he tried to get me to invest in some Internet porn company. I don't know. It was very strange."

"Internet porn?" Linda asked, glancing at me. I remembered the article clippings we had found in Hector's room.

"Big industry now, so maybe I should've invested. But that's the last I saw of him."

"How did he seem?"

"Raul? Okay. Older, like me. He had some money. Drove a Beamer."

"My father?"

"That's right. Your brother was also surprised. I liked him, Hector. I took him and his girlfriend out for drinks, and I liked both of them. But then I didn't hear anything from him, until I read about the accident."

"Girlfriend?" I asked. "You mean Gloria? You met her?"

"Sure. They seemed pretty close. I met her twice."

"Do you know her last name? How can we find her?"

"Sorry. I don't know. She didn't tell me much about herself."

"What did she look like?" Linda asked.

"Short, pretty. Her hair was dyed red. Very red."

"You wouldn't happen to have a photo?"

"No, sorry," he said.

"What did you two talk about?" Linda asked.

"He asked me about your father, about what we did. He was just trying to find out more."

"Did he and Gloria talk about anything?"

William thought about this, then said, "Going to parties or something like that."

"Did they ever mention anyone else? Names or places or anything?"

"Not that I can remember. Oh, once they were going to meet someone for dinner, I think."

"Who?"

William shook his head. "Tyler? Taylor? Something with a 'T'? I'm not sure."

Linda pulled out a small pad and wrote this down. Then she asked, "So, what was he like? Raul, I mean."

William smiled. "Nice guy. We got along. He could be tough, maybe a little mean if you crossed him, but generally a good guy."

I asked, "Did Hector tell you if he found him?"

"Well, the last meeting we had was strange. He showed up, thanked me for my help, and took off."

"He found him," I said. "And he thanked you."

"That's right. He didn't want to talk about it though. I didn't push it."

"Why not?" Linda asked.

"Not my business, but he didn't seem very happy," William said. "I don't think it went well."

"But he did find Raul," Linda said. "Is that what you're saying?"

William nodded. "Yes."

After grilling William for another twenty minutes, with Linda finding out what he and Hector had talked about—names, dates, and relationships with former contractor-related colleagues—and taking more notes, she finally thanked him and apologized for tiring him. William shook hands with me again and led us out the front door. He waved as we drove away. Linda flipped through her pad, rereading her notes. She said, "Hector was really looking for him. I can't believe it."

"And found him," I said.

"I don't get it." She leaned back, easing her head carefully against the seat. "Why would he do that? And why now?"

"And it might be connected to his accident," I said.

She told me to continue on PCH for another few miles. After a minute I asked, "Are you going to follow Hector's trail?"

"I don't know."

"Do you want to find your father?" I asked.

She lowered her seat back and said to the roof of the car, "Hector never talked about him. He never showed any interest in Raul to me. I just don't understand."

"But you haven't been around recently."

"I know," she said. "I know that, but still."

"So what are you going to do?"

"I don't know."

I wondered what had she meant by "just a friend"?

She looked out the windshield and pointed ahead. "Luego Canyon is your next right."

I signaled, then turned onto a road that began winding and rising into the hills. Almost immediately I lost sight of PCH and was surrounded by thick trees and brush, crumbling rock faces to our left. I tried to be understanding, since all this news about her brother was undoubtedly a shock. I said, "What else do you remember about him?"

"Raul? Some things more than others. He wasn't around a lot. He was a loser."

"But he was okay to you."

She said, annoyed, "He bullied my mom, he bullied Hector. It just made it worse that he was nice to me."

"Why would Hector look for him?"

"I don't know. You don't think I'm trying to figure this out?" she asked, an edge to her voice.

"Take it easy," I said. I kept driving up the narrow road. If I veered too close to the edge, I could see the sheer drop below, and we were only climbing higher.

Linda finally said, "Sorry."

"Hey, it's none of my business, right?"

"He used to call my mom fat and ugly right in front of us, and sometimes when they fought, Hector would cry. That would set Raul off."

"How?"

"He'd call him a girl, a fag, a sissy. He'd push him and tell him to defend himself. Stupid crap like that. I mean, Hector was only five or six years old."

"How come you never told me this stuff before?"

"It never came up."

I didn't answer as we made a hairpin turn. I was perplexed by how much I didn't know about her. We soon ascended to a view of the Pacific Ocean, slivers of beaches on the fringes. "What was the code you two used?"

"The what?"

"The code. Your mother said you and Hector used to speak in code."

"What? When did you speak to her about this?"

"Last night."

"You two talked last night?"

"I had trouble sleeping."

She fell quiet, and after a few minutes said, "Yeah, we had a code. But that was later. I made up a version of Spanish pig Latin. I taught it to Hector, and we used it to drive her crazy. I had forgotten about that." She stared out her window.

I said, "If Hector was with his girlfriend while he was doing all this—"

"Then she'd be able to tell us exactly what he was up to. I know. We should find her." She pointed to a series of houses clustered beyond the main road. "We'll pass through that and turn onto McIntyre."

"How do you know?"

"I asked the police. They told me how to find it."

I realized she had memorized the directions. "I didn't know there were neighborhoods up here."

"Oh, sure. They go way up."

We threaded through the narrow streets, gleaming white houses with large wooden slat fences surrounding them, then continued up McIntyre, a narrow road that hugged the side of the mountain. There were no guard rails, and it would have been very easy to drive off the edge and down into the steep ravine. We were leaving a trail of dust that rose up, then zipped away in the wind.

Linda said, "Okay, about a half mile. There'll be a sharp turn and a wide dirt shoulder. The policeman said I'll see a slippery road sign right before the turn."

Slippery road? I slowed the car, worried about maneuvering a big sedan. Linda usually made fun of or grew annoyed at my careful driving, but not today. Instead she faced forward and stared blankly at the view as we climbed higher. About six months ago we had driven up to a Sonoma bed and breakfast, intending to visit vineyards for an extended weekend. She had complained about the way I stayed behind a slow truck, refusing to pass it. I had said, "What's the hurry? The B&B isn't going to go anywhere."

"I'd like to get there before it's dark," she replied, even though it was ten in the morning.

I told her to relax, but I felt her tension. We had planned the weekend months ago, and it no longer seemed like such a good idea, especially with our fights increasing and her problems at work. I found that I didn't know what to say to her anymore, and I ended up not talking for the rest of the ride.

What was it that tripped up a relationship, making it stumble forward or lurch to the side? What was it that transformed a couple who used to shower together to something more tame, to . . . *just friends?* I had thought the comfort and stability of our relationship would make it even better, but then again, what the hell did I know? I've never been married, like Linda. I was sure there were things I just didn't understand.

Thinking about this now confused me. I watched the canyon road and saw the yellow sign ahead—a car with wavy tire tracks behind it. I pulled onto the dirt shoulder, seeing nothing unusual. I wasn't sure what I expected. Remnants of a police scene?

We left the car and walked to the edge, looking down. Only then did I see the trees and shrubs along the side of the ravine torn and blackened. The few large rocks embedded in the side had been scraped deeply, with large bushes around the rocks uprooted. Linda said, "They had to drag the car back up."

I stepped back and looked out over the lush green valley. I then noticed how quiet it was. None of the traffic noise from PCH reached us here. I heard only the wind rustling trees. I watched Linda stare down into the ravine for a long time, then back away and take in the view. She said, "What a waste. He could've done something with his life."

She turned to me. I nodded.

"Goddamn this. I'm probably going to have find him now," she said.

"Raul?"

"Yes."

"Because he'll tell you what happened to Hector?"

"Because Hector found him, and something happened."

"And his girlfriend."

"Gloria. Yes. Maybe she's first. She'll know more."

"You'll need help."

"I will," she said slowly.

I saw a speck of a plane in the sky that left a white trail. I said, "I'll call Larry tonight."

A gust of wind blew back her hair. She said, "He's going to be mad."

"What's more important: videotaping a pissed-off sweaty guy stealing money from an insurance company, or helping you find out what happened to your brother?"

"You tell me."

"Helping you is more important."

"Are you sure?" she asked.

I was sure, but I also wondered if I could do the job.

"What's wrong?" she asked.

"Nothing."

She held my gaze, then looked out over the valley. She said quietly, "I know you want to talk about the other stuff."

I held my breath. I struggled with my need to ask questions and my knowledge of her grief. I kept waiting for her to say something else, but she didn't. Her expression changed, a look of apprehension settling into her eyes, and she surveyed the valley slowly, the wind feathering her hair. She said quietly, "It's nice up here."

Ten

When **I called** Baxter Investigations, I expected to leave a message but was surprised to hear Larry answer the phone. "You're in," I said, knowing that his workload must be heavy for him to be there on a Sunday.

"I think I'm going to take on a new law firm," he said. "They want us to interview people and find some possible witnesses in a big civil lawsuit. Tomorrow we'll meet up with the contact—"

"Hold on. I'm still in L.A."

Larry paused. "You flying up tonight or tomorrow morning?"

"That's the thing," I said. "I might have to stay down here for a bit."

"A bit? What's that? A day or two?"

"Maybe, but I'm thinking the week."

"Ah, shit, Allen," he said, the sound of his chair creaking in the background. "I'm shorthanded here."

"I know, I know. But Linda needs my help—"

"*I* need your help. Christ, a week? I don't know if I can handle the law firm alone."

"Linda was hurt today. Not too serious, but a tail pulled a gun on us and we had a small accident."

Larry breathed heavily. "Is she okay?"

"Yeah, just a bump."

"Took a shot?"

"No. We made him and it looked like he panicked, but we didn't get a plate."

Sighing, Larry said, "Why a tail?"

"I don't know. We don't know. It might have something to do with her brother."

He was quiet. I could imagine him squinting up at the ceiling as he weighed this. Larry was a big man with long salt-and-pepper hair he kept in a ponytail, and assumed this odd arching posture when he needed to make a decision; he searched for answers above him. He reminded me of a pro wrestler, beefy arms and chest and a thick neck, and he had the strength— the few times I'd worked out with him, I watched him bench-press three hundred pounds. I knew Linda's dislike of him had something to do with his blustery attitude and the way he used his bulk to intimidate. When he felt uncertain about a situation, he tended to swell up and raise his voice. I had to admit that when I first met Larry on an assignment, I didn't much like him, either, but then I soon saw that he meant well. He was earnest. He rarely had ulterior motives. Larry finally said, "I've been looking over the PI requirements."

"I have, too."

"I can certify you for two years, but you'll have to get ProServ to certify a year. Can you do that?"

"I think Polansky will if I ask him. He's also a licensed PI."

"Perfect. How about this: you take as much time as you need down there, but you promise when you get back you apply, using Polansky for that extra year, and take the exam."

"What's the exam like?"

"Hundred questions, multiple choice of procedures, laws and stuff. It's pass/fail. If you apply soon, you can take the one coming up next month. In fact, let me send you the paperwork so you can fill it all out down there."

"So I work the PI business with you? What if executive protection comes up?"

"Christ, we take it. But it's just not happening right now. If that starts picking up, I'll get licensed, but until then you help me."

I wanted to ask what would happen if I refused, but already knew the answer. And he was right: I wasn't contributing enough. I said, "Okay. Send me the application material and maybe something to help me start prepping for the test." I gave him the condo address.

We hung up, and I thought, So that's that. I'd have to call Polansky and reveal my new career path. He had given me a chance at ProServ when I had only in-house security experience and no executive protection background. Starting me on group work and letting me move up to paired fieldwork, Polansky had promoted me fairly quickly though the ranks. Our relationship became strained two years ago during the Mess, when the second-in-command, Charles Swinburn had to fire me to protect the firm.

I returned to the living room and found Linda lying back on the sofa, listening to the TV. She opened her eyes and said, "How'd it go?"

"Fine. How do you feel?"

"I took more Tylenol. Larry was okay?"

"Sort of. We have a deal. What's next?"

"Find Gloria. I was thinking about asking Tim Jacobs again. He must know more."

"I agree. If Delgado was right, then Hector and Gloria were close."

"And Tim and Hector hung out together," she said, slowly pulling herself up. "I'll call."

"No. Let me handle this. You rest."

"I should go, too," she said, her voice thin.

"You're exhausted. Rest. This isn't that important. I'll talk to Tim, come back here, and tell you what happened. Save your energy for the important things."

She hesitated.

"It's next door, practically. I'll be back in twenty minutes."

She lay back down slowly and waved me away.

I talked to Kate on the phone and learned that Tim was working at the café in Santa Monica, so I headed directly there from the condo. During the short drive I thought about becoming a PI and what that meant. I remembered

Polansky joking with Charles about a PI who was trying to get a job with them; they called him a "Dumpster diver" and made fun of the guy's résumé and cover letter, which were riddled with typos and had phrases like "action oriented" and "quick footed." While they were showing the letter around the office and laughing, I couldn't help but feel sorry for the guy, since I had been looking for a better job not too long ago. I had moved from sitting at a console and watching security cameras, and I knew that I had made as big a leap as this PI wanted. Maybe they had made fun of my résumé as well, though I certainly hadn't used language like that.

I was worried what my former colleagues would think, what everyone would think. I knew the rep: PIs were usually washed-up cops and cop wanna-bes, or if they were specializing in security they called themselves "security experts" and strutted around with dark sunglasses and oversize hand guns. Larry was a little like that, and I had to admit to myself a slight prejudice against this type.

Why didn't I tell Linda about this deal? Because I knew she disliked the work PI's did, and she had told me so on many occasions. She had called it a "seedy job," and I guess I was a little offended by that. Yet maybe I felt the same way but just couldn't admit it.

The café was off Wilshire, a tiny coffee bar with tables out on the sidewalk, mountain bikes racked up against the parking meters. Customers in bright Lycra cycling gear and helmets at their feet sipped coffee and watched traffic pass by. Inside, a few worn wooden tables were filled with people talking and reading. The acidic smell of burnt coffee beans surrounded me. Faces looked up as I headed for the counter.

Tim, wearing an apron and ringing up a customer, saw me approaching. Another clerk behind Tim rushed back and forth with mugs. Tim stopped, then thanked the customer and began helping the next one in line. I watched him glance up uneasily, then try to ignore me. I stood off to the side, waiting. He had combed back his messy hair, and had shaved, so he looked much younger. He could've been a teenager.

The other clerk whipped up foam for a cappuccino. The sound of slurping and fizzing momentarily drowned out the customers' murmurs. Tim dropped some change. He scooped it up from the floor and said to the other clerk, "Can you take over for a second?"

The clerk, a younger kid with a nose ring, nodded.

Tim took off his apron and moved around the counter. He said to me, "This isn't cool, coming here to my work. How'd you know I was here?"

"Kate."

He frowned. "This is harassment."

"I haven't done anything. I just want to talk."

"Where's Hector's sister?"

"Recovering," I replied. "Someone almost took a shot at us, and we had a small car accident."

Tim said, "What?"

I repeated myself.

"Who did it?" Tim asked.

"I don't know, but someone is getting nervous."

It took a second for Tim to process this, and he shook his head. "Wait. Someone tried to shoot you with a gun?"

I nodded. "We're trying to find Gloria. She was with Hector a lot. There has to be a way to get hold of her—"

"Are you fucking crazy?" Tim raised his voice. A few customers turned to us, and he whispered fiercely, "Someone took a shot at you because of Hector, and now you're coming to me?" He looked around. "Oh, fuck me."

"How do I find Gloria?"

"I told you I don't know her! I've only met her a few times."

"You were good friends with Hector, but didn't know his girlfriend?"

He shrugged. "He had his own life. I only met her at raves."

"At raves," I said. "When's the next one?"

"God, there are raves all over the place."

"When's the next one that Gloria might go to?" I asked.

"How the hell am I supposed to know?"

"Hey!" I snapped. "We almost got killed today. You're going to give me shit now? What kind of raves did they like? Where might she go?"

"Hector liked hardcore Trance. That's all I'm telling you."

"How would I—"

"Don't ask me nothing else. You want the info, the map point, or anything else you talk to someone else."

"Who? The what point?"

"Shit, you don't know nothing. Don't bother me anymore. This is just so not cool."

"If you were really Hector's friend, you'd want to help me."

"Yeah? Well, fuck you. Don't bother me again, you got it? I don't know what Hector was into, but I don't want to get mixed up in it. So, fuck off." He turned and disappeared into the back room. I rubbed my forehead, smelling the roasting coffee. I leaned against the counter, and listened to the cash register ringing up orders.

I was telling Linda what I had learned when her parents walked into the condo. Neither of us were prepared, and we froze. Marianne bustled into the living room, then halted in mid-sentence, her gaze locking onto Linda's forehead, her surprise jerking her body back. Luke turned and saw the bandage as well. There was a brief hanging moment, and then both Linda and Marianne started talking at once.

"What happened to your—"

"Mom, don't worry—"

They stopped. Linda said, "I'm fine. It was a small accident."

Marianne rushed over and examined Linda's head. She said, "Were you hurt? What happened?"

Luke's eyes darkened. "This doesn't have anything to do with Hector, does it?"

Linda said, "Why do you think that?"

"A bad feeling," he said.

She immediately tried to downplay the accident by telling them the road-rage story, and not mentioning the gun. Marianne kept repeating, "Right here? This happened around here?" Linda explained that she had told the police what had happened, and they were working on it.

Luke said grimly, "Road rage? Did it seem like road rage?"

Linda shrugged.

Luke turned to me and said, "What do you think?"

They waited for my response, and I shook my head slightly. Linda quickly added, "It's too early to tell."

"This is my fault," Marianne said. "I've made a mistake."

"No," Linda said.

"This is because of Hector somehow," Marianne said. "Isn't it? Why would someone try to run you off the road? It makes no sense."

Linda sighed. "Maybe. But your instincts might have been right. Something was going on with Hector."

Marianne started to reply but seemed unable to continue. Her face, conflicted as she looked down at her daughter, revealed a grief I felt embarrassed to witness. Her mouth tightened and she closed her eyes. Then she said softly, "You found out something?"

"Allen and I just found out that he may have found Raul."

"In Mexico?" Marianne asked.

Linda said, "No. He might be in California, maybe not too far away."

"What?" Marianne stiffened. Luke put his thin arm around her shoulder. Luke asked us, "Do you know where?"

"Not yet."

"Oh, but you can't do this!" Marianne said. "Hector shouldn't have tried to! You shouldn't . . ."

Linda waited for her mother to finish, but she just trailed off and shook her head. Linda said, "Mom, it'll be okay. I have to know now."

"No."

"But why? You wanted to—"

"Because he's bad," Marianne said. "You know that! He's . . ."

Linda winced, and touched her temple.

"Are you okay?" I asked.

"What did the doctors say?" Luke asked.

"I'll be fine. Just a bad headache. The doctor said I should rest."

"Then you'll rest," Marianne said, shaking off Luke's arm and carefully pulling on Linda's arm. "Let me help. You can use our bed." She wrapped her arm around Linda's waist and walked her to the bedroom. "I'm so sorry," she said. "This is my fault."

"Oh, Mom, I'll be fine." Linda rested her head on her mother's shoulder, and I was surprised to see this gesture of affection.

Marianne and Luke sat me down at the dining room table and asked me more questions while Linda was sleeping. I explained in greater detail where we had gone and what had happened, and as I was finishing up, Luke grimly stood up and left the room while Marianne opened and closed her thick fists

on the table. She said, "Why didn't Linda tell us about the gun you saw?"
She had changed out of her skirt and blouse and now wore a purple sweat
suit.

"She didn't want to worry you," I said.

"Why are you telling us?"

"I think you need to know that this might be getting a little dangerous."

"But she won't stop now, will she," Marianne said.

"I doubt it."

Luke returned with a wooden box. He rolled up his sleeves. Marianne met
her husband's eyes and nodded. Luke asked me, "You've got a permit?"

"Firearms permit?" I said. "Yes."

Luke opened the box and pulled out a stainless steel revolver wrapped in
a rag. He handed it to me, holding the muzzle with his skeletal fingers. The
gun, a Smith & Wesson Model 638, had a shrouded hammer. I said, "Nice. A
pocket pistol. Yours?"

"I used to show commercial property in bad neighborhoods."

"I don't have a concealed-weapons permit for this area," I said. "I'd have
to apply."

"Just hold onto it," Marianne said. "Luke doesn't need it anymore."

"What do you want me to do with it?"

"Protect Linda," she said. "I don't want her getting hurt again."

I checked her eyes, which were deadly serious. When I opened up the
cylinder, Luke said, "No bullets. You'll have to buy some."

"We just want you to look out for her," Marianne said, her voice hard and
steady. "It's what you do, isn't it? I want you to protect her."

"I'll try, but she's pretty strong-minded—"

"You can't let this happen again. Do you understand? I will not allow her
to get hurt again."

I suddenly saw where Linda had inherited her toughness. I said, "I'll hold
onto this, but I'm not sure if I'll actually use it."

"Just in case," Marianne said. "I know I can't tell her to stop, but I'll feel
better knowing you're helping. You'll protect her, okay?"

"She can look out for herself."

"No, she never knows when to stop. She always goes too far. Promise me
you'll protect her."

I said, "I promise." I replaced the gun back into the box. After a moment I asked, "Do you know why Hector would look for Raul?"

"No," she said, placing her fists in her lap.

"He never said anything recently?"

"No. He didn't talk much to us."

Luke turned toward the bedroom and said, "I think I woke her when I got the box."

Marianne told me, "Check on her. She won't admit she needs help, but she does."

I left the dining room and knocked lightly on the bedroom door, peering in. "You awake?"

"Hey. What're you guys talking about?" She raised her head and squinted as the hall light shone in.

"They just gave me a gun."

"What?"

"Luke had a small revolver. Your mother wants me to protect you."

"I didn't know they had a gun," she said. "Protect me?"

"Unloaded, no ammo." I walked into the room, closing the door behind me. Threading through the darkness, I sat on the edge of the bed. My eyes slowly adjusted. Shapeless, blurry forms danced around me. I whispered, "I didn't realize how tough your mother is."

"She is. Hector's death threw her though. What do you mean 'protect me'?"

"Just keep an eye out, I guess."

She said, "With a gun?"

We fell quiet. I asked, "Tell me about when Raul left. He just walked out?"

Linda rolled onto her side, the bed squeaking. "Yes. They had a big fight. It was late at night. The next morning he was gone. The TV and bank accounts were gone, too."

"He left you with nothing?"

"Nothing. My mom just shut down. She couldn't get out of bed, she lost her job, and Hector and I were really scared for a while." Linda explained quietly that her mother eventually snapped out of it when Hector became sick, but for a week she barely moved from her bed, ignoring all phone calls or visitors. Linda said, "I remember that time pretty vividly. We didn't know what to do at night without the TV. There was a big blank space in the living room."

"How did Hector react?"

"Scared," she said. "He couldn't really understand what was happening. He wouldn't let me out of his sight. I think my mom's reaction scared him more than anything. He ended up getting some kind of intestinal virus, which was probably brought on by stress."

"How'd *you* take it?"

She breathed heavily through her nose, and her disembodied voice surrounded me. "I was angry at everyone, even my mom for letting it happen, and then letting it get to her. I was angry at my brother for being scared. I just wanted everyone to forget about him."

"Why would Hector want to find him now, after all these years?"

"For answers, maybe. If he was depressed it might make sense." Her voice weakened, and I heard her lying back.

"You're tired. Sleep. We can talk tomorrow."

"Wait. We have to follow up on what Tim said."

"I'll take care of it. I was thinking of calling Serena to ask her about it. You just rest." I started to move off the bed, but when she didn't respond I said, "You okay?"

"Uh-huh," she said.

I waited, then asked, "You want me to stay here a bit?"

"If you want."

I thought about what her mother had said, about Linda not asking for help. I sat back against the headboard, and she moved closer to me. I ran my fingers through her hair, something that calmed her. I couldn't count the number of times I had done this while we had lain in bed or on her sofa, reading or listening to music. Those quiet nights pleased me, the drama of the day melting away. I paused, then continued. I would miss this the most. Perhaps it was these comforts that worried Linda, the domestic routine of it. She had once told me that she would never again feel trapped like she had with Manny, that she would always be free and unencumbered by attachments.

Attachments. What a word. I certainly didn't want to be an attachment.

The room grew darker, quieter, with Linda's breathing slowing. She liked it when I let strands of her curly hair fall through my fingers. I did this now, and I thought I heard Luke and Marianne's voices in the living room. I knew they were talking about Linda, worried about her, and I wondered if she knew how lucky she was. People cared for her. I cared for her. Perhaps I should begin to steel myself, sever the attachments.

After a few minutes I slid off the bed and went to call Serena.

I found the number among the papers in Linda's planner, which she had left on the small sofa in the office. I looked at her weekly appointments, most of this past week blank, but at the end of last week I read "Lunch w/ Harlan" in the noon slot. Harlan. I hadn't known about this. But why would she have to tell me? I closed the book with a familiar sting of jealousy. He was just a colleague at work. Right? I stared at the leather cover, which had Linda's business card in a clear sleeve. I was tired. I was having trouble understanding the point of relationships.

Dialing Serena's number, I felt an irrational flare of resentment toward Linda, then regretted it. I had trouble ordering my thoughts. Serena answered the phone and I told her who it was. She said, sounding pleased, "Hey, Mr. Bodyguard. What's up?"

I smiled. "I have a question."

"The answer is yes."

"I haven't asked it yet."

"Sorry. Go ahead."

I told her about my meeting with Tim and our search for Gloria. "Do you know anything about finding the next rave, especially with this Trance band?"

She laughed. "It's not a band, it's a kind of music. And it's really easy to find them. It's all online. You want to see if Gloria shows up?"

"How would I do that? Do I just show up at the rave?"

She said, "Depends. If it's an illegal one, you have to find the map point, then find the actual location. Sometimes you end up driving all over the place."

"I probably wouldn't get very far," I said.

"You probably wouldn't," she said.

"Maybe I need help."

"Like a guide?"

"I guess. It's bad enough everyone seems to think I'm a narc."

She laughed again, a lightness that startled me. She said, "I can check and find one. Actually, hold on."

I heard her fumble with the phone. She said, "I'm checking right now."

"Online?"

"There's a site that lists most of the upcoming raves. Ah. Here's one that's all Goa Trance. It's in L.A. Tomorrow night."

"Tomorrow? That's perfect. She might be there."

"It's been ages since I've gone to one. It might be fun. You want to go?"

"You'll help me?"

"Sure. It'll be a fun date."

I hesitated.

Serena said, "Oh, wait a minute. Is this with Hector's sister, too?"

"I'm not sure."

"I don't know about that. I'll go with you to have some fun, but I won't do this if it's just you going to act like a cop. I don't want to do that."

"What if we find Gloria?"

"Then ask a few questions, but nicely. None of the narc stuff."

I heard someone walking into the bathroom and shutting the door. I was in a strange house with strangers. I said, "All right. No narcs. But if I find her, I'll want to ask a bunch of questions."

"Just you and me?"

I looked down at Linda's appointment book and said, "Just you and me."

Eleven

My package from Larry arrived the next morning, an overnight-express box filled with applications, forms, and a textbook. Larry's note read, "Don't forget. As soon as you fly back, you finish this and we get to work." He signed it, "Your partner." I saw this as a reminder to keep up my end of the bargain. The textbook, *A Complete Guide to Private Investigations*, was worn and dirty, Larry's name scribbled in the front cover. Tucked inside was a copy of the California Private Investigator's Act, a series of laws governing California's PIs, full of legalese, with another note from Larry: "This will be on the test, too."

I glanced at a section that read, "The proceedings under this section shall be governed by Chapter 3 (commencing with Section 525) of Title 7 of Part 2 of the Code of Civil Procedure, except that there shall be no requirement to allege facts necessary to show or tending to show lack of adequate remedy at law or irreparable injury." I stared at the words, which refused to make any sense. I reread them slowly and tried to piece together the meaning. The letters seemed to crawl off the page. They danced and waved at me. I suddenly remembered the old, moldy medical textbooks I had once found in my aunt's basement—the only evidence of my father's desire to be a doctor—and wondered if he had encountered similar difficulties.

Linda walked into the living room, glancing at the sheets and blankets on the sofa. She tugged at her pajamas and asked me, "You slept out here?"

"No," Marianne said from the kitchen. "Your father did. I slept in the office. We didn't want to wake you."

"But mom! You didn't have to—"

"How do you feel?" Marianne asked.

"So much better. My head feels almost normal. I was just so tired last night."

"Your father carpooled to work, so you can take his car again. He said there's no real damage to it."

"Sorry about denting it, though."

Marianne waved this off and said, "I'm about to go to Ralph's for groceries. You want anything?" She headed into the kitchen.

Linda shook her head, then noticed the papers in front of me. She nodded to them, her eyes curious.

I said, "PI application from Larry, for when I get back."

"So you're really doing it?"

"I am."

She was about to reply, but her mother returned with a list in her hand. "I'll be out for a while. Will you be okay?"

Linda said she'd be fine and kissed her mother on the cheek. After Marianne left, Linda asked me, "Did you talk to Serena?"

"Yes. I'm going to a rave tonight with her to look for Gloria. She might be at this one."

"Great. What time? Should we take my father's car? Maybe I should rent a car while I'm down here."

I thought about how to phrase this, then said, "Well, the only way I could get Serena to agree to this was by telling her I'd go alone, and I wouldn't act like a cop."

"Alone?"

"Without you."

She flinched, then her expression set rigidly into a nonreaction, one that I recognized as her poker face. She said calmly, "And why is this?"

I straightened the papers in front of me, and answered, "She didn't want to help unless we were going for the rave, not for Gloria."

"But why can't I go?"

"I guess . . . I guess she's thinking that this is a kind of date."

"And did you discourage her from this idea?" she asked.

"Not really. If I had, she wouldn't have agreed."

She folded her arms. "So what you're telling me is that you're going out with Serena on a date tonight, and maybe, just maybe, you'll look for Gloria if you're not having too much fun?"

"Uh, wait a minute—"

"That while I'm sitting here with a concussion and my brother's dead and who the hell knows what he'd been up to with my biological father—you'll be dancing with this girl who's obviously coming on to you and using this as an excuse? That I have to sit here and twiddle my goddamn thumbs while you're *out on a date?*"

"Those are the terms she set," I said quietly. "What're you so pissed about? That fact that you're excluded or the fact that there's some woman interested in me?"

"So you admit she's interested in you? Did she say something? What the hell is going on here?"

"You want me to cancel?" I said, my face heating up. "Give me the phone. I'll cancel right now. Better yet, why don't you cancel for me." I clumsily gathered up my papers and textbook. I couldn't see clearly. "The number's in the office. You call her up, and tell her the guy who's about to lose his job, the guy who came down here at your beck and call, who's getting dumped by you for no good fucking reason—this guy who's trying to help you, help *you*, this loser is no longer *allowed* go to a stupid illegal dance club where he'll be twice as old as everyone there, trying to pretend to have fun and then look for some stranger who's no doubt going to spit in his face." My heart was thudding, and I tried to stop myself from saying anything else, bitter thoughts tumbling through me, and I headed for the door. The papers almost slipped from my unsteady hands; I held them close to my chest. I didn't look at Linda, but said, "*You* want to break up with *me*. You think I'm stupid and can't see that? *You* asked *me* down here to help. You think I need this shit? You think I *want* this?"

I slammed the door behind me.

Remember when you two used to take a shower together? Linda preferred a hard sea sponge to soap herself, the abrasive fibers rubbing her skin raw and red. She would hand it to me and say, "Do my back, please." I would scrub her back, but she would want it harder, and I would comply, surprised that the red welts didn't hurt. I'd admire her curved back, tracing her spine down to her buttocks, and would finish scrubbing her, then press myself up against her, feeling the warm water running down between us. It became a Sunday morning ritual for a while, after brunch, though often one or both of us would have to work later that afternoon. I remembered these mornings clearly but wasn't sure why they'd stopped. I couldn't pinpoint the last time we had done this. Vague images of water dripping between her breasts flashed before me. She'd slick back her hair, straightened and flattened by the shower stream. I'd startle her by squirting water into her ear.

I tried to focus on the PI application in front of me. I sat at a pastry-and-coffee shop down the block from the condo and stared at the blank entries. Some of this information was already on file at the BSIS, and I probably wouldn't need to resubmit a fingerprint card, but the Certificate in Support of Experience would have to go to Larry and Polansky to verify my work with them. I'd have to call Polansky this afternoon.

I had trouble shaking off the post-fight darkness. Back at home after a heated argument, I'd go running, pushing myself beyond my usual routes. Exhaustion would replace gloom. Without my gym clothes, though—no sneakers, no sweats—I was trapped here in shoes and slacks. At home I'd also return to my apartment and sulk in silence, in familiar solitude. I'd find comfort in the street noises outside my window, the Cal-Tran train blaring its horn a few blocks away.

But I was in limbo down here. At some point I'd have to return to the condo and deal not only with Linda but her parents hovering. Everything, even this neighborhood, was Linda's, and I needed to escape.

I looked around this shop. A few office workers bought coffee and dough-nuts at the front counter, then hurried out. I watched them walk down the street, and I longed for the stability I imagined them having. While I had been at ProServ doing paired work with Paul and living a quiet, solitary life, I had chafed at the repetition of my day, and felt the dis-ease encroaching. Yet now

I looked back at that time with nostalgia. At least I had been free of this tumult. At least I had function with some degree of contentment, though perhaps I hadn't known it. Engagement is elusive. It hides behind you as you look for it, and you notice its absence only when you walk away.

I noticed a familiar figure across the street, and then recognized Linda's gait. She moved briskly forward, leaning slightly ahead as if pushing through the air. She crossed at the light, looking into stores and offices, and I realized she was searching for me. I sighed inwardly, and started filling out the application, refusing to look up. I heard the front door open and listened to Linda's shoes click on the floor. She sat down across from me. I still didn't look up.

"Detective Harrison wants us over at the Homicide Bureau at noon to sign a report," she said.

I glanced at my watch. Ten o'clock. "I'll meet you at the condo."

"I'm sorry about before. I didn't react well."

I shrugged.

"It's just that she was so blatantly coming on to you last time, so when you said it'd just be you two . . ."

I looked up. "What's going on with you?"

"What do you mean?"

"What is it you want from me?"

"What?"

"What do you want? You're not happy with us? Do you want to break up? Do you want me to sit around and wait for you to decide something?"

She stared at the application in front of me, and replied, "I don't know."

"Let me ask you this, and I want you to be honest."

She nodded.

"Why do you want to break up?"

I saw her hesitate, about to deny this, but then she sighed. She looked down and said gently, "I know what you want, but I don't want the same thing."

"What do I want?"

"You want a family. You want us to move in together and maybe someday get married, have kids, that kind of thing. You want stability. You want what you never had."

Surprised, I considered this. I had never articulated it, but she might be right. I said, "And you don't?"

"No, Allen."

"Then what is it you *do* want?"

"I don't know. To answer just to me. To be free. Things haven't quite worked out like I thought they would, and I can't . . . worry about another person."

"Is this because you're turning thirty next month?"

She shrugged.

"But you definitely don't want any of those other things?"

"No. I've done it. I've been married. I've been shoved into that slot before. I don't like it."

"So, when I bought that VCR for your place, you saw me, what, moving in, taking over?"

She almost smiled. "Something like that."

I said, "And your dinners with Harlan?"

She jerked her head up. "What's that got to do with this?"

"A little flirting, a little testing? Just making sure you're not tied down?"

Her cheeks reddened, something I'd rarely seen. Although I had suspected this, it was a shock to see I had been right. I felt an initial flicker of relief that my jealousy had been well-founded, but then the truth pierced my chest. I let out a slow breath and couldn't meet her eyes. Finally I said, "All right. I need to finish this application. I'll meet you at the condo at eleven-thirty."

"That's it?"

I looked up at her. "What else is there?" I knew she wanted to ask about tonight with Serena. I was daring her to bring it up. A brief glint of sadness passed across her gaze, and I wavered. Then I thought about my being called down here, not invited for the funeral but to ease her mother's fears, to help her with a job. She had needed me not as a boyfriend but as a grunt, a worker ant. I said, "Yes?"

She shook her head. "Eleven-thirty, then." She pulled herself up and walked swiftly to the exit without looking back. She struggled with the door for a second, and I resisted the urge help her. She didn't want me crowding her? Okay. Open the door yourself. She did, and walked out onto the street. I watched her push forward through a gust of wind.

The meeting with Detective Harrison was brief, since he seemed to be juggling many cases and needed us only to review and sign the statement he had prepared. He told us that he hadn't found any bullets, and there were no witnesses that could identify the driver or the SUV. When Linda asked him about the possible connection to Hector, Harrison told her that the narcotics division would get back to him, but it wasn't promising. He said, "None of the officers had heard about your brother or any connection to him with the known local meth dealers. It might be a stretch."

We read the statement, which summarized our stories but deemphasized the gun I had seen, and the annoyed look on Linda's face prompted Harrison to say, "Homicide is still handling this. We're taking the possibility of a gun threat seriously. However, we just don't have much to go on."

We signed it and talked with Harrison a bit more about Hector—the coroner's report was available, though Linda didn't think she needed to see it. When Harrison received a phone call, he thanked us for coming by, and we left.

On the ride back, Linda was quiet. I drove because she was feeling tired. We hadn't spoken about this morning's argument, and that was fine with me. I was still thinking about how I'd ask Polansky for the certification and also wondered how I would meet Serena tonight.

"By the way," Linda said. "Julie and her daughter might be flying down here."

"It's getting crowded. I guess I should find a hotel."

"No, no. They'll stay at a hotel. They've got the money."

"What about Frank? He's not coming?"

"No. I think because of work."

We fell silent. Frank, Julie's husband, worked for a credit card company and seemed to have more money than anyone I knew. Their huge five-bedroom house in Walnut Creek (for the three of them), felt wasteful to me. I asked, "Why is she coming down?"

"Paying respects, seeing our parents. Nora got over the flu."

We entered Marina Alta and headed for the condo. I asked if I could make a few long-distance calls to the Bay Area.

"For what?"

"Take care of this application."

"Sure. I'll be at the library. I'm going to see what I can find out about Raul."

"Like what?"

"His address, for one thing. Especially if he's in the area. I can access my Lexis-Nexis account from there, and do some news searches."

"You want to find him."

"I do."

"If I find Gloria, you'll want to talk to her at some point."

"Yes," she said. "How will you find her?"

"If she's a regular, maybe I can ask around. I'll want to check Hector's photos again. I think there are shots of his friends."

"Sounds good. Can you drop me off at the library?"

"Right now?" I asked.

She nodded. I felt the coolness rolling off her, her polite answers depressing me. I passed the condo building and drove her four blocks to the local library.

"Should I pick you up?"

"No, thank you. I can walk it," she said, shutting the door before I could protest. I sat back and rubbed my forehead.

Returning to the condo and letting myself in with Linda's extra key, I went through the photos in Hector's room and set aside the shots of him at a rave. I recognized Tim and Kate in one photo. In another, Hector was standing with a short red-haired woman in black leather pants. She smiled at the camera. She had large eyes and bushy eyebrows with heavy make-up, dark brown lipstick that made her white face whiter. Delgado had mentioned her hair, and I thought this woman could be Gloria. I pocketed the photo.

I spread out my PI application, preparing to call Polansky, but I kept going over my fight with Linda. I should never have come down here. With Julie arriving, I would be the only non-family member and completely out of place. And Julie didn't even like me. She hid it well, and was pleasant to me, but the plastic smile whenever she greeted me made me want to flee. It had started with a very bad first meeting—Linda had asked Julie to help me when

I had been in trouble with the law—and Julie's image of me was forever tainted with this. Her words to me at the time were, "Like she needs any more losers in her life."

I shook this off and began making my calls.

Twelve

Serena had agreed to pick me up outside the condo, so I waited on a small brick ledge surrounding a garden. Upstairs, the family was having a late dinner. The only thing Linda had said when she returned from the library was, "You find a photo?" After that, she had disappeared into her parent's bedroom. I didn't think I could handle dinner with them, so I excused myself and was now waiting for Serena, thirty minutes early.

I had worked on the PI application and had sent off the certification forms to both Polansky and Larry. Polansky had been surprisingly agreeable on the phone and said he'd gladly certify me. We had talked briefly about how business was going, and when I explained why I was adding a PI license to work both ends, Polansky said it was a good idea. "Executive protection is slowing down. A lot of companies are having cash problems."

"I know," I said. "Larry's getting more PI business."

"Drop by sometime. Maybe we can talk about throwing extra work your way."

I thanked him and hung up, wondering if I should have stayed there. I'd probably be doing solo work by now, at the very least heading up the teams. If working with Larry ultimately failed, and I needed a job, I could probably return to ProServ. Yet the prospect of having my own firm pleased me. Baxter & Choice. B&C Investigations.

I found Larry's textbook useful. I learned the legal parameters of workers' compensation investigations and realized that my taping of Smith while on his property could cause problems. There were minefields. I had spent an hour engrossed in a case, *Noble* v. *Sears* in which a PI, investigating an injury law-suit had sneaked into a hospital room and had tricked a patient into revealing a new witness. However, since the PI was working for opposing counsel, and wasn't allowed to interview the patient without the patient's lawyer present, the new witness was inadmissible in court.

I worried about the video of Smith and hoped Larry didn't get into trouble with it. There was a lot I had to learn. It struck me that I was completely changing careers. I tried not to let all this instability dizzy me.

A new silver Volkswagen Beetle pulled up at the curb, glittering in the streetlights. The car kept its engine running, and I froze, on alert. But there was a short honk, and the passenger-side window eased down. "Ready, Mr. Bodyguard?"

I walked over and looked in. Serena, dressed in yellow vinyl short-shorts with a tiny white sleeveless T-shirt, waved me in. "Hey," she said.

Still looking at her outfit, I climbed in. Her T-shirt had a Japanese cartoon character on the front, and she had slicked back her hair. I said, "Won't you be cold?"

She smiled. "Not when I'm dancing. You might be too hot in that."

I was wearing khakis and a button-up shirt. I felt old. As we drove off, I noticed a small backpack near my feet and pointed to it.

"Supplies," Serena said.

"What kind?"

"Open it."

I did, and saw bottled water, lollipops, a collapsible windbreaker, and a pacifier. I told her that Hector had a bag filled with pacifiers in his room.

"Sucking reflex when you take E. It keeps you from grinding your teeth."

I turned to her. "You brought Ecstasy?"

"You okay with that?"

"I don't know," I said uneasily.

"I only take it when I dance, and I don't dance that much anymore."

"How do you know if it's safe?"

"I had it tested. I bought a bunch a while back, and at some raves they have tables set up to test it for you."

"You're kidding. Right there?"

She nodded, her slender neck glittering. "I don't know what you've heard, but raves aren't bad places." She drove us away from L.A., which confused me. When I asked her about this, she told me that the LAPD was cracking down on illegal raves, and promoters were setting them up wherever they could. "The cops know most of the tricks, and the regular dance clubs—the establishment—are mad at losing money, so they've been telling the cops where the raves are. So now it's trickier."

"How'd you find out about this one?" I asked, zipping closed her back-pack. I noticed a few condom packets in the side pockets.

"Online. This one is definitely for Goa Trance fans."

I didn't understand what she was talking about, and asked, "Hector did all this?"

"Totally. It's more than just dancing. There's a kind of ethic to it. You know, the PLUR stuff and—"

"The what?"

"P.L.U.R. Peace, love, unity, respect. That's old now, but that's part of it." She smiled. "I know it sounds stupid, but early on, a lot of people really got into it, including Hector."

"Not anymore?"

"Not anymore. The media's gotten on the drug cry, and a whole new generation of kids are showing up who know nothing about the music. For most people, like Tim, it's about the music. For Hector it was about escaping, about feeling good and having fun."

"When you two were going out, how often did he go?"

"A lot. A lot more than me. He felt at home there. I was getting tired of it." She turned on her signal and exited the freeway.

"Where are we going?"

"To get the tickets. Pasadena. Then we'll go to the actual location."

"And you found this . . . ?"

"E-mail list. You can sign up on the Web."

Two blocks ahead I saw a line of cars idling. The freeway noise hummed in the distance. Car stereos clashed with competing bass rhythms. A group of five climbed out of a minivan and stretched their legs, their clothing like Serena's, baby-girl pigtails, tight pants, and shorts, cartoon logos on T-shirts, and backpacks. A couple of girls attached teddy bears to their packs. The sight of all these brightly dressed kids in a drab commercial area with run-down storefronts was jarring. Serena then said, "There he is," and pointed to a man in a leather jacket, counting money as he moved away from a car that sped off. He waved on the next car, which pulled forward. He leaned into the passenger window.

As we slid forward in the line, I watched the small groups forming on the sidewalk, people greeting and hugging each other. One guy wore an angel costume complete with small wings and a halo.

We continued moving forward, and when it was our turn Serena told me to lower my window. The man leaned in, smiled, and said, "Evening. How are you?"

"Pretty good," Serena said. "It's going to be DJ Snow and Watchtower tonight?"

"Yeah, but we're trying to keep it smaller," he said. "Sorry, but I gotta ask this. Top-three Trance favorites?"

"A test?"

The man nodded. "This is for fans only."

"Let me see," Serena said. "How about Astral Projection, 303 Infinity, and maybe Juno Reactor."

"Juno Reactor?" the man said. "Whoa. Classic fan."

"No. Just getting old."

"Fifteen each," he said, flipping out two cards.

I counted out thirty dollars and handed it to the man, who gave me two tickets and a photocopy of a computer-printed map. The man said, "No buying tickets at the door, so don't lose them."

"Thanks."

The man withdrew and moved to the car behind us. Serena drove off and asked me to direct her. I read off the directions, and said, "It looks like a place in Glendale."

"Off the freeway?"

"When we intersect the Five. Near railroad tracks."

"It's definitely for Trance fans. They never do that."

"Test?"

"Yeah. If Gloria is really a Trance fan, she should be there. Hector would've."

"Good," I said.

After a few minutes Serena asked, "So what's the deal with you and Hector's sister? Are you guys going out?"

I wasn't sure how to answer that. I thought about this for a while, then finally said, "I'm not sure."

"You're not sure?"

"We were, but I'm not sure about now."

"Ah. One of those situations."

I turned to her. "You know what I'm talking about?"

"Of course. One of you wants to break up, the other doesn't. Or both of you do, but aren't sure about it. That cover it?"

"I guess."

She smiled. "What you need is a good time."

The warehouse flashed and pulsed from inside, the dirty and mesh windows high above the street shimmering reds and greens, a steady pounding shaking the air. Serena had parked two blocks down and we walked with a few others toward the music. A teenager with silver paint on her face crossed the street and hugged Serena, then me. "I'm so glad you came!" she sang.

Serena smiled. The girl hurried to another group and gave them hugs as well.

"You know her?" I asked.

"No."

I was about to remark on this but saw others standing in line at the door, laughing, greeting each other, arm in arm and holding hands. "Is it always like this?"

"No," she said. "Remember that this is for hard-core fans, so I'm sure a lot of them know each other." We joined the line. One guy ahead of us was wearing a dust-filter mask, another had a pacifier hanging around his neck. I smelled something medicinal and minty. I sniffed again and Serena said, "Vicks VapoRub."

"Why?"

"Helps the E."

I noticed the smell came from the guy with the mask and realized that the Vicks was on the mask itself, forcing him to inhale the fumes directly. He noticed me staring, and winked. The line moved forward.

We handed our tickets to the man at the door, who looked Serena up and down, and as we entered the warehouse, I found myself staring at Serena's legs. Her calves curved up, tightening as she walked. Thigh muscles gave her legs long, smooth lines. She turned to me and I looked up quickly.

Laser lights shot around us, sweet-smelling smoke blanketing the floor. About fifty people were crowded in the center, a low stage with stacks of speakers and electronic equipment along one side. Colored lights with psychedelic patterns rotated on the ceilings and walls, a small strobe light flickering in the corner. Serena grabbed my hand as she led me through groups of people; she leaned near my ear and yelled over the music, "It's going to be tough to find her!"

She smelled of bubble gum. The heavy beat reverberated into me, and the electronic synthesizer music warbled and buzzed in rhythm. I saw two people onstage, one at a turntable spinning records, headphones hanging from one ear; the other man sat at a computer and electronic panel, turning knobs and checking the monitor. Dancers with fluorescent sticks wrapped around their hands and fingers waved their arms wildly as they spun across the floor, the blurred streaks of light arcing around them. Two young men, holding hands, walked by us and waved. We waved back.

She turned to me, nodded toward the stage, and led me through more people. I tried to tell her that we had to look for Gloria, but the music was too loud. Serena let go of my arm and danced, her body loose, her arms rising above her head as she spun back and forth. She met my eyes and smiled. I saw that I was the only one not dancing, and joined her. She clapped and moved closer to me. Her shoulders curved with small muscles when she pressed her palms together and swayed to the beat. She said into my ear, "Relax! Have fun!"

"What about Gloria?" I yelled.

"Too early! We have all night!"

She reached into her tight shorts and pulled out a piece of folded paper. She shook out a pill. I touched her hand and said, "Shouldn't you wait until we find her?"

"You wait. I'll help." She swallowed the pill, which made me flinch. "I'll save you some," she said.

I saw this deteriorating around me and pulled her away from the stage. She grinned and skipped next to me. I showed her the photo in the poor lighting and said, "Let's look for her now. Then we can relax."

She squinted at the photo and said, "All right, boss. Funky red hair? That's her?"

"Yeah. I'll start on the far end. You start near the door. We'll meet up here?"

"Then we dance?"

"Then we dance."

We separated, and I edged my way through dancers who had spread out and filled the warehouse main floor. I saw many more teens here than I would've thought. How did their parents let them out on a school night? I scanned all the faces around me, searching for Gloria. The music grew louder, the dancing more wild, and I kept getting bumped and pushed. I saw a short woman with red hair who looked a little like the person in the photo. I approached and said, "Gloria?"

She turned to me with a dazed smile and shook her head.

I circled back, blinking through a haze. A skinny teen, flinging his arms and hopping up and down, hit my arm. He apologized and I held up my hands and mouthed "It's fine." I saw Serena up ahead talking to a man with spiky hair and wearing an oversized silver jumpsuit. He was shaking his head to something Serena was saying. She glanced at me, and waved me over.

"Allen, this is an old friend of mine, Rocket Man."

I said hello to him, and asked Serena, "Gloria?"

"Not yet, but if she's into Trance and likes E, she should be here."

Rocket Man said to Serena, "You're looking hot!"

Serena rolled her eyes at me, and I asked him, "Where do you buy E?"

He smiled, revealing a missing front tooth. He said, "Follow the vowels. The vowels will set you free."

"Huh?"

Serena grabbed my arm and pulled me away. She said, "I think I saw someone selling near the water table."

"Vowels?"

"A for acid. E for Ecstasy," she answered, leading me to the side exit where a long table had cases of water bottles for sale. A line of sweaty people, many of them still dancing in place, moved forward. A few others gathered near a man with a backpack and an Oakland A's baseball cap. I saw a woman with bright red hair talking to a girl. I nudged Serena and pointed.

We walked toward them, and I noticed multiple bands around the woman's bare arms, loops of plastic digging into her biceps. She had on a sleeveless silver jacket and silver shorts. I called out her name and she turned. She looked confused as I waved.

"You're Gloria, right?" I asked.

She smiled, her teeth white against her black lipstick. "I know you?"

"What's your last name?"

"Katz." She glanced at Serena.

I turned to the other girl, a rail-thin teen, her face sparkling with glued-on glitter, and said, "What's your name again?"

Puzzled, she replied, "Valerie."

I said to Gloria, "I'm Allen, and I was wondering if we can talk? Maybe outside?"

"About what?"

"I'm in town with Linda, Hector's sister—"

Gloria stepped back, grimacing. She looked at Valerie, their eyes meeting. Valerie quickly slipped into a crowd.

"Wait. It's okay," I said to Gloria. "We just need to find out what was going on with Hector."

"How'd you find me?"

"Can we talk outside? It's too noisy—"

"How'd you find me? How'd you know who I was?"

"Hector's photo. Can I have your number? Maybe we can talk tomorrow, then—"

"Jesus. You shouldn't have . . . I shouldn't be talking to you."

"Why?"

"I can't have anything to do with you. I'll be—just leave me alone!"

"Why?"

"Oh, man. This never fucking ends. This is too much. I gotta go—"

"Please," I said. "Just for a minute—"

She ran. I went after her, but she was quick. She dodged the crowds, weaving around dancers, and raced for the main entrance. By the time I reached the doorway, throngs of people pushing forward, Gloria had disappeared.

When I looked for Serena, I saw that she was talking to Valerie. I hurried over to them, and the girl, backing away, was saying, "Leave me alone! I don't know anything!"

Serena said to me, "Something's up."

"Please," the girl said. "Bangs will kill me."

"Who?"

"Lowell Bangs. I can't."

"What's going on?" Serena asked. "Maybe we can help."

"You can't help."

I said, "Can we talk? Anywhere you want. Where do you live? No one will know."

"No, I can't. I can't talk to you."

"Who's Lowell Bangs?"

"I can't. Please leave me alone." She glanced fearfully around the dance floor. Glitter sprinkled out of her black frizzy hair.

"Tomorrow," I said. "Let me call you. What's your number? No one will know. It's really important."

She looked at Serena, who said, "No, he's not a narc. I used to date Hector. He's friends with Hector's sister."

Valerie hesitated. "You dated Hector?"

Serena nodded.

"I liked him."

"Then help us," Serena said.

Valerie said, "Tomorrow night. Six."

"Where?"

"Here. Out in front."

"Let me have your number just in case—"

"No. Tomorrow." She turned and ran off, glitter sparkling to the floor in her wake. I was about to chase her, but she zipped easily through the darkness.

Serena said, "Well?"

"I guess it'll have to wait until tomorrow. She knew Hector, though. That's good."

"They both ran as soon as the name came up," she said.

I nodded, then motioned to the door. "Let's go."

"Oh no you don't," she said, pulling me toward the stage. "You promised."

"Now?" I resisted.

"What else are you going to do?" She tugged harder. "Come on. You promised."

I didn't feel like dancing but joined her, thinking about what Gloria had said, and planning my and Linda's steps tomorrow. Look up Gloria Katz. Look up Lowell Bangs. Try to meet Valerie for more information. It felt good to make progress. Serena watched me, pulled out her folded piece of paper, and shook out a pill. She danced closer to me. I thought she was going to take it, but she held it up to my lips. I danced back and shook my head.

"You'll loosen up," she said in my ear. "You'll be fine. I promise."

"I've never done that," I said.

She smiled, danced up against me, and said, "Aren't you open to new experiences?"

New experiences. I felt old, reacting to her as a man with children might, worried about the future. It struck me that when I saw these teens here, I thought of their parents first. Something was wrong with me. Linda once said I acted as if I were twenty years older, and it was true. When did I ever act like a kid and live carefree? When did I ever have *fun?*

Serena grinded her body against mine, laughing quietly as I thought about this. She said, "Let yourself go a little, Allen. You're so tightly wound up."

She lifted the pill to my lips again, and I remembered Linda's planner with the "Lunch w/ Harlan" entry, her quick handwriting familiar, but this image melted away in the lights now suddenly strobing all around us, all the dancers suddenly moving in slow motion, ghostly kids flickering around us in a circle, arms and heads disconnecting from bodies and floating. I thought, What does it matter? Let me have fun. Serena kept dancing next to me and opened my mouth with her other hand, then dropped the pill in. I let it sit on my tongue, tasting the bitterness, suppressing the fear that this was poison, and swallowed.

I didn't think I felt anything at first, yet as I continued dancing the music became muted, less harsh on my ears, and I felt the beats deep inside my chest, then I realized it was my heart thumping to the same rhythm as the music—my heart was filling the warehouse. I was driving the beat in the speakers. My limbs felt looser, and I danced without seeing anyone but Serena, who kept watching me and touching my shoulders. Sweat beaded down her face and she didn't seem to care, so I leaned forward and wiped her forehead, which made her smile. When I wiped my own face my hand was drenched, and I looked down in surprise at my wet shirt sticking to my chest. Serena ran her finger down my neck and held it up. My sweat trickled down her palm. As we continued dancing I felt a lightness in my chest that I knew was forgiveness. I forgave Linda for bringing me down here. I forgave her for wanting to break up with me. I would help her, and this warmth and generosity spread through me. I laughed, and danced, and grabbed Serena's hand. We moved closer to the stage. The music from the speakers and my heart thudded through my body. Smoky lights flashed around us with lasers crisscrossing over our heads, and a pleasant calmness overtook me as Serena twisted her body with abandon, and I couldn't help but join her, and for an instant, before I lost myself in the pulsing lights and the blurs around me, the strobe flashes filling me with bubble gum tastes, I wondered if this was what Hector liked, this immersion into sounds, beats, movements, and I tried to follow this thought, which scurried away, and I kept dancing and was soon gone.

Thirteen

woke up in my boxers, my legs so sore that I had trouble turning my head. An invisible thread held everything together, so even my breathing sent a spasm of pain ricocheting to my toes. I tried not to blink. A soft sheet wound around my bare chest, and a heavier blanket bunched up at my feet. I didn't recognize the room—African masks and rainbow-colored fabrics hanging on the walls—and when I looked on the floor I saw Gracie, Serena's German Shepherd, lying on a folded towel. Gracie raised her head and stared at me.

"Oh, man," I said to the dog.

Gracie lowered her head.

I cleared my throat and called out, "Hello?" A spasm of pain tightened my calves.

No answer. The small alarm clock on the nightstand read nine forty-five, and I saw a note. With some straining I reached for it and read: "Had to run to work. I had fun! Please lock up when you leave, and give me a call later." Beneath that was her work number, and she had signed it "S."

I couldn't remember leaving the rave, nor could I recall how I had ended up in bed.

No. Wait a minute. An image came to me: Serena framed in the darkened doorway. Last night, almost four in the morning, we had stumbled into the house, exhausted, our ears ringing. I heard the world as if through a damp cloth—sounds muted, fuzzy—and watched Serena's lips with fascination as she spoke to me with little if any sounds coming out. She repeated herself, then laughed and pushed me gently to the bedroom.

I watched her peel off her clothes as she glided to the bathroom, a wake of shorts, her shirt, her panties, and socks littering the hallway. Flashes of bare skin in the darkness. When she turned on the bathroom light, I covered my eyes, and she turned to me. Her face was shadowed, her blurry figure outlined with light. Her arms sparkled. She stared at me, completely unembarrassed and unself-conscious about her nakedness. Then she grinned and closed the bathroom door. I felt an unsteady beating in my chest. Gracie padded down the hall and sat by the bathroom door as I heard the shower sputtering on.

Now, as I pulled myself up painfully and limped to the bathroom, I remembered talking too much in the car ride to Serena's. Something had freed my thoughts, which came out without much censoring. Perhaps it was Serena's casual questions, her interest in my background. "You're Korean American, aren't you?" she had asked.

It had begun with the story about my last name, how my father, once immigrating here, had Americanized his name, Choi, by looking for the closest word in the dictionary—"choice." She then revealed her last name as Yew, which is usually Americanized as Lee, though her parents had opted for a more unusual variation. I turned to her, thinking about Luke's last name as well, and was startled to realize that last-name changes weren't unique. I told her about Luke trying to use Korean on me, and she smiled, but her lack of a response made me ask if she spoke Korean. She nodded.

"You do? Fluently?" I asked, surprised.

"Well, it's basic, but I can get by," she said.

I wondered if it was just me. She glanced at me, then changed the subject by asking me about my parents and where I had grown up. I ended up telling her all about my aunt and the Mess of two years ago. As I revealed this, I heard something in my voice that I didn't recognize, a bitterness.

"Sounds like you're still a little mad about it," she said.

"Maybe."

We arrived at her house, and I was surprised that she hadn't driven me to Marina Alta. She saw my confusion and said that she was too tired for the drive up, and I could crash here for the night. I hesitated, which drew a smile from her as she said, "Now, now. We'll be good, if you want."

When she walked naked into the bathroom, her slender back curving as she turned to me, I gaped for a second too long. I started to feel drawn to her, so I backed slowly away. I was excited, and knew what could happen. I knew I wanted it to happen. Yet I was tired, so tired, not just physically but of the complications of relationships, of couplings, of affairs and the intricacies of dating. I lay on top of the bedcovers, listening to Serena shower and was instantly reminded of the many times I had stayed over Linda's and heard the rhythm of the water drubbing the shower curtain, the massage setting she liked set on high as she pounded herself with alternating jets. She would hunch over and let the stream move up and down her spine, humming to herself with her voice vibrating.

As I lay on the bed listening to Serena shower, I drifted in and out sleep, waiting for her. She suddenly appeared next to me wrapped in a towel, her hair wet and combed back. The hall light fell on her bare shoulders, and she rested her hand on my arm. "You can shower, too," she whispered.

I nodded and sat up. Her hand was warm and damp. She said, "What do you want to do?"

She smelled clean, soapy. I wanted to touch her. I wanted to run my hand up her leg. I wanted to feel her against me. But what I said was, "Maybe we should just get some rest."

She replied, "Okay" through a smile, and moved to the bureau, where she shed her towel and pulled on a nightshirt. I walked to the bathroom, took a quick shower, and returned to find Serena curled up in bed. I was glad for the darkness. I slid under the covers, keeping a few inches away, and felt her shifting her weight. I was aroused and tried not to think about Serena just a few inches away from me, in only a nightshirt. I rolled onto my side, my back to her.

Serena moved closer to me, our legs touching. I let out a slow breath. She then spooned herself against me, and rested her arm on my waist. A small jolt traveled up my chest, and yet with her hand there, her body snuggling up to me, I felt comforted. I touched her hand and we linked fingers. She rested her forehead against the back of my neck, and I felt her warm breath. I knew very little about this woman, had just met her, and yet this felt natural. We settled against each other and fell asleep.

Now I called a cab and wandered through Serena's house, Gracie following me. A small electronic keyboard lay on the kitchen table, with sheet music and an *Introduction to Piano* booklet. I thought of my own textbook to study, and the reminder of my impending job change—no, my career change—weighed on me. I wondered if my life would ever feel settled.

Linda was right. I needed stability. I yearned for equilibrium.

I could still feel Serena's breath on my neck. As she fell asleep her breathing had steadied, deepened. Warm, then cool air had encircled me as she exhaled, then inhaled. Warm, then cool. Her fingers occasionally tightened in mine, small movements as she dreamed.

Studying her bookshelves, I found rows of computer manuals and technical books—her night school ambitions. I admired this and wished we had talked more about that rather than dancing all night. The pain in my legs had worsened, and I walked stiff-legged, Frankenstein-style.

The cab pulled up in front of the house, and I petted Gracie good-bye, locking the front door and walking gingerly down the steps. On the ride back to Marina Alta I went over the events at the rave. I took out the card with the map to the warehouse and studied it, worried that Valerie wouldn't show up tonight. And I couldn't forget the shock on Gloria's face when I had mentioned Hector's name. Marianne's instincts, that something wasn't right about her son's death, were on target. It hadn't been just hope. I wondered if my own mother, had she lived, would've been so protective. She had never even had the chance to hug me as a newborn. She had died while giving birth, and all the photographs I had of her were pre-pregnancy shots, a tiny, frail woman with a tentative smile. I was always surprised by how thin her arms were. In one shot that my father had always shown me, my mother held a tie up to the camera, a Christmas present for my father, she was pointing and smiling. But I always looked at her bony forearms and thought they seemed to be shaking under the weight of the tie.

When I arrived at the condo I paid the cab driver and let myself in the front entrance. I wasn't sure what to tell Linda, if anything. Did she even have the right to ask? A flicker of resentment passed through me. I resisted the urge to be petty and vindictive.

Even though I had the key, I knocked. Linda opened it. She stepped back, taking the sight of me in, and said, "You look like hell."

"Thanks," I said. "But I met Gloria."

"Good. I found Raul."

Yesterday Linda had spent hours on the library computer, searching through news databases and had come up with a number of references to different Raul Gamas, none of whom seemed to be her father. The phone and address searches, however, produced a few Raul or "R." Gamas in the area, and with those in hand Linda began trying to narrow them down. She told me this after I changed my clothes. We sat at the kitchen table while I had coffee, wondering if Linda suspected anything or if she was just excited about her find. She said she had tried contacting all the Gamas, not revealing who she was or what she wanted, and the R. Gama in Laguna Beach was the most likely one.

"How do you know?" I said.

"I asked if they still did construction and carpentry work."

"And the one in Laguna Beach said . . . ?"

"He hadn't done it in years, and he wanted to know how I had found out about him."

"What'd you say?"

"I hung up. I was surprised I found him."

"You're not definite, though."

"Pretty definite. His voice sounded familiar, if that's possible." She studied me. "Rough night? Tell me about Gloria."

I did, describing what had happened, and showed her the map. "I don't know who this Lowell Bangs is, but he might be important. I hope this Valerie shows up."

"We'll ask her tonight. How did it go with Serena?"

"Fine."

"Did you dance?"

I nodded. "It was fine. I was probably the oldest person there, but I can see why Hector liked it."

"You can?"

"The music isn't really music. I guess that's why they call it Trance. It's hypnotic. A steady beat with electronic stuff. It was like those ritual Indian dances or something."

"Did it just end?"

I shook my head and said carefully, "No. I crashed at her place because it was so late. I only got a couple hours of sleep."

Linda didn't reply and reached over to sip some of my coffee. I could see her trying to formulate a question, so I said, "What are you going to do about your father?"

"He's not my father," she said. "I want to talk to this Valerie first, maybe find Gloria, find out what Hector was doing."

"Did you tell your mother?"

"No. I don't know how she'll react." She sat back.

I pointed to the bandage and asked, "How's your head?"

She said, "Better." She continued staring at me.

I didn't know what else to say, and I tried not to shift in my chair. I finished my coffee and wondered where Marianne was. Luke was probably at work.

"So we go meet Valerie tonight," Linda said.

"Yes."

"I'll try to find something on Gloria Katz or Lowell Bangs at the library."

"I have to finish my application, and maybe study a little."

"Meet back here later this afternoon?" she asked.

"Sounds good."

She stood up, a small frown on her face. I asked her what was wrong.

She hesitated, then said, "I guess you're not going to tell me about last night."

"I just did. I found Gloria."

"You know what I mean."

I said, "No. What do you mean?"

Her jaw set rigidly, and she swung her body to face me directly. "What's this, a punishment or something?"

I was about to argue, but held back. Instead I said, "Do you remember the time I woke up in the middle of the night and found you talking to Harlan on the phone? Whispering in the living room?"

She narrowed her eyes. "Yeah, so?"

"When I asked you about it, you got mad at me. All I did was ask who it was and what you guys could possibly be talking about at three in the morning. You accused me of all sorts of things."

"I told you I was sorry about that."

"When I asked you what your problem was, you remember what you said?"

"No."

"You said to me, 'You're the problem.'"

Linda shook her head slowly. "What's your point?"

"How does it feel?"

"How does what feel?"

"How does it feel to have that weird feeling in your stomach? To want to ask, but then feel too embarrassed. How does it feel to be jealous?"

She began walking away and said, "I don't need this now, Allen. Okay? I've got other things to worry about."

"Good," I said. "You're the one who brought it up."

She was about to reply but instead held her hands up. "Let's concentrate on Hector," she said.

"Okay."

She continued walking, then stopped. She turned. "Oh, by the way?"

"Yes?"

"You've got a hickey on the side of your neck." She locked eyes with me, then left the room.

In the bathroom I examined the small red welt on my neck, and couldn't figure out where it had come from. Serena had slept close to me, but I would've remembered a hickey. When I touched it with a wet tissue, it stung, and I suddenly remembered this had been from Serena's ring. While we were dancing she had wrapped her hands around my waist, moving in rhythm with me, then raised her hands onto my shoulders and then my neck. She had clasped her fingers around the back of my neck, and we continued dancing this way for a while. Her rings might have scraped the skin, even though I hadn't noticed at the time. A pinch on my neck was the least of the sensations I had felt last night.

I considered explaining this to Linda, but decided it wasn't worth it. I spent the rest of the morning finishing my PI application and studying for the test, focusing on the criminal and civil liability laws, jotting notes as I had done in college. My mind kept wandering. I pictured Serena's naked back as she walked into the bathroom. I heard Linda's biting tone, *Oh, by the way?* and sighed. I tried to focus on the Controlled Substances Act. There were five schedules to categorize various drugs, and as I read through the Schedule I drugs, it struck me that I had violated the law last night in many ways. The rave had been illegal. Ecstasy was a Schedule I drug.

Had I really taken some Ecstasy last night? What was I doing?

I had been so forgiving and sympathetic after taking the drug, an odd magnanimity filling me. In the light of day, however, I felt more petty. I wanted Linda to think something had happened last night. Then I regretted it. Then I regretted regretting it. I spun in circles while trying to read the textbook.

I longed to return home. I wanted my routines. I missed my extended and relaxing runs. I scolded myself. Concentrate. Study. Read.

I suddenly wondered if I had something worse than the dis-ease.

Maybe there were schedules, like drug classifications. Maybe there were many tiers of dis-ease.

This thought depressed me further, and I buried myself in drug classifications.

I met Linda at the condo in the late afternoon and studied her eyes for clues. I wasn't sure if she was angry or jealous or if she simply no longer cared. I asked her about Lowell Bangs, and she told me she hadn't found anything on him at the library. "And there are way too many Gloria Katzes to be of any use."

I said, "About this morning—"

"Forget it. None of my business."

"You don't care?"

She glanced at her watch. "You coming with me to meet this kid?"

"Of course," I said. "She's expecting me. You don't want to talk about this?"

"No." She faced me. "Let's just get through this. Once we finish down here, we can figure the rest out."

I said, "Don't you want to know what happened?"

"I know what happened."

"I don't think you do."

She let out a laugh that tightened at the end. "Allen, I just found out my father, who abandoned us, has been living twenty minutes away for all these years. Think about it. I just found out Hector might have met with him." She tilted her head and almost smiled. "You and I will deal with this other stuff later. Okay?"

"Okay," I said. "You're right. Let's go."

We took Luke's car back to Glendale, following the map. I drove carefully, making sure we weren't being followed. In daylight everything looked different to me. I recognized almost none of the buildings and began doubting my memories of last night. The only thing that matched was the warehouse itself, though in the light I noticed graffiti bluntly spray-painted along one side. Even the streets were unfamiliar—shiny and moonlit eighteen hours ago, they now had a dull grime layered over oily soot. There were no angels hugging one another. There were no rocket men.

"This is it?" Linda asked.

"It is. We're early."

"I wonder why he stayed in the area," she said.

"Your father—I mean Raul?"

"And he never contacted us."

"Why would he?"

She shook her head. "It's just strange."

"I guess Hector was wondering the same thing."

"I'm worried what he found," she said.

"What do you mean?"

"Hector didn't want to tell William Delgado anything. Remember? Maybe something happened."

"It could've just been him not wanting to reveal—"

A figure appeared by Linda's window, causing us both to jump. I barely recognized Valerie without her make-up and glitter, and I said, "Jesus. Where did she come from?"

Linda unrolled her window. "Valerie?"

"Let's get out of here," she said, and climbed into the backseat. "Go."

I drove off. In the rearview mirror I saw her checking the street around us. She wore casual clothes—jeans and a tight T-shirt that exposed her belly— and had moussed her hair back; she looked even younger than at the rave. She put her hand on my seat and peered out the front windshield. She smacked gum in her mouth. I asked, "Something wrong?"

"Were you followed?"

"No."

"You sure?"

"I'm sure. Why?"

She said, "I got a call at home. A warning."

"A warning?" Linda asked. "About what? From whom?"

Valerie said, "You're Hector's sister?"

"I am."

"You look like him."

Linda blinked but didn't reply.

"Who warned you?" I asked.

"Bangs knew I talked to you," she said, her voice unsteady. "He knew where I was, what you were up to."

"Who is Bangs?" I asked.

Valerie said quietly, "He probably killed Hector."

We were silent, and I continued driving. I began counting cars, waiting for Linda to take up the questioning. When she finally did, she said, "How do you know Hector?"

"I saw him and Gloria at raves. They were nice to me."

"Is there a way we can talk to Gloria?"

"Only time I've seen her was at raves."

"Who is Lowell Bangs?" Linda asked. "What happened to my brother?"

Valerie leaned forward and said, "Your brother tried to screw over a drug dealer."

We waited for more, and when she didn't add anything, Linda said, "Bangs is a drug dealer."

"He dealt meth, but was doing more E, and your brother used to sell locally for him."

"Sell Ecstasy for Bangs?"

"Yeah. Gloria said he was Bangs's right hand. I mean, small time, but making a lot of money for him."

Linda exhaled slowly and said, "How did Hector cheat him?"

"I don't know. She didn't say, but she told me to be careful. Look, I'm meeting with you because I liked Hector. But you can't mess with this."

"How do you know Bangs killed Hector?"

"Gloria said it, but isn't it obvious? Bangs is supposed to be crazy. He has killed people for looking at him wrong."

"But you're sure Hector was selling drugs?" Linda asked.

Valerie said, "Well, yeah. I bought off him all the time."

I was about to ask how old she was, but I stopped myself. Instead I said, "How do we find Bangs?"

She met my eyes in the rearview mirror, and said, "Are you dumb? Didn't you hear what I just said? I'm here to tell you to get out of this while you can. And I *don't* want you talking to me or asking me questions at raves. I mean, you're going to get *me* killed."

"If you really liked Hector, why won't you help us?" Linda said. "If he was murdered—"

"You don't know nothing about me! You don't know shit! I'm just trying to pay him back for being nice to me. Pull over," Valerie said to me. "I'm getting the hell out of here."

"Calm down," Linda said.

"Pull over!"

"Wait—"

"Stop the car!" she screeched at me.

I slowed, and drove up to the curb. She opened her door and said to us, "I talked to you because of Hector. I'm telling you now to forget about this. Gloria told me he fucked up and ended up dead."

"But I need to know more," Linda said.

"That's all I know. I swear," Valerie said. To me she said, "And don't go looking for me anymore." She slammed the door shut and hurried down the block, almost tripping in her clunky shoes.

"Damn," Linda said. "Should I go after her?"

"I doubt she knows much more."

Linda shook her head and let out a tired sigh. "What the hell was my little brother doing?"

Fourteen

In the condo no one seemed to want to talk. Luke watched financial shows and Marianne cooked dinner, the sounds and smells of frying vegetables mingled with stock quotes. I conducted a quick check for listening devices, puzzled by how Bangs could know what our steps had been. He must have had someone at the rave last night, watching us, or had even himself been at the rave. Without RF probe equipment like the kind Larry had at the office, I could only do a hand search, sweeping furniture and listening to the phone for triggers—a change in volume or a clicking. I had also swept the car again, finding nothing.

Marianne bustled out of the kitchen, announcing that dinner would be ready in a few minutes, then stopped at the sight of me running my fingers around a picture frame. "Dust?" she asked.

"No," I said. "Just checking for something."

"What could possibly be up there?" Marianne asked.

"Listening devices. Bugs."

"In here?"

"A precaution."

"You don't seriously think . . ."

I turned. "Two years ago, when Linda was helping me, we found bugs in our apartments and cars. Since then, I've been very careful."

"In your apartment?" she said.

"Yes."

"Linda never told me that."

Linda appeared in the hallway and asked, "Told you what?"

"Listening devices?" Luke said.

Linda watched me wipe my hands on my pants. I said, "It seems okay in here."

"You never mentioned that," Marianne said to her daughter. "Did something happen today? You two are so quiet."

I saw the stack of clean dishes on the table, ready to be set. Linda and I began arranging the place mats and utensils. The microwave in the kitchen beeped. Marianne withdrew. Luke moved to the dining table, sitting down and said, "Julie and Nora will be coming in this weekend. I spoke to Julie this afternoon."

Marianne brought out serving dishes filled with rice and vegetables, steam rising around her arms. She sat down, and everyone began passing the platters around.

"How's Nora?" Linda asked.

"All better."

"I can stay at a hotel," I said.

"Of course not," Marianne said. "Julie likes hotels, anyway—"

"And as much as I adore Nora," Luke said, "she can be a handful."

Marianne lowered her voice. "I think there's something going on with Frank."

"There's nothing going on," Linda replied.

"They might be having problems."

"Mom! You don't know that!"

"I'm just saying it sounded like—"

"I don't like it when you do that," Linda said. "Gossip like that. Has she said anything to you?"

"No."

"What about you?" Linda asked Luke.

"No."

"Then why," she said, turning back to Marianne, "why would you say that?"

"Julie mentioned Frank would be coming, but now he's not. She's being vague."

"That's it?" Linda asked.

"It's a feeling," Marianne said, glancing at me. "I could hear something in her voice."

"You did not," Linda said. "You're probably just hoping something's there. You think Frank is bossy. I know you do—"

"How can you say that? I just want her to be happy—"

"You used to do the same thing with me. I know. I remember—"

"Please," Luke said. "Can't we have a nice dinner for once?"

Marianne raised her voice. "But she just accused me of—"

"Please!" Luke snapped. He glared across the table. "I had a long day at work and would really appreciate a nicer atmosphere here."

Although Luke left for work in the mornings, I hadn't imagined him actually doing much, since he was moving toward retirement. I asked, "What happened?" My voice seemed to jar Marianne.

Luke smiled. "Nothing really. I'm trying to leave, but a crisis keeps appearing. Sometimes I feel I'll never be able to retire."

A long silence followed. I heard the TV drone on about interest rates.

"There's something I don't understand," Linda said to her parents.

Both Marianne and Luke turned to her.

Linda asked her mother, "Why did you say Raul went to Mexico?"

"I thought that's where he'd go. He once mentioned it. He had relatives there. Do we have to talk about this?"

"How come he never contacted us?"

"Because he was a terrible man! How many times do I have tell you I don't want to talk about him!"

"Let's talk about Hector, then," Linda said. "Tell me more about why he wanted to move out."

"I told you. He was twenty-seven and thought it was time."

Luke said, "He talked about starting over."

I watched Linda as she chose her words carefully. "I guess that would entail him thinking about Raul." Linda stared at her mother.

"What did you find out?" Marianne said.

Linda said, "Raul is in Laguna Beach."

Marianne's expression froze, then quickly recovered. "Impossible. He can't be."

"Why?"

"He just can't."

Linda said, "He's in Laguna Beach, and it looks like Hector met with him—"

"What? When?"

Luke said, "I'm sure we can talk about this rationally."

Marianne said to Linda, "How do you know this?"

Linda briefly described William Delgado's story, then added, "I found a Raul Gama, formerly in construction, living in Laguna. It's almost certainly him."

"How long has he been there?" Luke asked.

"Years."

"It can't be," Marianne said. "He was never in Mexico?"

"He might have been, but he's been back for a while."

"What—what are you going to do?"

"Well, talk to him—"

"Absolutely not! I forbid it!"

Linda blinked. "You forbid it?"

"I don't want you seeing him! He almost destroyed us! He almost sent us into the streets! I don't want you—"

"You asked me to look into this. *You* wanted me to find out more!"

"I know. I was wrong. If I knew that he—that Hector—that all this . . . please. This is too much."

Luke asked quietly, "Why did Hector find him?"

"We're not sure, but like Mom said before, maybe he wanted to figure out things."

Marianne said, "I don't want you stirring it up."

"We're just seeing what Hector was doing. That's all," Linda said.

Luke rubbed his temples and said to Linda, "Just be careful."

"No! She can't," Marianne said.

"But if Hector found him—"

"No! I'm sorry I ever asked this! It was just a foolish mother's need for answers. I don't want to know about Raul!"

"How about we just try to have a quiet dinner," Luke said. "Everyone. Let's calm down and have this nice dinner before it gets cold."

But after a moment, Marianne stood up and left the dining room. We heard her bedroom door slam shut.

Linda and I glanced at each other. Luke sighed and followed his wife. I tried to imagine myself as Hector, twenty-seven and living with my parents, dealing drugs on the side and partying all night. How could he live at home? I had wanted to flee my aunt's house as soon as I could. I wanted to be on my own, working, relying on no one, since high school. I couldn't imagine living at home in my twenties. And I definitely wasn't suited for all-night raves. My legs still wobbled in pain whenever I put too much weight on them.

Linda stared at her food. The phone rang, and Linda left the table.

My aunt Insook used to follow me around the house, berating me for failing my classes, and without my father running interference, I could only escape her by leaving home. She was right, though. I could've done better. But I had never been a good test taker. I had been a mediocre student and had flunked a handful of exams from nerves and poor timing. I'd spend too much time on one problem, only to look up and realize I had only ten minutes left for the rest of the exam. Rattled, I'd try to rush through the exam and make careless mistakes. I still remembered that sense of panic as my attention leaped from question to question, flustered, a sense of doom shaking my pencil.

A startling thought flashed through me: What if I failed the PI exam?

Linda walked out of the kitchen and said to me, "It's for you."

"Who is it?"

"Serena."

Linda walked by me and sat back at the table without saying anything else. In the kitchen I picked up the phone and said hello.

Serena said, "Hey, Mr. Bodyguard. You're alive."

"I am." I lowered my voice and said, "Thanks for letting me stay over."

"No prob. I wanted to let you know about a party tomorrow night."

"Party? I don't know if I'm up for another night."

"Low key. Just a friend of mine leaving for New York. A good-bye party."

I said, "Have you heard of Lowell Bangs?"

"The one that kid mentioned?"

"Yeah. Apparently a meth dealer who's selling Ecstasy."

"No. I don't think so," she said.

"You should be careful," I told her. "This guy might be watching me."

"What do you mean? How?"

"I don't know, but he knew I had talked to Valerie. He knows what I've been doing." I leaned against the refrigerator, suddenly tired.

"Should I be worried?" she asked.

"I'm not sure. I don't think anyone really connects you to Hector."

Serena was quiet, then said, "Did you say he sold E?"

"Selling more stuff, and used Hector."

"There's a guy I know who could help you. He'll probably know who Lowell Bangs is."

"Who?"

"I can invite him to this party. It's in Balboa."

"Tomorrow night?"

"We can go together. What do you think?"

I kept still, hearing Linda speaking to her parents. I said, "This guy knows Lowell Bangs?"

"Probably. He sold E at most of the raves in L.A. for years. Not anymore, though."

"This isn't a rave, is it? I really don't think I can handle another one."

She laughed. "No. Small party. I promise."

"Okay. That might be helpful."

"I can pick you up again. Around eight?"

"Thanks."

I hung up. I couldn't stand parties, and yet here I was going to them. I thought about her question to me late last night, *What do you want to do?* When I closed my eyes I saw her naked in the bathroom doorway, framed by darkness.

Linda walked into the kitchen with an empty water glass. I stepped away from the refrigerator. She refilled her glass, and I said, "There might be a guy who knows Lowell Bangs."

"Who?" She watched me carefully, sipping her water.

I told her what Serena had said.

"So you'll talk to him at this party?"

"Yes. Do you want to come?" I asked.

She remained expressionless. "I wasn't invited."

"Doesn't matter," I said.

"No." She shook her head. "But are you coming with me to visit Raul?"

"Of course. What time?"

"Tomorrow morning. I'll call to make sure he's home, and then we'll show up."

"You'll call?"

"Just to see if he's home. Then we'll make an appearance. I want to see how he reacts in person."

"No warning? Is that a good idea?"

She put down her glass and frowned at me. I held up my hands in surrender. "Never mind," I said.

"It'll be fine."

I watched her tighten her grip around her glass. I asked, "How will it feel to see him after all this time?"

She shrugged. "This isn't about me. It's about my brother."

"You have no feelings at all?"

She said, "He was a loser who pushed people around and stole from us. I just want to find out what happened to Hector."

I said, "Okay."

"Why should I feel anything?" she said. "Just because he knocked up my mom? He was nothing. He was the enemy."

"Okay," I said, softly. "Okay."

She said, "If he did anything to Hector, I'll kill him."

Fifteen

The next morning we drove to Raul Gama's house. I asked Linda while we were approaching Laguna Beach what she remembered about him, if she even recalled what he looked like. She didn't seem to hear me at first, and when I repeated the question she said, "Just a big guy with meaty forearms. He was really strong."

"From construction work?"

"I guess."

Her description resonated with me, since my father, who was a driver for a shipping company, was similarly built. I remembered his gnarled hands from the years of moving heavy crates, his fingernails blackened from minor accidents. His forearms bulged. Once, wanting to show me the insects that hid underground, he lifted a huge, broken slab of concrete with one hand. I remembered looking at his arms and not the insects.

Raul's neighborhood was farther up the hill in Laguna Beach, well beyond the tourist trap intersection with high-end boutique stores lining the main coastal road, small restaurants and shops crowding for pedestrians' attention. The houses in the upper residential areas were densely packed, overlooking the ocean. We parked, and searched on foot. The higher we walked, the more worn in and settled the buildings looked, with small houses and apartments jutted up against one another. Raul lived off Second Street, but as we neared his address, Linda slowed her pace. The sidewalks were gritty. I smelled the salty air mingling with burnt wood.

"Did you have pictures of him?" I asked.

"Thrown away, by my mom." She stopped. "I think I recognized his voice on the phone, though."

I had been watching the cars and people around us, and felt safer once we moved away from the center of town. We were in unfamiliar territory with unseen enemies, and I felt a tension in my back that surprised me, something that hadn't happened to me in years. One of my early jobs with Paul—covering an Argentine diplomat with death threats against him—had made me similarly agitated. I realized I was out of practice, my security skills softening.

Maybe I was getting too old for this. Both Polansky and Swinburn had left the field for management, and Polansky had once talked about burnout. At a certain point, he had explained, you just don't feel like getting in front of a bullet for someone, especially for a spoiled, rich, and condescending executive.

I thought more about the PI license.

We walked along a narrow, crooked side street, Linda checking the numbers and leading us farther up. A breeze kicked up some dust. I heard a seagull crying. Linda said, "There it is. The stucco one."

I followed her pointing finger and saw the pale gray two-story wedged in between more modern-looking ranch houses. The red-tiled roof with broken shingles added some color to the drab stucco walls. Across the street a young man was washing his Honda, sudsing up the hood. Linda turned to me and shrugged in a gesture of forced nonchalance. "Shall we?"

"Have you thought about what you'll ask?"

"Yes. I'll start off easy."

"So you'll tell him who you are?"

She nodded. "I want to see his reaction."

We walked up the front steps. Linda rang the doorbell. She took a deep breath and stepped back. A voice from the other side of the door said, "Who is it?"

"Mr. Gama?" Linda asked. "Raul Gama?"

"Who is it?"

Linda said, "We need to talk to Raul Gama."

Security chains clinked. Two deadbolts slid unlocked. The door opened, and a bald man with wire-rimmed glasses looked out. Smooth-shaven, neatly dressed with a button-down white shirt, the man's eyes went from Linda to me, then back to Linda. He had large shoulders and a thick neck.

"Uh, Raul Gama?" Linda said.

"Yes. What is it?"

"Do you have a few minutes?"

Raul opened the door further but didn't move from the entrance. He folded his large arms and said, "I'm not religious and I don't want to buy anything." He kept staring at Linda, though.

"We're not selling," I said.

Linda cleared her throat. "We have a few questions for you."

"Who are you?" he asked.

"I'm Linda. I'm your daughter."

Raul kept still, but didn't seem surprised. He nodded slowly, glancing at me. The bright sky reflected off his lenses. He said to Linda, "I was wondering when you'd show up." He stepped back, pulling the door wide open.

Raul Gama was about my height, with a slight middle-age paunch, but he had a quickness to his movements that belied his mass. The way he walked, pushing forward, reminded me of Linda. He had shaved his head, but I noticed the fuzz growing on the back and sides of his head. He unbuttoned and rolled up his sleeves as he led us to a small living room. I saw Linda taking everything in, squinting at the framed photos of sunsets and beach scenes on the wall, assessing the furniture and TV system. Raul said, "How did you find me?"

Linda looked up. "You're in the book. But also Hector's girlfriend told us."

Raul took off his glasses and rubbed the bridge of his nose. His forehead was shiny. "I heard about Hector."

"That's what I want to talk about."

"It's good to see you," he said, putting his glasses back on.

"Is it?"

Raul smiled, and I was startled by how similar his facial features were to Linda's. Both had an angular nose and dark eyebrows, though Linda's cheekbones were harder, more prominent, than her father's. He said, "It's not as surprising the second time around."

"Second time? Hector?"

"Hector. That was a shock."

Linda shoved her hands into her pockets and leaned back, her expression puzzled. I stepped forward and introduced myself as a friend. Raul gave me a brief nod but focused on Linda. He said, "He showed up like this, without warning, and I was pretty surprised."

"I understand it didn't go well," Linda said.

"He told you that?"

"What happened?" she asked.

Raul shook his head. "The kid finds me, then hits me up for money."

"What?"

"That's right. He said I owed him. I had to cut the visit short."

"You owed him?"

"That's what he said. And it wasn't like he wanted some cash to buy a dinner. He wanted big money."

"How much?"

"He asked for twenty grand to start with."

"Why would he . . . I don't understand."

Raul started to reply, then grimaced. "It got bad. I lost my temper."

"Did he say why he needed the money?"

"He blamed me for ruining his life. He said I screwed everyone up, and he wanted money to start over."

"And what did you say?"

Raul threw his hands up. "What could I say? Some punk kid shows up asking for twenty g's because I was tough on him as a kid? I told him to forget it. I told him to get lost. And then he tried to shake me down."

"What?"

"Threatened me. Told me he'd make trouble. I didn't want to, but I had to throw him out."

"I can't believe that," Linda said. "How did he even know you had money?"

"Did his homework. He knew about my business."

"Internet porn?" I asked.

Raul glanced sharply at me. "How did you know that?"

Linda answered, "We do our homework, too."

"Are you going to ask for money now?"

Linda tensed. "No. I just want to know about Hector."

Raul said, "When I heard about the accident, I didn't know what to think. What happened? Was it drugs?"

"We're trying to find out."

"If I had given him the money, would he still be alive?"

Linda shook her head. "We don't know."

"I think he might've started some trouble for me. Some guy left a few ugly messages."

"Like what?"

"The guy said Hector owed him money, and that now with Hector dead I had to come up with it."

"Did you tell the police this?" I asked.

"No. What could I tell them? It wasn't a threat, not yet. And I haven't heard from him in a week."

"Did he tell you his name?" Linda asked.

"No. Just that I better start raising cash," he said. "I've read some of your articles."

Linda's head snapped forward. "What?"

"Your articles from that San Jose paper. On the Internet."

"How did you know I wrote for a newspaper?"

"Hector mentioned it. I didn't know you married."

"And divorced."

"You kept his name," Raul said, studying her.

"I did," she said. "What else did you and Hector talk about?"

"He wanted to know why I left."

Linda waited. When the silence extended, she asked, "What did you tell him?"

Raul stared down at the floor, and almost smiled. He said, "As a reporter you know that there are always different versions of a story, right?"

"What's your version?"

"Hector told me what he thought, what your mother said. It wasn't quite like that."

"You didn't abandon us? You didn't empty the bank account? You didn't leave us stranded?"

I glanced at her, trying to warn her, but she continued glaring at Raul.

"Here we go," Raul said to me. "Can you feel the poison?"

Linda held up her hands and said, "Okay. What did you tell Hector?"

"Your mother kicked me out."

"Oh, bullshit!" Linda said.

"Hey, watch your mouth—"

"She didn't kick you out, and how come if you were wronged, you never contacted us? Don't tell me that it's also Mom's fault."

"She warned me away," Raul said. "She said she'd call the cops and have me ruined."

"What? What kind of crap is this?" Linda laughed. "Ruined for what?"

He shook his head. "Ask your mother. This was how she wanted it."

Linda turned to me. "He takes off and blames my mom. Can you believe this?"

"You don't know," Raul said. "Neither did Hector. Ask your mother what happened. Ask her about the charges she made."

Linda kept still. "What?"

"Ask her."

"No, you tell me. What kind of charges?"

"She threatened me. But ask her. Ask her for the truth."

"You are so full of it!" Linda said. "You can't even take responsibility—" She stopped and turned away. She held a finger up into the air, and composed herself. She lowered her voice and said, "Just tell me what else you and Hector talked about, and I'll go."

"That's it. He wanted money. He wanted, like you, for me to own up. But it's not that simple. We argued and I kicked him out."

"Argued about the money."

"About the money and about your mother."

Linda's lower jaw jutted out. "Don't you dare talk about my mother."

Raul sighed. "You know what? Maybe you should leave. I didn't ask you here."

"You didn't," she said. "That's right. Both your children had to find you. And you couldn't care less."

"That's not—to hell with this. I'm done being insulted. Get out. You come by after you've calmed down."

"Calm?" Linda stormed to the door and I followed. She muttered something then, while on the steps, turned and said, "If I wasn't calm I'd tell you what you really are, a sniveling selfish son of a bitch who almost destroyed his family."

"Get the hell out of here!" Raul yelled.

I went down the steps and Raul came out. "She poisoned you two!" he said to Linda. "You go ask her what really happened!" He turned back into his house and slammed the door behind him.

The man across the street was still washing his car, and he stopped running the hose spray, staring at us. I stared back. He looked away and continued spraying. I caught up with Linda, whose cheeks were blotchy and red. She muttered, "I lost it."

I didn't say anything. We walked back down the hill, and she said, "I'm not done with him. Once I talk to my mom I'll want to see him again."

"You believe Hector tried to get money from him?"

"It's possible. Maybe Bangs found out about being cheated and wanted Hector to pay him back. So Hector went to Raul, who has some money."

"And when Raul turned him down—"

"Bangs killed Hector. And then maybe gave Raul a call."

I nodded. After a moment I asked, "What did he mean about the charges? What kind of charges?"

"Good question. I don't know."

"Abuse charges? Physical abuse?"

"I don't know," she said. She looked up at the sky for a moment, then followed me to the car.

"What are you going to tell your mother?" I asked.

She hesitated. "I'll have to be careful, but I need to know more about Raul. Maybe you can run interference. We'll do zone."

"I might not be back until late," I said.

"Right." She nodded, not meeting my eyes. "I forgot."

"I don't have to. I can cancel."

"No. If you can get more on Bangs, it's good."

"You sure?"

She faced me. "I'm sure."

I searched for signs of hostility, but couldn't find any. I pointed across the street. "There's a beach there. Let's check it out."

"Now?"

"You in a hurry to get home?"

She scowled and shook her head.

Linda told me that after her mother started working two jobs to support them—all day at the fabric company, and then from six to ten as a cashier at a women's clothing store—Linda and Hector had to keep house by themselves. Even something as small as grocery shopping became difficult. Normally their mother would buy groceries on the weekends, but sometimes she worked extra shifts. Linda and her brother would find themselves without any food toward the end of the week, and often they had to call and remind their mother to bring something for them from the mall.

"Dinners at ten-thirty at night," Linda said. "And usually something from the greasy food court."

"You never told me that."

She shrugged.

"It was sort of like that when it was just me and father, before he died," I said.

"That's right. I forgot. You guys ate junk, too. I remember a few times we were so hungry we couldn't wait—we'd go to the grocery and pretend to shop, but just eat whatever we could in the aisles."

"That's terrible."

She laughed. "It was like the Tasmanian Devil cartoon. We'd walk through an aisle and there'd be nothing left."

We moved into the center of town, pausing at a few store windows. In front of one souvenir shop a table had been set up outside with trinkets and postcards. Traffic was backed up on PCH, the sidewalks beginning to crowd with tourists in khaki shorts and clean tennis shirts, stringy-haired surfers lounging on benches and curbs. We crossed the street and walked onto the beach, Linda's pace slowing as she looked out over the ocean. I thought again of the last time we were at a beach and said, "Remember when we went to Muir?"

She nodded. "That was nice."

"Remember that old naked couple?"

She smiled and continued toward the water. I followed. She stopped and took off her shoes. She said, "Jeez, that was weird, seeing him. I didn't know what to expect."

"For it to be happier?"

"What was it like when you saw your aunt after a dozen years?"

"That was different," I said. "We never got along. We were both glad I left."

"You didn't expect a happy reunion?"

"No."

"I don't understand how someone can be such a bastard. He doesn't care about his kids. That's so bizarre. Is it me?"

"No. It's not." The waves lapped up closer, and I stepped back. Linda dipped her bare foot into the water. A breeze sprayed mist on us, my skin becoming sticky. I wanted to ask her more questions about her brother, about how she'd confront her mother, but she pressed her foot into the wet sand, sinking in. Another breeze blew her hair back, and she raised her head into the wind. She closed her eyes and let the sun warm her face, and she held out her arms, the wind flapping her sleeves. I stayed quiet, just watching her, listening to the waves breaking around us.

Sixteen

The party on Balboa Island was at a small beach house overlooking a black, glistening channel. There didn't seem to be a moon tonight, and I found the shivering and inky water to be disturbing—it looked as if it could go miles deep—and I couldn't stop staring. The ripples beckoned me.

Serena had driven us again, and after winding through hills with fresh condominiums, then inching in traffic onto the island, the small, almost comically miniaturized buildings cramped and overlapping around us, we had finally arrived at the house. The party was already lively. Music, lights, guests spilled onto the porch and front steps. Beer bottles and empty plastic champagne glasses sat on the railing. Serena had introduced me to her friend, Anne, an actress moving to New York for stage work, but the man whom I was here to meet, the Bangs connection, hadn't yet arrived.

I found myself standing by the kitchen window as Serena moved through the partygoers with her arm linked in Anne's, greeting old friends and whispering in Anne's ear. I wanted to be back at the condo with Linda, eavesdropping on what her mother had to say about Raul.

Serena now glided into the kitchen with two mixed drinks in her hand. She said, "How about a Long Island Iced Tea?"

I thanked her and asked if her friend had shown up yet.

"No. He'll be here, though. He's hot for me." She winked.

"Hot for you?"

"For a long time he tried to date me."

"I don't blame him," I said.

She raised an eyebrow. "Hey, is that a compliment?"

I nodded. "It is. And thanks for helping me out."

She raised up her drink and clinked my glass. She was wearing a sleeveless blouse, and when she brought the glass up to her lips, a small knot muscle appeared on her biceps. I was about to ask her about working out when she said, "The thing about these aspiring actors—they bartend and know how to make a good drink."

Tasting the Long Island Iced Tea, which had a faint tea flavor masking the alcohol, I said, "It's good. How do you know these people?"

"I wanted to act for a while. That's why I was down here."

"Really? Did you get any roles?"

"No. They wanted me to be Asian prostitutes or Kung-Fu sluts."

I smiled.

"Which is why I've gotten realistic," she said. "I'll settle for being an Internet millionaire."

"Is that all?" I asked, laughing. "Is that why you're moving north?"

"Soon as I finish up my XML and Java course work, Silicon Valley here I come."

"I'll show you around when you get there."

"I'd like that." She drank with both hands, peering at me over the rim. "I don't know anyone up there."

"Where's your family?"

"New York," she said.

A voice from the doorway said, "Serena?"

We turned, and I saw a tall, athletic black man in a navy blue sport jacket. He had on silver sunglasses that glinted the kitchen light. He smiled, which softened his hard jaw, and pointed his finger at Serena. "There you are. Been a while." He took off his sunglasses.

"Mack! Glad you're here! This is my friend Allen."

Mack? I nodded to him, but he locked his eyes onto Serena. "You're look-ing great."

"Thanks. Growing in your hair?"

He ran his hand over the dark stubble on his head. "Got tired of shaving it."

"So, my friend here is trying to find a guy named . . ." She turned to me.

"Lowell Bangs," I said.

Mack didn't reply. He scratched his head and gave Serena a big grin. "Why would your friend want to do that?"

I said, "I'm helping someone. Lowell Bangs seems to be connected to what I'm trying to find out."

Mack said to Serena, "How'd you get sucked into this?"

"Just doing my civic duty."

He turned to me. "You don't want to mess with Bangs."

"You know him?" I put my drink down. Mack gave me a half-shrug and started to reply, but stopped. He said to Serena, "Is that why you called me?"

"Yeah, and I also know you never turn down a party."

"You know I'm out of it. I haven't dealt in a while."

"I know."

Studying her with amusement, he said, "Let me get a drink and hang out a little, okay? I feel kind of bait and switched."

"So is that all I am? Bait?"

"You know it," he said. "And you use it well."

Serena put one hand on her hip and cocked her head back. "If I'm bait, then have you been hooked?"

He laughed and shook his head. "No. Not yet. It's good to see you."

"We'll be out back, and thanks, Mack."

"Don't thank me yet," he said, turning smoothly and gliding out of the kitchen. "I haven't done anything."

Serena and I walked out onto a small wooden deck with rocky sand a few feet below. The alcohol was warming my stomach. Serena said, "I used to know him in my crazier days. He worked the raves, selling acid and E."

"Did you end up dating him?"

"No. He's a little too slick for me. But he'll help us."

I caught the "us" and said, "Why are you doing this?"

"I'm doing this for Hector. Don't forget we went out."

I had forgotten, and said, "Linda and I visited his father, the biological one, today."

"The one Hector talked about."

"Yes. Did he ever mention some kind of charges against his father?"

She shook her head. "No. Police charges?"

"I don't know. The father wasn't very nice. He said Hector tried to extort money out of him."

She said, "So he found him. He talked about it once, but I never thought he would."

"What did he say?"

"Rambled on when he took too much E. Something about how everything went wrong because of his father. He was so angry about it."

"Did he talk about him a lot?"

"No. Just a couple times."

The side door opened and Mack sauntered out. He said, "You out there?"

"Over here," Serena said.

He peered along the deck and saw us. He walked over with a glass of wine. To Serena he said, "What have you been up to? Last time I saw you was what, half a year ago?"

"At Jason Voll's party."

"Right, right. I hear you're doing some kind of computer thing. Great."

"So you know of Lowell Bangs?" Serena asked.

"Yeah," Mack said. "He ended my dealing career."

"How?"

Mack said, "I wasn't that serious about it, just making a little extra money, but this guy Bangs was moving more into E. He began getting rid of all his competition. Including me."

"How?" I asked.

He smiled. The light of the kitchen window slid across his face. He put down his wineglass, shrugged off his sport jacket. He then unbuttoned the top of his silk shirt. He pointed to a small, puckered scar. "See that? A guy stabbed me with a screwdriver and told me to stop dealing E. So I stopped."

"It was Bangs?" Serena said.

"Someone he sent. My selling was just on the side. But these meth dealers are crazy. A lot of them are users. I didn't need that kind of shit. Why do you want to know about him?"

"There was a guy helping him, then cheated him," I said.

"Hector cheated him?" Serena asked, turning to me. "I didn't know that."

"Cheated Bangs?" Mack said. "This guy still alive?"

"No," I said.

Mack nodded. "Figures. And what do you want to do?"

"Get more information. Maybe bring in the police—"

"No way," Mack said. "Nothing with the cops. I can't have anything to do with the cops."

"Okay," I said. "Just tell me what you know about Bangs."

"Not much. Started out selling meth, making it himself. When he saw that E had a better markup he just started selling his meth as E. But with all the testing now, people knew it wasn't pure. So he started making high-quality E, and stamping it 'BE.'"

"Oh," Serena said. "I've used BE."

"Yeah, it's got a good rep, 'Bangs's Ecstasy,' but other people started using that stamp. So Bangs decided to put us all out of business."

"How does he make it?"

"Probably just modified his meth labs. It's the same reductive alkylation process as making meth. Anyway, he had to keep the franchise clean, the BE franchise, so he got this reputation for hurting anyone using the stamp or even selling E at raves."

"Have you ever met him?" I asked.

"No."

"Have you heard of Hector Gama?"

Mack turned to Serena. "Didn't you date that guy?"

"Yeah."

He said, "And this Hector was the guy who cheated Bangs?"

I nodded. "Looks that way."

"And now you're trying to get the cops onto Bangs?"

"I don't know," I said.

"Oh, friend, not a good idea. Look," he said to Serena. "Sorry about Hector, but you really got to stay out of this. You're lucky Bangs didn't come after you because of Hector."

"No, we broke up a while ago."

"How would you find out more?" I asked Mack. "Where would you go?"

"Easy. Find someone dealing BE, and start with him. Work up the chain. But you'd be crazy to. He gets wind of it, and you're dead."

"Is BE still showing up at raves?"

He smiled at Serena. "I haven't been in the scene for a while. I remember when you were really into it. The good old days."

Serena said, "It's a blur now. They were kind of wasted years."

"Nah," Mack said. "You were just having fun."

"I don't have much to show for it," she said quietly.

They began talking about people they knew and where they were now. I drifted to the other end of the deck, thinking about how in her mid-twenties Serena thought she had wasted some of her years. I was thirty-two and still wasn't sure what I was doing. Were my twenties also wasted? It struck me that I was older than my mother had been when she had died. My father died in his mid-forties. That gave me only thirteen years left.

Voices rose on the beach below. Someone yelled, "Well, fuck you, too!"

I peered over the railing and saw two men pushing each other. Both seemed drunk, staggering across the sand and throwing wild punches at each other that missed. Mack and Serena looked over the railing as well, and more partygoers filtered out onto the deck as the two men yelled louder.

Anne, the host, called out to them, "Hey, can you two take this somewhere else?"

One of the men said, "Hey, are you a cunt?"

The second man punched the first, and they began rolling in sand. Because it was dark I couldn't tell who was winning, but one of them scrambled aside and pulled out a gun. Everyone on the deck backed away. Someone said, "Shit. Call the police."

"You think you can fuck with me?" the man with the gun said to the other. "You think you can do that to me?"

Mack called down to them, "Someone just went to get the cops. You guys should leave."

The man looked up, squinting in the light. "Why don't *you* take your black ass and leave," the man said.

Mack's face closed up. He asked, "What did you just say?"

"Take your black ass and leave."

"Tough guy with a gun," Mack said. "Why don't you come up here and say that?"

"Uh, Mack," Serena said. "What are you doing?"

I watched the man look around, surprised, and then he registered his small audience. He said to his opponent, frozen on the sand, "I'll deal with you later, shithead." The man then approached the deck, and everyone stiffened. To Mack he said, "You got a fucking problem?"

"Come on up here and be a tough guy."

I couldn't understand what Mack was doing. As the man with the gun climbed up onto the porch I saw he had a cheap .38 and was sprinkling sand wherever he walked. Sand caught in a crappy .38 wasn't very safe. The man looked around and said to Mack, "Who the fuck you think you are?"

Mack replied, "You're ruining this party. Take your gun and your friend and your foul mouth and get going."

The man nodded, raising the gun and approaching. "Fucking hero, is it? Superman? Super Black Man?" He pointed the gun at Mack, getting even closer. "You think I care if I waste a fucking jungle bunny?"

The side door opened and Anne said, "I called the cops!"

The man turned toward her, and I saw Mack step lightly forward, and in one quick motion grabbed the gun with one hand. He turned his body and held the gun up, then backed into the man and thrust his elbow into the man's solar plexus. Mack then yanked the gun away as the man doubled over and gagged. Mack spun around to face him, and he held the back of the man's head with his other hand and threw his knee up as he pulled the man's head down. His knee slammed into the man's face, a muted *thunk*, making everyone draw back. The man collapsed and lay still. Mack looked around, then handed the gun to a startled partygoer. He said, "No cops for me."

He turned to Serena and said, "Walk me out? It's time for me to go."

Serena nodded. I followed them through the house. Everyone seemed stunned.

Mack waited for me to catch up, and when we walked out the front door, he said, "You got to be careful with Bangs. He's supposed to be really crazy."

"I can't believe what just happened," Serena said. "Why'd you do that? He could've—"

"He was drunk. He couldn't even see straight, let alone shoot straight." To me he said, "Man, you should've seen Serena back then. She'd dance for eight hours straight. She'd be all glittery with these silver tails flying around her."

I blinked. He acted as if nothing had happened.

"She was beautiful," he said to me. He pointed to a shiny black Mustang. "That's me. I got to get out of here before the cops show up. You don't tell them about me, okay?"

I nodded. Serena said, "Thanks, Mack."

"No problem. But next time? We can just talk on the phone."

She smiled. "You always knew how to entertain a crowd."

He climbed into his car, revved the engine, and sped off.

We watched the red taillights turn a corner. We heard a police siren in the distance.

I said, "This is the strangest party I've ever been to."

She said, "Let's get out of here."

We drove back to Marina Alta, and I asked her about Mack. She didn't know what he was doing now, and said, "But I don't think he's ever done anything legal. He mentioned sales, but didn't elaborate."

"He was . . . he was very cool."

She turned to me and laughed. "I'll tell him that. He'll get a kick out of that."

"He likes you a lot," I said.

Serena said, "Well, truthfully I think he just thinks I'm exotic."

"What do you mean?"

"He likes my hair long and silky, and sometimes he's a little too interested in my being Asian."

I thought about that, and said, "Long and silky?"

"It used to be long when I was going for acting roles. But yeah, long and silky. Asian fetish. Geisha-girl syndrome."

"Ah."

"Whereas you, even though you're Asian, don't even seem to think about it."

"About being Asian?"

"Yeah."

"I think about it," I said too quickly, then realized I sounded defensive. "When I have to."

"I don't mean anything by that. It's just an observation."

Why did that bother me? I became quiet.

Serena said, "What's wrong?"

"Nothing. I guess I don't think much about it."

"Why not?"

I shrugged.

"You never did?"

"Maybe when I was younger," I said. I told her about going to a Korean church as a kid because my aunt had forced me to. Since I couldn't speak any Korean, I was assigned to the kindergarten Korean-language class after the regular Bible study. I hated it and would slip out of the church before the language classes began. "I didn't fit in there."

Serena smiled and said, "I went to a Korean church for a while, too, back in New York. We didn't have any of those classes, though."

"You missed out," I said dryly. "Being force-fed culture is something all eleven-year-olds want."

She asked, "You didn't like it there?"

"The other kids knew about my parents. My father had just died. They didn't know what to make of me, and I kept to myself."

She nodded. "Like now, I guess."

I didn't reply. I remembered what Linda had said about my wanting stability, how she seemed to know what I wanted. Why was everyone analyzing me?

"So tell me," she said. "Are you and Linda broken up?"

I sighed heavily.

She laughed and said, "Never mind."

"I don't know. I think she wants to, but there's too much else going on."

"Have you ever dated a Korean American woman?"

This stopped me. "No. Why?"

"Just curious."

I told her that except for the brief time at the Korean church, I didn't know that many Korean Americans. Anticipating her next question I said, "No real reason why. It just worked out that way."

"Do you have a lot of friends up north?" she asked.

"Some," I said, but except for Linda, there were none. This disturbed me. My former partner, Paul, had been a friend, though it grew out of work. I suddenly wondered if what Linda was reacting to was this focus. She had other friends, but I didn't. I tended to want to spend my time with her. Was the pressure coming from that? I was saddened by this thought.

We exited the freeway and Serena drove us to the condo. She said, "I'd invite you over to my place, but I've got work and class tomorrow. I have to study tonight."

"Me, too," I said, telling her about the PI exam.

"I also have exams coming up. Maybe sometime we can study together." She pulled up in front of the condo. "Hey, don't worry. We'll take it easy."

"Studying?" I asked.

"No. Things between you and Linda are weird. I see that."

I nodded.

"I'm good with the skittish type. You're the skittish type."

"I am?"

"I have to use breadcrumbs and I can't make any sudden movements."

"Or else?"

"Or else you'll fly away." She winked.

I hesitated, then climbed out of the car. She met my eyes as I looked back at her, and she held up an imaginary phone and dialed with her other finger. She mouthed the words, "Call me."

I nodded, then entered the building lobby, thinking, This never happens to me.

Seventeen

used the extra key to let myself in, and found the condo dark and still. I crept down the hallway, the carpet dampening my steps, and saw a line of light under the office door where Linda was sleeping. I then heard her whispering. I stopped. I knocked lightly, and she shuffled something, a chair creaking. She said, "One sec."

I opened the door and saw her quickly wiping away tears with one hand, the other hand holding the telephone. After a startled moment I said, "Sorry. I heard you talking—"

"I said, 'One sec.' Give me a minute." She motioned for me to close the door. Her eyes were red, her cheeks wet.

I shut the door and waited. Linda whispered something to the caller, and hung up. After what seemed like a long minute she said, "Okay, Allen."

I looked in again. She was sitting at the desk, her face dried but still red. I asked what happened.

"Nothing. It's fine. How did it go?"

"Who were you on the phone with?" I asked, but knew.

"No one. It doesn't matter. Did you find out more?"

I stepped in and closed the door behind me. "You were crying. Why?"

"Don't worry about it. I was just upset. It was because of an argument with my mom. Tell me about tonight."

"First tell me who was on the phone," I said. "Was it Julie?" I knew it wasn't.

She shook her head.

"Harlan?" I asked quietly.

"Yes," she said.

"Why . . . why were you crying?"

"Look, it doesn't matter. It's no big deal—"

"Just tell me please. You never . . . just tell me why."

She said in a tired voice, "I was fighting with my mom. I needed to talk to someone. I called Harlan and we talked, and I got upset again. That's all."

She had never cried in front of me before, and this news stung. I tried not to show any expression and asked, "Why didn't you wait for me? Why'd you call him?"

"I didn't know when you'd be back. Last time you spent the night with her."

"Oh. So this is about Serena?"

"No. It's about me. You weren't here. Harlan was home. You got a problem with that?"

I didn't know how to answer this, and felt my stomach tightening. The confusion of the moment seemed to immobilize me. Finally, I asked, "What happened with your mother?"

"Raul wasn't lying," she said. "She did threaten him with charges, child abuse charges."

I stared at her. "Did he . . . abuse you?"

"No. She claims she suspected something with Hector."

"What kind of—I mean—how . . . with Hector?"

She let out a slow breath and looked up at me. "The pushing around stuff I told you about. But also she says she caught Raul coming out of Hector's room late at night. She said she just knew something was wrong."

"But is it true? Did Hector say anything?"

"I don't *know*," she said, loudly. She held up her hand, and lowered her voice. "I kept pressing my mom, and she said Raul denied it, and Hector never admitted it, but she suspected something. Plus, the fact that Raul started working in the porn industry convinced her."

"He started the company back then?"

"Sort of. Something about a construction project leading to a porn film company. She said it would've been enough to get the police and courts believing her. So Raul stayed away." She met my eyes and pressed her lips together. I heard the wall clock ticking. She said, "I was just so pissed. She always made it seem like he just abandoned us, but she had some role in it. It was much more complicated."

"But if she thought Hector was being abused—"

"But we don't know."

"Would she make it up?"

Linda rocked back and forth in the chair, then stopped. "I don't know. She was really upset at the time. If he left her but wanted to keep in contact with us, she could've been so angry . . . maybe . . . ? I don't know."

"Hector never said anything?"

"Never." She lowered her voice and cracked her knuckles. "I have no idea what to believe." She then clicked off the desk lamp. The darkness disoriented me. She said, "My mom kept trying to turn it around tonight, saying I was being deliberately hurtful. That just made me madder." She rocked back and forth in her chair, then stopped. "What did you find out at the party?"

I summarized what Mack had told me. "He warned me away from this. Bangs has a bad reputation."

"And Hector was working for him?" she said, her voice tired. "A brilliant career move."

"I'll let you sleep," I said. "We can talk tomorrow."

"Was Serena there tonight?"

"Yes. She gave me a ride."

"So, are you dating her now?"

"No. She's just helping," I said.

Linda didn't respond.

"How come we never talk anymore?" I asked.

"I don't know, Allen."

I couldn't find the words to reply, a feeling of something loosening between us, and as my eyes adjusted to the dark I saw her fuzzy silhouette against the pale wall, her head bowed forward. I asked, "How's the bump?"

"Fine. A twinge now and then, but pretty much normal."

"What should we do about Bangs?"

She didn't reply for a long time. Then, "I don't know."

"Is your sister coming—"

"Allen? I'd like to be alone."

I wanted to say, But you just called Harlan! Instead I left the office without uttering another word, closing the door and leaving her in darkness.

So this is how it ends, I thought. There was a brief moment last year when we had been kidding around, making fun of Linda's last appearance on *This Week in Northern California* on KQED, when another journalist had contradicted Linda's take on the Silicon Valley economy. I had perfected an imitation of the condescending voice this man had used, and was making Linda laugh by repeating what he had said but adding jokes like "And I'm hot for your body, but since I'll never have you I'll put you down in front of thousands of viewers." Linda had laughed so hard that she couldn't catch her breath. We rolled together on the sofa. I lay on top of her, and kissed her. I thought, I'm nuts about her.

As I walked into the guest room now, I pulled up the blinds and stared out over the marina. A few of the boats were lit up inside. I left the lights off and listened to my breathing. I tried to pinpoint a time when things had gone wrong. I thought back and picked apart my conversations with Linda, and searched for the signs of change. The problem was that our relationship had been based on a common goal—Linda helping me learn more about my father's death. Once our goal had been attained, we lost our momentum. We didn't have much in common, and except for a physical attraction that I had felt early on, I wondered why we had started dating in the first place.

It struck me that I had come down here for that common goal again. I wanted to help her as she had me. Maybe I thought it could be like old times.

I tried to sleep, but couldn't. I turned on a small lamp and leafed through my PI textbook. The impending exam depressed me. Being down here depressed me. I paced, waving my arms wildly, trying to shake off the dis-ease.

I didn't belong down here.

My aunt Insook, who was hiding out somewhere in Korea, had resented being forced to raise me, and I always had a sense of being a burden. I felt that way now, my presence here only taking up space. Someday, I thought, I'd feel at home.

The space here only became more crowded when Julie and her daughter Nora arrived the next afternoon. I had spent the morning studying at the coffee-and-pastry shop, and when I returned to the condo, I found Nora curled up on the sofa with a paperback book, her eyes hidden beneath her severe blond bangs. She looked up at me, blinking into focus, then said, "Hi."

"Hi. You and your mother just get in?"

"Uh-huh. She's in the kitchen with Aunt Linda."

"What're you reading?"

She held up the book, and I saw a witch on the cover. I said, "If it's good maybe I'll read it, too."

"It's for kids," she said very seriously.

"I can read kids' books, can't I?"

"But why?"

I smiled. "I didn't read much as a kid. I have to make up for lost time."

"Okay, but you have to read them in order or else it's wrong."

Julie looked out of the kitchen and greeted me. I noticed that she had lost weight. The last time I had seen her, she had had a fuller face, her cheeks rounder, her arms fleshier, and back then she had worn her curly blond hair long, covering her face, but now it was cut short. Her cheeks had thinned. Her chin was sharper. She said to her daughter, "You remember Allen, don't you?"

Nora nodded.

Linda appeared behind Julie and said, "They just arrived. I've been filling her in."

"About what?" I asked.

"Everything," Julie said.

Linda motioned me into the kitchen, and I followed them. Julie said to me, "I thought you were a bodyguard. How did you let her get hurt?"

I stammered, "What?"

Linda said to her, "I told you he got me to pull away in time."

"Not in time to avoid a concussion!"

Linda replied calmly, "It wasn't his fault."

"And what the heck is this all about? Why are you even bothering with all this?" Julie asked.

Linda said to me, "I told her what we've been doing."

"Do you remember anything about child abuse charges?" I asked her.

"No. But my father and I didn't come in until a couple years after Raul left." She turned to Linda and said, "Why are you doing this? It's just going to drive you crazy. Hector got himself into it, and you should just let it go."

"But she lied to me—"

"She didn't lie. She just didn't tell you everything. And why should she? You were just a kid."

"I need to know," Linda said. "I don't like these secrets."

"What do you intend to do?" Julie asked. "You're not going torture Mom with this—"

"I want to see Raul again. I need his side of the story."

Julie closed her eyes for a moment, then said to me, "You've got to talk her out of this. This thing with Hector's got her all confused."

"Why didn't you come down for the funeral?" Linda asked.

"I told you. I couldn't. Nora was really sick. Plus you moved it up without much notice."

"Admit it," Linda said. "You and Hector hated each other. This was just the final way of showing it."

"Oh, come on!" Julie said. "I'm here now!"

"And where's Frank?" Linda asked. "He's part of the family."

Julie said, "He had to work."

But it was the way she said this that caught my attention, a slight turn of her head and then a turn back, as if she were forcing herself to keep a normal expression. I recognized it as a sign of trouble, something that I had done once when Larry had asked me about Linda. I said, "So Marianne was right."

"About what," Julie said.

I said, "About you and Frank."

Linda turned to her and said, "You're having problems?"

"Mom said that?" Julie said, her eyes widening. "She said that to you?"

"Is it true?" Linda asked.

Julie put her hands on her hips, and demanded, "What did Mom say?"

"It *is* true," Linda said.

"What did she say?"

"Just that she thought something might be up between you two."

"How in the hell did she know that?"

"What happened?" Linda asked. "I thought you guys were fine."

Julie glanced at me. I started walking toward the door, but Julie said, "Hell, you know already." To Linda she said, "It's true. We're separating."

"No. You guys have been together for what, nine years?"

Julie shrugged. "It happens."

"What about Nora?"

"It's hard on her."

They fell silent. I knew that Linda wanted to ask more but was waiting to be alone with her. I said I'd be in the living room and left them. I heard Linda saying, "But why? You guys seemed okay that last time we met . . ."

I didn't hear Julie's response and wasn't sure if I wanted to. Relationships were falling apart everywhere I looked. Tenuous bonds disintegrated around me. I knew this would give Linda more reasons for our own break-up. I sat across from Nora, who looked up from her book. She said, "Where's my grandma?"

"I don't know. I saw her leaving this morning to run errands."

"And grandpa?"

"At work."

"Why aren't you at work?"

"I'm taking a break."

"Like my mom."

"Yes," I said, searching for signs that she knew about her parents. "How are you?"

"I'm fine, thank you," she said.

I smiled. "You're very polite."

"My mom taught me to be polite."

I realized that like her mother, Nora seemed thinner, paler. I said, "You were sick for a while, weren't you?"

"I had the flu. I was in bed for three days."

Linda and Julie came out of the kitchen. Julie said to her daughter,

"Honey, your aunt Linda and I are going for some coffee. Can you stay here with Allen for a little bit?"

I turned to them, surprised.

"It's just for thirty minutes, an hour max," Linda told me.

"Okay," I said, though wasn't sure I wanted to baby-sit.

"Just read your book or watch TV," Julie said to Nora, as she followed Linda out the door. "We'll be right back."

I watched them leave, and I grabbed my PI textbook. I sat down at the dining room table and said to Nora, "I guess I'll just read here." Nora watched me, then moved from the sofa to the table, sitting down across from me. "I'll read, too."

I nodded toward the door and said, "I guess they want to do girl talk."

Nora wrinkled her nose.

I said, "I agree."

Dinner. Marianne had made another large feast. I sat at the table next to Julie, whom I hadn't spoken to since this morning, but Linda had filled me in. Julie and Frank had split up last year in a trial separation, had reconciled for a few months, but were now divorcing for good. When I asked why, Linda said, "They kept fighting."

"About what?"

"Money, for one. Frank blew a lot of their savings in the stock market. Then Julie wanted another child, but Frank didn't."

"When we went over to their house—"

"I know. Everything seemed normal." She had a lost, distracted expression. "It's hard to believe."

During dinner Marianne kept asking Nora about school and friends, and a few times I caught Linda and Julie exchanging knowing looks. Marianne seemed to be ignoring Linda. Linda ignored Marianne. Julie tried to talk to everyone. I stared at Nora, wondering if she knew her parents were splitting. I remembered that my late partner Paul's marriage had been deteriorating, and again I hadn't suspected anything until Paul's wife mentioned it to me. I didn't understand how a couple could hide this kind of tension. I knew I couldn't. I constantly felt like my stomach was upset. I barely recognized my uneasy expression in the mirror.

I had asked Linda earlier what her sister thought about the abuse charge, and Linda had answered, "She said something interesting—she always thought our mom favored Hector. She figured it was because he was a boy."

"And you said he was always sick."

"But it could've been something else. I have to talk to Raul again, and I'll get the truth."

Now, while Luke praised the dinner, telling his wife the spicy chicken was delicious in an oddly formal way, I watched everyone pretend how normal this occasion was. Marianne smiled and told us that the recipe included jalapeños and basil. Nora glanced at the TV and asked if she could watch "Jeopardy." Julie said, "Not during dinner."

"You must be so smart!" Marianne said.

The phone rang. Linda went to answer it and came out, pointing to me. "It's Serena."

Julie glared at me.

I went into the kitchen and heard Marianne asking Linda who Serena was. When I said hello, Serena greeted me with, "So I hear there's this really big rave tonight in the desert, and from the people I talked to it's pretty certain to have a BE dealer there."

"How do you know?"

"Because this one is being widely advertised in clubs and record stores. There are going to be five different DJs there."

"Tonight?" I asked, tired at the thought of another one. "Don't these people sleep?"

She laughed. "This will be a younger crowd I think. You could probably find a BE dealer and ask about Hector."

"Can I call you back?" I asked.

She said yes, and that if I wanted to go, she'd accompany me.

"Why? Don't you have work tomorrow?"

"Work and night classes. But hey, I like hanging out with you."

I smiled to myself. "Thanks, but this might be getting risky. If I talk to a BE dealer—"

"You can just ask. You don't have to do anything crazy."

"Okay. Let me call you back."

I walked out into the dining room and they looked up at me.

I motioned to Linda to talk in the kitchen.

"No, you can say it here."

I paused, then said, "There's another rave tonight and . . . BE might be there."

"So, you're going?"

"I don't know. I wanted to ask what you thought—"

"Go. See what you can find." She shrugged.

"Well, if you're not okay with this—"

"I said go. See if you can find out more on Bangs."

Julie tilted her head at her sister, hearing the sharpness. I didn't like this dismissive tone, and said, "Can I talk to you in private?"

"If this is about her, then it's fine. We don't have to talk about it."

I thought about all the time I was putting into this and tried to keep my anger in check. Luke and Marianne studied their wineglasses. I said curtly, "All right. I'll let you know what I find."

Julie said to her daughter, "Will you stop playing with your food? No TV until you've cleaned the plate."

I suddenly had to get out of this apartment. I felt myself bombarded by people, the air being sucked from me. I grabbed my jacket and my PI text-book, and, apologizing to Marianne and Luke for not finishing my dinner, I bustled out the door, ignoring their puzzled looks. I heard Nora say, "But *he* didn't have to finish his dinner!"

Eighteen

About four months ago when Linda and I stopped having sex, it felt like a natural and inevitable progression, the consequence of a strained yet routine relationship. Because of work or travel or exhaustion, we went days, weeks, then months of not having sex, and never talked about it. I knew it was on her mind, though, because of the awkwardness that arose whenever I tried. Early on we used to throw ourselves at each other, but soon an uncertainty crept into our actions, and when I began doubting her desire for me, I found myself hesitating. Something had been depleted from us, and there were times when we would be in bed together, and I would feel very close to her, but just couldn't bring myself to try anything more than an innocent kiss good night.

Of course we were affectionate, but any passion seemed to be channeled into a fight. As I drove with Serena to an outdoor rave called "Desert Moon," I felt a familiar twisting in my gut, a queasiness that was becoming a natural state. After I had left the condo, I had called Serena from the pastry shop, and then had tried to study while waiting for her. I wasn't able to read more than a few pages. I kept thinking how Linda had acted as if she were doing me a favor by letting me go out tonight. No, it was more than that. She had pretended it didn't matter, that everything I was doing didn't matter. But I was doing all this for her.

She helped me, though, when I needed it.

No, I argued with myself. She helped me because it was her job. She wanted a story.

She did more than that.

I thought about this now and shook my head, which Serena noticed. She asked, "Everything all right?" She was dressed differently this time, in long black pants and a zippered vinyl vest with a windbreaker over that. She had told me that it gets cold in the desert at night. She asked me again if I was okay.

I said, "I need to be meaner."

She laughed. "Why?"

"I just do."

The rave was outside Palm Springs, and we had already bought tickets at the map point in Riverside. Now we were leaving L.A. on a quiet highway, the radio on low. I asked, "Have you met any BE dealers?"

"A few times, but this was a while ago," she said. "We have to be careful, if what Mack said is true. What's your plan?"

"I don't have one," I said. If I were meaner, Linda wouldn't take me for granted. Maybe that was what Harlan was like. Certainly her ex-husband was a bastard. Then I remembered when she had dated a lawyer around the time we had first met. He had led her on, slept with her, then dumped her all within two or three weeks. And she still liked him. I had heard her tell her sister on a telephone call that she had really liked him and that he was nice. Nice? Slept with her and dumped her, and he was nice. Maybe she wanted that kind of coldness from her relationships. Jeez, I just couldn't figure this out.

Maybe I should become a tough guy. I should be like Mack—cool, menacing, and decisive. The way he had subdued the drunken man at the party had been impressive. Why couldn't I be like that? I should never let anyone else take control. I should be Mack.

"You're not really going after Bangs, are you?" Serena said. "You remember what Mack said."

"I remember." What would Mack do tonight?

"Is something the matter?" she asked.

"Why?"

"You seem distracted."

"I'm pissed off at Linda."

"Ah."

"I'm going to knock some heads tonight," Mack said.

Serena glanced at me but didn't reply.

Because it was dark, and the route to the parking area was convoluted, Serena followed another car through the dust as we left the highway and headed into what seemed to be private land. A few signs warned trespassers away. I read off the directions from the map. Serena said that the car ahead was going to the same place. Her headlights pushed through waves of glowing red dust from the car's brake lights, and I saw lights behind us, a caravan driving deeper into the desert. The dirt road became rockier; pings of pebbles hit the wheel well. Soon, there was thumping in the distance and Serena said, "I hear something!"

I peered ahead and thought I saw lights flashing. "It's close."

Serena bounced in her seat. "Finally!"

I smiled. "Is it going to be the same kind of music?"

"No. Well, one DJ is into Trance, but the others are into Hard House and Detroit Techno."

"Are we going to dance?"

"Of course," she said. We drove over a hill, then saw the rows of cars parking, lights lining up side by side. A man with two flashlights was guiding drivers to the far end of the clearing. I said, "Organized."

"There are now professional companies that do this now. I bet whoever owns this land gets a cut." She pointed to the cars and said, "This is bigger than I thought."

I saw the familiar groups of oddly dressed kids clustering around cars, hugging and talking, glow sticks being shaken on. We parked and climbed out, stretching our legs. We followed the other groups down a path and beyond some picnic tables with people selling drinks. A row of portable toilets lined one clearing, and as we continued farther down the path the heavy thumping beat grew louder, lights shooting up into the sky. A film projector was running a Kung-Fu movie onto a white sheet. We walked over another hill and immediately saw a small bonfire at the center of a clearing. At least a hundred kids were crowded around the fire, dancing. A stage had been set up next to a cluster of boulders with generators behind them, and two large speakers pumped electronic music toward the fire. Some kids danced on the boulders.

I noticed that most of the dancers were teenagers. I said, "Younger crowd."

"Typical crowd," Serena said.

"How do we find a dealer?" I asked.

"Not yet. You'll look like a narc. Just take everything in. You'll soon see where the E is."

I turned to her. "The E will come to you."

She laughed. "The Zen of E," she said. "Are we flying tonight?"

I stopped. "You brought some?"

"I did."

"Are you?"

"I don't know," she said. "It depends on you."

"On me?"

"I don't want to fly alone."

"You won't, but I want to find a BE dealer."

"Then afterward?"

"We'll see."

She smiled and linked arms with me, and we began walking around the clearing, watching kids drinking beers and sodas. Many of them danced in small groups near the fire. Laser lights shot against the boulders, but the bonfire was the best light show, with the flames growing higher. The man who had been trafficking the parking area now fed the fire with logs. Each time he threw one on, a flurry of sparks scattered upward and people cheered.

The music was different from what I remembered, but it still had the same heavy, drilling beat. This time the computer effects were harsher, with synthesized grating sounds overlaying the rhythms, buzz saws set to electronic drums. More kids flowed into the clearing, crowding up toward the fire. Serena pointed ahead to a table with a line, the man behind the table checking a pill with a flashlight. We approached and saw the sign Rave Help—Testing taped to the bottom of the table.

I glanced at Serena, who nodded. We walked up behind the man, and someone in line yelled, "Hey, no cutting!"

The man turned. He was baby faced with an ill-fitting thin mustache.

"I have a quick question," I said.

The man said, "Yeah?"

"Have you seen any tablets stamped with B-E?"

"Sure. That's at every rave."

"I mean, tonight? Here?"

He nodded. "Just tested one a few minutes ago."

"Who was it? Do you see that person?"

The man squinted through the darkness. "Can't remember. It's pretty busy."

The girl at the front of the line pointed to a blot of liquid on a dish and said, "Can you hurry?"

The man shined his light onto the plate and said, "See that orange color? It means it's something other than MDMA. It's not E. Probably some amphetamine. I can do another test to see if there's any LSD—"

"Nah," the girl said. "No wonder it was cheap. You can chuck it." She disappeared into a crowd.

The man said to me, "If you hang out here, I'm sure another one will turn up."

Serena and I moved away from the table as the man took another pill, scraped off some shavings with a razor, then added a drop of liquid onto it, mixing it on a plate. I told Serena, "I think I'll wait here until he gets a BE."

"What if takes a while?" she asked.

I noticed her moving her body to the beat, and said, "Go dance. When I'm done here I'll join you."

She smiled. "You sure?"

I nodded and she skipped off toward the bonfire. I watched her raise her arms above her head, her windbreaker and vest pulled up, her midriff exposed. The flames flickered dangerously near her, but she didn't seem to care. Her face shone.

I started talking to the drug tester, who was nicknamed "Doc" for the obvious reason that he was an M.D., doing his residency at U.C. Irvine. I was surprised that he volunteered one night a week at raves, not only testing drugs but handing out information pamphlets and drug hot-line numbers. I stood at

Doc's side while he tested different pills and asked him why he did this. He told me he used to go to raves as a teen and college student, and he was glad when this organization started putting up these booths. I asked about the testing liquid, and Doc said, "It's Marquis, a reagent. Sulfuric acid and formaldehyde, and it reacts to MDMA and MDA."

He shaved off bits of a pill with a razor blade, centered the shavings on a white plate, then added the liquid. I asked, "How did you know that other pill was an amphetamine?"

"I've tested so many of these, I can recognize some of the other colors. It gets purplish with opiates and sort of brownish purplish with Ecstasy, sort of orangelike with amphetamines." He shone a bright halogen flashlight onto the plate. "See this brownish tinge? This is E."

I looked at the small puddle and nodded, though I wasn't quite sure. Doc shivered and put on a sweatshirt. The line was growing shorter, and I asked him what he knew about BE.

"It's usually pretty clean. I think once I saw a few fakes, some with nothing in them—probably just aspirin—but usually when you see that stamp it's Ecstasy."

A skinny teenage girl with sunken cheeks and wearing a tassled ski cap moved behind the table. "Hey Doc. Got any extras for me?"

"No, Betty. I told you I can't do that." Doc smiled sadly.

"Nothing?" she said, her hands shaking. "You're just gonna throw it away, anyway?"

Doc shook his head. "The discards are garbage for a reason." He met my eyes and frowned. To Betty he held out a card and said, "Here's the address of a treatment center. Will you please check it out? I'll go with you if you want."

Betty pouted, which made her seem as young as Nora. I couldn't understand how her parents had let her stay out this late. Then I realized I was doing it again—I automatically allied myself with her parents. This startled me. Doc said to her, "Will you at least call me if you need help?"

Betty then stuck up her middle finger at Doc and ran off.

Doc sighed and tested another pill. He paused, then looked up. He motioned to me, pointing to the plate and mouthing the letters "B.E."

I nodded and moved away from the table, checking the customer: a teenaged boy with a leather jacket, his hair slicked back. I watched Doc tell something to the boy, handing him a pamphlet, which the boy refused. The boy took the pill, popped it into his mouth, and headed back to the bonfire. I caught up with him and said, "Got a sec?"

The boy stopped, looked me up and down. "Yeah?"

"Was that BE?"

"Huh?"

"The tablet stamped B-E?"

He looked surprised. "How'd you know that?"

"Where'd you get it? I like that brand."

"By the chill spot. There's a guy with a winter coat on."

"The what spot?"

The boy stared at me. "The chill spot. Where you rest. It's by those rocks." He pointed to the other side of the clearing, away from the front stage. I saw the rocks and turned to thank the kid, but he was already moving toward the bonfire.

I searched for Serena by the fire, but there were too many people now. The flames sent distorted shadows across faces and bodies, the heavy beat shaking the ground. I moved around the clearing toward the chill spot, which was less crowded, and saw that behind the rocks a half dozen kids sat talking, a few of them sleeping curled up on the ground on blankets. A few rickety tables with tins of food leaned against the rocks. A sign—Free Ear Plugs!!!!—pointed to a plastic box. Then I saw a man with a ski jacket, the bright yellow and orange colors matching the outfits around him. The man was about to make a sale, as two girls approached him and talked for a minute. Then the man pulled out a bag from an inside pocket and handed them one pill each. One of the girls gave him some cash. They left.

I walked up to the man and said, "Is it BE?"

The man smiled. "A connoisseur. You bet your ass it's BE and it's the best of the best." The man, gaunt with red-rimmed eyes, bopped his head to the beat and said, "Interested?"

"How do I know it's real?"

"Stamped and certified. You take it to the testing booth. If it's not pure, you come back here and I refund your money."

"How much?"

"Thirty."

"Per pill? That's expensive, isn't it?"

"It's guaranteed, like I said."

"Whatever happened to Hector? I used to buy from him."

The man froze. "Who?"

"Hector Gama? You know him?"

"No, man. Hey, you want some or not?"

"You never met Hector? He dealt a lot—"

"Hey! Papa-san! Lay off all right? I don't know what you're talking about."

I kept still. Papa-san? I was getting sick of this. I remembered Mack being called jungle bunny and wasn't sure why people always resorted to race for a quick comeback. I stared hard at this man, who became more antsy, his eyes shifting, and I saw he was young, barely in his twenties. I thought, What would Mack do? Would he take this shit?

I grabbed the man's jacket and threw him against one of the large rocks. He stumbled back and yelped, "What the fuck!"

Leaning over him I clutched his throat and squeezed. "You know what?" I said calmly. "I don't like being called 'Papa-san,' especially by some piece of shit."

"Yo, asshole—"

I pulled the man up, then slammed him back down against the rock.

"Ah, fuck! What the hell's your problem?"

"Are you working for Lowell Bangs?"

The man reached inside his jacket, and I quickly stopped his hand, grabbing the wrist as he struggled. I tightened my other grip on his throat and yanked his hand from his jacket. He had a small lock-blade knife still closed, and I said, "You have got to be kidding me."

"Go fuck yourself."

I pulled the man's knife hand up and dragged his entire body off the rock. While still holding his neck I threw my knee up into his midsection, connecting deeply, and the man tried to double over, but I held his neck. The man started gagging. I loosened my grip and asked again, "Do you work for Lowell Bangs?"

"No, man. Not directly. Fucking shit. Why'd you do that?" He kept coughing.

"Who do you get your supply from?"

"Not from Bangs. I'm no one, man. I buy from another dealer—"

"Who?"

"I can't tell you, or they'll fuck me over—"

I tightened my grip on his throat and said, "A name."

"Ah, fuck! I don't even know her name! I just meet her every couple of weeks and I buy off her!"

"A woman?"

"Yeah. I don't know nothing. I just do these big raves. That's all!"

"Where do you meet? Who is this woman?"

"I told you I don't know! I just beep her and we meet. I buy more BE off her."

"Give me the number."

"I can't do that, man. They'll mess me up if I—"

"Drop your knife."

He did.

I stepped on the knife and said, "What's the number?"

"I can't tell you—"

"You think I'm joking? You think I'm doing this for fun? Give me the number or I end your career here and now."

"It's in my wallet, but—"

I spun and shoved his body against the rock, letting go of his wrist and pulling out his wallet. I moved away and checked his driver's license. Thomas Corman. I searched through the billfold, ignoring the thick wad of cash, and found a worn and folded piece of paper with initials and phone numbers. One number had "page" next to it, and I said, "Page?"

Thomas rubbed his neck and watched me with his lip curled. He said, "Asshole," and jumped at me, swinging his fist. I blocked it easily and stepped in with a quick backfist strike to his nose. He staggered back, holding his face, blood seeping through his fingers. He cursed and said, "Give me back my fucking wallet!"

I took the piece of paper with the numbers and checked the license again, memorizing the L.A. address on Pico. I threw him the wallet and said, "I'm keeping the knife. Thanks for your help."

"This isn't over, asshole," he said, turning and walking away, still holding his nose.

A few people from the chill spot were watching. I glanced back toward the fire and saw Serena standing by the clearing, staring at me. She tilted her head, a puzzled expression on her face. I shrugged my shoulders. She wagged her finger in a disapproving gesture. I shrugged again. She turned her hand and crooked her finger, beckoning me. She made a dancing motion with her hips. I picked up the knife, pocketed it with the phone numbers, and walked to her.

Gracie met us at the door. She nosed my hand as I followed Serena into the house, staggering on wobbly legs. "She knows me now," I said as Gracie trotted next to me.

"She likes you. Want some water?"

I said I did, and we sat at the kitchen table, gulping glasses of tap water. It was five in the morning, but I felt alert. We had danced near the bonfire the entire time, the heat of the flames keeping us warm, and it had been Serena who suggested we leave. She had to be at work in less than four hours. Neither of us had taken any of her E, and yet I had achieved a similar sense of envelopment in the music, a sense of everything disappearing except for the heat on my face and the pulsing in my chest. I felt better than I did earlier tonight. I was no longer angry, and I looked around with a sense of serenity. The kitchen had old yellow wallpaper with grease stains near the stove. I asked her if she owned this house.

"What? Are you kidding? No. I'm renting. Someday, though."

"It's expensive in the Bay Area."

"That's okay. I'm going to be rich."

I saw that she was serious, and said, "Good for you."

"You don't believe me."

"I do."

"You had fun tonight," she said.

"I did. I liked the bonfire."

"You can see why I used to like it a lot, why Hector liked it."

"I think so. But I was the oldest guy there."

"Probably."

"Some of those kids taking E were really young."

"I know."

"It can't be good for them."

"Probably isn't." She had a tired smile, and said, "The novelty wears off, though."

"Did it for you?"

"Yeah. I'm doing this because of you."

I hesitated at the change in her tone. I said, "Thank you."

"What happened tonight, with that guy?" she asked.

"I don't know. I got mad. I was tired of hitting dead ends."

"I was surprised. You normally seem so . . . steady."

"Steady? Boring?"

"No. Steady. I like that."

I thought I knew where this might be heading and wanted to tell her about Linda, how nothing was quite resolved yet. I started to speak, but she held up her finger. She put her glass of water down slowly and leaned toward me. "We don't have to talk anymore."

My heart let off an erratic thump. Should I even be here? I heard Gracie clicking across the floor. Serena stood up and held out her hand. I clasped it, and she led me down the dark hallway toward the bathroom. At the door she stopped and turned. I couldn't see her expression, but as she moved closer to me, I felt her hand tighten around mine. I heard our breathing in rhythm. I missed having someone close to me, and I put my hand on her waist, drawing her against me. When we kissed, her other hand went up to my neck and touched me lightly, her fingers warm. Then, a pang of conscience caused me to draw back. I said, "I'm not sure . . ."

She whispered in my ear, "Okay. I'm going to take a shower. You do what you want to do."

With this, she touched my neck again, letting her fingertips drag down over my shirt, lingering for a moment before she walked into the bathroom. I felt myself wanting to follow her in but stopped at the doorway. I heard her taking off her clothes—unzipping, unbuttoning, the swish of cloth onto the floor—and withdrew. I knew that I wasn't thinking clearly, that if I moved purely on desire I'd regret it later. Serena ran the shower, but she still didn't turn on the lights. I listened to her pull back the shower curtain and climb in. The image of her standing there naked, accepting me if I wanted to join her, excited me. I closed my eyes and wavered.

Gracie sat by the bathroom door. I knelt down and petted her, whispering, "What should I do?"

She lay her head down on her paws and didn't reply.

I called a cab and left a note for Serena, telling her that we both had a lot to do in the morning and that I wanted to see her this weekend. I was waiting on the front steps when the cab finally arrived, though I had heard movement in the house that meant Serena had finished her shower and had read my note. I waited for her to come out to check on me, but she didn't. Instead a light went on in the bedroom for a few minutes, then went off.

By the time I reached the condo in Marina Alta, it was almost 6:00 A.M., and I planned on sleeping for a few hours before following up the pager number I had taken from the dealer. But when I let myself into the condo, all the lights were blazing, and I stepped back in surprise. Luke was on the couch, but sprang up at the sight of me. Marianne was pacing.

"Is she with you?" Marianne asked.

I stopped. "Linda?"

"She hasn't been back all night," Luke said. "We were getting worried."

"Where'd she go?"

"Don't you know?" Marianne said, her voice rising. "Where were you?"

"I was finding out more about Hector," I answered. "Where did Linda go?"

Luke and Marianne turned to one another, confused. Marianne said, "She told us she was meeting you!"

I shook my head. "When did she leave?"

"Around nine o'clock."

"She took the car?"

"Yes," Luke said.

"Did anything happen before she left? Did she say anything?"

"During dinner," Luke said. "She argued with her mother."

I turned to Marianne, who said, "It's just that she wanted to stir everything up! I couldn't stand listening to it anymore."

"So she said she was going with me?" I asked.

"That's what she said."

I remembered Linda had mentioned her plans to visit Raul again, and asked, "Did she mention going to Raul's?"

"What?" Marianne cried. "Why would she do that?"

To Luke I said, "Can I borrow a car?"

"Take my company car."

"Oh, God. It's happening again!" Marianne said.

"No, no. It could be anything. She could be with Julie. Have you called Julie?"

Luke said, "Not yet. We just realized that Linda hadn't come home."

"How?"

"The sofa bed wasn't slept in. The car's still gone."

"Call Julie first and check." I hurried to the office and checked Linda's belongings. No purse. Her planner was missing, so she was going to take notes. The sofa bed was neatly made. I tried not to scare myself. I didn't want to consider the possibilities, but I did know this—while I was out with Serena, Linda could have been in trouble. I cursed. My limbs were sluggish, not responding well as I quickly washed up, trying to get more alert. I told myself that she was probably sick of staying with her parents and went to sleep over at Julie's hotel. Maybe she was watching Raul's house and fell asleep in the car.

Marianne met me in the living room and said with barely controlled panic, "She never went to the hotel! Julie hasn't seen her since last night's dinner!"

I nodded and felt a coldness in the back of my head. I couldn't help wondering if this was somehow my fault.

Although I didn't remember the precise address, I knew how to get to Raul's, and drove quickly on the freeway as the cold morning light began filtering through the sky. There was already traffic, and I wove dangerously around slower cars, imagining the worst possible scenarios. I suddenly remembered the gun Luke had given me and regretted not buying bullets and not bringing it with me. I tried to think of reasonable explanations for Linda's absence. Maybe she met with Raul but this time their conversation had gone well; they had stayed up all night talking. That was possible. Linda was in a better frame of mind. Maybe Linda had met an old friend in Laguna. Maybe she wanted some time alone, away from her parents, and checked into a motel. Maybe she was sleeping at this very moment in some bed and breakfast near the beach.

Yet somehow I knew this wasn't the case. Something didn't feel right. She wouldn't just disappear without calling. At the very least she would've let Julie know where she was. And why had she told her parents she was meeting me? Because she had just fought with Marianne and hadn't wanted to admit to seeing Raul again. Unless she was actually planning to meet me? No. Not possible.

Random, bizarre thoughts popped into my head. Maybe she went to Serena's and saw us?

I entered downtown Laguna Beach, and searched for the street to turn up into the hills. It was quiet, too early for tourists. I saw a familiar restaurant and made the turn, revving the engine and searching for Second Street. I recognized Raul's street and sped toward his house. When I saw Luke's big sedan, the one Linda had driven, I pulled into Raul's driveway. I hurried to the front door and knocked. No answer. I rang the doorbell and knocked again. Still no answer. I looked through the front curtained window but couldn't see much.

Circling the house, I found a slate patio and approached the back sliding glass doors. I knocked and yelled, "Mr. Gama? You in there? Is Linda there? Mr. Gama?"

I checked the handle and found it unlocked. I called for Mr. Gama and slid the door open. There was a stillness to the kitchen that scared me. The orange dawn shone in from a side window, bouncing off the counters. I smelled something odd. I walked in, calling out Mr. Gama's name again and realized the smell was urine. A cat? A puppy? When I moved around the center counter, I stopped. Raul was lying on the ground, his arms awkwardly bent over his chest. A puddle of black liquid was beside his torso. As my eyes adjusted to shadows, I saw it was blood. A kitchen knife lay on the ground. Raul's glasses were crooked.

I ran past him and called out Linda's name as I looked frantically around the dining room, then a hallway, and then, in the living room I stopped. Linda was on the floor. I jumped to her, checking for a pulse, found one, then put my ear to her mouth, listening for her breathing. It was faint, but I heard and felt the warm air. I patted her cheek, trying to wake her. I yelled her name and looked for a wound of some kind, but then I was afraid to move her. I gently pulled up her eyelids and checked her eyes. Her pupils looked strange, not quite matching in size. I ran to the telephone to call for help.

PART III

THE BLOCK
IN A VOID

Nineteen

t was a foreign language of pain. Medical terms were thrown at us with dizzying speed and alacrity, the doctor's melodic voice counterpointing the starkness of the hospital and the chill of the clinical Latinate descriptions. Julie scribbled notes; intending to research all of this on the Internet; she asked for clarifications and spellings. She stopped the doctor and wanted the layman's terms as well as the proper medical definitions. She refused to let her sister drown in nomenclature.

Cerebral edema: increased brain water content. Swelling of the brain. Linda had fallen into a progressive coma from the intracranial pressure. She had suffered a blow behind her ear, and this had caused bruising and pressure under her skull, endangering her brain. The worst case, the doctor explained as Julie wrote furiously, was cerebellar herniation, in which the brain is actually displaced. The brain shifts and becomes damaged.

Displaced. Shifted. Moved. Removement. We are displaced from the center and search to return.

The memory of her mismatched pupils shook me. I thought again of Paul and his bloodied eye and wondered if this was my curse, to witness the hurt of those close to me through their eyes.

The doctor asked Julie about the previous injury to Linda's forehead, and when she explained the car accident and concussion, the doctor told her that the brain could handle only so much abuse. The swelling, he said, was a protective measure to help cushion the brain, but at the same time this could damage it. I thought, The body helps itself to death.

The doctor described their course of action: corticosteroids to help ease the swelling in Linda's head. They had more drugs on hand—diuretics to drain the excess fluids—but they wanted to wait before doing anything more. They could also try an experimental shunting procedure, but they were reluctant.

"We never like going inside if we don't absolutely have to," he explained.

Inside. Inside the head? I visibly snapped to attention and everyone turned to me. The doctor told us they would monitor Linda closely and hoped the drugs worked. But the risks were clear. If the swelling continued, they might have to operate. Linda could suffer debilitating and permanent neurological damage. The part controlling her breathing could be affected. She could need a respirator for life. She could fall into a permanent vegetative state. She could go into cardiac arrest. Her brain could shut down one or two vital organs.

I thought, There are too many ways to die.

Marianne kept rubbing her hands and squinting at the doctor; a sheen of sweat covered her brow. Luke was pale and rigid. Julie cried, took more notes.

At Raul's house, after calling the police and an ambulance, I had been afraid to move Linda, worrying about spinal and brain injuries, but checked her for wounds. Blood caked on her scalp, near her ear. I was terrified, but somehow, after the initial shock, I began thinking very clearly. I saw the kitchen knife next to Raul, then quickly ran through scenarios, trying to determine what had happened. My first thought was that they fought, Linda stabbed him, Raul struck her with an object that I couldn't locate, and they both went down. But I knew that she would never do that. Would she? I remembered her anger, and even her words, *If he did anything to Hector, I'll kill him.* No. I knew her too well; she had a temper but she would never. . . . And then I looked at the kitchen knife again and worried that her prints might be on it.

The scenario that made more sense to me was that Linda had arrived at the wrong time, with Lowell Bangs there. He had made threatening phone calls. He wanted to collect Hector's debts. Bangs had killed Raul, and Linda had walked in. Bangs had hit her and run. And yet I stared at the knife, then looked at Linda. I saw Raul's blood on the blade and handle of the knife and then calmly checked Linda's hands, looking for blood. There was none, but I still debated whether or not I should tamper with evidence. It came down to this: Did I believe Linda had anything to do with this? I decided she didn't. I left the knife alone.

When the police and paramedics arrived, Investigator Frank Vines from the Orange County Sheriff's Homicide detail commanded the scene. He and a number of other investigators and officers cordoned off the house and quickly began looking for evidence and witnesses in the area. Flashing police lights drew a large early-morning crowd. Vines questioned me at length, but I had trouble forming coherent answers. I spoke in fragments, non sequiturs; I just wanted to follow the ambulance to the hospital. I told him what I had found, that I hadn't touched anything except the phone, and checking Linda, and blurted out that Lowell Bangs probably had done this. Vines, an unusually tall man with a gaunt face and receding hairline, tried to be patient with me. He waited until I made my accusations, then asked me if I needed to lie down. He wanted to bring me to the police station. I insisted on going first to the hospital. He said he would tie up the scene, leave his partner here, and drive me to the hospital. He would question me there.

After the doctor briefed the family and me on Linda's condition, Vines took me to a private room and used a tape recorder to take my statement. But when I tried telling him about Bangs, everything came out garbled. I kept backtracking, then leaping forward. There was too much to keep straight.

"Please, Mr. Choice," he said calmly, rubbing his forehead with oversize hands. "How about you begin with why you flew down here?" He checked his notes.

I nodded. Yes. Yes. That made sense. As I told him about Hector's death and Linda's search into the details, he wrote this down, the pad and pen looking strangely small in his grip, and he urged me to continue. He double-checked the tape recorder. I told him about Hector's drug dealing and the connections to Lowell Bangs, which in turn connected to Raul Gama. I said, "After Hector died, Bangs probably turned to Raul Gama and killed him, too."

Vines revealed no expression, and asked, "Did you tell the L.A. Sheriff about Hector Gama's possible dealing?"

"We did. We told a Detective Harrison after the car accident. He thought it was road rage. He haven't heard from him since then."

"Tell me again why Ms. Maldonado visited Raul Gama."

"The first time it was to talk about Hector—"

"And you went with her?"

"Yes. The second time was last night, and she went alone—"

"Where were you again?"

"I told you. I was with Serena Yew. We went to a rave. When I got back Linda still hadn't come home, and so I went looking for her."

"And you're certain you didn't disturb the crime scene, didn't take anything?"

"I tried to help Linda and I called the police, that's it," I said, unable to erase the image of her lying on the floor. She had been on her side, one arm extended under her head, the other arm limp over her chest. Her hair had covered her face. When I examined her, checking her breathing, her pulse, a spot of blood rubbed off on my hands from her scalp. Everything in me had grown eerie and still.

"You didn't see anyone?" Vines asked. "A car driving away? Another person in the vicinity?"

"No."

"You saw the knife, but not another weapon on the floor? A stick of some kind?"

"No."

"How would you describe their relationship?"

"Whose?"

"Ms. Maldonado and her father."

"They didn't really know each other. This is the first time she's seen him in years."

"Were they friendly?"

I hesitated. "Not really."

He tilted his head. "Unfriendly?"

"No. Cautious."

"How so?"

I said, "Look, you have to find Lowell Bangs. Every minute you're here you're wasting—"

"Mr. Choice, we're doing everything we can. My partner will be working with our Narcotics Division. Did Ms. Maldonado and Mr. Gama have some kind of fight?"

I knew then that Linda was a suspect. And the fact that I had found them and was Linda's boyfriend might put me under suspicion as well. I said, "They were wary. Raul had abandoned the family, after all."

"Did either of them make any threats?"

"No."

He continued writing and said, "Are you certain?"

"Yes."

"Do you have Serena Yew's number? We'd like to talk to her as well."

"She's not involved in this."

"Yes, but if you don't mind we'd like to cover all the bases."

I gave him Serena's phone number. Slowly, I organized my thoughts and tried to anticipate what would happen next. They would analyze the crime scene evidence, then begin looking into motive. I said, "Check his phone records. He said he got threatening phone calls from someone who might have been Lowell Bangs."

"That's useful. Thank you," Vines said, writing this. "Did he say exactly who it was, and when they called? Did he report it?"

"He didn't, but it must have been recently. All Raul said was that this guy wanted money that Hector apparently owed."

"He told you this?"

"The first meeting. He told Linda and me."

"Why did she visit him again?"

I said, "To find out more. She had a lot of questions about why he left the family, that kind of thing."

He finished jotting this down and turned off the tape recorder. He said, "Can you come to the Aliso Viejo station for a little while?"

"Right now?" I asked. "I'd like to stay with Linda."

"It'll be just for a couple hours. We want to type this statement up for you to sign, and we want to get some evidence off you."

"Off me? Why?"

"You've contaminated the scene. We need your fingerprint, hair, blood, and clothing samples to separate you from the real suspect."

I agreed to go with him.

"The press already has wind of this. Don't talk to them. Refer them to me."

"It was Lowell Bangs," I said. "You have to find him."

"We'll do everything we can, Mr. Choice. I'll meet you out front." I told him I'd be right there and went back to the main waiting room, where I saw another doctor talking to the family. As I approached, Marianne turned to me with such a look of despair that I stopped and almost tripped over my own feet. Her eyes barely registered me, and then she turned back to the doctor. He was speaking to Julie. I joined them. He was saying that to measure the intracranial pressure more precisely, they had one of three options: an intraventrical catheter, which was a tube near the brain; an epidural sensor, a device placed right underneath the skull; or a subarachnoid bolt, which was essentially a bolt screwed into the skull. Julie wrote down these terms. The doctor waited, then she told him to continue. The most accurate measurements came from the catheter, he said, but it took too much time. They wanted readings quickly. So they were going with the bolt. "We have some of the best neurologists next door. It's a standard procedure."

"A bolt?" Julie said. "You're putting a bolt in my sister's head?"

I couldn't listen to this. I spun abruptly and walked down the hall, knowing that they were all watching me. I left the hospital and looked for Vines, startled to find it sunny and hot outside.

After I gave my samples and signed a preliminary statement that Vines had quickly typed, a deputy drove me back to the hospital, and I was able to visit Linda in the ICU. What had shocked me the most was that the doctors had shaved her hair. She had tubes running from her nose and an IV in her arm, wires running from patches on her torso and temple. An EKG and another machine stood beside her. A plastic cap had been fitted over her head, but I saw her bare scalp around it, and some kind of tube ran out from underneath the cap. Her skin at the hairline was white. Her face was puffy, shiny. I couldn't process this; it didn't seem like Linda, but some wax mannequin with a faint likeness. I wanted to touch her hand but was afraid to disturb any of the machines.

I stared at her pale scalp lines and remembered a story she had told me while we were in bed and I was stroking her hair. Marianne had once shaved Linda's head as a child because she believed the hair would grow in thicker and curlier. Linda wasn't sure if this was true, but she did have the thickest and curliest hair of her family. I joked that we should shave it again to test the theory, and she told me she had actually thought about cutting her hair really short. "Long hair is a pain to take care of," she had said. "I was thinking about one of those butch crew cuts." I was about to protest, but then realized that my objection wasn't to how she would look, but to the fact that I wouldn't be able to do this anymore. My stroking and playing with her curls soothed her, and I knew it wouldn't work with short hair. I wanted to be wanted. I clung to what few links we had.

Someone walked up behind me, and I turned. It was Luke, and he looked down at his daughter with exhaustion. Deep, dark bags hung under his bloodshot eyes. He whispered to me, "How did . . . how did this happen?"

"I'm not sure. I think she could've come in on that drug dealer—"

"But she said she was with you. Where were you?"

"I was working another end. She said that not to worry you."

Luke squeezed his eyes shut, and touched his forehead with his shaking fingers. "I don't know what to do."

"I'm really sorry. I should've been there. I didn't think she'd go without me." I realized that they were all trying not to blame me. I had been invited down here to help and this was what happened. Seeing Luke grope for more words unnerved me. I said, "I promise I'll find who did this."

Luke nodded, not really registering me. I waited for his anger, his disappointment, for some recognition of my failure, and braced myself. Yet nothing came. He stared at Linda and shook his head. Then I realized how petty I was, thinking of my own guilt rather than of Linda, and I felt even worse.

Julie drove me to the condo a few hours later. The doctors had been constantly checking on Linda, testing her reflexes, monitoring her breathing; she wasn't allowed any more visitors until tomorrow afternoon. Julie wanted to bring

Linda's nightgown and buy dinner for the family, who were all still at the hospital.

It had grown dark out. I had lost my sense of time. Had the entire day passed? With no sleep and a tight, tense feeling in me all day, I found myself looking at the world through a gray fog. Colors were muted. Shadows accentuated. Dark fuzzy halos encircled lightbulbs. I stared at the oncoming traffic, the headlights pulsing. I said to Julie, "Tell me what happened last night after I left. Marianne told me a little."

My voice had made her jump. She said, "They fought."

"With Nora there?"

"Nora went to watch TV."

"What did they fight about?"

Julie sighed. Headlights from traffic across the street glided over her pale face. "Linda wanted to know about the abuse charge."

"And Marianne didn't want to talk about it."

"She didn't, but you know Linda."

I turned to her. "I *do* know her."

Julie looked confused, but continued: "Marianne admitted it. She said she did threaten to bring the police in."

"For child abuse?"

"Yes."

"For sexual abuse?"

"Yes."

"Was it true?"

"That's what Linda wanted to know."

"And what did Marianne say?"

"She said that she had no proof, but she was almost certain of it. She said the fact that Raul went running was proof enough."

"But didn't Marianne ask Hector about it?"

"She did. He denied it, but she didn't believe him."

"So no one really knows?"

"She says she does."

I couldn't wrap my thoughts around this. A kernel of anger grew within me, but I had nowhere to direct it. I said, "Linda was mad because she never knew."

"Because she never knew, but also because she felt lied to."

I asked slowly, "What about Linda herself? Was she in any way—"

Julie said, "What?"

"Did Raul do anything to her?"

Julie remained quiet for a long time, then said, "I don't know."

"Did you ask her—"

"Jesus, you're pushy."

My limbs felt tired, heavy. Nothing made sense to me. I heard the car engine roaring as Julie sped up. I said, "I'm just trying to find out what happened."

She said, "I didn't ask her anything."

"I did, and she said no."

"You asked her?"

"Yes. She said no."

"And did you believe her?" Julie asked.

I hesitated. "What do you think?"

"I don't know what to think."

I asked, "What do you guess?"

She said, "I don't want to guess."

"But can you think back and—"

"Stop. Just stop. I don't want to talk about it."

"No one wants to talk about anything," I said, more to myself than to Julie.

"Don't you know one of the signs?"

"What signs?"

"The signs of abuse. One of the signs is an eating disorder."

It took me a moment to connect this to Linda's weight problems as a child. I sunk into my seat. "But that doesn't mean . . ." I trailed off.

She turned to me quickly, snapping, "Why are you here, Allen? Why don't you go home?"

"I'm here because of Linda," I said.

"Well, a lot of good you've been," she said.

I kept still.

She said, "Sorry. I didn't mean it like that."

I thought, Yes you did.

"By the way," she said. "Nora and I are going to stay at the condo. My parents need me with them."

I turned to her, not sure why she was telling me this, then understood. The condo would be crowded. I imagined hostility or blame wherever I turned. I said, "I can find a motel, give you guys space."

"They want you to stay," she replied.

They wanted me to stay, but not her. I knew then that the family had discussed me at the hospital. But I knew I couldn't remain at the condo without Linda there. "No, I'll go. I'll find a motel close to the hospital," I said. "I should be nearby, anyway."

"If you want."

I said, "You know I'd do anything for her. I . . . I'll watch out for her."

"Even though you guys are breaking up?"

I turned to her. "We are?"

"Aren't you?"

"Did she say that?"

Julie said, "Never mind. Just help her."

"I will."

She was quiet for a moment, then let out a sharp *tsk*, saying, "Why is it that whenever I see you, things are all screwed up? Why is that giant police officer asking me questions about Linda? Is she a suspect? What the hell is going on?"

"I'm going to help Linda," I said, my voice unsteady. My vision was blurring. "I'm not leaving her like this."

"Then *do* something," she said, her voice edged. She stared at the road. "Find out who did this and *do* something, goddammit."

Twenty

After Julie dropped me off outside the condo and went to buy dinner for the family, I quickly packed my things, wanting to get out before she returned for Linda's clothes. I remembered the photo of Linda as a teen and shook it out of the crossword puzzle book, slipping it into my PI textbook. I also packed Luke's Smith & Wesson. I left the door key on the dining room table and took a cab to a cheap motel off the 405, near the John Wayne Airport, close to Linda's hospital. I paid for both the cab and the motel room with my credit card. My expenses were rising. I thought about Larry wanting me back up north, but there was no way I could return home yet.

Do something.

In my motel room I thought about buying ammunition for the gun, but needed to break it down and clean it first. I needed a shower. I needed to sleep. The silence around me was unnerving after the day filled with hospital sounds. I turned on the TV and watched the six o'clock news. I heard the anchor talk about a late-breaking story, "a gruesome murder in sleepy Laguna Beach," and I turned up the volume. The correspondent didn't have much to report, except the initial findings of Raul Gama's death and an unidentified woman in a coma. The screen cut back to the anchors, and the woman said, "The murderer might still be at large, and the Orange County Sheriff's Department will be holding a news conference tomorrow morning. Residents of the Laguna area are advised to report any suspicious people or activities immediately."

I searched for more local news on other channels. There was another report, but this was from the hospital, the reporter stationed right in front of the main entrance. The young man was saying to the camera, ". . . believed to be the victim's daughter, Linda Maldonado. It's unclear the extent of her injuries and if she's a suspect or also a victim of this vicious attack. We have unconfirmed reports that the victim and Ms. Maldonado were estranged, but we'll have more tomorrow after the news conference, which we'll bring to you live."

Startled by the speed and speculation of the reports, I turned the TV off. An odd paralysis overtook me. I found myself unable to move from the bed and listened to traffic sounds drifting across the motel parking lot. Linda had been lying in a coma while I had been dancing in the desert, while I had been kissing Serena. The memory of Serena goaded me off the bed and toward the telephone. I had to let Serena know that the police would be contacting her. She wasn't in, but I left a long, rambling message on her machine, telling her what had happened and where I was, then hung up.

I lay still and could feel the ache over my ear where Linda had been struck, and I hated this sense of helplessness. She had always come to my aid. She had helped me find out what had happened to my father. She had encouraged me to take on better jobs. She had made me stronger.

Do something, goddammit.

I remembered the time she was worried about my job at Black Diamond and came home with printouts of local high-tech firms that could use executive protection. She had spent hours searching databases to help me find leads for potential customers. I listened to her pitch as she explained how she had culled this data, and I was stunned that she had done this for me. I was even a little guilty that she had worked harder than I had in finding these contacts. I thanked her, but she shrugged it off. "I just want to help," she had said. No matter how often we fought, or how angry I would become with her later, I'd remember that look on her face as she came through the door, holding up the papers. Her cheeks were flushed, her eyes tired from staring at the computer screen. Tired, but excited. She smiled and waved the papers at me, saying, "Guess what I got!" She was happy to be helping me, and I was amazed.

Whenever I closed my eyes I saw Linda's white scalp, tubes and wires attached all over her. I saw no meaning behind this. She didn't deserve this.

I had a strange thought. My philosophy of removement was a desperate attempt to order a chaotic and illogical world. The truth was that there was no order or logic to anything. There was no rational reason for Linda to be hurt so seriously. There was no reason why she might die like this, so brutally. That I would attempt to structure my world was foolish, laughable. It was building scaffolding on quicksand. The sooner I accepted this, the better off I'd be. The dis-ease is a way of life. Engagement is never found. We are alone. We are helpless.

I thought, You must accept loss forever.

"I will," I said aloud.

I realized I was in a strange motel, in a strange town, with strangers all around me, and I was trying to be a detective without a license, without any idea of what I was doing. Give me an executive to protect, give me a threat assessment to analyze, give me a partner to watch my back, and I know what to do. But this . . . What the hell was this?

I fell asleep.

The shrieking telephone pulled me out of a nightmare, and I bolted upright in my bed in a sweat, my clothes damp and hot. The phone continued its shrill cry—the volume had been set on high—and I scrambled to the side table, checking the clock. Almost 9:00 A.M. I answered the phone and Vines recognized my voice. "Mr. Choice, you should tell us if you move. We had some trouble finding you again."

"I couldn't stay at the condo anymore. I'm at a motel."

"Yes, well, we learned that through Ms. Yew. I wanted to ask you a few follow-up questions based on some new information we've been gathering."

I waited. "Yes?"

"You mentioned that first meeting with Raul Gama. In your statement you said that they talked about Hector, but then once they started talking about why Mr. Gama left, they became, in your words, 'wary.'"

I didn't like the sound of this. "Yes," I said.

"Did they actually argue? Did either of them make any threats?"

"No threats. Linda didn't like Raul's version of the past, but no one made any threats."

"Are you certain about that?"

I said, "What's this about?"

"So would you characterize the exchange as a fight?"

"They disagreed."

"Raul never yelled at both of you?"

I hesitated.

"Mr. Choice, I realize Ms. Maldonado is your girlfriend, but you're not helping the case by lying to us—"

"Whoa, whoa. I'm not lying." I sat up, shaking myself awake.

"We have a witness who says that Raul was angry, that he yelled something to the effect that he ought to poison you two."

"What? There was no one else there." Had there been another person in the house?

"He didn't order you out of his residence?"

Then I remembered the neighbor and said, "The guy washing his car? He's your witness? He was across the street, over a hundred feet away."

"Would you like to recharacterize your version of the events?"

"No," I said. "The guy misheard it. Raul said that Linda's mother had poisoned her kids against him. He said, 'She poisoned you two,' or something like that. As for ordering us out of the house, we were already leaving."

"You didn't mention this before, Mr. Choice."

"I told you they disagreed about the past."

"But obviously they argued."

"Oh, Christ. Don't tell me you haven't even looked into Lowell Bangs!"

"We are exploring every possible avenue, Mr. Choice. Was Raul Gama alive when you found him?"

"No. I told you that. Why?"

"The coroner determined that death wasn't instantaneous."

I thought about this, then said, "Oh, wait. You're not considering some ridiculous scenario?"

"What scenario would that be?"

"That they fought and she stabbed him, and then—" I stopped.

"Mr. Gama knocked her unconscious before he died. That did cross our minds. Would it be possible for you to come back to the station for a few more questions?"

"What? Again?"

"In light of this new information from the witness, I'd like my partner to interview you again."

"Am I a suspect?"

"No, not at this time. It would help us out if you filled us in with more of the details you left out."

"I didn't leave anything out! That guy across the street misheard it!"

"Can you come by this afternoon? Say four o'clock?"

"Should I bring a lawyer?" I asked.

"As I said, you're not a suspect. This isn't custodial, but of course you're perfectly entitled to legal representation. However, we're just trying to get to the bottom of this."

I said I'd be there and hung up. I realized my hands were shaking. I stood and paced, wondering how I'd find a lawyer down here. I knew better than to go in for another interview without a lawyer, even though I was certain I couldn't be a suspect with my alibi. But Linda was exposed. I wasn't sure about motive, but she definitely had opportunity, and without hard evidence of another suspect, the police would first focus on what they had.

I called Julie's cell phone and reached her at the hospital. I asked her how Linda was doing. She said, "Better. Much better. The pressure went down overnight. The drugs are working, and they don't think they have to operate."

Sitting down and exhaling, I said, "And the coma?"

"She's still unconscious. They don't know how long it'll be."

"But she'll come out eventually, when the pressure is normal, right?"

"I don't know," Julie said.

"What did they say about the prognosis?"

"They can't predict the consequences of this kind of head injury. They mentioned memory loss, confusion. They even talked about possible personality changes."

"What?"

"They just don't know."

"Personality changes?"

"It's the brain, and it depends on which parts get affected."

I suddenly had an image of Linda raving and unstable, and this frightened me. I said, "But that won't happen, will it?"

"I said they don't know."

"Be careful of what you tell the police."

"Why?"

I revealed what Vines had said and how the police seemed to be focusing on Linda.

"Shit, I knew it," Julie said.

"They don't have anything else."

"What about the drug dealer!" she cried.

"I know. Don't worry. I'm going to talk to them again."

"Allen . . ." she warned. "Don't mess this up."

"I said I'll talk to them."

She didn't reply, but her meaning was clear. She then said, "Fine. Keep me posted," and hung up.

I went to take a shower, engrossed in thought. I'd have to find a lawyer, and I wanted to bring something harder to the police. As I considered what evidence I had, I realized why the police hadn't given Bangs much weight. I hadn't presented anything credible. I had a ghost of a suspect, someone who might have run Linda and me off the road, who might have killed Hector. As for Raul's murder, the motive I had put forth was weak. Why would Bangs kill someone he was trying to extort? Wouldn't he threaten and injure, intimidate in any way possible?

No wonder the police were more intent on figuring out Linda's role in this than pursuing Bangs.

After my shower I dressed, going through my pockets, and was startled to find the list of numbers I had taken from Thomas Corman, the BE dealer from the rave. I had dismissed Corman during the turmoil of Linda's injury. I hadn't even mentioned him to Vines for my statement; all he had wanted was confirmation of my alibi, and Corman was just some foot soldier. But maybe this was important. I hurried to the phone, about to call Vines.

I stopped. Could this be used against Linda in some way? I didn't trust Vines. I thought of Julie's warning. I looked down at the numbers. The pager was Corman's BE contact. Vines hadn't even checked on Bangs yet—why would he look into this? I decided to wait until I had something more concrete. I also wanted to get legal advice before the second interview.

With a pocket full of quarters, I walked out of the motel and down the street to the nearest pay phone. I found one at a gas station. I stared at the slip of paper, the smell of gas strong around me. I wasn't sure how to do this.

Cars pulled up at the pumps. I stared at the shiny windshields. The sun illuminated the oil-stained pavement, and I squinted at the glare. I was still very tired, knowing that I could probably use another six or seven hours of sleep, I dropped coins into the phone and called the pager number. At the tone I punched in the pay phone number, then hung up. I waited, looking at the other numbers on the piece of paper. My head throbbed.

Personality change? Did that mean Linda would wake up a completely different person? I couldn't bear to think about this.

The phone rang, and I stepped back with surprise. That was fast. The phone rang again.

I picked it up, and listened.

Silence. Then a woman's voice: "You paged?"

The voice sounded familiar. "Who is this?" I asked.

"You paged me. Who's calling?" she asked.

The voice. The voice. I knew this voice. It had the same high-pitched inflection I had recently heard from somewhere else.

"I need to talk to Lowell Bangs," I said.

"Is this the fuckhead who knocked around Tommy? Who the fuck you think you are?"

Then I recognized the voice: Gloria. I said, "Gloria? Gloria Katz?"

A pause. "Who the hell is this?"

A cold rush surged through me. The BE dealer had Gloria's pager? Gloria supplied BE? *Gloria* was working with Bangs? *Gloria* took over for Hector? I said, "You fucked over Hector, didn't you."

She hung up.

I tried to piece this together, but my thoughts stumbled into each other. There were connections everywhere. I focused on this: Gloria was a BE supplier. At the rave Gloria had acted as if she were afraid for her life and had fled, but she was working with Bangs all along.

Begin at the beginning.

Begin with the premise that Hector had dealt BE for Lowell Bangs. Maybe Hector tried to cheat Bangs, skimming cash, thinking about going solo. Either Gloria told Bangs, or Bangs somehow bribed her to help him. She sold Hector out. Bangs killed Hector, and now Gloria was taking over Hector's role. It was so simple, so clean.

Why hadn't I thought of this before?

But why kill Raul? Whether it was Bangs or Gloria, it didn't make sense, especially if they thought Raul would pay back Hector's debts. Maybe Raul hadn't given in, and even threatened to go to the police.

I didn't know what to do, and my first instinct was to tell this to Linda. And for a split second I almost called her, but then remembered where she was. Something tightened within me. Bangs and Gloria did this. They could have killed her. I needed to find them, and I had to start with Gloria. She would lead me to Bangs.

I dialed Vines's number. I had to let him know this. But someone else picked up. When I asked to speak to Vines, the man on the other end told me he had just gone to give a press conference. Did I want to leave a message? I thought about it, then said I'd call back. I hung up.

Question: How did I find this connection to Gloria in the first place?

Answer: Thomas Corman.

And I knew where he lived. I had checked his driver's license at the rave, and had seen his L.A. address. I stared out over the highway, trying to remember. Corman lived on West Pico Boulevard. I closed my eyes and pictured the license. I saw an eleven as the first two digits—an address in the eleven thousands. The apartment had a *D* in it—3D or 4D. I hurried back to the motel. I needed the Smith & Wesson. First I'd rent a car, then I'd buy ammo, and then I'd find Thomas Corman.

I had a few more questions for him.

No, Mack had a few more questions.

Twenty-one

I **wasn't always** able to show Linda how I felt. Once, when I began spending more time at her place, not quite moving in but sleeping over enough to warrant a toothbrush and razor in her bathroom, I saw her snag her foot on an extension cord and fall painfully into a table. She banged her hip and thigh and thudded onto the carpet. I ran over to her to help, and she cursed through a smile and said she was a klutz. I then checked the extension cord, and immediately unplugged it. I tried to rethread it under the carpet, making sure this wouldn't happen again, and Linda, still on the ground, watched me with some astonishment. Later that evening we had an argument about washing dishes, but it soon came out that she was annoyed at me for another reason. She didn't like that I had attended to the extension cord with more eagerness and care than I had attended to her, and when I tried to explain that I had only wanted to remove the cause of her accident, she said, "If I get hit with a baseball bat, do you check on me or do you destroy the bat?"

Of course she was right. At the time, though, I felt wrongfully accused of something, of apathy or heartlessness, and my first impulse was to defend myself. I began to realize how little I knew about this business of relationships. I was not conversant in this language, and everyone I knew while grow-ing up expressed their affection in this indirect way.

The warmest gesture from my father had been a pat on my head. I still remembered it: I had surprised him by decorating a Christmas tree he had bought and propped up in the corner. My father had a sentimental side that he rarely revealed to me, though I knew Christmas held some meaning for him. I guessed it had something to do with my mother. The box of Christmas decorations stored in the attic was labeled in handwriting that wasn't my father's, and the various sparkling balls and flowers, the kinds of frilly things my father would never have bought on his own, seemed old and worn, and were most likely my mother's. One night while my father worked late and my aunt had left me alone, I stared at the bare pine tree in the corner, only two days before Christmas, and I dug out the box of decorations.

He came home that night and stopped in the hallway. I was watching TV. He stared at the ornaments and tinsel. I hadn't been able to reach the top, and he added the final silver star himself. He stood back and studied the tree with a sadness that I thought I had caused, but then he leaned over me and put his two callused hands on my head. His palms were heavy and warm. He said, "You're a good boy."

I went to sleep happy that night.

The memories hurt me as I drove in search of Thomas Corman. The thought of Linda forced the regrets forward, the inconceivable prospect of her dying eclipsing everything else, and I bounced from anger to fear within seconds. I tried to focus on where I was, heading on West Pico and counting the address numbers, but my mind wouldn't stop leaping ahead and back, anticipating and grieving. I wanted to punish someone.

I drove underneath the 405 overpass, and saw worn-out liquor stores, a few dying mom-and-pop delis, tiny restaurants and bars, a sunlit grunginess that extended as far as I could see. At the eleven-thousand mark, I parked my rental car, a Hyundai, and went on foot. A homeless man with rags as clothing shuffled along the sidewalk, a series of red and blue bandanas tied around his arms. I had been watching the cars around me, suspicious of everything. I thought back to when I found Gloria at the rave. She had seemed terrified, but now I understood that she was reacting to me as an enemy, as someone who had startled her by being too close. Then Bangs had warned Valerie to keep quiet.

The street was busy with traffic, and I stopped when I saw a small apartment building with iron bars on the first-floor windows. I counted three floors, the fire escape scaffolding on the side pocked with rust. On the left side was a carpet store and on the right a video and CD store. The sidewalks were cracked and uneven, grass and weeds sprouting up in the gaps. The loud, chatty voice of a radio DJ blared through one of the barred windows. I looked up and down the street and didn't see any other apartment buildings.

The front entrance was protected with a grill-iron door; an intercom panel next to it had a listing of the residents. Many of the buttons had no names in the slots, and apartment 3D was blank. No fourth floor, so maybe I had seen 3D on Corman's driver's license. I stepped back and looked around. I was hot in my windbreaker, but I needed it to hide the gun in the back of my waistband. Now what? If I didn't feel so pressed for time, with Linda in the hospital and Vines probably working on a case against her, I might've waited. Instead I decided not to follow my instincts. I pressed 3D. After a moment an older woman's voice came on: "Yes?"

"Is Tommy there?"

"He's sleeping."

"Can I come up and wake him?"

"Who's this?"

I said, "It's Mack. We met at a rave the other night."

"He's sleeping. He'll be mad if I wake him."

"I can wake him. Is this Mrs. Corman?"

"Yes it is. I don't know—"

"Tommy told me to come by. I'll take the blame for waking him."

After a pause, the buzzer sounded, and I opened the security door and hurried into the building. I took a deep breath and prepared myself. No more messing around. I needed results, and this guy was my only chance right now. I went down a dark hallway and found the elevator with an Out of Order sign taped to it, so I went up the side stairs to the third floor. The stained carpets lined a narrow hallway, with most of the light fixtures missing bulbs. Apartment 3D was at the far end, and as I approached the door I thought, Be Mack.

I knocked lightly. A tiny gray-haired woman opened the door tentatively, and said, "He's going to be awfully mad you woke him up."

"Mrs. Corman, he told me to come by this morning."

"Well, if he told you," she said, stepping back. Her unsteady hands pulled the door farther open.

When I walked in she pointed to a door down the hall. The apartment smelled musty and old. I moved across the stained orange carpet and tried to open the door, but it was locked. I knocked. No answer. I knocked harder, and I heard a groan. "Oh, man," Corman said.

I knocked again.

"What! What do you want, Ma!"

I turned to Mrs. Corman and put my finger to my lips, smiling, and I knocked again.

"Oh, for chrissake! I told you not to wake me up!"

I heard him getting out of bed and creaking across the floor. He said, "What the hell! It's not even twelve yet!" I put my hand on the doorknob. As soon as he unlocked it, I pushed open the door and stepped in, saying, "Tommy, you told me to come now."

He backed up confused, and I closed the door behind me, pulling out my gun and whispering, "Shhh."

He stiffened and looked wildly around. His hair was greasy and sticking up, sleep lines on his cheek. I said, "Laugh. Say something that'll keep your mother quiet." I raised the gun and aimed it at him.

Corman let out a nervous laugh and said loudly, "No prob, man. You're here."

"Good," I said. "Sit down."

He sat down on the bed with Batman sheets. He was in his underwear and T-shirt, his arms and legs thin. The room smelled of cigarette smoke. He was watching the gun while tapping his fingers on his knee, and said, "You're the asshole from the desert. You're pissing a lot of people off."

"You told Gloria about me."

His head jerked back at the name. I said, "You lied. You knew who she was. She wasn't just some supplier."

"You're a dead man."

I stepped forward and swung the revolver into the side of his head, which sent him sprawling off the bed. He let out a curse and clutched his ear. I said, "Quiet."

"What's your fucking problem, man? What the hell you want from me?"

His mother knocked on the door and said, "Everything all right in there? You want some coffee and doughnuts?"

I aimed the gun at him and whispered, "Tell her to leave us alone."

"It's fine, Ma. We don't need anything."

We waited. I heard her walk away and turn on the TV. Then I said, "How do I find Gloria or Bangs?"

"I told you. I just page her—"

"I've had it. I'm sick of this shit. You tell me what I need to know or else I'll—"

"You'll what? Anything you do can't be worse than what Bangs will do to me. You don't get it. He won't just kill me. He'll fucking chop me up while I'm still alive. So you can go fuck off you piece of shit."

I listened to his mother change channels and turned my head slightly toward the door, not sure if she was returning to check on her son. Corman tensed. He misinterpreted my gesture and shot up. He said, "You touch her I'll fucking—"

"What? You'll do what?" I said, aiming my gun at him. "You little piece of shit." I stepped forward and backhanded him in the face. I said, "Tell me how to find Gloria Katz or Lowell Bangs. Don't make me hurt you or your mother."

He rubbed his ear and stared at the gun.

"I'll ask you one more time. How do I find Gloria Katz?"

He shook his head and sighed. "Fuck, man. I didn't even know her last name was Katz."

"How do you meet her?"

"I page her and she tells me where to go."

"Could you do it now?"

"No, man. She's all pissed off for telling you anything. I told her you got the pager number and she cut me off. She said she and Bangs got to see if they still want me to sell for them."

"How did you start working with them?"

"I started with Hector. I sold for Hector and he got killed and then Gloria took over for him."

"How'd you meet Hector?"

"We kinda already knew each other from the raves."

"He was dealing?"

"Yeah. Him and his friends."

"Gloria."

"Yeah."

"Who else?"

"I don't know them. I hardly knew Hector. I used to buy off him and he just asked if I wanted to sell for him."

"Just like that?"

"He was moving up, I guess."

"Who were some of his friends?"

"I told you, I don't know. It's not like I hung out with them." He sighed. "Could you just leave me alone? I don't want to do this anymore."

The faint whine made him seem much younger. I said, "Tell me how to find Gloria. Where did you usually meet?"

"In Malibu."

Startled, I said, "Luego Canyon?"

"Yeah. Different places, though. Sometimes in Venice or Santa Monica."

"Was she alone?"

"Yeah."

"You don't remember any of their friends? What about Tim and Kate?"

He shook his head.

"Tim Jacobs. A surfer-type with blond hair?"

He perked up. "Yeah, there was a surfer guy, bleached-blond hair."

"He was Hector's friend?"

"Yeah. He and his girlfriend. I didn't know their names, but they sold for Hector, too."

This stopped me. "They sold for Hector? They sold BE?"

"Yeah. When I met them they did. This was before I started. So, maybe they moved up like Hector did." He shrugged. "Maybe they're dead, too."

"The girlfriend was really thin, messed-up hair."

"Yeah, that was her. A lot of freckles on her face."

I thought, Goddamn these people. I shoved the gun into my pants and left the apartment.

Everyone lied. Linda had once told me I assumed the best in people, and that was a mistake. She never trusted anyone she didn't know well, and even then she was always aware of covert motives, minor deceptions. She had said,

"You'll be constantly disappointed. Not me. I get what I expect." I knew it was a smart way to deal with everyone, a way to protect yourself, and yet it saddened me. I couldn't help but wonder if she expected the worst from me, if she always questioned my motives.

As I drove into Venice and parked a block away from Tim and Kate's house, I forced myself not to think about the revelations of abuse. Linda had denied it, and that was good enough for me. I didn't like Julie second-guessing her sister, and was annoyed by her dime-store psychological reading of Linda's childhood obesity. I was getting too much information to process. I no longer knew what to believe about anybody.

I walked slowly to Tim's house; I didn't see any cars in the driveway or out front. What did I know? I knew that Linda was seriously hurt. I knew that Tim had lied to me from the beginning and that he held some answers. An image of Linda flashed before me, and my stomach tightened. *Do something. Do something.*

Instead of heading to the front, I slipped around the side facing the brick apartment building, then circled the house, checking the windows. The back-yard had a small patio with a barbecue grill and rusting lawn chairs. Broken and chipped slate tiles lined the patio, with weeds overtaking the dying lawn. I moved quietly to the wooden back door with small glass panes. Inside was a dining room. I checked the doorknob. Locked.

I pulled out my gun and used the handle to hit the pane of glass near the deadbolt. The glass cracked with the first hit, then tinkled apart on the sec-ond. I waited, listened. I turned and looked around the yard. After a moment, I reached through the opening, unlocked the deadbolt, and turned the door handle. I swung open the door and walked in, my shoes crunching the broken shards. I thought I heard a sound, a floor creak from the living room, and I raised my gun.

I moved quickly down the hall, checking a bedroom and bathroom, then stopped at the living room entrance. I heard another creak. Then a teenager jumped out into the hallway, brandishing a fire iron. "Get the fuck out of here!" he yelled.

He saw my gun and quickly dropped the poker and held up his hands. "Take what you want. I don't live here."

"Who are you?" I asked, motioning with the gun for him to move away from the fire iron. He stepped back, his hands still held up. He couldn't have been more than seventeen or eighteen, peach fuzz on his chin and acne on his forehead. Freckles spotted his cheeks and arms.

"No one. I just crashed here for the night," he said.

"Where's Tim?"

The boy said, "Surfing." Then he added, "Sir."

"Where's Kate? Why are you here?"

"I'm Kate's brother. She went to the grocery. Please don't shoot me, sir."

"When will they be back?"

"I don't know."

"What's your name?"

"Julian, sir."

"I'm going to have to tie you up and gag you while I look around here."

"That's fine, sir. Just don't shoot me."

I guided him to the kitchen, where I found a roll of duct tape. I bound his wrists and ankles to a chair. Before I covered his mouth I asked, "Do you know who Lowell Bangs or Gloria Katz is?"

"No, sir. I just came here from Arizona. I'm crashing here for my vacation."

I taped up his mouth. I asked him if he could breathe. He nodded.

Next to the bathroom was a doorway and a set of stairs. I climbed them slowly, holding my gun poised, and peered up over the railing. It was another bedroom with a large-screen TV and a stereo system against the wall.

Returning to the downstairs bedroom, I searched for anything connecting to Bangs. I turned up dozens of small sandwich bags filled with pills. A few bags were rubber-banded together and I saw that these pills were stamped BE. The other pills were different sizes and colors. I also found a large rectangular block of marijuana wrapped in plastic. Lining the bureau beside the bed were different bongs and pipes. I couldn't find any papers or addresses. Plenty of drugs, though.

Upstairs, I saw more drugs, two eight-millimeter handguns, both Glocks, and a small safe. On a night table lay a laptop computer, and when I opened it, the screen lit up, the hard drive stirring to life. After a moment the screen came into focus and I saw a map of the Malibu coast with a tide timetable. There were a series of numbers, temperatures and wave heights. I tried to exit the program but the screen kept returning to this map.

Then I heard the sound of brakes squealing outside. I looked out the window. A small station wagon pulled into the driveway, a surfboard sticking out of the back. I hurried downstairs and aimed my gun at Julian, putting a finger to my lips. He nodded quickly. I hid in the hallway, waiting. I heard Tim singing as he entered the front door. I took a deep breath. I let my anger focus my thoughts.

Twenty-two

The house shuddered as Tim slammed the front door closed. He yelled out, "Julian? You up yet, you lazy bum?" He held out a dripping black wetsuit, shaking the water over the living room floor, then threw his backpack onto the sofa. Sand sprinkled everywhere. He was in cutoff jeans and a ripped T-shirt, his face red and his hair combed back. The strong fishy smell of the ocean slowly rolled through the house. I watched him from the hallway as he hung his wetsuit on a wall hook and yawned. The phone rang. He reached down to the coffee table and picked up the cordless handset. He said, "What's up?" and listened.

"No shit," he said. "This is getting messed up." He nodded as the caller spoke, then he said, "I don't know where she is. Hold on." He lowered the handset and yelled, "Kate! You here? Kate? Julian?"

He waited, then said into the phone, "No idea. She might be hanging with her brother." He said good-bye and threw the phone onto the sofa.

I stepped out of the hallway, holding the gun up, and approached. Tim turned to me, and stared with a puzzled expression. It took him a full few seconds to realize who I was and he bolted toward the door, but I made it to him before he could open it all the way. I kicked the door closed, then pressed the gun into the back of his neck. "I'm back," I said. He tried to swing around to hit me, but I stepped out of reach and aimed the gun at his face. "Don't do anything stupid."

"Fuck!" he said. "What the hell do you want?"

"You've been lying to me." With the gun still aimed at him, and my other hand balancing me, I gave him a quick roundhouse kick to the head, snapping my foot back and watching him stagger to the floor. He cursed and rubbed his head.

"What the hell you talking about!" he cried.

I kicked him in his ribs, which made him howl, and he tried to crawl away. I kicked him again, and said, "You've been working with Gloria."

"I told you everything, man!"

I brought the gun down hard on the back of his head, and his chin hit the floor. I said, "You've been working with her all along. You started with Hector, and after he was killed you went with Gloria. Both of you screwed Hector over."

"I don't know what the hell you're talking about," he said with less conviction.

"Linda's in the hospital, in a coma. You know that? Bangs did that to her; he killed her father, Hector's father."

"I didn't do anything. Why the fuck are you bothering me?" He tried to slide away.

"How do I find Bangs?" I moved closer to him.

"You've got to be shitting me. What do you think you're going do? Pull a gun on him?" He laughed. "You don't know what the fuck you're doing."

Something clicked off inside me as I thought about Linda in the hospital. I just didn't care anymore if I hurt anyone. They didn't care about Linda, so why should I care about them. I looked down at Tim who was still smiling. I aimed the gun at his sneaker. He stopped smiling and said, "Wait a minute—"

I pulled the trigger; the gun exploded, kicking back, and the floor seemed to shake.

There was a stunned silence as both of us looked down at his foot, and then he howled in pain and screamed, "You fucking shit! What did you do?" I saw blood slowly staining the sneaker. The bullet had gone straight through and was lodged in the wooden floor.

I kicked him in the ribs as hard as I could and he curled up, twisting and moaning while trying to clutch at his sneaker. He cried out for me to stop, and whimpered that he needed a hospital.

"Tell me where Bangs is."

"I'm bleeding!"

I pointed the gun at his knee. "I'm going to ask you one more time. Do you understand that I couldn't care less if you ever walk again? Do you get that? I'm going to blow out your knee. Where is Bangs?"

"He has different places! I swear I've never gone to them!" he cried. "I only meet with Gloria! I swear!"

"She double-crossed Hector?"

"I don't know anything about that." He gritted his teeth and sucked air. "She asked me to help, so I did."

"You fucked over your friend?"

"He was dead! What was I supposed to do? Oh, man, my foot! I got to get to a hospital!"

"Where is Gloria? Where does she live?"

"She used to live in Marina Alta, when Hector was alive. I don't know anymore. I swear to God!"

"Where in Marina Alta?"

"An apartment off Lincoln. Concord Apartments."

"But now?"

"I don't know. I just page her and we meet. Please. Call an ambulance." He was untying his laces slowly, wincing. Blood dripped down the sneaker treads.

"Why did you lie? Why didn't you tell me about Gloria—"

"They're fucking crazy, don't you get it? You see what happened to Hector? Bangs just burned him up. He did it while Hector was still alive. That's just fucked up. I'm helping Gloria out because she asked and because I was afraid to say no." He slowly pulled off his sneaker and moaned. He wasn't wearing socks. I saw that I had shot him in between his first and second toe, the soft tissue now all bloody. "Oh, man," he said, his face crumpling. "Look at it."

He glanced up, something catching his attention. I saw a brief shadow pass near the sofa, and I whirled around. Kate was flying toward me with the fire iron. Tim yelled, "He's got a gun!" Kate was wild-eyed, her teeth bared, and swung at my head. I heard the air slice near me. I stepped back and raised the revolver, but Tim then leaped onto my legs from behind, trying to climb up me to grab the gun. Kate almost fell over from missing me, and she regained her balance and spun around, rearing back with the iron over her head. She let out a deep-throated cry. I punched Tim in his mouth and tried to kick him away, yanking my gun hand free from his desperate grasp. I accidentally stamped on his bloody foot, and he screamed. Kate then ran toward me and brought the iron down onto my shoulder, the pain erupting through me, and this sent both Tim and me onto the floor, struggling with the gun. I pulled Tim over me to protect myself from Kate, but he went wild, biting my hand and cursing, kicking and twisting away from me while yanking at the gun. My left arm was numb from the blow, but I still managed to hit Tim in the neck, loosening his grip. Kate swung the iron down again, like an ax, and chopped into my other arm, and the pointed barb ripped through my shirt and tore open a small gash. Tim almost grabbed the gun free, but I aimed it toward him and I pulled the trigger, the gun going off. He let go and cried out, holding his arm.

I turned toward Kate with the gun, but she swung the iron and knocked the gun out of my hand; it clattered and slid along the floor and into the hallway. She screeched, "You shot him!" and swung again, the blow glancing off my arm as I jumped out of her range and ran for the gun. Before I reached it, though, I saw Julian stoop over, the duct tape hanging from his wrists, and he picked the gun up and aimed it at me. I jumped out of the way, and scrambled toward the front door, but Kate barreled toward me, the iron poised, and Tim hit me from behind with something that clanged against my shoulder blade. I spun, falling, and saw the small fireplace shovel in Tim's good hand, his other arm clutched to his ribs, and Kate, Tim, and Julian descended on me, Kate bringing down her iron onto my stomach, missing me as I rolled to the side, but Julian then kicked me, and when Tim slammed down the small black shovel, aiming for my head, I thought of Linda and wasn't able to block the hits coming from all directions.

Twenty-three

I felt my breath on my face, moisture dripping down my cheeks and chin, the heat reflected off a rough fabric scraping my nose. Some kind of hood had been drawn over my head, and a cord choked it tightly around my neck. I blinked, but saw only darkness. I heard heavy footsteps clomping on the wooden floor, and slowly other sounds filtered through and I recognized Tim's hushed voice say something about Gloria, a throbbing in my head cutting out every other word. Kate's voice pulsed around me.

I told you this would happen. I told you not to get mixed up in this! I told you it's never easy money!

I'm sorry, baby, I'm really sorry. You're right.

Look at you! We have to get to the hospital.

Not yet. Not until Gloria gets here and takes care of him. God, this fucking hurts.

I could've killed him! Look what you made me do!

I'm sorry. Let's get the hell out of here as soon as we can. Let's go to Kauai or something.

Look at your foot! What'll you tell the doctors?

I was cleaning my gun. It was an accident.

Oh, Tim. What have you done? What have you done?

Kate's exasperated and sympathetic voice faded as the pounding in my head grew, and slowly a pain spread from my left shoulder, and I remembered the gash Kate had given me. I tried to move my arms, but they were tied behind my back, my limbs frozen. When I tried to roll over, my shoulder exploded and I let out a sharp gasp. The voices around me stopped and I heard Tim say, *Yeah you don't like it motherfucker? How about this?* And he kicked my shoulder, which set off fireworks in my vision, the darkened hood now bright with sparklers and red flares, and the throbbing was so loud that it shook the backs of my eyes and loosened my teeth and pushed me out of consciousness.

I woke up again when I was being carried, my wrists still tied behind my back, my ankles bound; two sets of hands roughly pulled up my arms, almost popping them out of the sockets, and the pain in my left shoulder jolted me into a chilled, sweaty state of agony. I kept my body limp, tried not to moan or breathe too heavily. My feet dragged behind me. A woman's voice said, "In the trunk. Hurry." Gloria.

I heard a trunk opening. I tried to muster up some strength to struggle, but my limbs wouldn't respond. I couldn't even raise my head from its lolled, slumped position. I felt myself being lifted up and then dropped into the trunk, my head hitting the floor hard, and I let out a soundless, breathless yell. They slammed the trunk closed; my eardrums shuddered against the air pressure change. I imagined my impending suffocation and tried to move my limbs, but the knots were too tight.

The car rocked back and forth as they climbed in, and three doors closed with an even rhythm. They started the engine. I shifted and slid on a loose mat as the car backed up, turned quickly, then sped forward. I struggled with the cord, which bit into my skin. My shoulder was numb, which worried me more than the pain. I heard the faint murmurs of a conversation, Gloria's higher-pitched voice cutting into the lower registers of men's replies.

The hood made it difficult for me to breathe, so I tried to rub it off by scraping my cheek against the trunk floor. My back ached from this awkward position, but I managed to pull the hood away from my mouth, giving me more air. I smelled motor oil. My lower back began cramping up.

After struggling for a while, breaking into a sweat and cutting off the circulation in my hands, I stopped moving. My head ached. I was tiring myself out. I needed to save my energy and try to figure out where I was going. I relaxed against the floor, listening to the traffic sounds. We were on a freeway, moving fast. I heard us passing cars, engines and tire noises approaching, then falling away. The talking in the car had stopped. Occasionally I felt a series of turns, but I wasn't sure.

Tim said they had burned Hector alive. This fear gave me more energy, and I tried sawing my hands free again but only cut into my wrists. I still couldn't feel my shoulder.

When I felt the car struggling up an incline, my body sliding down, I kept still and listened. Pings of gravel hit the wheel well. We had turned off a paved road. I immediately thought of where Hector had died and imagined a similar fate for me. Maybe they were heading to a secluded area of a canyon. I thought, But I still have thirteen years left to live. My father didn't die until he was forty-five, so that gave me thirteen years. Until then I was invincible.

I rolled over and somehow pushed myself onto my knees, with my forehead supporting my upper body; my neck strained under the weight. I slowly positioned myself so that my upper back rested against the top of the trunk. I began lowering myself, then rising quickly and banging my shoulders against the trunk lid, hoping to break the latch somehow. Each time I did this I was thrown off balance. The pain was slowly coming back into my shoulder, and I tried to ignore it. I repositioned myself. After the fourth hit, someone in the car said something. I kept doing this, hurting my back, my body pulsing. If I broke the latch, maybe I could buy some time.

The car slowed, then halted. Gloria said something that sounded like, "Check it out."

I heard the car behind us skid in the dirt.

A car door opened. The weight of the car shifted. Footsteps coming around. Then, "Oh fuck. He dented it!"

The trunk opened, and sunlight shone through my hood. The man said, "You dickwad, you put a bubble in the metal." He pushed me down.

"Fuck you," I said.

"What's the holdup," another man's voice said.

"Dickwad is making a racket."

"This is kidnapping," I said. "I told the cops all about Lowell Bangs and Gloria Katz. If anything happens to me—"

"Yo, shut the fuck up," the man said. He punched me on my ear, which sent me headfirst into the trunk. I let out an *oof* as I cushioned the fall with my bad shoulder, and a burning flare crossed my darkened vision. The blinding pain burst through my arm, spreading quickly into my entire body, and I let out a low groan. It felt like something clawing into my wound. My face instantly flushed and yet my body was cold. I shivered.

The man laughed and slammed the trunk lid shut.

We finally stopped, and the cramped position had put my legs and arms to sleep; I felt as if my limbs had disappeared. My cheek stung, and when I stared into the darkness, my face now dripping with sweat and condensed breath, I saw the little stars in my vision forming shapes and designs. A stick-figure man waved at me. I had lost track of time, and when the trunk opened, I kept still, confused.

Someone reached down and pulled the hood tighter down my face. Then I heard tape stretched out, torn, and felt it being wrapped around my head. Gloria said, "Put him in the backseat. You guys take off. I'll go from here."

They lifted me out of the trunk and threw me in the back. I bounced off the cushion and fell onto the floor, wedged in behind the front seat and foot rests, my shoulder coming back to life. The sharp tearing I felt shook me awake. I then heard the others getting into another car, and drive away. I was confused by all the changes, and tried to hear sounds of our location. Gloria said, "You've been causing a lot of problems." She was in the driver's seat and started the engine.

"I can't . . . breathe," I said, muffled. The tape had blocked off most of the fabric around my nose and mouth. I was getting dizzy. My voice sounded alien to me.

"Good."

"The police know . . . about Lowell Bangs."

She sighed heavily. "I didn't want to do this, but you just wouldn't go away."

"Do what?"

"You might want to say your prayers. Sorry."

"If I end up dead, the police will look into it," I said, my head clearing.

"Oh, I know. It doesn't matter. It'll take them a while to find you, and then we'll have disappeared."

"Why did you do that to Hector? Wasn't he your boyfriend?"

She didn't answer.

The movement had put some feeling back into my hands, but the pins and needles were coming, and I groaned as the slow scraping crawled up my arms. My shoulder pulsed. "Where are we going?"

"Lowell wants to meet you before you die."

"Why did he kill Raul Gama?"

"I don't know anything about that. I want you to know I'm sorry. I don't like all this."

This surprised me. I said, "Then let me go."

"Then I'd be killed."

"I can make it look like I got away—"

"Sorry. No can do. And I loved Hector. I still do."

"But you helped Bangs kill him."

She was quiet for a while, then said, "Don't even try to figure it out."

Was I wrong? The lack of air making me nauseous and lightheaded. I had trouble focusing my questions. I tried to take a deep breath, and said, "Where are we?"

She didn't answer me. I calmly considered if I was going to die. I wasn't ready. I hadn't done anything. I hadn't yet lived.

The car made a series of turns, went over a steep hill, then came to a stop. Gloria left the car for a moment, then opened the rear door, and a pair of hands pulled me out. The man grunted as he tried to carry me, but put me down. He said, "Too heavy by myself."

"All right," Gloria said. She cut the cord around my ankles, but I couldn't get up. I had no feeling in my legs.

"My legs are asleep," I said.

"Wake 'em up," the man said, and kicked my thigh, which sent a ripple of needles to my toes. I struggled up. The man grabbed my arm, making me yelp in pain. He pulled me up roughly and dragged me forward.

The cord around my wrists seemed to have loosened, and I made sure I didn't hear Gloria behind me before slowly moving my hands back and forth, trying to pull apart the knots, each small movement making the pain in my shoulder throb. I still had the hood taped over my face, and stumbled over roots and rocks. The man tightened his grip on me. I heard the deep rumbling of a growling dog, which stopped me, and a new, scratchy voice said, "Down, boy."

"This is him," Gloria said.

"Bring him inside," the new voice said. I thought I heard a flurry of whispers around me.

"Hello?" I asked.

No one replied, but someone pushed me forward.

I tripped on some steps and walked up, my weight creaking the floors. It felt unsteady in here, not quite like a house. Maybe a trailer. The lightweight floors reminded me of one of my father's former coworkers, Junil Kim, who was killed two years ago in the Mess. He owned a trailer in Milpitas, and I remembered how he had taped up samples of his calligraphy—his hobby—on thin papers throughout the interior of the trailer. The rice papers had curled and yellowed in the sun. I was suddenly saddened by this. Whatever happened to those drawings? I should've taken a few. I had liked Junil Kim.

I was pushed into a chair and felt my wrists almost free themselves. The voice said, "You guys wait outside."

"You're not going to do it now, are you?" Gloria asked.

"Why do you care?"

She lowered her voice. "I don't want another Jameson."

"Wait outside."

I tightened my body, preparing my movements: pull out my hands, tear off the hood, and get ready to fight or run. I plotted my steps to the door, about five paces. My limbs felt like liquid, oozing from my body. Maybe I could splash to the floor and spill out of the trailer. I could throw myself into the air and evaporate away.

"How's that woman," the voice asked.

I snapped back. I wasn't sure if I was being addressed.

"How's Hector's sister?" he asked again.

"Linda?" I said, surprised. "You almost killed her. She's still in a coma, and she has a bolt in her head."

He was quiet.

I said, "Why'd you kill Raul Gama? He was nothing. He had no connection to all this."

"That guy was an asshole."

"I take it you're Lowell Bangs?"

"You've been trying to find me. Here I am."

I said, "I was hoping to find you under different circumstances."

He snorted, then said, "I don't get who you are and why you're here."

"I'm Linda's—was Linda's boyfriend. I'm here to help her."

"Was?"

"Now we're just friends."

"This isn't . . . this isn't how it normally is. I want you to know that. We're not killers. We just started dealing more and it got really complicated."

"You're going to kill me, though."

"You're causing too many problems. You've been making too much trouble. I have to set an example. You get it? I have to keep everyone afraid."

"Like Mack. I met a guy who got a screwdriver from you."

"A screwdriver?" After a moment, he said, "Oh, right. He was lucky he lived. We decided it was enough."

"His name is Mack," I said, listening to him move across the room. What would Mack do?

Bangs didn't reply.

I worked my hands freer, loosening the cord around my wrists and said, "Mack is very cool."

After a moment, Bangs said, "Yeah, whatever." I heard him pick something up, and my heart tightened. I sawed at the cord even more, and felt the knot loosen.

I slowly pulled my right hand free. I kept my arms behind my back, my heart quickening. Wait for an opening. Listen.

I asked, "How are you going to do it?"

Bangs answered from another part of the room, "You're very calm."

"You're not the first person to want to kill me."

He let out a small laugh. "We'll put a bullet in your head and dump you in the woods. Very simple."

"Why the knife for Raul, then? That must have been messy." Listen. Now?

I heard him clink something, ignoring my question, and I quickly tore off the hood, and stood up, but was startled by the darkness. The fresh cold air slapped my face. I stepped back, dizzy. The blurry, slim figure next to a table, Bangs, said, "Oh, what the fuck—"

I grabbed something that looked like a narrow beaker filled with fluid and threw it at his head, aiming for the baseball cap. He dove to the ground, and when the beaker shattered against the wall, he yelled, "Fuck! That's lye! Are you fucking crazy?"

The sudden intake of fresh air roused me, my eyes quickly adjusting. I saw a long table with all kinds of beakers and burners, glass tubing and large metal canisters. I grabbed another beaker, threw it, then stumbled for the door. Bangs yelled, "He's loose! He's loose!" and ducked again as the beaker skidded off the table and crashed to the floor.

Unable to keep my balance, and my legs still wobbly, I tripped over a chair and fell heavily to the ground. Bangs rushed toward me. I pulled myself up, but he jumped on me and forced me back down. We struggled as he reached for my throat with one hand, then yelled, "Hurry!"

I punched his chest, then kneed his leg, and tried to roll away. He cursed, and grabbed my wounded shoulder, and I yelled in pain, trying to scramble away, and he gripped me harder. I kicked him in the knee, which loosened his grip, and I kicked him again. He rolled away, cursing.

Jumping up and staggering out the door, I was surprised by the darkness. It was night? I saw a man with a flashlight moving quickly toward me, and he had a gun. I heard a shot as I zigzagged toward the woods. The dog, tethered to a chair, a glowing white pit bull, started barking ferociously as I ran past a hissing lantern and flew through some bushes. I heard Gloria yell, "What the hell happened?"

Bangs called out, "Go after him. I'll bring Blood."

I crashed through small trees and thick, low branches, running blindly through the dark with my hands in front of me, guiding me. I slammed into a fallen log at waist level, and flipped right over it, knocking the wind out of me. I stopped and listened. The dog was snarling and the sounds of trampling through the brush approached. Flashlight beams waved back and forth. I pulled myself up, my shoulder hurting more. When I touched it, I felt my shirt stiff with dried blood. I heard the dog in a howling frenzy and continued running away from the sounds.

"This way!" the other man yelled.

As I ran I picked up a small stick. I tried to move as quietly as I could, but there were so many dead leaves and branches around that I kept cracking and crinkling. I stopped. I then threw the stick as far as I could back toward the trailer. I waited. Nothing. They stopped, listening. I heard Bangs say, "Where is he boy? Come on boy! Sic 'em! Sic 'em."

I moved more slowly, trying to keep quiet. I felt my foot slip over loose rocks and I reached down to pick one up. A hefty baseball-sized one. They stopped again. I threw the rock as high and far as I could. After a moment I heard a deadened thud as the rock hit something metal. A voice that sounded only a hundred feet away said, "Wait. Did he circle back? Shit. Did he get the keys to the car?"

They thrashed noisily back toward the clearing, and I stood up and walked carefully over dead leaves and branches. I looked up but had trouble seeing stars through the high trees. I had no idea where I was.

Their voices called out to me. Bangs yelled, "You're in the middle of nowhere! You'll die from exposure before you find anything!"

I kept moving.

"I'm letting my dog loose. He's a trained attack bull. Tell me not to, and come back."

This stopped me.

Gloria yelled, "We can make a deal!"

My eyes were adjusting to this darkness, and I patted the ground, looking for a weapon. I found a thick dead pine branch, the sap sticky. I stripped off the twigs and swung it back and forth. Better than nothing. I continued forward and found that some areas were more dense than others, and if I kept moving downhill, I could avoid the thicker brush.

The dog began barking furiously, and Bangs yelled, "Go get him, boy! Sic 'em! Good boy!"

I could barely see, let alone fight off a pit bull. I turned and ran down another incline, hitting a tree and bouncing off. I stumbled through more brush as I thought I heard the dog growling. Farther up ahead I thought I could make out some boulders. My throat constricted when I heard the dog barking and speeding in my direction.

I ran wildly toward the boulders and scrambled up them, turning, the branch still in my hand. A small glowing figure moved incredibly fast toward me, zipping through the air, and the growl had deepened into something murderous. I cursed and shoved the branch ahead of me as the dog leaped off the ground, flying toward me. The dog landed on the rock, its claws scrabbling, but he slipped and fell back, the growl catching in his throat as he barked and flipped quickly onto his feet. His barking had turned into deep-throated spasms, and he backed up, preparing for another jump. I tried to get farther up the rock. I heard Bangs in the distance, yelling, "Sic 'em! Sic 'em!"

I found another branch and threw it down. The dog ignored it. He ran back, turned, and gained more speed.

The dog leaped up again and this time made it farther along the rocks, his claws still not catching. As he tried to get his balance, I jumped forward and jammed the branch into his head, and I connected, one of the smaller offshoots digging into an eye. The dog let out a sharp cry and stumbled back, falling off the rock and landing heavily onto his side; he let out another yip. He pulled himself up and whimpered. He shook his head, dazed. He then tried to leap back onto the rock but misjudged the distance and slammed his face into a smaller rock, his bark cut off in pain. I climbed down with the stick and began jabbing him and yelling, the Y-shaped branches confusing him. I stabbed his neck and he yelped in pain. He snapped at me, but this time I swung the branch and another offshoot tore into the side of his neck. I yanked it back and ripped open his skin around his eye, and at the same time I kicked him as hard as I could in his chest. He whimpered and ran back in the other direction. I could barely hear anything over my slamming heartbeat and fled blindly into the dark.

Twenty-four

When I stopped running, the adrenaline easing off and my body shaking, I listened for any sounds near me but heard only my head pounding. I tried to slow my breathing. I heard crickets. I wasn't sure if I had lost Bangs and Gloria, or if they had given up. I continued forward. I touched my shoulder and winced. I felt the protrusions of ripped flesh, dried blood; the pain made me queasy. Some of the blood had dried along my arm, flaking. I worried about infection. I sat down. I listened. I had no idea where I was. I didn't have a flashlight, a compass, or a map, and I didn't know how far they had driven me from Venice. How long had the drive been? I couldn't be sure. I looked up at the stars, now more visible, and I tried to find the Big Dipper. I thought I found it, with the two stars at the end of the pot lining up with the North Star, but I wasn't certain, and I hadn't looked at the stars like this since I was a kid.

I assumed Bangs had set up camp in the woods farther up past Malibu, and I had to head south to hit the ocean. But there was no way to know this. I needed to rest. I wasn't thinking clearly. I wasn't sure how much blood I had lost. Was that pit bull going to recover and come back for me? Oh, shit. That fucking thing was scary. I needed a better weapon. The pine branch was too unwieldy. I searched along the ground for more branches, but I could barely see a few inches from my face.

I looked around the darkness. I tried to simplify my tasks. I needed to find help. I needed to call the police and tell them about Bangs. I needed to get out of the woods. I stared up at the sky. I couldn't depend on the stars, because I wasn't certain about navigating by the Big Dipper. What was the best source of direction? The sun. Sunrise in the east. At dawn, I'd see the sunrise and would get my bearings. I needed to stay warm until the morning. I had to listen for the pit bull. I had to be ready to fight again.

I kicked together some leaves and pulled down a few low branches to make bedding. My sweat was chilling me. I shivered, just beginning to realize how cold it was. I lay down on my good side, curling up to retain my body heat, and continued listening for any sounds. If the dog recovered, and Bangs sent him back after me, it wouldn't be too difficult to find me. I had been sweating heavily, leaving a nice long scent trail. Pine needles dug into my side. I tried not to touch my wound, which was still humming. I still smelled the faint hints of motor oil.

A twig snapped nearby, and I sat up. I waited, poised to jump up and run. But it fell quiet again. I leaned against a tree, pulling my knees up to my chest, and tried to rest in this position. I put my head down. I reviewed the sounds I had heard while in the trunk of the car, hoping to reconstruct the route for the police. But the only thing I could tell them was that we had gone off a main road. That was it.

I couldn't stop shivering. I regretted never joining the Boy Scouts. I regretted not taking the survival training Polansky had offered some of us when the army was testing a civilian program. We would've been the first group to take their course, but at the time I was still trying to learn my job. I had already taken defensive driving and was tired of the extra course work.

I didn't know how to start a fire without matches. Goddamn city boy.

Something happens after the rush of adrenaline fades: you crash. A fatigue sets in, a depletion of spirit as your breathing slows and your head clouds. Your limbs feel dead. The bigger the rush, the harder the crash, and you feel the faint quivers in your chest, the last remnants of energy rattling your heart, and yet your mind is still active, but your body no longer responds. Let me rest, it says. You juiced me too much, it cries.

I had trouble shaking off the snarls of the pit bull, the homicidal barking like nothing I'd heard before. What the hell is it with me and dogs? And at the moment I was more worried about the pit bull than about Bangs. I felt safely hidden in the dark from Bangs, but that damn animal could sniff me out.

Once I grew accustomed to the competing cricket chirps and no longer jumped at the movement in the brush—realizing it was a nocturnal animal foraging nearby—I curled up and tried to sleep. I couldn't stop shivering. I thought about the bonfire at the desert rave and wished for that warmth right now. Serena and I had been slick with sweat, the heat from the fire so strong that we had to dance away from it. A few kids had taken off their shirts, their bodies glossy in the firelight.

My teeth chattered. I wished for sunrise. My mind wandered. I tried to ignore the spreading pain in my shoulder. I thought about Linda in the hospital and told myself that I was okay, that Linda had it worse, and at the first hint of feeling sorry for myself all I had to do was consider a bolt in my head.

Linda was tough. I knew that while in a coma she would fight to get better. Maybe she was even aware of everything; I wanted to visit her and try talking to her. I could tell her I understood better why she needed to be alone. I could tell her everything would be okay.

I was suddenly sorry for all the fights we had had. Besides the VCR fight, the last big argument had been about one of her editors who disliked her. Linda had come home in a testy mood, and she told me about having her story ideas shot down every time she worked with this particular editor, who was growing in power at her department. I was annoyed that whenever she came home, she barely even said hello. She dumped this on me almost every day. I had my own problems, first at Black Diamond, and then with Larry, yet I tried not to burden her with it. She didn't seem to care.

I grew impatient. I told her she should switch departments, go to the business section. She liked business. She shook her head irritably and told me I didn't understand. I said she should work at a different newspaper; she had enough clout to jump. Maybe even the *Chronicle* might be interested, I said. She snapped, Why do you always have to do that? I didn't know what she meant and she wouldn't elaborate. I grew angrier and accused her of something—I no longer remembered what it was. She then said I made things worse by my attitude. From there it degenerated. We ended up shouting for a few minutes, and then I stormed out. I went back to my apartment and brooded. I mumbled to myself. I thought of better comebacks.

This memory pained me. She had wanted comfort. She had not wanted career advice. It was the extension cord incident all over again. Hadn't I learned anything in two years? Obviously not.

Why hadn't I been more sympathetic? Instead I accused her of inaction. Why? I didn't like being dumped on. I didn't like being the repository of her bad day.

I was selfish. I was petty. I wanted to start over.

The regrets compounded with each shivering minute. I sat up, the cold ground too hard to sleep on, and leaned back against a tree. No wonder she started confiding in Harlan. I had just made her feel worse.

If she didn't recover from the coma, then these would be the last things she would remember.

The shoulder wound pulsed electric waves through my arm and chest. I was sorry, and I vowed that I would redeem myself. I had to make things right.

The next morning, having barely slept, I headed south at first light and hiked for hours. I kept being detoured by steep ravines and dense brush. My shirt kept tearing on branches, and I had to protect my shoulder, shielding it from whip-like saplings. My mouth and throat were parched, and I worried about dehydration. Only then did I wonder if Bangs might be right, that I was too deep to ever find my way out. Was it a mistake to run? I kept imagining how I could've handled last night better. Maybe I should've tried to take Bangs hostage. Instead of throwing a beaker and fleeing, I should've attacked him. I could've used him as an out. Though, without a gun I had little leverage.

What surprised me was how calm everyone was. I had expected a raving psycho, but Bangs seemed very normal. He was almost businesslike and talked about killing me as if I were a deal to close. And Gloria was apologetic? How strange.

I thought I heard someone calling my name. I froze. Bangs? They had waited until daylight to search for me. I moved quietly into the bushes, waiting for an attack, but when I didn't hear anything else, I wondered if I had imagined it. I continued hiking, using the sun to keep heading south.

I heard my name again, and whirled around.

Nothing.

"Shit," I said to myself. My voice sounded strange. "You're hearing things."

I couldn't remember when I had had a normal night of rest, and my senses were jittery. I kept smelling menthol. Vicks VaporRub. At first I tried shaking it off, but then I realized I liked the smell, and inhaled deeply. But after a few deep breaths I became light-headed, and needed to keep still. I stopped walking and touched my chapped lips, in danger of splitting. I tried to lick them, but my tongue was dry. I felt my lips scraping against each other.

I looked ahead and thought I recognized a small rock formation. The three-peaked jagged top was oddly familiar. I squeezed my eyes shut, then opened them again. The rocks were still there. I checked the sun. I seemed to be moving south, but it was easy to veer off course without landmarks. And it was difficult to use landmarks when everything looked the same: tall trees everywhere.

My stomach grumbled. I looked down at my filthy hands, dirt and tree sap covering them, and noticed that they were swollen. My bruised wrists still hurt from the tight cord. When I checked the gash on my shoulder, I saw that I kept opening the wound with my movements. Dried blood traced the edges, but fresh blood kept seeping out.

I quickened my pace, worried that if I didn't find my way out of here soon, I would have to spend another night without food or water. I forced myself to think of something other than where I was. Just keep moving south, I told myself. Keep moving.

I picked up a branch and stripped the bark to make a hiking stick. I noticed that my hands had swollen even more. I hurried my pace. I heard my name again, but ignored it. I said aloud, "Just keep moving."

There was another steep ravine, but I didn't want to detour and waste more time. I climbed down slowly, straining my legs, my street shoes slipping on the dirt and rocks. I used the hiking stick to stabilize me. I stepped on a large rock, thinking it was secure, but it fell away, and I lost my balance. I dropped the stick and went scrabbling along the loose dirt, tumbling onto my side and hitting a thorny bush. I lay still for a while, my legs and ribs in pain. I had rolled over smaller rocks that had dug into me. Some thorns had ripped into my neck. Every small movement deepened them. I stifled the growing anger that nothing would go right with me. Gritting my teeth, I yanked myself away, feeling more skin tear. I stood up, and with my neck stinging, my ribs pulsing, I staggered down the rocky slope. I thought my shoulder smelled funny, but I ignored it.

I passed a set of boulders with three jagged peaks, and stopped in shock. Had I circled back? "No fucking way," I said aloud. I looked around, and didn't recognize anything else. Staring at the rocks I felt a dread creeping up the back of my neck. I was dead if I was circling. I found two sticks and lay them on the lower peak in a cross. If I saw this cross again, I would die. I looked up at the sun, now halfway up the sky, and continued south.

I smiled at a good memory. Linda and I got drunk after celebrating a story of hers that the wires had picked up, running it in newspapers around the country. It was a story about an elderly woman who had been cheated out of her life savings by her own son. The woman had to go back to work as a cashier to live, and yet she didn't want to press charges against her son. The DA was prosecuting for fraud, but the woman said, No matter what, he's still my son. All the local TV news stations carried the story as well.

After a few martinis, Linda and I walked arm in arm through downtown Monte Vista, giddy and tipsy. This is what it's about, she told me. People read it, and they're affected. This is when it's worth it.

I hugged her. She laughed, her eyes shining. She said, I'd call this a blockable moment.

The Block in the hot sun. The Block unable to think clearly, exhaustion and thirst affecting his judgment, his perceptions. The Block keeps seeing glitter on the trees and small boulders. Everything glistens and twinkles. He hears rave music in the distance. The Block stops, finds it difficult to continue. He contemplates lying down and sleeping. The Block is losing momentum. His hands are oddly puffy. His shoulder wound keeps opening, the scabs tearing. He worries about gangrene.

The underbrush is thick, and the Block moves slowly, trailblazing. He tries to push aside the thorny bushes with his walking stick, but has little energy for the task, and ends up walking through the thorns, his clothes tearing. His shirt is in tatters. He looks down at his pants and sees it torn at the knees. He thinks, What a way to die.

He's bleeding and thirsty.

Bleeding and thirsty. Bleeding and thirsty. He tries to keep his hiking in rhythm, walking steadily to the beat. He hopes this will keep him moving forward, diverting his mind from the pain in his shoulder. His legs feel fine, however. It's a good thing I run a lot, he thinks. Then the Block remembers that he hasn't run in over two weeks, and maybe his legs don't feel so fine after all. He loses his rhythm and stops when he sees a tall set of boulders with three peaks. He rubs his eyes. He stares. Uncertain if it's the same set of boulders, he approaches it. He thinks in the third person: The Block creeps forward cautiously. The Block, sensing danger, is poised to run.

He circles the boulders but doesn't see the cross he left to mark it. A bubble of gratitude wells up inside him, and he pats the rock and thanks it. The Block looks up at the sun, orients himself south, and marches forward. He thinks about everything he has ever done wrong, offended people, lied, cursed, killed. Yes, he has killed, and he doesn't like thinking about it, even though it was self-defense and it was during a struggle for a gun, and, moreover, if he had not shot the man, he would not be here today. Still, the idea of taking another life is something he hasn't really adjusted to, and he can't understand how murderers, real murderers, were not affected by it. The sum of all experiences of that man, Durante, came down to a bullet in his chest. The Block did not mourn for Durante, a killer himself, but neither did he relish the justice of the act.

His regrets pursue him. He wonders if this is what happens as you approach death. Your life doesn't flash before your eyes; your regrets whisper behind you. He remembers the time he had called his aunt a lonely and bitter woman to her face; he was a teenager, chafing at her restrictions and authority. He had a curfew that contracted with every failed test, and he failed many tests. They fought almost every night toward the end of his high school career, and he called her lonely and bitter for taking everything out on him. That was a moment he wanted to withdraw. Her face fell. Her eyes registered his own contempt, glowing with mirrored understanding. And he knew he should've apologized, taken those words back quickly, but he didn't. He let it pierce her. He let it fester. He did not stay with his aunt much longer.

Where is she now? No one really knows. Despite all that has happened between them, he wants to see her again.

He stops walking. The ties of family. He understands this a little better now. He understands why perhaps Hector searched for his father, why Linda searches for answers about Hector.

His stillness in the brush, the absence of crunching leaves and branches, triggers his hearing. There's something in the distance, the sound of trickling water. He straightens and cups his ears. The sound fades. He waits. The sound returns. He tries to home in on the sound—it's toward his right—and he walks slowly in that direction, stopping every few steps to listen.

It *is* water. He resists the impulse to go crashing toward the sound. Instead, he moves steadily in that direction, the sound growing louder. His throat aches with dryness.

Then, climbing through more brush, he finds a tiny stream, the trickling of water over rocks and down a small crevice. He kneels down, examines the clarity of the water, hesitating only for a moment as he considers viruses and bacteria, then he says, Screw it, and begins slurping away.

Streams lead somewhere. Of what little he knows about hiking and survival, he does know that streams lead to other, larger streams, to lakes, to the ocean. The Block washes his cuts, which now mark his entire midsection and arms from the thorny brush, and carefully tends to his shoulder, which stings and bleeds more in the cold water. He drinks until his stomach is full. Then he begins following the stream. His head clears. His thoughts sharpen. Energized by the cool water, he hurries downstream, often splashing into the water's edge and soaking his shoes and socks.

He wants to see Linda. It has been almost twenty-four hours since they put the device in her head, and he has no idea how she is progressing. He needs more than her sister's updates—he needs to see her for himself.

He realizes that he tends to do that, to watch her without her knowing, and he isn't sure why. He watched her in the mornings as she sprung out of bed and prepared for work. He watched her as she talked on the phone.

Once, just a few months ago when she sat out on her balcony and read in the sun, he was sitting in the bedroom and saw her through the window. The balcony jutted out and gave him a direct view of her as she sat cross-legged on the ground, despite there being a chair behind her. She was snapping the pages of a magazine, her eyes skimming the articles, until she came across something that stopped her. She leaned forward, her hair falling over her face. She flipped it back and deftly pushed it behind her ears with her two index fingers. She then hugged her stomach as she read, her brows furrowed.

Perhaps he was a little amazed that this woman wanted to be with him.

The Block stops walking. The stream has grown wider and deeper, the underbrush thinning. He has more room to hike. He looks up at the sky; the sun passed the midday mark and it's now in the early afternoon. The brief surge of energy has worn off. He trudges forward, slipping a few times on rocks. His shoes have flat soles and no treads.

He hears an engine. At first he thinks he's imagining it. But it grows louder. He splashes across the stream, and pushes through some high, thorny bushes. After a hundred feet, he runs over a hill and stumbles down onto a dirt road. Dust floats around him, slowly settling, and the engine sound fades. A car? He runs along the road, yelling, and passes through thicker clouds of dust. His legs weak, and his voice thin from exhaustion, he pushes himself forward. Up ahead he sees some kind of tractor pulling a low, wide hoeing machine that's churning up the sides of the dirt road and smoothing the surface. He yells and waves his arms. The driver eventually notices him and stops, turning off the machine. The Block coughs through the dust and runs forward.

"Hey, this fire road is closed off to the public," the man says. He is looking the Block up and down.

"I need help," the Block says, the relief making him unsteady. The world spins and warps. "I need the police."

"Police? I can radio—"

But his vision blurs, his legs buckle. Losing his strength, he sits down on the ground, puffs of dust billowing up over him, and says, "Help me."

Twenty-five

Sun. Stars. The light of the sun, or what I thought was the sun shining hotly on my face, tinted red through my closed eyelids, pulled me from my drowsiness. I began to raise my arm to cover my eyes, but then felt a jolt of acid running through me, centering in my left shoulder. I groaned and opened my eyes, and saw strangers looking over me. I was in a small hospital room, lying on an angled bed with my body propped up, an IV attached to the back of my hand, and generic flower prints hanging on the yolk-colored walls. "Where am I?" I asked. The fluorescent lights buzzed above me.

"A private hospital," said a man in a suit. "I'm Detective Henry Bowler of the Ventura County Sheriff's Department. You were found wandering in the Santa Monica mountains. You've suffered from heat exhaustion, dehydration, and a pretty severe tear in your shoulder. You've lost a lot of blood."

Blood? Blood. I had heard Bangs call his dog "Blood," and with that memory everything came back to me. I blurted out, "I was kidnapped. A drug dealer named Lowell Bangs kidnapped me. I got away, but you have to find him before he—"

"We already have a copter searching the area. You told us some of this before they put you under."

"Put me under? Why?"

A young doctor in a white coat and a stethoscope hanging around his neck cleared his throat and said, "We had to do a little repair work on your deltoid—cleaning and stitching. You were in a lot of pain so we gave you a general anesthesia."

"How bad is it?"

"It was infected. You'll have to stay on antibiotics for a week. Your shoulder should fully recover in a month or so."

Detective Bowler then introduced the others, though the only name I caught was of the DEA agent, David Wallace. Next to him was a park ranger and a deputy sheriff. Bowler said, "I head VCAT, the Ventura County Combined Action Team, and we work the narcotics end with the DEA. When you mentioned the lab in the trailer to the deputy, he called us."

"It's Lowell Bangs's trailer. Have you heard of him?"

"Not until now," the DEA agent, Wallace, said. "Which is why we need to know everything that happened."

The park ranger said, "I have a map of where you were found. It would also help if you could possibly retrace your movements."

I said, "Yes. You have to call Vines of OCSD homicide. He needs to know what's going on."

"He's on his way," Bowler said. "We contacted him once we looked at your wallet and saw who you are."

"What? Why?"

"There's an APB on you. Investigator Vines thought you were trying to flee the area."

Flee? Then I remembered I was supposed to be interviewed by him again and had missed the appointment. I shook my head. "Bangs is the murderer. He was planning on killing me—"

"Why don't we start from the beginning," Agent Wallace said, pulling out a pad and pen.

My hands had swollen from an allergic reaction to pine sap. The park ranger had told the doctor that the stream water in the area was probably contaminated with Giardia, a microscopic parasite that the antibiotics should take care of. The tear in my shoulder had required fifteen stitches, and I had purple-and-orange bruises on my legs and body. As the doctor checked my bandage and dressed the lacerations on my legs from the thorns and branches, I tried to tell them everything I could. I focused on Bangs and Gloria. When I mentioned the trailer and what I had seen inside it, they were alert, anxious. They asked me to describe as much as I could, but my recollection was hazy. It had been dark, I had been tied up, and I had wanted only to escape. I was fairly certain it was a lab, though. When I told them about the test tubes, beakers, and throwing the lye, Wallace said to Bowler, "Must be meth."

Detective Bowler, an overweight, ruddy man who talked in a deep, hoarse voice, was less concerned about the overall story than about finding the trailer. He asked me to describe the car ride, to trace the route into the mountains. He had a tendency to scratch his chubby cheeks, the corner of his mouth pulled down every few minutes as he listened to me carefully. I told him what I could, but I had been too disoriented to recount anything worthwhile.

"What about when you got out, when you ran from the trailer?" Agent Wallace asked.

"It was dark, and I had fought Bangs off. I was running as fast as I could and didn't see much. They had a pit bull."

Wallace looked up from his notes. I said, "I headed south—or what I thought was south—until I hit the stream, and then followed the stream until I got near that fire road."

"But this was at night?"

"No. I rested until daylight."

"So they have a twelve-hour head start," Wallace said.

Bowler laid out a map of the Santa Monica Mountains, and said, "Most of this is a national park, but the area around it is private property." He pointed to a fire road and said, "This is where the park service crewman found you." He pointed to a penciled line drawn near the road. "The stream you followed isn't even marked on the map, but Sean here," he nodded to the park ranger, "said it's fed by dozens of smaller ones." He pointed to an area north of the penciled stream. "Depending on how long you followed the streams, if you go far enough, this is private property, unmapped."

"That must be it," I said.

Wallace asked, "Why didn't you run away along the road that took you up to the trailer?"

"I didn't know where it was. I just tried to get away. It was dark."

"Did you see guns? Weapons of any kind?" Bowler asked.

"They had guns. One of them took shots at me as I ran into the woods. They also have my gun, a revolver."

They stopped. Wallace flipped through his notes. "Why do you have a gun again?"

I sighed and leaned back into the bed. "It was my girlfriend's father's. I have a permit. I had a gun for when I talked to Tim Jacobs. He's the one I shot in the foot and arm before I was kidnapped. He might even be in a hospital right now."

Bowler said to Wallace, "I'll ask someone from VCAT to finish this interview. We should expand the aerial search."

"Thanks, Mr. Choice," Wallace said to me. "We'll be back tonight."

Bowler asked, "Is there someone you want to call? To let them know you're okay?"

I thought about this, and said, "Do you know if Linda Maldonado's condition has changed?"

They shook their heads. Bowler said, "Investigator Vines can update you on that."

I said, "Serena Yew. I should call her."

The doctor brought me a cordless phone, and the others left the hospital.

I dialed Serena's number, relieved that they were taking over.

Serena had been worried when I hadn't answered my motel phone all night and wanted to come pick me up right away. I told her I'd explain everything when I saw her. I then called Julie's cell phone, wanting to check on Linda. Julie heard my voice and said, "Where the hell have you been? Do you know the police are looking for you now?"

"It's a long story. How's Linda?"

"Have you spoken to the police? Do you know what's happening?"

"Happening? Which police? Vines is coming up here—"

"Don't talk to him," Julie said quickly. "Do you understand? Don't talk to him without our lawyer. Vines is definitely targeting Linda as the primary suspect and we've hired a lawyer. Do *not* tell him anything else without a lawyer."

"Wait, there's more. I saw Lowell Bangs and he pretty much admitted to killing Raul."

"Where are you?"

"A hospital in Ventura County, I think."

"Why are you up there—never mind. Come and meet with the lawyer. We've got to sort this out. You found Lowell Bangs?"

"Not quite. The local police here are going after him."

"Good! Finally! You won't believe the crap that's been happening. When can you be back down here?"

"Not for a while. I still have to talk to the local sheriff, and then Serena will be picking me up."

"Are you okay?"

I pulled up the sleeve of my hospital gown and looked at the gauze over my shoulder. A large swath of orange stain spread out beyond the bandage. My wrists were bandaged from the rope cuts. I said, "I've been better."

I said, "How is Linda? How's her head?" I tried to picture Linda's face but couldn't. I gripped the phone. The only image I had was of her in the hospital bed, her face swollen and shiny, unrecognizable. That wasn't Linda.

"Almost normal. The doctors think any time now she could wake up."

"Why is Vines focusing on her?"

She said, "The media are putting more pressure on them. They have no other suspect."

"But Bangs more or less admitted to it."

"The police found a motive."

"What? For Linda?"

"Raul named Linda and Hector as beneficiaries in his will and life insurance."

"So?" I said. "They were his only children."

"But they weren't close. They hadn't seen each other in years. It just doesn't look good."

"That's all they have? What about the crime scene?"

"Not much. Her fingerprints weren't on the knife. But don't talk to Vines without our lawyer."

"Call me if Linda wakes up. It doesn't matter when, what time, just call me."

"Where will you be?"

I gave her Serena's home number, and said, "Try that first, then the motel."

"Allen," she said. "You've got to find Bangs."

"I know."

We hung up. I lay back down on the bed and felt the past two days catching up with me. A deep exhaustion shivered through my body, and I closed my eyes, concerned about Vines. A life insurance policy was an obvious motive, but Bangs had admitted to me that Raul deserved to die. He had said Hector was the connection, and I assumed it had something to do with the money Hector had stolen. Unless they caught Bangs, however, it was only my word; the fact that I dated Linda biased me. Nothing held together without Bangs. Too many loose ends. Too many contingencies.

The faint hope I felt for Linda's improvement was tempered by my fear of the damage. Julie had mentioned the possibility of a personality change. I tried not to worry about this and focused on helping her. I needed to find Bangs. He had asked about her. *How's Hector's sister*, he had said. So he knew she was alive.

I opened my eyes. Why had he been curious? He was worried about what she knew, what she witnessed? What if Linda woke up and could identify him as Raul's killer? I wasn't sure if I was thinking clearly, if she was in real danger. I'd have to tell Vines about this possible threat; he could assign guards. If Bangs had wanted to get to Linda, he could've plenty of times before now. Maybe Bowler and Wallace were making some progress. I lay back down, closed my eyes. I was waiting for Serena. I was waiting for Vines. I always seemed to be in some kind of holding pattern.

Linda was a little better. That was all that mattered. Was she aware of her coma? Was she conscious on some level? She and I were both in hospital beds, and I imagined I could see her right now if I shut my eyes. We were linked. I heard her thoughts. I felt her lumpy pillow under my neck, the same scratchy sheets over my legs. She was dreaming but at the same time fighting to wake up. Her limbs were held down by invisible straps. She struggled, slowly freeing herself. I saw her swimming up to the surface in a deep green sea, scissor-kicking, bubbles swirling, but in her dream her head hadn't been shaved; her hair was long and flowing, suspended and ghostly in the murky water.

Twenty-six

The deputy sheriff, the one who had originally called in VCAT, visited my hospital room and told me the helicopter search hadn't yielded anything yet, and that it was possible Bangs could've taken the trailer out of the woods. They'd continue searching until nightfall and then reconsider their options. He told me that I could leave, that they'd draw up the formal complaint against Bangs and file the police report tomorrow. As I dressed, borrowing hospital scrubs because my clothes were filthy and torn, I knew somehow that Bangs had slipped away. He was a guerrilla fighter, disappearing and reappearing to cause havoc. He did what anyone would've done when I had escaped—he packed up and left the area. I wasn't sure how a trailer could be hidden and transported through the woods unnoticed, but I knew he wouldn't be stupid enough to hang around.

I was filling out forms at the front desk, knowing my insurance wouldn't cover all this. Larry had enrolled us to a high-deductible plan, and I expected a large bill in a few weeks. As I sat in the waiting room I worried about money. My short weekend stay down here was turning into a huge expense, and with my leaving Larry shorthanded, I was costing him money as well. The move into PI work was now necessary. I hadn't cracked open the textbook in a while, and I ignored the thought of the impending exam. It was another universe.

Vines arrived before Serena, and I knew immediately that he found my story difficult to believe. As I told him what I had told Wallace and Bowler, Vines kept asking why I hadn't gotten a better look at Bangs, and what exactly Bangs's words were regarding killing Raul Gama. Vines had brought a tape recorder and pointed to it, saying, "Repeat again exactly what you said about Raul Gama and Lowell Bangs's response, please."

I did, stating that Bangs had said Raul "deserved it" and he had admitted that using the knife was messy. I watched Vines's long-faced, disbelieving expression as I retold this; his large forehead shiny, his pupils pinpricks as they focused on me. He was wearing a wool sports coat that was obviously too warm, but he kept it on. I told him to look for Tim Jacobs at local hospitals—the shot to his foot and arm would require a doctor. I said, "Tim Jacobs is a link. Get him and you might get a lead on Bangs."

When Vines began asking me about Linda, though, I hesitated, then said, "Linda's family advised me not to talk about this without a lawyer."

Vines sat up, his large torso looming. "And when did they tell you this?"

"Just before you arrived. I talked to Julie on the phone."

"Christ," he said quietly. "That woman . . ."

"She said you're looking at Linda as a suspect? Are you serious?"

"You don't know what we've found out."

"I have a good idea," I said.

"Are you aware of the insurance policy? Or the will with Linda as beneficiary?"

I said, "She was his only daughter. Of course he'd name her in his will. Plus she was almost killed. You can't possibly think she had something to do with Raul—"

"Did Linda mention the insurance policy?"

"No. There's nothing unusual about a father naming his children as beneficiaries."

Vines narrowed his eyes. "A few weeks before his death? Expanding the policy? I'd say that was suspicious."

I thought about this, then said, "Maybe Hector's visit triggered his guilt.

He abandoned them when they were just kids. He expanded the policy to include them out of new guilt."

"Tell me again about the argument Linda had with her father at his house."

I shook my head. "Not until I talk to the lawyer."

"These tactics aren't used by the innocent, Mr. Choice."

"By the way, Bangs knows about Linda," I said. "If he thinks she witnessed something in that house, her life could be in danger."

Startled, Vines asked, "Did he threaten her safety?"

"No, but he asked about her. He was curious."

Vines was quiet. Then he said, "Mr. Choice, are you aware of the financial difficulties facing Linda?"

"What?"

"Did you know about her credit problems and her unpaid vacation leave?"

"What credit problems?"

"She recently needed to bring in a credit arbitrator to deal with her debt load."

"A what?"

"To prevent filing for bankruptcy."

"What? Impossible."

"We have her paperwork."

I shook my head, but then asked, "And the unpaid vacation?"

"The *San Jose Sentinel* is having problems and began layoffs. Some of the staff took unpaid, extended vacation leave to avoid losing their jobs completely. She has very little money, Mr. Choice."

I didn't reply. I knew about the Silicon Valley economy having trouble, but Linda hadn't mentioned anything about her newspaper job.

"Mr. Choice, how well do you know Linda?"

I stood up slowly. "This interview is over. We'll continue this after I've spoken with the lawyer."

Vines turned off his tape recorder and towered over me. He said, "Isn't it convenient that right as we begin focusing on your girlfriend you disappear then reappear with a story about a confession from a small-time drug dealer? I'm going to talk to Detective Bowler now. What do you want to bet that this Lowell Bangs is nowhere to be found?"

I said, "I hear that the press is beginning to make some noise about your case."

He kept still.

"I respect what you're trying to do," I said. "But you're going to look even worse if you finger Linda. She's innocent. I know she is."

He pulled out a handkerchief and wiped his forehead. He gave me a hard stare, then said, "We'll see about that."

I waited for Serena outside the hospital and wondered if Vines had been telling the truth. Maybe he was trying to rattle me. I suspected Linda sometimes maxed out her credit cards and paid only the minimum balance. But she had never once referred to an arbitrator, to bankruptcy. I would've known about this. I would've seen signs of it. She had also told me about taking vacation time, though I wasn't certain if she had said it was unpaid and in lieu of lay-offs. No, she hadn't. I would've questioned her about possible layoffs.

It occurred to me that we hadn't gone out to eat as much in the past few months. When we had first met we ate out every other night, and I remembered even remarking on her preference for Chinese restaurants. Except for that trip up to the Sonoma bed and breakfast, something planned much earlier, we hadn't recently done anything that required money. I thought we were being careful because of my job instability. Maybe there was something more going on. She never talked about her bills. I had no idea what her bank balance was.

Was I that blind? Another thought arose: What if our problems stemmed from that? I had been wrapped up in my job, my worries, and although I knew she was having difficulties at the *Sentinel*, I never even considered the possibility of her having money problems. *Things haven't quite worked out like I thought they would*, she had said.

Jeez. What kind of boyfriend was I if I couldn't even see something so important?

It wasn't obvious, though. She was good at her job. She seemed to be in demand. Hell, she had been on TV. If all this was true, I felt slighted. Why hadn't she told me? Maybe she was trying to spare me, especially after the way I had reacted to hearing too much of her work problems.

If she hadn't told me, it was because I hadn't made it very easy for her.

I looked up. Serena's silver Beetle had pulled into the parking lot, She honked and parked at the curb; she jumped out of it as soon as she cut the engine. "Allen!" she said, walking quickly toward me. "Are you okay?" She wore a tight gray skirt with a crisp white blouse, the top buttons opened and revealing a silver pendant. Her heels clicked on the pavement. She had on light makeup and nail polish.

Heartened by a friendly face, I stepped up and hugged her. She laughed and hugged me back, saying, "I was worried about you." But her hand grazed my left shoulder, and I winced. She pulled away, her brows furrowed. "You're hurt." I shook it off and hugged her again. "Are you okay?" she whispered.

I didn't want to let her go, and smelled her neck, a hint of sweat rubbing against my cheek. I was so tired.

On the car ride back to Costa Mesa, I explained to Serena what had been happening. I opened my window a few inches to let the air blow onto me and felt safe here with her. We were in a silver bubble that floated down the highway. When I described my running from Bangs and the pit bull, getting lost in the woods, she let out a small cry of surprise. "No way! A pit bull?"

I smiled at her response, liking her sympathy, and said, "I spent a night in the woods, and I eventually found my way out." I then told her about Bowler and Wallace now searching for the trailer.

"Why didn't you call me earlier? I could've helped."

"How?" I asked.

"When you were looking for that E dealer in L.A. Or when you were waiting for Tim. I could've helped. I could've waited outside and called the police when Gloria showed up."

"You would've done that?"

"Of course."

"But . . . it would've been dangerous."

She frowned, and tightened her grip on the steering wheel. I waited for her to reply, but she just stared straight ahead. I said, "It would've been too risky."

She shook her head.

"Don't be mad," I said. "I didn't want to impose."

"Impose? I've taken you to two raves and a party where someone pulled a gun. I've been late to work three times, missed two night classes, and left work early today, pissing off my boss." She glanced at me sadly, meeting my eyes, then turned back to the road. "I'm trying to help you."

I started to thank her but stopped. I said, "You're right. You've done a lot for me already, and I haven't really included you. I'm sorry."

She said, "You can be pretty closed off, Allen."

Closed off? I wanted to deny this, since I was always looking for engagement. I needed to be open, accepting. I asked, "How do you mean?"

"Not asking for anything. Not relying on anyone."

"I rely on people," I said lamely, though it was true that I didn't like making demands. I wondered if Linda thought the same way.

Serena said, "You know, sometimes people want to help. Sometimes they like to feel useful."

"I just don't want to be a burden," I said.

"A burden."

"I don't want to bother people."

She fell silent. I watched her drive. After a full minute she said, "Maybe as a kid you were a burden to your aunt." I was about to interrupt, but she continued, "Maybe you were even a burden to your father after your mother died, but things change. You were just a kid."

This stopped me. Aunt Insook had always complained that I had made her life harder. She never let me forget how I had been foisted onto her. I said, "You don't fool around, do you?"

She shook her head.

"You might be right," I said.

"I know I'm right."

"You're also pretty smart."

"I know I'm smart."

I turned to her. "And modest, too."

She gave me a half shrug. Then she said, "How do you feel? You look pretty tired."

"I'm exhausted. My shoulder really hurts."

"Let's pick up your things from the motel, and take you to my place."

I started to protest, but she glared at me, raising her eyebrow. She said, "Yes?"

I nodded. "Yes. I'll check out of the motel. My expenses are getting out of hand. Also, my rental car is in Venice. I'll have to pick that up."

She watched the traffic crowding ahead of us, and she said, "Let me help you, okay?"

I said okay, and we drove down PCH in silence. I struggled with the question of why she wanted to help me, but then decided just to accept it. I tried to think of my next moves, of what I had to do to help Linda; I couldn't stop searching for Bangs. With Vines turning his attention to Linda, I had to bring more evidence to light.

Serena seemed lost in thought. I watched her stare out over the road, some of the wind from my window brushing against her short hair. She had on faint traces of eye makeup and her lips were light red, her nails dark red against tanned hands, but I thought she looked good without any kind of makeup. I wanted to tell her this, but instead I reached over to her and touched her arm. I said, "Thank you for helping me."

She smiled.

By that evening, after checking out of the motel and getting my rental car from Tim Jacobs's street, I heard from Detective Bowler, who told me that they hadn't found the trailer but had found unmarked trails that led off the national park area and into private land. "Bangs probably used one of these newer trails. He's probably gone by now," Bowler said. They would continue the search in the morning, looking for evidence, but it didn't look promising. I asked him about Tim Jacobs, and he said, "That's out of our jurisdiction, but I believe Investigator Vines is getting help from the L.A. Sheriff and looking at hospitals. They want to pick him up for questioning but are having trouble finding him."

I also spoke to Julie, who wanted me to meet her and the lawyer at the hospital in the morning. She said, "What did you tell Vines? He put a policeman at the ICU door."

"Good. I told him about Bangs being interested in her status. She might be a witness. She might be able to identify him."

Julie let out a sharp breath. "You don't think he'd come after her, do you?"

"Depends on what she's seen."

"I can't believe this is happening," she said. "This is a nightmare."

"How is she?"

"She's going to come out of it any time now. The doctors said everything has stabilized."

"What does that mean?"

"They took the bolt out. The danger's gone."

I sat down on Serena's sofa. I was so relieved that I couldn't speak. Gracie walked across the floor and rested her head in my lap. I scratched her ears. After a moment I was able to say, "That's good."

"Come to the hospital tomorrow at ten, okay? The lawyer will be there."

I agreed and hung up. I hugged Gracie, who tried to lick my cheek. Serena walked in from the bedroom, dressed in red pajamas, and stopped at the sight of me nuzzling and cooing her dog. She gave me a curious look, but didn't say anything. My biggest worry—of Linda getting worse—seemed to have been allayed, and I was able to breathe again. I said to Serena, "Linda is recovering."

"Her coma?"

"Still unconscious, but the pressure in her head is back to normal."

She sat cross-legged on the cushion next to me, and Gracie moved away from me, drawn to Serena. "What will you do now?"

"Find Lowell Bangs," I said.

"How?"

"I have no idea," I said, slumping back and closing my eyes. "Bangs is slippery. He always seems to be a couple steps ahead of everyone else."

"Maybe you should find Gloria first."

I opened my eyes. "Maybe I should."

"I doubt she'll be going to raves—"

"No, but she's much more accessible." I wondered if her pager number could be traced. I had told Vines about it, so I hoped he was looking into it.

Serena said, "Did you learn anything when you saw them? Did you see a license plate on the car?"

I shook my head and told her what had happened. "It was too dark," I said. "And I was blindfolded for most of the time." But I had heard them. Both of them had spoken to me, and I went over their words. Then I remembered a reference. I said, "Gloria did say to Bangs something I didn't understand. It might have been about me, but she said, 'I don't want another Jameson.' "

"Jameson?"

"She was worried that Bangs would do something to me right away, and she said that she didn't want another Jameson."

"A person?" Serena asked. "Another person they went after?"

"Possibly," I said. I had mentioned this to Bowler and Wallace, but it was only a passing reference, and they didn't seem interested. They had just wanted to find the trailer. I said to Serena, "Maybe they did something similar to a person named Jameson."

"We can check for the name."

"Online?"

"The local papers have search engines on their sites. Also the UCI library has back issues on CD or on microfilm."

I knew we had to begin searching, but I could barely keep my eyes open. A heavy blanket seemed to weigh me down as I tried to pull myself off the sofa. Serena grabbed my hand to help me upright. I felt my stitches pulling, and I winced. She stopped and said, "Hey, you need to rest. Lie on the bed while I go online. I'll read you what I find."

We went into her bedroom and I lay down diagonally across her bed, keeping my head away from her pillows; I resisted sleep. She began clicking the keyboard and said, "When I was in college I used to write my papers late at night like this. My roommate told me that she couldn't relax without the sounds of my typing."

"What did you study?"

"Drama. With a minor in English. What about you?"

"Never finished," I said. "Started as a biology major and dropped out."

"Biology. Don't tell me you were premed."

I smiled, staring up at her ceiling. "Blame my aunt."

"Jeez. Does every Asian American major in biology?"

"Well, not this one. It was organic chemistry that pushed me over the edge."

She laughed and continued typing and clicking her mouse. She said, "The strange thing was that I was pretty good at biology and chemistry. I probably could've been premed."

"Why not, then?" I asked. I watched her with half-closed eyes, the small desk lamp shining over her arms and hands, shadowing her face. Papers were scattered over her desk, with a Tweety mug overflowing with pencils. She leaned forward and stared at the screen, saying, "I like being different. A whole lot of Jamesons in the news."

I mumbled that we could take care of it tomorrow. She nodded to me, then turned back to the screen. I stared at an African mask on the wall. The long oblong face, carved with large eyes and a small mouth stained dark brown, seemed to pulse in the dim light. I began drifting off. After a few minutes Serena walked to the bed and pulled a sheet over me. I mumbled a thanks. She returned to the desk and put on a pair of headphones, and I heard the drilling beat of rave music filtering out as she bopped her head back and forth. She began typing, and I watched her dance in her chair, her bare feet tapping the wooden floor, and I thought, *I am not a burden.*

Twenty-seven

Ten hours of deep, dreamless sleep rejuvenated me; my body, with almost every joint and muscle aching, nevertheless felt energized, reminiscent of a hard workout. My bruises had changed colors and were now a deeper shade of purple, bordering on brown. My shoulder stung, but only really hurt when I raised my arm too quickly. Most important, I was thinking with a sharpness and clarity that only comes from rest and perspective.

On my way to the hospital to meet with Julie, I brought a sheaf of print-outs that Serena had left me before going to work. Last night she had found only a few references to different people named Jameson, including a Los Angeles congressman and a lawyer representing a stock broker accused of fraud, but the one listing that seemed interesting to her was an obituary, which she had printed from the *Orange County Register*:

HAMMOND JAMESON, 46, PASSED AWAY ON MARCH 14. "HAM," AS HIS FRIENDS AND COLLEAGUES CALLED HIM, WAS BORN IN SAVANNAH, GA, AND MOVED TO CALIFORNIA TO ATTEND U.C. BERKELEY AND U.S.C. FILM SCHOOL. HAM CONTINUED TO WRITE, PRODUCE, AND DIRECT SMALL-BUDGET FILMS WHILE FOUNDING AND RUNNING AN INTERNET COM-PANY. HE SETTLED IN THE IRVINE AREA, RAISING A LOVING FAMILY AND ENJOYING HIS HOBBIES OF WINDSURFING AND

HIKING. HE IS SURVIVED BY HIS WIFE, JERI, AND HIS THREE CHILDREN, SONS MATTHEW AND HAMMOND JR., AND DAUGHTER MARY. FAMILY AND FRIENDS WILL ATTEND A PRIVATE BURIAL AT SEA APRIL THE 28TH. IN LIEU OF FLOWERS, DONATIONS MAY BE MADE TO THE SIERRA CLUB.—SEASIDE PLAINS MORTUARY DIRECTORS.

Serena's note to me said, "No cause of death even though other obits usually mention it. This is the only 'Jameson' (first or last name) in recent L.A. and O.C. papers that might be linked." But she had also included printouts of the stories about the congressman and the lawyer, with "just in case" scribbled on them. I had read through them as soon as I had woken up, thinking again about Gloria's worry of "another Jameson," and agreed with Serena's instincts. I decided to follow up on Hammond Jameson after meeting with Julie and the lawyer.

I was stuck in traffic on the 5, an accident miles ahead backing everyone up, and realized that this rental car didn't have air conditioning. I was sweating, but relished the heat after my night in the woods, the chill still lingering in my bones. My memories of shivering on the hard, prickly ground mingled with my faint recollections of promises I had made to myself. I had vowed to be more sympathetic. I needed to redeem myself.

My regrets, no longer pursuing me with the same ferocity as two nights ago, still loitered nearby. Their quiet rumblings kept me hurrying forward.

When I finally arrived at the hospital, almost an hour late, I found Julie in the waiting room and was startled by her appearance: her face haggard and wan, her eyes rimmed with sleeplessness, and yet she seemed happy and ran over to me. "Linda woke up this morning," she said to me before I opened my mouth.

"What? How is she? Can I see her? What'd she say—"

"Still really tired. We spoke for less than a minute, and the doctors examined her. She's sleeping now. She's going to be okay."

I wasn't sure what to think, and it took almost a full minute for this to register. And when I did, my legs were unsteady. I reached out and held Julie's arm, which she interpreted as a comforting gesture. She pulled me to her and we hugged. She grazed my bad shoulder, which hurt, but I didn't say anything. After an awkward moment, we broke apart and looked away. She said, "I already called everyone." A man in a suit approached, and Julie waved him closer. She said to me, "The lawyer."

He walked to us, clearing his throat, and Julie introduced us. Carlos Cielo was slim, boyish, and seemed to be in his late twenties, his crisp, tailored blue suit looking out of place on him, like a teen playing dress up. My expression must have betrayed my thoughts because he immediately said, "I know I look young. I'm a junior partner and have gone to trial in over two dozen cases."

"Carlos's parents know my parents," Julie said. "He works at a big L.A. firm."

"I have to let you know that I represent Linda, not you, though at this point your interests are the same."

"What did she say? How is she?"

Julie said, "She was actually surprisingly alert. Just tired. She said she didn't see who the attacker was."

"What happened at Raul's?"

"She said she went into the house but he was already dead. There was someone and she surprised him."

To Carlos, I said, "Have the police found anything more?"

"No. I just learned that Tim Jacobs seems to have disappeared, and the Ventura County Sheriff's Department haven't found anything in those woods you were in."

I sighed. I told them about the possible Jameson lead, though I said it was a stretch. "It was just a passing reference I heard. It might be nothing."

"No, it's good. You should look into it," Carlos said, fixing the knot of his red tie. The collar of his shirt was starched white. He said, "The case against Linda is extremely flimsy, and with your testimony it should fall apart. But having another suspect, one with harder evidence, is vital."

"Is what Vines said about Raul's will and life insurance true?"

Carlos and Julie nodded. Julie said, "So are some of Linda's financial problems, but—"

"But that's all they have," Carlos said, "No evidence at the crime scene, and they can't find the weapon that hit Linda. She said the attacker must have taken it. And she can't ID him; it happened too fast. The sheriff is only looking at Linda because he has nothing else."

"I'll get more," I said.

"Vines will be coming by later to interview Linda," Carlos said. "And then he'll probably want to talk to you again. I want to hear everything from your end first. I need to know how badly Linda is exposed."

"Can I see her?"

Julie said, "Once they move her out of the ICU, she can have more visitors."

"When?"

"Tonight."

"I have to warn you again," Carlos said, "that I'm not your lawyer, but Linda's. And I'm going to do everything I can to defend her, not you."

"I'm not worried about me."

"You should be. You can be named an accessory, obstructing justice, aiding and abetting. You should have your own lawyer."

"I would really like to see Linda. Can I?"

"You can see her but I don't think you should wake her up," Julie said. "She needs to rest."

"What did she say?"

"How about you tell Carlos here everything that's been going on, while I check with the doctor. Afterward you can see her," Julie said. "Okay?"

"Here? Now?" I asked Carlos.

He said, "Let me get my briefcase, but yes, the sooner the better."

We spent the next hour in a corner of the waiting room as I retold the series of events leading me here, answering Carlos's questions and occasionally asking my own about the case against Linda. He was convinced there wasn't much the police could use against Linda, and that at this stage they wouldn't try to file charges. "There are a lot of wealthy and influential people in Laguna Beach, so the pressure is on the sheriff. But I doubt the D.A. would take this case as it is."

When I described the kidnapping, Carlos asked if the hospital in Ventura County had documented my injuries. They had. As he was taking notes he said, "This is perfect. A practical confession from Bangs."

"But isn't it hearsay?"

"You're now a witness. You're establishing his guilt. It'll fly at a hearing."

I went on and told him again about Jameson, and he said, "I'm not sure how that'll help Linda except for pointing to a pattern for Bangs, but anything you can get to incriminate him helps."

After a few more questions and clarifications, I asked if I could see Linda. Julie, who had been listening, nodded, and led me down a hall. She spoke to a nurse who walked us to the ICU. My hands began sweating, and I chided myself for being nervous. A uniformed policeman was sitting next to the door, and he stood up as we approached.

Julie said, "He's a friend."

The officer, a muscular man with a crew cut, looked bored, checked his clipboard, and said to Julie, "Ma'am, I told you it's just immediate family."

"He's a close family friend," Julie said. "It's just for a minute."

"Another friend?" the officer said. "I don't know—"

"One minute. That's it."

The officer sighed, but gave Julie a small grin. Julie smiled back, and the officer sat down. I glanced at her, and said, "What other friend?"

She hesitated.

I didn't know Linda had any friends down here, but then I immediately thought of Harlan and said, "From the Bay Area? What friend? Is Harlan here?"

She froze at the name, which was all I needed. I asked, "When did he come?"

"He flew down on his own. He called and I told him what happened."

"Where is he now?"

"He took them out for brunch."

"Brunch? He took your parents out to brunch?"

She shrugged.

I was dumbfounded. I wondered if I had been expected to do something like that. Why hadn't anyone told me? I felt defeated on all fronts. I hurried into the ICU and saw Linda lying in bed without all the wires and tubes connected to her, a paisley scarf wrapped around her head. Her eyes were closed, and I was surprised to see how gaunt her cheeks were. All the puffiness was gone—the contours of her face were sharper. I stood closer to her and listened to her slow, steady breathing and reached down to touch her hand. Her skin was warm.

Her eyes flickered open. I stepped back in surprise. I glanced back at the door, but Julie and the officer were talking away from the window. I leaned over the bed and said hello.

She focused on me, and answered in a clear voice, "Hi."

I felt my chest constricting. I said, "I'm so glad you're awake."

She said, "Me, too."

"You look much better than before."

"Did you know that they drilled into my head?"

I nodded.

She blinked her eyes slowly, deliberately. "Julie and the lawyer filled me in. You've been doing a lot."

"I've been trying to."

She said, "I couldn't help them. I didn't see much."

"You mean at Raul's?"

She nodded slowly. "It was all so fast. It was dark."

"That's okay. All that matters is that you're better." I searched for personality changes, but she seemed normal. I heard Julie's voice outside, and Harlan's presence gnawed at me; I resisted asking about him. Instead, I said, "How do you feel?"

"Antsy. I want to get up."

I smiled. Same old Linda. She gave me a tired smile back, and her obvious effort at this almost unhinged me again. I turned away and looked at another patient on a respirator. I said, "I was worried about you."

"I don't feel as if I've been in a coma."

"What's it like?"

"My head hurts. Everything aches. Like a bad hangover."

I tried to laugh, but it came out as a nervous bark. "Do you remember anything? Did you dream?"

"No. I don't think so. I can't believe that the police think I might have . . ." She sighed, then said, "Did you talk to the lawyer?"

"I did," I said. "You'll be fine. I'm going to get Bangs."

She nodded. I didn't know what else to say. I thought of Harlan taking out her parents. He was moving in quickly.

She looked at me. "I keep thinking about Hector, about what my mom said."

I didn't move. "About the abuse?"

"Just thinking about things. Going back and remembering small details, like the way Hector really clung to me. And he was scared of Raul as a kid. I mean, scared in a weird way."

"Like how?"

"Never wanting to be alone with him."

"But that's because he was so hard on Hector."

"True, but now I wonder . . ."

I sat down on a plastic chair next to the bed. "Do you think your mother was right?"

"I have no idea."

I asked tentatively, "What about . . ." I hesitated.

"What about what?" she said.

"What about you?"

"What about me?"

"Did Raul—"

"No," she said quickly.

"No?"

Her eyes met mine. "No. Not me. I'm sure about that."

"But you think with Hector?"

"I don't know what to think."

"What kind of abuse do you think—"

"Please don't ask me that."

"I'm sorry," I said. "It's really none of my business."

"No, I'm sorry." Her voice thinned. "I'm sorry about a lot of things."

"Let's not worry about that. You just get better."

"I can see it happening," she said. "Hector wanting to start fresh, but needing to figure out things with Raul."

"Asking for money?"

"Maybe going to him for help. You know? Getting in too deep with the drugs, and giving Raul a chance to make things right."

"But then Raul throws him out."

"And then Hector tells Bangs about him, knowing what Bangs would do." She closed her eyes for a moment, then sighed. "Allen? It's okay if you want to go home. There's not much else you can do."

I thought of Harlan being here. I said, "No, I'm close. I have a new lead."

"What?"

I told her briefly about Jameson and about what Gloria had said. "It's something worth looking into. Maybe there's a connection. I have to find out how and why he died."

"Let me know what you find," she said, sinking deeper into her pillow. "Just be careful. . . ."

"I'll let you rest. I'll come back tomorrow."

She nodded.

"Linda?" I asked.

She turned to me. I touched her cheek, and kissed her forehead, which made her smile.

Although I had plenty to do, I didn't want to leave her side yet. I watched her sleep, and I let myself relax. The relief of seeing her recovering, the easing of tension that I didn't realize was permeating my entire body, fatigued me. I inhaled and exhaled slowly, steadying myself. Linda would be okay. My guilt abated.

I noticed a patient in the bed across the room, his face bandaged with gauze and silver strips of metal. I looked around at the others, everyone in different stages of distress. Faint announcements and requests for doctors floated down the hallways outside, quick steps passing by. Voices. Something in the wall hummed, then stopped. I turned back to Linda and saw that her scarf had shifted on the pillow, exposing a part of her shaved scalp. I reached over to pull the scarf down and saw dried blood over black stitches, a dime-sized area where her skin had pulled up into a small pucker and stitched. Carefully, I moved the scarf over the wound. She stirred, then kept still. It didn't matter if Harlan was around and cozying up to her parents. Linda and I were over. That much was obvious. I had to let go of any jealous feelings. I needed to be a better person. It didn't matter. It didn't matter. No, what mattered was her getting better and me helping her. What mattered was making everything right. I stared at her sleeping: I stared at her mouth slightly open, her breath fluttering the sheet near her chin. I had to redeem myself. You'll be okay, I thought. I promise you. I lay my hand over her forehead, and thought, *Heal.*

Twenty-eight

The woman who answered the door looked at me blankly, waiting for me to say something. I was taken aback by her pale, almost translucent skin, needle-thin blue veins tinting her cheeks. She had wispy carrot-colored hair and lifeless green eyes. When she acknowledged with a small nod that she was Jeri Jameson, I realized she was probably still in mourning. I had to be delicate about this. I asked her if this was a bad time, and she said in an unsteady voice, "Bad time for what?"

I introduced myself and told her I was looking into a few things for a friend. When I offered my hand to shake, she extended hers tentatively, and I saw how bony her fingers were. I tried not to squeeze too hard. Her skin seemed to be pulled too tightly against her skull. She waited for me to explain. I said, "I'm looking for someone, and I'm not sure, but there's a chance that he had known in some way your . . . your late husband."

"My late husband," she said.

"Ham."

She blinked. "You knew Ham?"

"No, I'm sorry. Do you have time for a few questions?"

"Can I see some ID?"

I pulled out my wallet. "I have my private patrol card and my gun permit, but I don't have a PI license yet." I also showed her Larry's business card with my name on it. "I work for Baxter Investigations."

She barely looked at the cards and didn't seem to hear me. She nodded and said, "I have a little time before my kids come home from school." She stepped aside and let me in.

The apartment was almost empty. Except for a few pieces of furniture, all the shelves and tables were bare. I asked, "Are you moving?"

"Yes." She sat down on the sofa.

I looked around curiously.

She said, "I'm selling the place."

I sat across from her and said, "I'm really sorry to bother you about this, but can I ask about your husband?"

She nodded. "How did you hear about it?"

"The obituary. And I looked you up in the phone book."

She nodded again.

"How did he die?"

She met my eyes and said, "He committed suicide."

Then I realized why the obituary hadn't listed the cause of death. I said, "I'm sorry to hear that." I didn't know how to continue. I asked, "May I ask if he left a—"

"Note? No. A lot of people ask that for some reason. The police did. The insurance company did. No. He stuck a gun in his mouth and pulled the trigger."

"So the police looked into it?"

"Yes. Not to my satisfaction, but yes."

"What do you mean?"

She was quiet. She sighed. "Do you know what my husband did?"

"Something about an Internet company."

"It was an Internet porn company. He used his knowledge of film and video and founded a Web porn site."

I froze. "Was he friends with Raul Gama?"

"Who?"

"Raul Gama. Also in the same business."

She shook her head. "I didn't know much about Ham's business. I didn't like it, but he did very, very well. Or so I thought."

"What do you mean?"

"He was very much in debt. When my lawyer helped sort out the finances, I was shocked. Ham had leveraged everything. Maybe that's why he killed himself."

"What did the police say?"

"That he probably was on the verge of financial ruin. That he dealt in pornography when he once wanted to make great films. He loved Orson Welles. He loved Goddard. Now he dealt with teen cheerleaders. They did their routine investigation and found it was most likely suicide."

I asked slowly, "Does the name Lowell Bangs mean anything to you?"

She shook her head.

"Hector Gama? Gloria Katz?"

"No. Why?"

"I'm trying to find Lowell Bangs, and I have reason to believe he might have had some kind of contact with your late husband."

"Was he in the business?"

"I don't think so."

"So who was he?"

I said, "Just someone I'm trying to find."

She frowned. "I've been direct with you and you're not returning the courtesy."

"I'm sorry. Lowell bangs is a drug dealer. During my investigation I heard the name 'Jameson' arise in the context of . . . regret? Of something not working out? I searched the newspapers for this name and found the obituary of your late husband."

"Are there others?"

"Yes, but no deaths."

Mrs. Jameson straightened and said, "Do you think this drug dealer could've been involved with my husband's death?"

I held up my hand and said, "I don't know. I don't want to mislead you. There might not be any connection, but I had to see—"

"But that would make sense. Sometimes in that business Ham ran across bad elements. He said that drugs are often a problem. Maybe he tried to help one of the actresses. Maybe he got this dealer mad."

"Mrs. Jameson, I don't know. Did your husband have records or something that I can look into? What about employees or—"

"His partner. Jim Sarman. You *must* talk to him immediately."

"Frankly, I don't know if there's any connection—"

"You don't understand. Ham was very responsible. He loved his kids. He had a two-million-dollar life insurance policy that was void if he committed suicide. He would never, ever have done it and wasted all those premiums. Never. If he wanted to commit suicide, he would've done it and made it look like an accident."

"I'll talk to Sarman, of course. I can't guarantee anything."

"Mr. Choice, never mind me or the state I'm in. If you can prove Ham was killed, my kids will be okay. We have nothing right now. Nothing. And I wouldn't be so angry."

"Angry?"

Her mouth tightened. "I loved Ham, but if he did kill himself like this, I can never forgive him. It would've been the most selfish act he could've committed."

I returned to Serena's, armed with Mrs. Jameson's directions to her late husband's company and a promise from her that she'd tell Sarman to expect a call from me. She warned me that Sarman was very "odd" and that he used to let her husband deal with the public. Sarman was now in the process of shutting down the company.

Serena was still at work, so I made myself a quick snack and rested. I felt guilty for eating her food and sleeping in her bed. Then I told myself to accept her help without compunction. She wanted to help.

I tried not to think about Harlan. But that thick feeling of jealousy kept rising up in my throat. I had never met him, and yet I felt as if I knew him. He was worming his way into the family. He was getting on everyone's good side, whereas I seemed to have messed everything up.

Enough. I focused on Hammond Jameson and Bangs. I tried to find a link. Drugs? Money? It was possible that I had misheard Gloria, that it wasn't "Jameson" at all. Or maybe "Jameson" was a nickname. Too many possibilities. However, the coincidence of Jameson involved in the same industry as

Raul Gama was too obvious to ignore. Maybe Raul and Jameson were linked, and Bangs started to shake down Jameson?

I couldn't stop returning to Linda. Julie had been wrong about her sister. Linda denied any kind of abuse. But would she admit it to me? She had no reason to tell me the truth. She hadn't even told me about her financial trouble. And it really wasn't any of my business. There were many, many things she probably kept from me. Harlan, for one. I knew whatever connections we had were quickly dissolving. Maybe they were never there to begin with.

Some of this was beyond my comprehension. I wondered how much Julie actually knew but wasn't revealing to me. I remembered Linda describing how close she and Julie were when they were in their teens. Linda told me a story about how they had discovered in their attic a box of old disco records. Julie thought it might have belonged to her late mother who had always shopped at rummage sales, impulsively buying junk. Linda had laughed while telling me this, saying, "All the disco greats: Village People, K. C. and the Sunshine Band, Gloria Gaynor." I watched her as she lost herself in the memory, describing how she and her sister would play the records when no one was home, dancing wildly around the living room. "We would've died if anyone saw us, but it was so much fun. I think that's when we clicked. It wasn't until then that we started becoming friends."

I could picture her with Julie. I closed my eyes and saw her dancing and laughing. But my vivid imaginings of Linda as a kid were darkened by her memories of her father, of Hector. It seemed that everything joyful was tainted with the complications of families.

I was preparing to call Sarman when Serena appeared. I glanced at the clock and said, "You're not at work?"

She threw her knapsack onto the sofa and said, "I quit."

"What? Why?"

"My boss was giving me a hard time about my lates and leaving early."

"Oh, no. This is my fault."

"It isn't. I also got word back from a few companies I e-mailed my résumé to. I sent it to five companies, and four want interviews. I'm going to fly up next week."

"Four? That's amazing. I thought the economy was really bad."

"It is, but they're replacing more expensive programmers, laying them off, and hiring entry-level people like me to take their place."

"Out with the old?"

She shrugged. "Some of these 'old' programmers are my age. They just started earlier. I'm not mourning their stock options. What're you up to?"

I thanked her for finding Jameson's obituary, then recounted the events of my morning. She listened, then asked, "You think there's a link?"

"No idea. It can't hurt to check," I said. "If there's nothing we can try the other Jamesons. Maybe the criminal lawyer."

"So, were you serious about your offer to put me up while I'm in the Bay Area?"

"Of course. I owe you big time."

"It's just because you owe me?" she asked.

"No. It's because I like you."

She smiled. "All right, what's next, boss?"

"I'm going to arrange a meeting with this partner of Jameson's."

"I'll go with you. You want company?"

"I do," I said, picking up the phone.

Jim Sarman met us in his office, part of a large glass complex near the Fashion Island shopping center, and immediately told us that without Jeri Jameson's plea he would never do something like this. "I told the police what I know. I don't like private detectives."

"Why not?" I asked, studying him. He was an overweight man with tiny oval eyeglasses, his large face spreading down to his collar. He folded his arms, his sleeves rolled up.

"You profit from other people's misery," he said. "And I don't like what you're doing to Jeri."

"Doing to her?"

"Giving her hope!" he yelled.

Both Serena and I stepped back, startled. We glanced at each other. I said, "Excuse me?"

Serena said to him, "Profiting from misery? And what you do isn't profiting from women's misery? You're not exploiting them?"

"I knew it!" he said. "You're here to give me shit!"

I held up my hands. "No. We're here to ask about Ham." I took a better look around the office and realized that there were no signs of what this company did. I couldn't even find the name of the company in here. Downstairs in the lobby this office was just listed as "JS Enterprises."

"Ham, oh yes, Ham. He ate a bullet and now we're screwed." Sarman rubbed his forehead ferociously.

Serena met my eyes, then asked him, "Screwed, why?"

"He took care of the business. I took care of the technology. I can't do it all alone," he said.

Serena said, "Is everything off-site? Do you use a server farm?"

Sarman brightened. "No! Everything's here. We run it all in the back."

"What kind of servers?"

"Sun Enterprise series."

"Are you using their SANs for storage—"

"No way! Cost is important. We've been using NetApp's filers, because of their scalability. You want to see?" He smiled.

Serena nodded. I gave her a thumbs-up signal and followed them as Sarman began telling Serena about their computer systems. We moved out of the front office and down a hallway, where thick tubes of wires snaked all across the floor. There were three empty rooms with beds, cameras set up on tripods and aimed at the beds. I reached into the one room and flicked a light switch. Five bright spotlights shone onto the bed. I turned off the switch and caught up to Serena. Sarman directed us into a smaller room filled with computer equipment stacked high, wires running everywhere, small lights blinking, a low-pitched humming surrounding us. Serena said, "They're all on."

"We're still getting a lot of traffic, and we're still charging the subscriptions, but nothing live anymore," Sarman said. "Soon people will be canceling. I'll sell off the equipment."

"That's it?" I asked. "That's the company?"

"That's all you need," he said. "You just have to have a lot of storage for all that video."

"Can we ask you about Jameson?" Serena said.

He rubbed his forehead again. "I can't. I can't."

"Did you know Raul Gama?" I asked.

Sarman looked up. "Yes. I know him. Knew him. I heard he was killed. What's going on?"

"What? No. Wait. You knew Raul?"

"He was Ham's friend. They almost merged companies. But Ham didn't want to get into the kiddie stuff. The international stuff."

"Kiddie porn? Raul did that?" I asked.

Sarman nodded quickly, avoiding our gazes. "Through an Amsterdam company."

I said, "What about Lowell Bangs? Have you heard of him? Met him?"

Sarman's face blanched. "Oh no, no, no. Is that what this is about? Is this about him? Oh no. I knew something was wrong."

"What do you mean?" Serena asked. "You knew Bangs?"

"No. I mean yes. No. I knew Ham was doing something with him. Something illegal. I didn't want to know. It was drugs, wasn't it? That guy had 'drug dealer' written all over him. I knew something was wrong."

"Tell us what you know about Bangs," I said.

"Nothing. I didn't want to know. Ham was getting worried about money, his future. The company wasn't doing well. He began associating with lowlifes. I didn't want to get involved."

"What did Ham say?"

"Something about being the money front man for some big deal. I assume he meant drug deal, but I didn't want to know. I didn't ask. I just take care of technology. That's all I do."

"Did you ever meet Bangs? Do you know how to find him?"

"He came here once, but I didn't want to meet him. I didn't want anything to do with it."

"Did you see him?" Serena asked. "When was this?"

"A couple of months ago. He was in the front office. I passed by."

"What did he look like?"

"I didn't see closely. He had a beard. Kind of scuzzy. He had a baseball cap. He was with some other guy."

"Who? Another man?"

"Yes. I forgot his name. Tanner, I think. But Bangs was the main guy."

"Can we search Ham's files? Is there anything we can look through to help us find Bangs?"

Sarman shook his head. "If it was illegal, he wouldn't have any records around. Maybe encrypted on an off-site server, but I don't know."

"Did you tell the police this?" Serena asked.

"God, no! I can't get involved. I mean, it could've been suicide. Anything's possible. I didn't want to get mixed up in this. I just take care of technology."

"Don't tell Mrs. Jameson anything yet," I said. "We still have to look into this."

"Don't worry. I don't know anything. I never will."

"Thanks for your help," Serena told him.

Sarman led us out to the front office, then scurried back down the hallway. Serena and I walked out of the building and to her car. I said, "Bangs got money from Jameson?"

"Jameson wanted action," she said.

"Bangs could probably give him that," I said. "But then what, Bangs double-crossed him? Kept the money?"

"And killed him," Serena said. "But what about Hector's father?"

"Raul knew Jameson. Maybe Jameson told him something. Bangs was being careful."

"Jeez," Serena said. "And killed him, too?"

I sighed, unable to grasp the implications, and I suddenly had an image of Jeri Jameson, shell-shocked by her husband's death. Her eyes had been deadened by pain, and I'd be haunted by her for a while. Lowell Bangs had left a wide wake.

Twenty-nine

Serena and I took Gracie for a walk around the neighborhood as night approached. I needed to think. Serena had suggested a run, but my shoulder still ached, and I knew my legs hadn't recovered from my trek in the woods. However, the cool air and darkening sky did help, and as we moved farther from her house and into a quieter series of streets, where rows of single-family homes glowed from within, I felt cushioned by the monochrome of the night. The glare of the sun and heat of the day had worn me down. Gracie sniffed signposts, walked ahead, stopped and looked back, then continued. Dogs from inside the houses sensed her and barked at the windows.

Serena held my arm and moved in step with me. I felt relaxed, comforted. We didn't talk for five blocks, just taking in the neighborhood. I said this was nice. She smiled.

"How is Linda?" she asked.

I told her that Linda was being moved out of the ICU tonight. She had woken up this morning.

"Oh! How is she?"

"Tired."

Serena nodded but didn't ask anything else. I found myself getting winded and realized it would take a few months to get back into shape; my body had been severely punished the past few days. I took deep breaths and felt my skin tingling. Needing some distance. I tried to push all thoughts of Lowell Bangs away so that I could focus on what was waiting for me back up north: the PI exam. If I passed it, I'd be the new partner of B&C Investigations. That we wouldn't be B&C Security and I'd be moving out of executive protection didn't bother me anymore. I was learning to be flexible. Nothing like a cold night in the woods to put things in perspective.

Serena said, "Should I fly or drive up to the Bay Area?"

"With all the flight delays, it might be easier to drive."

"Do you have a return ticket?"

"No."

"Maybe we can drive up together. When do you go back?"

"Good question," I said. "I don't know. I can't stay down here much longer." I told her about the PI exam and the work situation. "I'm running out of money."

"I hope Linda appreciates what you're doing."

I glanced at her. "I think she does."

"She doesn't like me."

"Why do you say that?"

"The way she looked at me when you guys first showed up."

"After your run? Probably because I had to try really hard not to gawk." She said, "I know."

"You know?" I stopped.

"You don't think I know when I'm being checked out?" She saw my stricken expression and laughed, "Oh, come on. No big deal."

"No?"

"No. It was flattering."

We continued walking.

I said, "Tell me more about Hector."

"Like what?" she asked.

"Did he ever talk about being a kid? His parents, anything?"

"Not often. A few times. We were really casual. We'd hook up and go to raves, then come back and crash. It's funny, but we hardly saw each other during the day. Once I met him for lunch and I almost didn't recognize him in the daylight." She glanced at me. "I think I told you this. It was usually when he was high, he'd talk a little bit about how he hated living at home, not knowing what do with his life."

"Right. You mentioned he wanted to know about his real father, Raul." I thought of what we had learned from Sarman, that Raul had been involved in child pornography.

"Well," Serena said. "Hector blamed him for messing up everything."

"Messing up everything? Did he talk about being abused or anything?"

She stopped. "Abused? You mean physically?"

"Anything."

She shook her head, then took my arm. She was quiet for a while, as we passed a small park, then said, "He never mentioned that, but it's not like we ever had real deep conversations. We talked about which rave to go to. Was he abused?"

"Maybe."

"Like, how?"

"His mother accused his father of sexual abuse, one of the reasons why the father stayed away."

Serena squeezed my arm. "Everyone's so screwed up."

When we returned to her house, she played a message on her machine, and we heard Linda's voice: "Uh, hello? I'm looking for Allen Choice and was given this number. Allen, call me. I have a phone at the hospital." She listed a number, then said, "Where are you?" and hung up.

I met Serena's eyes, and she nodded to the phone. She said, "I'll be in the shower."

I called Linda.

"Whose number is that?" she asked, after I had said hello. "Julie didn't say."

"Serena's."

A pause. "Serena, Hector's ex-girlfriend?"

"Yes."

"You're *living* there?"

"No, just sleeping on her sofa. The motel was getting expensive. I'm running low on funds."

"And she let you sleep there?"

"Yes."

"Well," Linda said, but then fell silent.

I waited for more, but when she didn't say anything else, I asked, "How are you feeling?"

"Better. I should be able to leave in two days."

"That soon?"

"I feel okay, and, besides, I have to pay a percentage of this hospital bill."

"Oh. That must be a lot."

"I wanted to explain about Harlan," she said. "Julie said she told you. I didn't invite him."

"But why would he fly down here?" I asked.

"Because he was worried."

"I didn't know you guys were that close—"

"I'm not going to apologize for something I had no control over."

"Fine," I said. "I found out some more things about Bangs."

"Good. Vines is trying to find him. Carlos is doing a good job of deflecting them."

I told her about Jameson's widow, the connection to Sarman, and what Sarman had said. "I'm not sure I understand it all, but Bangs met with Jameson, got him involved in something. I'm sure it's connected with Raul, since Jameson knew Raul." I decided not to mention the child pornography.

"Wait," Linda said. "Go over that again. Tell me exactly what this Sarman guy said."

I repeated myself, emphasizing that Sarman had seen Bangs recently.

"And this other man? What was his name?"

"Sarman said 'Tanner,' but he wasn't sure."

"Not 'Taylor' or 'Tyler'?"

"He said 'Tanner.' Why?"

Linda was silent. After a moment she said, "I've got to go."

"Wait. What is it?"

"I have a hunch. I need to sort it out first. We'll talk tomorrow. Go hang out with Serena."

"Wait," I said. "Tell me. I've done so much of the legwork—"

But she had hung up. I said, "Hello?" and the line clicked off. I listened to the brief silence, then the dial tone came on. I stared at the phone. Did she just dismiss me? After all the shit I'd been through, she *dismissed* me and told me to hang out with Serena? What the hell was that? The motel had been costing me forty dollars a night. What did she expect me to do?

I hung up the phone a little too hard, and Gracie raised her head at me. I said to her, "Jeez, that's the thanks I get?"

I tried to calm down. She was under pressure. She was confused. She didn't have the patience to be polite, not even to me.

I sat down at the kitchen table and slumped in the chair. I gave up. I was tired of not knowing what to do or say to her. Tired of helping her. Tired of all this. I put my forehead down onto the table, feeling the coolness of the surface, feeling the vibration of the refrigerator travel through the floor. My head thrummed. The stitches in my shoulder prickled, and my body still flashed moments of deep pain whenever I moved too quickly. I felt a burst of self-pity. I was doing everything I could to help Linda, and it didn't matter. I probably shouldn't have come down in the first place. Maybe Linda would have been better off. Maybe without me she would've talked to fewer people, then had given her mother the truth—that Hector dealt drugs and was killed—and then it would've been over. She would've spent more time with her family. She would've returned home and broken up with me and would've hooked up with Harlan and I'd move into PI work and live my quiet life with none of these hassles, and I'd be healthy and sane and free.

Maybe not, but at least I wouldn't be feeling so shitty.

Why was it that people coupled? What was the point if all that happened was an eventual end, a painful one, which could be spared by simply staying alone? Engagement was a drug, an illusory one. Maybe it gave you a high, made you feel complete, but then it wore off. Maybe the true search was for an engagement with yourself, the only permanent and satisfying solution to dis-ease. A self-engagement. Why keep searching for connections with others, with externals? Why not reach inward? I knew what Linda would say to that—she'd laugh at me and say it was a nice name for being a recluse. I could even hear her voice as she snickered.

Then I saw how I tended to anticipate Linda's reactions to my thoughts.

She was a constant point of reference, and this bothered me. When anything happened I wanted to tell her, and I was annoyed with myself for this kind of dependence. It was a weakness I wanted to rectify. I had to be tougher, more self-reliant, and I had to protect myself from others.

I had to be Mack.

"Uh, Allen?"

I looked up from the table. Serena was in the kitchen doorway, wrapped in a large white bath towel, her hair wet and combed back. She said, puzzled, "You okay?"

My forehead tingled from resting it on the hard surface for so long. I said, "I was thinking."

"Being one with the Formica?" She smiled. Gracie padded up beside her. Serena leaned in the doorway, and I felt a jolt of attraction. She said, "Your turn, if you want."

I thanked her and stared at her freshly showered legs as she walked away.

We watched the late evening news for any developments on Raul Gama's murder and the search for Bangs, but there was nothing, and Serena asked me what I planned to do tomorrow. I said, "I guess tell Vines what I learned. The connection with this guy Jameson is important."

"It's definitely motive," she said, tugging on her pajamas pants and sitting cross-legged on the sofa. Her bare feet were pale against her red pajamas and the dark green sofa.

"This is getting exhausting," I said.

"Oh, come on. You're just feeling a little frustrated."

I nodded. "What're you going to do tomorrow?"

She slid closer to me. "I'm going to be researching the companies I'll be interviewing with. You sure you'll have room at your place for my visit?"

"Positive."

"And you'll show me around."

"Yes. You'll like it. By then I'll also be ready to go on some nice runs with you. Make sure you bring running gear."

"How long can I crash there?"

"As long as you want."

"Thanks," she said, touching my leg. "You're a pal."

My heart thumped out of rhythm, and I said, "Maybe when all this is over we can go out and do something nice. Dinner."

"Like a date?"

"A real date."

"You mean searching for a drug dealer isn't a real date?"

I smiled. "I guess dinner and a movie would be too boring for you."

"No," she said, tugging my arm. "I'd like that."

"You might be disappointed."

"I don't think so." She stroked my arm. I leaned forward and we kissed. I twisted too sharply, and my shoulder stung. I pulled away and lifted my sleeve. A corner of the bandage had peeled off. She ran her finger along my skin next to the bandage, and said, "Hurts?"

"A little."

She continued sliding her fingers up my arm, then across my neck. I smelled her lavender soap, which excited me, but I held her hand, pulling it slowly away. I said, "We shouldn't."

"Why not?" She searched my eyes.

"I don't know if it's right."

She smiled. "Were you ever a Boy Scout?"

"No."

"You should've joined. You would've done well." She brought my hand up to her lips and kissed my palm. "Have a good sleep," she said. I moved closer to her and we kissed again. I ran my hand over her legs, up her waist, then brushed lightly against her breast. She drew back, waving her finger in a warning gesture, and grinned. She held my gaze for a long moment, then stood up and walked down the hall to her bedroom.

I turned off the lights. Lying down on the sofa, my breathing erratic, I felt heat flush through me, and I had to take off my sweatshirt and fan myself cool. My erection was hurting, and I wasn't sure why I was being so careful. It seemed ridiculous. Why was I hesitating? Because Linda was in the hospital, because everything was so messy and unresolved.

A jolt of desire shuddered through me. The house had become completely still, and I wondered where Gracie was. I listened for Serena but heard nothing. Perhaps she had gone to sleep. I sat up. No. I could sense her awake. She was waiting. A small night-light cast a blue glow on the hallway floor, dim shadows stretching onto the living room ceiling. I stared at the furniture shrouded in semidarkness, the house settling with creaks and clicks. I stood and drifted into the kitchen and drank a glass of water. My back was sweating. I tugged at my T-shirt and thought, When did you start being a Boy Scout?

Gracie must have heard me, because she walked into the kitchen and waited for me to do something. I crouched down and scratched her ears. Then I moved silently through the living room, down the hall, and paused at Serena's closed bedroom door. I turned the handle. Unlocked. Opening it, and peering into the darkness, I could only see the faint blue light from the hall spilling onto the floor. I stepped in, exhaling nervously. My eyes adjusted, and I saw her darkened figure sitting up, watching me. I closed the door behind me before Gracie could follow and crept onto the bed. Serena kept still. I leaned toward her and touched her cheek. She held her hand over mine. When we kissed, she pulled me slowly on top of her, and I leaned on my elbows, keeping a few inches over her as she unbuttoned her pajama top. I drew circles around her nipples, but supporting myself on my arms hurt my shoulder. She sensed this and gently pushed me onto my back, kicking the sheets away. Straddling me, she rubbed side to side, the friction of her pajamas and my sweat pants aching, and she shed her pajama top and leaned down over me. I held her breasts, kissed them. Neither of us made any sounds. She climbed off me and slowly pulled down my sweat pants and boxers. She slipped off her pajama bottom, and I took off my T-shirt, and she threw her leg over me, her warm and slightly damp skin against mine, and she rubbed my erection with her hand then ran her finger up over my stomach and chest, kissing my neck. I needed to be closer to her, so I rolled on top and nestled myself between her legs without entering. I eased my weight on her, being careful with my shoulder, and felt her breasts against my chest. She opened her legs and tried to pull me in, but I teased her, touching, rubbing up and down, but not going in any farther. She grabbed my good shoulder with her hand, digging her nails in, and thrust her hips up, and as I moved into her, enveloped in warmth, neither of us uttering a word, though she exhaled sharply as I went deeper, I hugged her closely, ignoring the faint pains throughout my body, wanting only to be immersed and a part of Serena.

I woke up shivering. The sheets had slipped to the floor, and we had been sleeping huddled up against each other for warmth. I pulled the covers back over us, and Serena murmured a thanks as she curled up and tightened the sheet around her. She soon fell back asleep, but I lay awake. I climbed out of bed and went to the bathroom, checking my bandage. It seemed secure. My penis was sore, and I examined myself, wincing at the redness, but liking it. It began to stir right now, remembering. It was the newness of us, of this, and of pent-up desire for her. I was tempted to return to the bedroom to wake her up for more, but my skin was too tender.

I found a bathrobe hanging on the back of the door, and put it on, wandering through the house and finding Gracie sleeping in the kitchen. I gulped down two glasses of water, then sat down in the living room, a pleasant restfulness filling me. I was calm. The events of the past few weeks floated by, but I simply watched them with detachment.

The phone trilled and sent me jumping up to answer it before Serena awoke. I actually thought I saw sparks in the darkness, the electronic bell cracking the air around it. I fumbled with the handset before the next ring and croaked a "hello?"

"Is Linda there with you?"

"Julie?" I asked.

"Is she there with you? Is she there?"

"What? No. Isn't she at the hospital?"

Julie said, "What in the hell did you say to her tonight?"

"What?" My heart was thumping in my ears. "Where is Linda?"

"What did you say to her? What the hell is going on?"

"What are you talking about? Calm down."

"She left the hospital. I just heard from the night nurse. Linda put on her clothes and left the hospital."

It took me a moment to register this. "What about the guard? The police officer?"

"They took him off. After Vines interviewed Linda he didn't think she was in danger. She hadn't seen anything at Raul's. She couldn't ID anyone."

"She's not at the condo?"

"No! She's nowhere! What did you say to her? What happened?"

I immediately thought of my staying here at Serena's, but I knew that couldn't have caused any of this. "What about Harlan? Did you check with him?"

"Of course. First one I called. You don't know anything about this?"

She had called Harlan before me? I shook this off and tried to figure out what had happened. The reality of this slowly hit me. Linda wasn't that well. She wouldn't have left voluntarily. "Did anyone see her?"

"I'm on my way to the hospital right now."

"I'll meet you there," I said.

"Allen, you don't know where she is? Did you say anything to her?"

"I'm not sure."

She cursed quietly and hung up.

Thirty

scribbled a quick note to Serena, dressed, and sped to the hospital. I thought about the various possibilities for Linda disappearing, crossing them off as too unlike her. She wouldn't have been jealous of me at Serena's, definitely not enough to do something like this. She wouldn't have just walked away for no reason, worrying her family. She wasn't an amnesiac. Something had obviously happened. I could imagine her leaving without telling anyone because she was so wrapped up in her own thoughts—I'd seen that happen before, especially if she was working on an important story—but the unavoidable answer loomed nearby: she had gone unwillingly. It didn't make sense. If she couldn't ID Bangs, there was no reason for him to find her. Unless he didn't know this.

She had mentioned having a hunch about something, possibly the man named Tanner, and I hoped it was just this. I remembered the dozens of times she'd skip meals and or even leave a can half opened or the phone unhooked absentmindedly, all her thoughts on solving a problem. I knew better than to bother her in this state, since she would look at me, and barely hear a word I was saying.

When I arrived at the hospital, I found Julie arguing with a nurse. The lights seemed to have been dimmed, the waiting room empty, and I glanced at the clock in surprise. Three A.M.? Julie was saying, "What kind of procedures do you have? She was just in the ICU for chrissake!"

"Ma'am," the nurse said, an older woman with eyeglasses attached to a cord around her neck. "We're not watchdogs. We're not prison guards. Your sister apparently just got up and left. We didn't realize she was gone until a routine check."

Julie noticed me and hurried to meet me halfway, her purse slapping against her arm. She tugged on her oversized raincoat. "What the hell did you say to her? You spoke to her on the phone. I know you did. Don't deny it."

I stepped back. "I don't deny it. She didn't head back to the condo?"

"No. I just checked again. She called me earlier, and she sounded upset. She just got off the phone with you, so I know you said something to her. What did you say?"

"Nothing! I—"

"Bullshit. If you don't level with me, Allen, I swear I'm going to—"

"All I did was update her on what I've been doing: trying to find Lowell Bangs's trail. That's it. I don't know why she was upset."

"You didn't fight about that—that boy-toy chick? You didn't tell her anything that would've upset her, did you?"

I hesitated.

Julie saw my unease and said, "Allen, my God. She was just in a coma! She's probably all confused and scared. What the hell did you say?"

I admitted, "She wanted to know where I was staying. I just told her I was at Serena's—"

"You stupid ass. You don't think that would've upset her?"

Flinching, I said, "No. Look, she broke up with me—"

"Screw you, Allen. I've had it with you. I don't want you near her again."

"Wait, we should call the police. If it was Bangs—"

"Don't you get what's happening?" she explained to me deliberately, as if to a child. "She's under suspicion. If we tell the police she's taken off, what do you think they'll say? She's a *suspect* for chrissake. She's a suspect and she took off."

"But what if it was Bangs? What if she's in trouble?"

Julie's face tightened.

I said, "What did she tell you on the phone? Exactly?"

Julie focused on me and took a deep breath. "Just that she was feeling better. She said she spoke to you and that I didn't have to shield her from anything. She sounded upset. She also spoke to our father."

"About what?"

"I'm not sure."

"Can you call him and find out? I want to talk to the nurse—"

"I did."

"Let me try. Call your father. Find out exactly what they spoke about."

I walked over to the main reception area where the older nurse was writing on a clipboard but also watching us. I said hello and apologized for Julie. "It's been really hard on her the past few days."

"Sir, this sometimes happens. The patient might have just gone for a walk. She might be in a different wing. I already sent two orderlies to look for her."

I glanced at her name tag and said, "Mrs. Guilfoyle, I'm sure you're doing everything you can. Do you mind if I wake the people next to her and ask if they saw anything?"

"Saw anything?"

"Maybe she even mentioned where she was going."

Mrs. Guilfoyle considered this and said, "I don't know . . ."

"I would appreciate it. I'm sure you're right, but just in case. After all, maybe one of the patients saw her leave. She might have even told one of them where she was going." I heard Julie talking on her cell phone.

Mrs. Guilfoyle said, "My supervisor should be coming down soon."

"Time is important," I urged. "If something bad did happen, then we need to move quickly."

She thought about this, then agreed, and led me down the hall. Julie looked up from her phone and started following us as she spoke quietly. Mrs. Guilfoyle stopped me at the door and said, "We really shouldn't be disturbing them. We should keep it short."

We walked into the large, darkened recovery room with six hospital beds—three on each side—separated by curtains. The bed in the corner was the only one empty, and I pointed to the adjacent bed, an elderly woman sleeping with her head back and mouth open. Mrs. Guilfoyle walked over and checked the clipboard at the foot of the bed. She turned on a small bedside lamp. I approached as she gently touched the woman's wrinkled arm and whispered, "Mrs. Kellerman? Mrs. Kellerman?"

The woman blinked awake and coughed lightly. She said, "Is it time for my operation?"

"You've had your operation, Mrs. Kellerman. I'm sorry to wake you, but your neighbor in the bed next to you seems to have left. Do you know when she left or even where she went?"

Mrs. Kellerman squinted, slowly waking up. Her thinning gray hair was matted to her forehead. She said in a croaking voice, "The young cancer patient?"

"It wasn't cancer, but her head was shaved, yes. Did you see her?"

"She left? I didn't know that."

"You didn't see her leave?"

"No, sorry. I've been sleeping all night. Nurse, this bed is lumpy."

"Is it? Sometimes it helps to raise the legs with a pillow." Mrs. Guilfoyle shook her head at me.

Across the room was another patient, a younger woman who had awoken and was watching us through the semidarkness. She had a large white bandage on her throat. I walked over to her, and whispered, "Did you see that patient leave?"

"She wasn't supposed to, right?" the woman said, sitting up, her frail arms poking out of her hospital gown. "I didn't think so."

"Do you know what time she left?"

"Around eleven," she said. "She got dressed fast and ran out."

"Alone? No one else?"

"No, just her."

"Do you know why? Did she say anything?"

Mrs. Guilfoyle approached and checked the woman's chart. The woman said to me, "It was right after a phone call."

I noticed that there was a phone on the table next to each bed. I had called Linda at around nine o'clock, perhaps a little earlier, and I had watched the news at eleven, so it hadn't been my phone call.

Julie then came into the room, closing her cell phone, and I asked what time Linda had spoken to Luke.

"Around nine to nine-thirty. What's going on?"

"She was making a few calls around that time," the patient said. "She drew her curtains closed."

"But you said she left around eleven."

"After she got a call."

"An incoming call?" I asked.

Mrs. Guilfoyle said, "That can't be. The switchboard doesn't let through calls past ten." She paused. "Unless it was an emergency."

"It looked like it," the patient said. "After the call she got dressed fast and left."

I asked Mrs. Guilfoyle, "Can you check on that? Is there a record of calls?"

She nodded. "But we don't know where the calls come from."

Julie asked the patient, "What else? Did she say anything."

"No. She just left."

"That's odd," Mrs. Guilfoyle said. "I was on at eleven. I didn't see her."

"Which way would she go if she was leaving?" I asked.

"Most likely to the main entrance."

"Are there people there?"

"Oh, yes. Security, orderlies. It can be fairly busy, even at night."

"I'll go down and ask."

Mrs. Guilfoyle said, "I'll ask the switchboard about incoming calls."

We thanked the patient and left the ward. Julie took the elevator with me down to the ground floor, and I asked her what Luke had said.

"She kept asking about Hector's friends, if he remembered who some of them were."

"Why?"

"He didn't know. She wanted him to wake up our mom, but he didn't. She got angry. She kept asking about old childhood friends. I don't get it."

"They're up now?"

"Yeah. They're frantic now."

The elevator doors opened and we hurried to the security kiosk. The guard, an older black man in a navy blue sport coat, was sitting behind a console. I had worked this kind of security detail before joining ProServ, and I remembered it as one of the most boring jobs I'd had. I introduced myself to the guard. I asked him about anyone leaving at around eleven this evening. He nodded and said a bunch of people, doctors and nurses going off shift, left around then.

"What about a woman with a scarf over her head, a paisley scarf?" I asked.

He scratched his chin and looked up. Julie said, "We're in a hurry."

The man frowned.

I said to Julie, "Wait over there."

She was about to protest, but I gave her a hard look.

The guard watched Julie walk toward the entrance, flipping open her phone, and he said to me, "A real pretty woman? No hair?"

"Yes, that was her. She had a scarf on her head."

"Yep. I seen her come out here and wait for her ride."

"Her ride?"

"One of those nice-looking SUVs."

"What?" I asked in disbelief.

"Sport utility vehicle? Pulled right up onto the curb out there."

"Did you see who was driving?"

"No, but another woman helped this one into the backseat."

"Another woman? What did she look like?"

"Red hair. Short—"

"Bright red hair? A fake dye job?"

The guard smiled. "Like them punk kids, yep."

A car pulled up, catching our attention. A man in faded jeans and a white dress-shirt jumped out. He had on horn-rimmed glasses that glinted in the spotlights, and when he saw Julie at the doorway, he waved. He opened the passenger side, and I was startled to see Marianne climb out. Both she and the man hurried toward us through the automatic doors.

"Harlan," Julie said. "Mom?"

My stomach churned as Julie introduced me to Harlan. I had trouble meeting Marianne's eyes and held back any questions as to why Harlan had driven her here. I told them what the guard had said, then added, "It was Bangs. I'm almost certain. Gloria has red hair; the SUV was probably the one that had been following us." I turned to Harlan, who was much different than I had imagined. Although he had dirty-blond hair, he was thinner and more weath-ered—his face had the roughness of too much sun in his youth, leathery skin around his mouth and eyes. He seemed older than I had thought. He said, "If this was the drug dealer, why would she go with him? Was it voluntary?"

"It seemed like it, but I don't know," I said. "We should call the police."

"Hold on," Harlan said. "What if she was taken hostage or was black-mailed to go with them."

"All the more reason," I said. "She could be in danger."

"If the police are targeting her," Harlan said, "then this might give them more ammunition. They'll think she's working with them."

"Look, these are killers we're talking about. Linda is with them for some reason. We have to call the police."

"What if she *is* working with them?" Julie said. "What if she made some kind of deal with them?" She glanced at her mother.

"What?" Marianne said. She looked disoriented, trying to follow our con-versation. "How could she do that?"

I said forcefully, "She's *not* working with them. Jesus. How could you think that? We're wasting time. I'm going back upstairs to check the incom-ing calls." I left them, heading to the elevators.

I found Mrs. Guilfoyle talking to a young man in a tie, and she pointed at me and said something to the man as I approached. The man stepped forward and held out his hand. "My name is Larkens. Joe Larkens. I'm the night supervi-sor. I'm terribly sorry about the mix-up—"

"Let me see the call sheet," I said, ignoring his hand. "I want to know who Linda called and what calls came in."

"Well, uh, sir, what's your relationship to Ms. Maldonado?"

"Listen, goddammit. It's very possible that Ms. Maldonado could've been kidnapped from this hospital. If that's so you'll be liable for anything that happens. Give me the call sheet—"

"I don't appreciate threats, sir. What was your name?"

Julie, Harlan, and Marianne appeared in a second elevator and hurried over. Mrs. Guilfoyle said to Larkens, "That's the sister."

Larkens was about to offer the same introduction but Julie was even more curt. He barely said two words when Julie snapped, "I don't give a shit who you are. My sister is missing and I'll have your balls in a sling if anything happens to her."

Larkens's cheeks turned pink.

I said to her, "He won't show me the call list."

"I'm her mother!" Marianne said. "I demand that you help us!"

"Ma'am," Larkens said. "Please calm down. We're doing everything we can to—"

Harlan stepped forward, pulled out his wallet and handed Larkens his business card with a quick flick of his wrist. He said, "I'm with the *San Jose Sentinel* and I'm doing a story about the lax security in this hospital. How badly do you want to keep your job?"

Larkens looked bewildered, and said, "Uh, we're doing everything we can to locate Ms. Maldonado—"

"She was taken by strangers," Julie said. "We have every right to see what calls she made." She turned to me. "Maybe we should get the police now."

"Can I sue?" Marianne asked Harlan. "Can I sue them for this?"

"Yes, you can," he replied.

Larkens said to Mrs. Guilfoyle, "Show them the printout."

Julie, Harlan, Marianne, and I looked at the sheet of paper with a list of phone numbers ordered by the time the call was made. A separate listing showed an emergency incoming call at eleven o'clock. I pointed to Serena's phone number and said, "That's me."

Julie pointed to a long distance number. "That's my cell."

"Mine's right under that one," Harlan said.

"That's our number," Marianne said, pointing to a series of local calls.

"What about the other local one?" I asked.

Julie shook her head. "I don't know."

Harlan took out his cell phone and began dialing, glancing at the call sheet. We waited as he listened, a frown tightening the skin around his mouth. He shook his head at us. "Answering machine," he said. "No name, just 'leave a message.'" He asked Julie, "Should I?"

"No," I said. "Can we find out who it is first?"

He hung up, and dialed another number. He said into the phone, "I'd like a reverse listing." He read off the phone number, then waited. He met my eyes and said into the phone, "Dr. L. Tanner? Thanks. Is there an address?"

Tanner? Bangs's partner? I tried to connect him to Linda.

Harlan said, "No address listing? Thank you." He hung up, then dialed another number, telling us, "Don't worry. It's late, but I have a few special contacts." He listened to his phone, then said, "Bob? Sorry to wake you. I need a header check." He nodded and replied, "I know, I know. I'm sorry, but this is extremely urgent. I've got a name and phone number." He relayed this information and added, "Anything, but a current home address would be good."

Harlan said to us, "He's booting up his computer."

I noticed Julie staring at her mother. She said, "Dr. Tanner?" Nurse Guilfoyle was speaking quietly to the supervisor. Harlan nodded into the phone, saying, "I'll owe you big time." I couldn't stop wondering why he was here. It seemed we were all suspended until Harlan finally said, "Good. Good." He pulled out a pen, and made a writing motion with his hand. Julie pulled out an envelope from her pocketbook. Harlan jotted something down. He thanked his friend and hung up. He said, "Dr. L. Tanner lives in Malibu."

"She called a doctor?" Julie asked.

Harlan was already dialing. I asked him what he was doing. He ignored me. He waited, then said, "I'm trying to reach Dr. Tanner. This is a medical emergency." He stopped, then winced as a loud voice came through his earpiece. Harlan said, "Sorry to bother you at home so late, but I really have a bad stomach ache—" He moved his ear away from the phone again. "I don't know where I got this number. You can't help me?"

Harlan looked at us and said, "He hung up. He's home screening his calls at three in the morning. Something's going on."

I looked at the address he had scribbled down, and said, "I'm going over there. I'll try to find out what I can."

"I'll go with you," Harlan said. "I have a map in my car."

"Wait," Julie said. "How do we know this is connected? What if it wasn't Linda who went into that car?"

We stopped. Marianne said, "Luke is waiting at the condo in case she shows up."

I said, "Someone should be here as well."

Marianne turned to Julie. "You stay here—"

"What?" Julie cried. "No way! I should—"

"No, you're right. We might be mistaken," Marianne said. "We have to make sure."

"Both of you should stay here," I said.

Marianne shook her head and replied, "That's not needed. Julie will stay here and I'll go with you two." She began walking toward the elevator before Julie could object, and Harlan and I followed.

Thirty-one

Tanner's house was in Luego Canyon, and I realized as Marianne read off the directions from the map that this area was a connection between Hector and Bangs. We were in Harlan's car and he drove slowly up the canyon road, his headlights only reaching twenty feet ahead into the complete darkness. Harlan peered forward and kept switching from his brights to his low headlights, trying to see the turns. Marianne was in the passenger seat with the map, and I was in the back. As we ascended, a fog rolled in, and Harlan's brights reflected only a glare back at us. He muttered and squinted.

Nothing looked familiar to me. Rocks and spindly shrubs loomed in the shadows, whiteness descending, and I felt disembodied in the backseat. I was in a car with a family who hated me and a man who had designs on my girlfriend—ex-girlfriend. Linda had disappeared. I said, "Hector died on this road."

"What?" Marianne said, turning to the backseat.

"Farther up ahead. He went over the side. Bangs killed him."

"And Tanner is connected?" Harlan asked.

"Tanner might have been working with Bangs."

"And Linda talked to him on the phone tonight?" Marianne said. "Why?"

Harlan said, "I don't think Allen is telling us everything."

They turned to me. I said to him, "I don't think you know what you're talking about."

"You've heard of Tanner? Why would Linda call him?"

"There's too much to tell," I said. "Why are you down here?"

He made a sharp turn and downshifted. "I was worried about Linda."

"What's going on with you two?"

"That's none of your goddamn business."

Marianne said, "Now's not the time."

Harlan nodded and mumbled to himself. I pushed this aside and tried to think of why Linda would go with Bangs and Gloria. Maybe I was mistaken, and the redhead hadn't been Gloria. No. It must have been. The SUV was Bangs's. Somehow all this fit together, but I just couldn't see it yet. Tanner, a doctor? Maybe some kind of supplier? Tanner and Bangs using Jameson's money somehow?

What would compel Linda to go with Bangs? Information, maybe. He could've tempted her with more details of Hector. Blackmail was another possibility. Bangs could've threatened her parents, Julie.

Marianne looked at the map and said, "Escalante Drive is coming up. Take a left and then keep on it until you hit Melody Drive."

Harlan pulled onto a rockier and uneven paved road, braking as we went down a steep decline. We passed a few houses sunken into hills, wooden split-rail fences and No Trespassing signs lining the road. Harlan said, "Melody," and made another left onto a dirt road. There were only two houses on this road.

"The address is One-hundred Melody."

"That one," he said, squinting at the house with the lights on inside.

I saw an SUV parked in front and said, "Stop here. That might be Bangs's SUV. All of them might be there."

Harlan parked the car. Dust caught up to us and settled over the headlights. The house next to us was dark, but up ahead Tanner's was blazing, all the windows bright, curtains glowing. I said, "All right. Call the police. Do you understand? I think that's Bangs's car. Linda could be in serious trouble. *Call the police now.*"

Marianne flipped open her cell phone as I left the car, but she hesitated when Harlan climbed out after me. I asked, "What are you doing?"

"I want to go with you."

I was about to object but then decided a backup wasn't a bad idea. I shrugged and said, "Suit yourself." I headed across the street and toward Tanner's house, checking for perimeter alarms. I stopped Harlan and pointed to the unlit spotlights with small sensors over the front door and windows. I said quietly, "Probably motion detectors. We'll go around the side."

The house was an oversize Colonial with additions to the sides and some kind of sunporch on the second level. A tall wooden gate blocked the way to the backyard, and I peered over it but couldn't see much. Dim reflected light bounced from curtained windows and onto the lawn. I searched for alarms or motion detectors but didn't see any. I opened the gate, which squeaked, and went through. Harlan followed. The air was cool, and I heard wind rustling the trees and brush around us.

He whispered, "I really do care for her."

This stopped me. I turned and looked at him in the semidarkness. I couldn't see his expression, but he was waiting for my response. I put my finger to my lips and motioned for him to follow.

We rounded the house and came up to a wooden deck raised off the ground and leading to large glass patio doors. I saw movement in the windows adjacent to the patio doors, and pointed. Both of us stopped when we heard shouting. Two men were arguing. We climbed up onto the deck and moved quietly to the glass doors, which led into a kitchen. We looked in.

I saw Linda. She was sitting at a table, covering her face with her hands, shaking her head. Bangs, in a baseball cap, was pointing his finger at another man, yelling, and then pointing to Linda. The other man cursed and said something in a low voice. Then Bangs turned to Linda and said loudly, "Who the fuck do you think you are?" and Linda frowned without answering. She rubbed her eyes. She tightened the scarf around her head. Her cheeks shone under the bright track lighting, and she said something calmly, quietly. With a start, I saw no fear in her expression. I thought, She knows him.

Harlan whispered, "What's going on?"

"She's not afraid. She knows him."

Both of us stared, confused. Linda shook her head and said something else, her mouth forming the words, *You're so fucking stupid.*

Something crumpled inside me.

A deep-throated barking suddenly filled the house, and a chill flashed through me. I recognized the bark. Blood. I said to Harlan, "Get the fuck out of here. A pit bull."

He said, "Huh?" But I was already running toward the back fence, flying across the lawn. A woman's voice yelled something, and Harlan must have realized what was happening because he suddenly jumped off the deck and followed me. I heard the patio doors sliding open and Bangs yelled, "Sic 'em! Go sic 'em boy!"

The dog let out a murderous growl and made it across the deck and onto the lawn in a millisecond, and I heard Harlan let out a terrified "Fuck!" I was already scaling the wooden fence, throwing one leg over and looking back. Bangs had a gun with him, watching Blood. Harlan wasn't going to make it. The pit bull was so fast that within three strides he had caught up to Harlan and clamped down on his leg. Harlan let out a loud yell and flipped onto the ground. He began kicking and punching, trying to get the dog off his leg, and Bangs yelled, "Good boy! Good boy!"

Harlan screamed for help as Blood lunged for his neck, and snapped at his arm. I saw that Bangs wasn't going to call his dog off and jumped back into the yard, running for Blood. Spotlights suddenly flooded the yard and I saw a bandage on one side of Blood's face. He noticed me and stopped.

He recognized me.

He immediately ignored Harlan and went straight for me without even barking. His teeth were bared, and a burst of energy helped me dive back up the fence. I yelled, "Linda! Help!"

I scrambled up, almost making it over the top, when I felt a deep bite in my calf, the pain quickly shooting through my legs and up into my chest. I cried out, and lost my grip, the weight of the dog throwing me back. The dog held onto my calf as we both fell, and I tried to cushion myself by landing on top of the dog, but he was quick, and let go of my leg. He twisted away, growling, then chomped on my arm. I felt the teeth sinking in and yelled, "Fuck!" and heard more shouts coming from the house, but now I was trying to kick the dog away, but he wouldn't let go of my forearm, and I felt something tearing, blood squirting from his teeth. His deep-throated growl shook my arm, yanking the socket, and he wouldn't let go. I tried punching his bandaged eye, and he began shaking his head back and forth, plunging his teeth deeper in me. I cried out.

Bangs ran over and yelled, "Heel! Down!" and yanked on the dog's collar. "Heel!"

The dog opened his mouth and backed away. I curled up, trying to stanch the bleeding, cradling my arm. I couldn't move my fingers. I couldn't even feel my hand. I was losing my breath, shaking, and heard Bangs say calmly, "Wow. He remembered you. He was really pissed."

Linda was on the deck, and said, "Harlan? Oh God, Allen, what are you doing here?"

"Me? What the fuck are *you* doing here?" I yelled, and almost passed out. Bangs and the other man lifted me up, and I let out a staccato yelp, a "cu-cu-cu-cu" as I tried to keep off my left leg and hold my left arm close to my body. Gloria and Linda helped Harlan as he stood up and limped. I couldn't stop shaking, the adrenaline still pumping through me. They carried me up the deck and into the kitchen. The man saw my arm and said, "Shit, it's not too good."

In a strange haze, I turned to Linda and said, "You lied to me. You knew Bangs all along."

Linda blinked, then shook her head. "No. No. We got it all wrong."

"You guys fucked everything up," Bangs said.

"You're with him," I said. "You—"

"No, Allen." She was pulling paper towels from a roll and came over to me. I tried to pull away from her. "No, Allen," she said. "This isn't . . . This isn't Lowell Bangs. This is Hector. This is my brother, Hector."

I whirled toward him.

The man whom I thought was Bangs glared at me, and said, "You and my sister fucked everything up."

Harlan was clutching his leg and said, "What the hell is going on here! I need a hospital!"

Thirty-two

They laid me and Harlan on the floor, and the man who I guessed was Tanner brought over a medical kit to clean and dress our wounds. He said to Hector, "They both need stitches. The ones on their arms are bad."

"Fuck 'em," Hector said.

"Hector!" Linda said.

Hector turned to her. "My name is Lowell Bangs. Hector died in that canyon out there." He took off his baseball cap and I saw that he had bleached his hair. He scratched his head, put his cap back on, and looked at us in disgust. He might have been the same skinny man from the photograph of Hector I had seen, but his goatee and mustache were thicker, still dark, contrasting his pale yellow hair. His eyes were bloodshot with deep bags underneath.

"Please," Linda said. "They're my friends."

"Goddammit!" he said, punching his leg. "If you hadn't stuck your fucking nose into everything, I'd be fine!" Gloria touched his shoulder and told him to calm down.

Linda said, "What . . . happened to you?"

Tanner wrapped my arm tightly with gauze, which sent jolts of pain through me. He then cut the bottom of my pant leg open to check my calf. He said, "This isn't so bad. Puncture wounds." The feeling was slowly returning to my hand. I opened and closed my fist.

"You're Tanner?" I said. "What're you doing with him?"

He glanced up, a brief flicker of panic crossed his face, but he didn't answer. He wrapped my calf with gauze, then taped it up. Harlan moaned, "What about me?"

"In a sec."

I backtracked, wondering how Hector had switched his and Bangs's identity, then said to Tanner, "Are you a coroner?"

"Dentist," he said.

I saw it immediately. "Dental records," I said. "They ID'd the burned body using dental records. You had Bangs's records, and gave them to the police as Hector's."

Hector turned to me, and I said to him, "But how did you know him?"

He stared at me with tired eyes. Linda said, "Lou is an old friend. When Hector was digging into old contacts he found out Lou was a dentist, and he got Bangs to go to him for his cavities."

"You knew?" I asked her.

"Only after the name came up. I knew the name 'Tanner' but wasn't sure from where. Once I called, it came to me."

I still wasn't sure how this came together. I asked her, "How did he find . . . How did he know who . . ." I paused.

Linda said, "This was when he was looking for Raul. He was looking up old friends. Lou's father knew Raul."

I turned to Hector. "But why kill Raul? Why kill Jameson?"

Hector said in a monotone, "Loose ends." His expression was deadpan, remorseless, and I glanced at Linda, who was also shocked.

"You almost killed me," she said to him, pulling off her scarf. A shadow of stubble was growing over her scalp. "See that?" She pointed to the stitches behind her ear. "They had to drill my skull."

"I told you I was sorry about that," Hector said. "I didn't know it was you. You just showed up out of nowhere. I had to get away."

"But why kill them?" I asked. "Your own father?"

Hector answered, but directed it at Linda: "He was beginning to figure it out. He knew Jameson was involved with me, with Bangs. Jameson told him stuff. I didn't realize."

Linda said, "So when Jameson died . . . ?"

"Raul suspected something, didn't believe the suicide. I screwed up when I tried hitting him up for money so soon after Jameson. He began asking around, trying to get info about me and Bangs. He was getting close. I had no choice."

"No choice?" Linda said, her voice rising. "How about *not* killing him? That's a choice! My God! How can you—what were you thinking for God's sake?"

"He was an asshole and you know it," Hector said. "I'm not losing sleep over him."

Gloria said, "What are we going to do? What about these guys?"

"Yes," Linda said. "What *are* you going to do? Are you going to kill them, and me? Kill everyone?"

Hector grimaced. "Fuck if I know."

"Why kill Jameson?" I asked.

"Shut the fuck up!" Hector said.

"Was it about money?" Linda asked.

"Enough!"

"What about money?" I asked. I knew I had gone too far by the look on Hector's face, a tightening of his eyes as he pulled out his automatic from his waist and walked calmly over to me. He timed his steps perfectly so that two steps away he hopped forward and punted my ribs, kicking me off the floor. I curled up, the shock of the blow paralyzing me. The pit bull jumped up and growled.

Hector lowered his gun to my face. "One more word, asshole."

"Hector," Linda said softly. "Hector."

Gloria walked to him and touched his arm. "We got to get out of here."

Tanner stood up, turning toward the living room. He said, "The front lights went on."

"Go check," Hector said. To me he asked, "Who else is out there?"

"Your mother."

"My mother? Oh, fucking hell!" Hector yelled at Linda. "You're bringing the whole fucking family?"

"Jesus, I didn't tell her to come here!" Linda said.

Tanner called from the door. "There's someone coming up. Not sure who."

Hector said, "Go and bring her in. Fast." Tanner pulled out a gun from his waistband and hurried out the front door. We heard Tanner's voice, and then Marianne say something sharp.

Then Marianne appeared in the doorway with Tanner behind her. She blinked at the lights, surveying us, and froze at the sight of Hector.

"What are you doing here?" Hector asked.

Marianne stepped back, continued staring, then turned to Tanner. She said, "You're Louis. Hector's friend."

Tanner nodded. "You remember me."

"I remember your name."

"Mom," Linda said. "Hector's okay. I'm fine. He was always alive."

Marianne started to speak, then stopped. She look at her son with a crumpled expression, and said, "What have you done?"

"We don't have time for this," Tanner said. "Are the cops coming? What the hell? Do they know about me now? I'm screwed!"

Hector turned to him. "You wanted to be my partner? Well, welcome partner."

"I don't understand," Marianne said. "What did you do? What's happening?"

"You called the police?" Hector asked her.

Marianne looked at him squarely. "Not yet."

"Everything's all messed up. Everyone's going to know!" Gloria said. "What should we do?"

Hector let out a quiet curse.

"My practice!" Tanner cried. "I'll lose everything!"

"We should drop everything and run," Gloria said.

"What about me?" Tanner said, approaching Hector. "You're not leaving me in this shit!"

Hector swung his pistol at Tanner's face, and Tanner went down. Marianne yelled Hector's name. He said tiredly, "Mom, you shouldn't have come here."

"What . . . I don't understand! What's going on? Tell me."

"Gloria and I are disappearing," Hector said.

"But where?" Linda said. "When the truth comes out—"

"We'll be long gone."

Linda's eyes met her mother's, which prompted Marianne to say, "No. You will stay here. We will find a way out of this, no matter what you did."

Her cell phone rang. Everyone turned to it, but Hector said, "Don't answer it."

Marianne said, "What if it's Julie—"

"Don't answer it," Hector said. "Give me the phone."

Marianne handed it to him, and he threw it onto the ground. It burst apart. He said to Gloria, "We'll just move up the exit date. That's all."

Linda said, "What are you talking about? The police will find you! I can help you. Mom and Dad hired a good lawyer—"

"For three murders? Bangs was a paranoid asshole, and Raul deserved worse, but Jameson . . . I shouldn't have killed Jameson."

Marianne whispered, "Three murders?"

Hector whirled toward her. He was about to say something but then waved her off.

Marianne ran over to Hector and grabbed his arm. "It's okay. We can say you had to do it. Raul was a bad man. You had to protect yourself."

Hector pulled away and glared at her. "Protecting yourself. You know about that, don't you."

Marianne stopped. "What?"

"You know all about protecting yourself, don't you? I got the full story from Raul."

"What do you mean?"

"Child abuse? *Sexual* abuse? Raul never touched me like that, and you know it. You used me, Mom. You used me to keep him away."

Linda said to her, "It's true, isn't it? You did threaten it, even though it wasn't true."

"Raul was a bastard," Hector said, "and I hated him, but he never touched me like that, Mom."

Marianne looked at Linda, then Hector, and said, "But he did! I know it!"

Hector was about to reply but instead shook his head. "It doesn't matter. It's over." He nodded to Gloria. "Time for us to go."

"You can find another way," Marianne said. "We'll—"

"It's ruined. They know," he said, pointing to me and Harlan. "The police will figure it out. Everyone will know about Bangs. It's over. I tried, but it didn't work."

"Why did you do this?" Marianne said. "Why?"

"I was so close. Man, I was close." To his sister he said, "You realize that no one really got to know Bangs that well except me? I understood him. I could've been Bangs for a while."

"But why?" Linda asked.

He smiled. He was utterly calm. He said, "Who the fuck wants to be Hector? That pussy living at home and sponging off his parents? Not me."

"Why did you kill Jameson?" Linda asked.

Hector was about to leave the living room, but stopped. He said, "I didn't mean for all this to happen. It was going to be simple. Lou was going to help me switch with Bangs. I look like him, no one really dealt directly with him. He was an asshole and a lot of people wanted him dead, anyway. I was doing them a favor. It just got out of hand."

"Jameson?" Linda asked again.

"We weren't making money fast enough. I knew it wouldn't last so we had to make a lot before my ID was blown, and then we'd disappear. Jameson fronted almost fifty grand for a bigger purchase. I didn't want to return it."

"Oh, Jesus," Linda said. "So you double-crossed him just for the money, and then Raul began making connections."

"And *you* started fucking around my business," Hector said.

Gloria moved toward the front windows and cursed. She said, "Turn off the lights in here."

Hector did and asked why.

"I think there are cop cars pulling up. No lights, though. They're being quiet."

I saw through the semidarkness Hector rubbing his forehead ferociously. "What the hell." To his mother he yelled, "I thought you didn't call the police!"

Marianne said, "You need help. We can help you. Give yourself up and we'll get the best lawyers—"

"Oh my God," Hector said. "You lied to me and kept me talking. Oh, fuck."

"Hector!" Marianne said. "I want to help you—"

"Mom, *please shut the fuck up.*"

Marianne stumbled backward from force of this.

To Gloria he said, "They don't want you. They want me." He checked the magazine of his automatic, then said, "I'll try the back. I'll send Blood out first, and then go over the fence. I can lose them in the woods."

"What about me?" she asked. "I want to go with you."

"Wait," Linda said. "Are you crazy? You'll be killed!"

He gave his sister a faint smile.

The phone near the hallway rang, and Hector aimed his gun at it and shot it, the electronic warble dying off-key. The loud gunshot reverberated throughout the house and seemed to echo into the canyon. Then the front windows were bright with the glare of spotlights. The sound of feedback and a short burst of a siren came on and died. A gravelly man's voice burst in: *This is the Los Angeles Sheriff's Department. We have the house surrounded. Come out the front door with your hands high above your heads. We don't want any trouble.*

The dog began barking wildly at the patio doors. Hector said to Gloria, "Blame it all on me. Okay? I forced you. I bullied you. You can put it on me."

"I won't let you do this," Linda said. She approached.

Hector held up his gun. "Don't be stupid, sis. You know I can't be caught. Three counts of murder one? I'll be on death row. No fucking way." He let out a quick whistle and Blood barked and trotted up next to him.

"Hector!" Linda cried. "Please!"

Hector said to his mother, "You lied to me like you've always lied to us."

"You . . . you killed people. How could you?"

He shook his head, then looked down and petted Blood. "Ready, boy? Ready?"

The dog barked toward the rear yard.

He kissed Gloria on the forehead and said, "Turn off the floodlights when I say to, okay?"

Gloria said, "You don't want me to go with you?"

"No need. They want me. And I told you I'm never getting caught."

Marianne sprung forward, but Hector saw her coming, and moved toward the patio doors, snapping his fingers, which made Blood stand poised at Hector's side. Linda stopped her mother from following Hector as he slid open the glass and nodded to Gloria, who paused, then turned off a switch by the dining room. The lights blazing in the backyard suddenly went off, instant darkness, save the faint bluish moonlight, and then everything happened at once. Marianne yelled for him to stop, but Hector stamped his foot and pointed out into the yard, telling Blood to sic 'em, go boy, sic 'em, and Blood barked and roared out into the darkness, and the sheriff called to us again from the front, warning us that he wouldn't ask us a third time, but Hector nodded to Gloria, and there were yells and barks and gunshots in the yard, brief flashes of light, and Hector slipped out through the doors, and Marianne broke free then ran across the kitchen, crying out, Don't shoot! Don't shoot! Don't shoot! but I heard the sound of Hector's automatic firing, and then a cascade of answering fire that sounded like M-16s, and Gloria blocked the patio doorway, not letting Marianne out, but then the front door exploded open, a concussive *boom* and a flash of light, and the SWAT team came crashing through the entrance, flak jackets and helmets and rifles swiveling around and around, everyone yelling for us to get down. Get on the fucking floor! Get down now! Boots clomping and Marianne running out into the back, screaming Hector's name, but the shooting had stopped and for a brief instant while the SWAT team surveyed us on the floor, flashlight beams swerving around in long arcs, and the only sound was of Marianne calling Hector's name. Gloria was staring through the window. I saw Linda by the patio doors, both her hands covering her mouth, her body hunched forward, frozen, her eyes wide and in shock and glowing in the blue moonlight.

Thirty-three

The Block shuffles into the large conference room along with a dozen others, long narrow tables arranged in staggered rows, a lectern and a large portable blackboard sitting in the front. The PI test administrator, a black woman eyeing the nervous test takers with some amusement, tells everyone to take a seat at least one chair away from the next person. Everyone spreads out, looks around, and sits in the small, creaking plastic chairs. There are a few women, but most are men in their thirties, like the Block. Two men seem to be older, perhaps in their fifties. Everyone glances at everyone else. No one speaks. The fluorescent lights flicker and cast a sickly yellow haze over them. The Block notices people looking over his head. He follows their gaze up. He sees that he's sitting directly underneath the clock, which means he'll have to strain his neck to check the time. He stands slowly, his left leg still tender, and is about to find another seat when the test administrator asks where he is going. Heads turn to him. He says, I want a better view of the clock. The administrator smiles and says, Don't worry, I'll tell you in half-hour increments how much time is remaining, and then during the last half hour I'll write on the blackboard every ten minutes how much time is left.

The Block sits back down uneasily and stares at his bandaged arm, which pains him with faint, constant twinges. He prefers knowing the time himself. But he's embarrassed to find another seat. He wishes he wore his watch. He wonders why he forgot it this morning. Maybe on some level he wanted to fail this test? It's a terrible thought, given the past week of intense studying. He has never read and memorized so many facts in his life. He dreams about the test. He has flashcards piled around his apartment.

The administrator places small packets of stapled pages—the exam book—and a separate answer sheet facedown in front of each test taker. The slap of paper is the only sound as she weaves up and down the rows. Once she finishes, she announces that they have two hours to complete the test, but they can't turn over the exam booklet until exactly ten o'clock. All eyes focus over his head. He strains his neck to see the time, feeling the faint aches in his shoulder; 9:55. They wait.

The Block takes a deep, slow breath, but this doesn't help. His heart is beating faster, his ears are warm and tingling, and he thinks, I hate tests. I hate tests. His new career rests on these answers. Too much pressure. Larry is depending too much on this, and he already began printing up business cards and letterhead: B&C Investigations. He has drawn up a partnership agreement that they signed, notarized, and are waiting to implement. All that is needed is this test and the BSIS certification.

A sheen of sweat breaks out along the Block's back and neck. He fans his shirt and wipes his forehead. One of the women test takers, two seats to his left, sees his nervousness and smiles. She makes a slow-down motion with her hands, and mouths the words, *Relax*. The Block nods quickly. He's back in high school. He's back in college. He's going to mess this up; he can just feel it.

He stretches his neck to see the clock; 9:56. He tries to focus on something else. He thinks about Serena, who left town early because he was so worried about this test. She didn't want to interrupt his study, which he appreciated. She had spent only two days with him. They had driven up together from L.A., and after interviewing with three software companies and one semiconductor company, she received two job offers on the spot. She accepted the offer from a large E-business software company, and they are giving her one month of free corporate housing so that she can find her own apartment. She'll be moving up here in two weeks.

Civil and criminal liability. Evidence handling. Undercover operations. Surveillance. Burden of proof. Preponderance of evidence. Torts versus crimes. Personal injury. Service of process. Witness testimony. Tax rolls. Real property. Marriage and divorce records. Death claims. Liens. Judgments. Drug classifications.

Everything swirls around him, a tumult of terms, definitions, procedures. The Block lets out a low moan. Heads turn toward him.

The administrator says, Are you all right, sir?

The Block nods.

The woman two seats down laughs quietly.

The Block strains his neck; 9:57. He closes his eyes, and sees Linda as she was two weeks ago. It was possibly the last time he'll ever see her. He didn't have a chance to speak with her until after the long series of interviews at the sheriff's department. It took three days for the DEA and the OCSD to sort out what Hector had actually done, and who was to blame. Despite Gloria's attempts to shift the guilt, she was charged as an accessory to the murders, though a plea-bargaining agreement in which she named all of Hector/Bangs's suppliers will reduce her jail time. Gloria spelled out Hector's plan, devised only after he had worked his way up as Bangs's second in command, and intended to last only until they had made enough money to flee and live comfortably. They wanted to start a new life. Instead, Hector was buried two days later; he had been killed instantly from the nine shots in the head and chest. Gloria is still on suicide watch at the L.A. County Jail.

The Block saw Linda shortly before he left Marina Alta with Serena. He met her at the pastry shop across the street from her parents' condo, and Linda, wearing a baseball cap to cover her peach fuzz hair, walked in with a briskness that surprised him. She looked strong. She had more color in her cheeks, quickly surveying the tables and locking onto him. She waved, and sat down. He asked her how she felt.

"Better. I've been sleeping more. Thanks for meeting me."

"I wanted to," he said. "How is your mother?"

She shook her head. "Not so good."

"Sorry."

"She'll be okay eventually. She's strong."

"Hector almost got away with it."

"Until we started looking into it. But it was a risky plan."

He asked, "How did he manage to convince Bangs's friends?"

"Bangs was getting more secretive and paranoid, so when Hector took over, they didn't think much of Bangs wanting to use Gloria as the main contact. And Hector wasn't planning to stay as Bangs forever. He just wanted to raise a lot of cash fast."

"What about Tanner?"

"Accessory. Also pleading it down. He's looking at jail time, but he seems to be small fry," she said. "Oh, and no one has found Tim and Kate. They disappeared. Even Kate's brother doesn't know where they are."

"Can I ask about Raul?"

Her face remained blank. She said, "If you want."

"He didn't do anything to you," he said. "As a kid."

"No."

"But to Hector?"

"No. My mother still believes it, but you heard Hector. My mother made it up."

"Made it up?"

"She was scared of Raul, what he could do. She had no leverage. She needed to keep him away."

"By lying?"

"I think she convinced herself it was true. She convinced herself years ago, and now it's fact."

"But Julie mentioned that your . . . your weight problem as a kid—"

"I know. She told me what she said to you. It's not true. I was fat because I ate too much. End of story."

He didn't tell her that he still had the photograph of her as a teen. He suspected she'd destroy it if he returned it.

After a minute, she said, "Listen, I wanted to let you know that I'm not going back up north."

"To the Bay Area?"

"No."

"What about the *Sentinel?*"

"You know it was getting bad there for me."

"I know."

"I'll find something down here."

"What about money?"

She said, "Raul's will and insurance."

"So it's true? He left you money?"

"It's true. Just like when I was a kid. He left me a gift."

"How long will you stay here?"

"I don't know."

"For good?"

She said, "For a while."

"What about your apartment?"

"Julie will take care of it. She'll need a place. I think she and Frank are going to sell the Walnut Creek house."

"You're staying with your parents?"

"Just until I can figure things out. My mom needs me."

"Oh. What can I do?"

"You've already done a lot."

"What about Harlan?"

She looked out the window, staring at people walking by. "What about Harlan?" she said.

"Never mind."

Linda said, "I need time to think. Alone. I don't know what to think. Everything I believed was . . . wrong. Everything I expected hasn't worked out. I just need time to figure things out." She stood up. "I'm sorry. I have to get back. I wanted to thank you for everything."

"No need to—"

"The DEA guy told me about the woods and how bad it got. You didn't mention that Hector was probably going to kill you."

"Yes, well."

She said quietly, "I'll miss you, Allen."

He couldn't speak. The sound of the cash register broke the silence. He looked up. He finally said, "I'll miss you, too."

She turned and walked out the door without looking back.

Now, as he sits and waits for his test to begin, the Block has many more things to say to her. He wants to ask her about Hector and what else they talked about at Tanner's house. He wants to ask about Harlan. Where is Harlan now? Is Harlan down in L.A.? Is he with her? There are many things he needs to know. He needs to know if he is supposed to forget about her, if he is supposed to erase the past two years. He needs to know how to do this.

Two minutes, the test administrator announces.

Once, when they were at the bed and breakfast in Sonoma, and they had argued briefly about what to do one afternoon, they had separated for an hour while he went for a run, and she visited a local bakery and vineyard. When he returned, sweaty and sunburned, his eyes stinging, he found her outside on a ledge, snacking on sourdough bread and staring over the small valley. She didn't hear him approach, and she shook her head to an unvoiced thought, silently disagreeing. He tried to imagine what she was thinking, and although he guessed it might have been about them, he knew somehow that it wasn't, that he just seemed to register very low on her radar. He realized that he had no idea what occupied her thoughts, that he couldn't even begin to enter her mind. They had been seeing each other seriously for almost two years and he still hadn't felt as if he really knew her.

One more minute, the test administrator announces.

And yet he did know her. He knew her at her best, free of the entanglements of her family, free of the baggage of memory and the past. When they were stripping off their clothes self-consciously at Muir Beach, the warm sun slapping his bare skin, and they grinned at each other like two schoolkids doing something bad, she said, "What if I talk dirty to you? Will you get turned on? Will you get . . . hard?"

"Please don't," he said.

"Will you be embarrassed?"

He stared at her breasts, but then squeezed his eyes shut. "Please don't." He inhaled her coconut scent.

She laughed and kissed him. "I'll spare you this time," she said, and she lay back; he lay next to her, their hands touching. They linked pinky fingers. "Does the Block want some sunblock?" she asked. "Does the Block need block?" He turned to her. Her eyes were closed, a thin sheen of sweat appearing on her brow, and she was smiling. The sun lit up her skin. She was so beautiful.

Now, there's a shifting in the room as everyone turns to the test administrator, awaiting her orders. The Block sits up, startled, pulled back into the present. What? What happened?

It's ten o'clock, the administrator announces. Turn over your exam booklets and begin. You have two hours.

The Block looks around, and watches the others turn over their booklet; they swish open the cover page in unison and hunch over. The Block stares at his booklet. He can't seem to move his hands. The woman two seats down watches him, and points to his exam booklet. She makes a flipping motion with her hand. He nods. Slowly, he turns it over and opens to the first page. The smell of fresh photocopy toner blows toward him. The sheets are still warm. Multiple-choice questions fill his vision. A, B, C, D, E. He studies the first one for what seems like a long time, the words not fully registering in his mind. He sees the letters and thinks he's reading them, but they mean nothing to him. Words, sentences. They don't penetrate. Nothing really matters. All this seems irrelevant, useless. He looks up at the heads bowed and pencils scratching. He watches the test administrator write on the board "120 Minutes Left" and he suddenly misses Linda with a strange and deep ache. Is it true that we struggle in a void, alone, reaching out? Is it true that we must accept loss forever? He can't seem to hold all these different thoughts in his head, and the only thing that remains is the softness of Linda's hair when he plays with it, the curve of her neck in the shower, the way she smiles wryly right before she teases him. The Block slowly picks up his pencil, for he is the Block, and the Block needs to move forward steadily, ploddingly, dutifully, even in a void.

Acknowledgments

Thanks to my advocates, agents Nat Sobel and Judith Weber, editor Sally Kim and associate publisher John Cunningham; to my early readers Cara Evangelista and Frances Sackett; to the students and faculty at Antioch's M.F.A. program for their support and friendship; to Mills College for its perfectly timed visiting writer position; to the ravers, the real Rocket Man and the Experts; and, finally, thanks to Gaby Rodriguez, Jen Temple, and Danielle Unis for their friendship.

About the Author

Leonard Chang was born in New York City and studied philosophy at Dartmouth College and Harvard University. He received his M.F.A. from the University of California at Irvine and is the author of three previous novels: *The Fruit 'N Food, Dispatches from the Cold*, and *Over the Shoulder*. He was recently the Distinguished Visiting Writer at Mills College and is on the faculty at Antioch University's M.F.A. program in Los Angeles. His short stories have been published in literary journals such as *Prairie Schooner* and *Confluence*. He lives in the San Francisco Bay Area and is working on a new Allen Choice novel. For more information, visit his Web site at www.LeonardChang.com.